D1561556

Gabriele Reuter
München
1896.

GABRIELE REUTER

FROM A GOOD FAMILY

TRANSLATED
AND WITH AN INTRODUCTION BY
LYNNE TATLOCK

CAMDEN HOUSE

First published 1999 by Camden House
Reprinted in paperback and transferred to digital printing 2009

Camden House is an imprint of Boydell & Brewer Inc.
668 Mt. Hope Avenue, Rochester, NY 14620, USA
www.camden-house.com
and of Boydell & Brewer Limited
PO Box 9, Woodbridge, Suffolk IP12 3DF, UK
www.boydellandbrewer.com

Hardback ISBN-13: 978–1–57113–149–2
Hardback ISBN-10: 1–57113–149–3
Paperback ISBN-13: 978–1–57113–406–6
Paperback ISBN-10: 1–57113–406–9

Library of Congress Cataloging-in-Publication Data

Reuter, Gabriele, 1859–1941.
    [Aus guter Familie. English]
    From a good family / Gabriele Reuter; translated and with an
introduction by Lynne Tatlock.
      p. cm. — (Studies in German literature, linguistics, and culture)
    ISBN 1–57113–149–3 (alk. paper)
    1. Tatlock, Lynne, 1950– . II. Title. III. Series: Studies in German
literature, linguistics, and culture (Unnumbered)
    PT2635.E85A813 1999
    833'.912—DC21

                              98-55669
                                 CIP

This publication is printed on acid-free paper.
Printed in the United States of America.

Translator and publisher gratefully acknowledge the generous translation
support provided for this book by Inter Nationes, Bonn, Germany.

Frontispiece photograph of Gabriele Reuter courtesy of Stiftung Weimarer
Klassik (Goethe- und Schiller-Archiv call number GSA 112/227.)

Cover: Gabrielle Reuter with her mother, Hannchen, and her four brothers,
Tom, Alti, Mani, and Lola in the 1880s. Courtesy Stiftung Weimarer
Klassik (Goethe- und Schiller-Archiv call number GSA 112/227.

Acknowledgments

I would like to express my gratitude to family, friends, students, and colleagues for their interest and aid in the project of translating, introducing and editing Gabriele Reuter's *From a Good Family*. Christl Griesshaber-Weninger, Meghan Barnes, and Eugene Gagliano's continuing interest in and work on Reuter buoyed my decision to begin this work. Alyssa Lonner, as my summer research assistant, energetically tracked down information for the notes for the first eight chapters, and Lorie Ann Vanchena proved infinitely helpful in locating, identifying, and assembling sources in Germany. Gerhild Scholz Williams, Alexander Schwarz, and Rose Treusch von Buttlar patiently assisted me in interpreting German locutions. Paula V. Mehmel offered help locating biblical references and understanding them in a Lutheran context, and P. Vincent Mehmel kindly identified and supplied the English translations of the Lutheran hymns quoted in the text. Jennifer Askey and Vanessa Van Ornam tested early drafts of the translation in their Women's Studies courses in the spring of 1998 at Washington University and Middlebury College respectively. Michael Sherberg and Peter Leach offered critical and supportive readings of drafts of the translation, and Michael Sherberg and Vanessa Van Ornam generously reviewed drafts of the introduction. Gerda Jordan, who painstakingly vetted the manuscript for Camden House, provided invaluable criticism and advice, and Angela Gulielmetti and Michaela Giesenkirchen generously aided in the final proofreading of the manuscript. Finally, Joseph F. Loewenstein meticulously read and commented on the penultimate draft, and both he and Michael Sherberg lent a sympathetic ear throughout my work on this project.

I am obliged to Washington University for facilitating this translation with a sabbatical leave, to Inter Nationes for supporting it with a subvention, and to the *Goethe- und Schiller-Archiv* in Weimar, Germany, for allowing me access to Reuter's papers, for granting Camden House permission to use photographs held there, and for generally facilitating my research in Weimar. I would also like to thank James Hardin for advocating the publication of *From a Good Family* with Camden House.

I dedicate this translation to my mother-in-law, Jean Loewenstein Lazarus, and my mother, Jeanette Busing Tatlock.

L. T.
January 1999

Introduction

> [Lily Bart] was so evidently the victim of
> the civilization which had produced her,
> that the links of her bracelet seemed like
> manacles chaining her to her fate.
> — Edith Wharton, *House of Mirth*
> (1905)

Aus guter Familie (From a Good Family, 1895), Gabriele Reuter's
first literary success, was nothing if not shocking. "Upon reading
[this novel] one's first thought is 'that's ugly'; the second one, 'but
[it's] true, true, frighteningly true,' this decayed existence of a girl
from the 'better middle class,'"[1] wrote the reviewer for *Die Frau*
(Woman). The feminist Hedwig Dohm (1833–1919) called it quite
simply a "shocking lament, a crushing indictment"[2] and even years
later in 1929 Helene Stöcker (1869–1943) passionately recalled its
impact in similar terms:

> A wake-up call, elucidation, encouragement without compare ema-
> nated from the book. It was given to Gabriele Reuter to express what
> thousands of women from good families had suffered . . . what hun-
> dreds of thousands still suffered: that nameless, petty, paltry fate of re-
> pressed women, of those who were not taken seriously, of the
> uninteresting women whom no one granted a fate of their own . . . .[3]

This story of a Prussian bureaucrat's daughter, caught between
conformity and rebellion, was a deeply disturbing book, for it struck
at the very core of the class that upheld the second German empire.
As Reuter herself reported, Fernand Labori (d. 1917), Emile Zola's
defense lawyer, recognized that fact; he characterized her novel as
worse than Zola, a novel signifying revolution.[4] A German contemporary, moreover, went so far as to declare it the female companion
to Johann Wolfgang Goethe's *Die Leiden des jungen Werthers* (The
Sufferings of Young Werther, 1774), the confessional novel that had
offered the first compelling account of modern male subjectivity in
the German language.[5] While the claim may seem exaggerated, it
was not entirely unjustified; like Goethe's novel Reuter's work im-

mediately became a best seller in Germany and something of a cultural event.[6]

From a Good Family catapulted its author from relative obscurity to notoriety as one of the best-known women writers in the German-speaking world. Throughout the remaining years of the Second Empire Reuter enjoyed an indisputable reputation as one of Germany's most significant living women authors — in 1904 Thomas Mann called her "the most superior woman currently living in Germany."[7] The eleventh edition of the *Encyclopedia Britannica* (1910), moreover, recognized her as one of the best German fiction writers of her age, along with Thomas and Heinrich Mann, Jakob Wassermann, Helene Böhlau, Ricarda Huch, and Clara Viebig.[8] While feminists like Dohm and Stöcker stressed the book's social impact, other contemporary critics remarked on its artistry. They declared it a "moving piece of literature,"[9] a literary work of "no small value,"[10] a "masterpiece of the first water."[11]

Reuter had scored no small coup in publishing her book with Samuel Fischer (1859–1934). This young and forward-looking publisher set a high literary standard in the final decades of the nineteenth century with the publication of such German naturalists as Gerhart Hauptmann and of such European naturalists in German translation as Henrik Ibsen, Knut Hamsun and Zola. In the 1890s he was also beginning to specialize in the European modernist fiction of the turn-of-the-century avant garde as well as the earliest works of Thomas Mann and Hermann Hesse. Reuter became one of a select few women writers, including Dohm, Ellen Key, and Rosa Mayreder, to be published by Fischer before the First World War. *From a Good Family* was in fact the first of Fischer's books to succeed with a wider reading public.[12] In the late twentieth century, however, the educated German reading public has forgotten Reuter, manifesting a cultural amnesia that seems unwarranted in view of the quality and historical significance of *From a Good Family*.[13]

Gabriele Reuter's Life and Works

Gabriele Reuter was born Gabriele Elise Karoline Alexandrine Reuter in Alexandria, Egypt, on 8 February 1859, the oldest of five children.[14] In the 1840s her father had been sent by the King of Prussia to the Prussian consulate in Egypt as a commercial deputy (*kauf-*

männischer Agent) and had eventually founded an import-export business there. On her mother's side Reuter was descended from the occasional poet and translator Philippine Gatterer Engelhard (1756–1831) who would one day become the subject of her last novel. Her mother's large and closely knit family assumed a central place in her upbringing, outlook, livelihood, and subsequent career as writer and provided in part the material for *From a Good Family*. During her early years Reuter and her family divided their time between Alexandria and Cairo in Egypt and Dessau in the German duchy of Anhalt. In 1872 her father died and her mother had to liquidate his business, after which the family was forced to subsist on a severely reduced annual income and the charity of relatives on Reuter's mother's side. After completing a brief stint at a boarding school for proper middle-class girls, partially funded by her wealthy aunt, Luise Nathusius, Reuter joined her mother and brothers in Neuhaldensleben not far from the provincial capital of Magdeburg where the family lived in genteel poverty in the shadow of the wealthy Nathusius family in nearby Althaldensleben. Reuter describes her mother's family as politically conservative, highly critical of the liberal Crown Prince Friedrich and Crown Princess Victoria in the 1870s and 80s, and of a marked religious bent. Reuter herself spent years seeking spiritual alternatives to the harsh and rigid piety that guided her cousins' lives. There were exceptions to the austere religiosity of her family, however. Reuter's liberal, freethinking cousin, Henne Achten, provided an atmosphere of intellectual stimulation and gaiety, encouraged Reuter to develop her writing talent and offered useful criticism of her work. Similarly, her cousin, Gustchen Overbeck, a former headmistress of a girls' school, provided moral and material support both to Reuter and her mother for many years in Weimar.

In the 1870s Reuter submitted sketches of life in Egypt to the *Magdeburger Zeitung* (Magdeburg Newspaper) under her mother's name, thus becoming a published author in her teens. The honoraria she earned for these vignettes financed the family's move to Weimar in 1879 where she continued to write. Weimar offered Reuter not only the friendship and support of family members — Cousin Gustchen as well as her uncle, the painter Hermann Behmer, and his wife Elisabeth — but also promised a more stimulating intellectual and social life than tiny Neuhaldensleben. Encouraged by her mother and relatives, Reuter continued to write sporadically, occasionally managing to place an essay, sketch, or short story with a newspaper or magazine.

In her autobiography Reuter represents her career as writer both as meant to be — she claims that one of her mother's friends predicted at her cradle that she would become a writer — and as highly precarious, something that very nearly did not happen and that, had her life taken a different course, she could just as easily have foregone. Certainly little in her adolescent years prepared her for such a career. She was not only largely self taught from age fourteen on but of necessity assumed many household responsibilities, among others, helping her mother care for her four younger brothers. Reuter describes herself as a voracious reader and a painfully shy and insecure young woman, longing to participate in intellectual and artistic circles, but habitually frightened of opening her mouth. Even as late as 1921, apparently still uncomfortable with the notion of ambition in a woman, she downplays in her autobiography what can only have been an iron determination. Given the picture Reuter paints of herself as a soft and shy young woman, we may initially be surprised, then, to learn that in the 1880s this same young woman, still an unknown author, attended three writers' conventions, one of them in distant Munich. In these same years she doggedly attached herself to intellectual and artistic circles in Weimar, Munich, and Berlin, living a life of bourgeois respectability on the fringes of an intellectual *bohème*.

In 1889 she formed a friendship with the Scottish-born German poet and anarchist John Henry Mackay (1864–1933), whom she met at a writers' convention in Munich. Mackay, who would serve as prototype for the final development of Martin in *From a Good Family*, urged Reuter to break free of Weimar and the family circle there. She should move to Munich, he insisted, and devote herself fully to her writing. When she announced this plan to her mother it met with enthusiasm; her mother declared that she would come too and so she did. Reuter's attempt to write full-time ended within a few short months when her mother's severe illness forced them to return to Weimar in 1891. For nearly four years, while caring for her mother, she worked intermittently on *From a Good Family*, which she had begun in Munich. Eventually and unexpectedly her mother recovered, and meanwhile Reuter had completed what was to become a best-selling novel.

Reuter had published two novels in the 1880s, *Glück und Geld. Ein Roman aus dem heutigen Egypten* [*sic*] (Happiness and Money. A Novel from Today's Egypt, 1888)[15] and *Kolonistenvolk* (Colonists, 1889), set in Argentina and based on her brother Tom's experiences there. In the late 1880s, still unknown despite these publications, she received what was to prove sound advice from the Berlin critic and editor Karl Frenzel (1827–1914): she needed to write about what she knew. Having read the naturalists — the Goncourt brothers, Maupassant, and all of Zola's works — she was familiar with the milieu studies that dominated contemporary European literature in the naturalist vein. Instead of the washerwomen, actresses, waitresses, and prostitutes who populated the demi-monde of naturalist fiction, she chose to study the young middle-class woman, a figure more likely to be the object of derision than the subject of high art in the naturalist literature of the day. When it came time for her to market the book, her friend Mackay suggested that she change her title from *Agathe Heidling* to *From a Good Family*. Thus from the outset the book struck the ironic tone that characterized its entirety and insisted, moreover, on the social moment. Mackay also recommended Reuter to his publisher, Samuel Fischer, but in the end it was Fischer's young wife, Hedwig (1871–1952), who successfully advocated publication of the book.

Reuter's novel achieved success nearly overnight and quickly sold out even before Fischer had decided on a second printing. Having become a public figure as a result of a novel that portrayed and questioned the constraints placed on middle-class women, Reuter was now expected to take a position on women's rights. Contemporary journalists repeatedly asked whether she was a suffragette, many a reviewer heaving a sigh of relief upon concluding that she was not but instead a truly womanly woman. While some stylized Reuter as a strident advocate of women's rights in *From a Good Family*, others pointed to her ironic depiction of the reformatory zeal of the women schoolteachers in chapter 2 of part 2 as evidence of doubt about the women's movement. Reuter can in fact at most be located at the periphery of political activism; indeed, she appears at times uneasy with the more aggressive factions of the women's movement; and true to her individualist leanings and her grounding in late century pessimism, she evinces a certain skepticism as to the ability of politics to remedy all social ills and all personal tragedy. In her autobiography she notes that although briefly active in the women's movement while in Munich in the late 1890s, she felt herself more an artist than a politician and had to live her life accordingly.[16] In retrospect the obsessive locating of Reuter, the person, on the political scale and the repeated insistence on her femininity by those who feared to find in her an incipient radicalism seems indicative of the paradoxical high profile and simultaneous precariousness of the women's movement in Germany before the First World War. The brisance of Reuter's critical delineation of the making of gender in *From a Good Family* can hardly be missed, regardless of its author's stance on individual issues and regardless of the extent of her political activism.

In the early 1890s Reuter made several trips to Berlin where she became acquainted with the circle of naturalist writers located in the Berlin suburb Friedrichshagen. When, however, she made her definitive break with Weimar in 1895, she chose to move to Munich where she became a part of the circle around the writer Ernst von Wolzogen (1855–1934). During her years in Munich, probably in 1897 or 1998, Reuter had a daughter, Lili, out of wedlock — she never revealed the name of the father.[17] In 1899 she left Munich for Berlin where she spent the better part of the remaining forty-two years of her life.

A long list of novels and short stories followed *From a Good Family*, the last of these, *Grüne Ranken um alte Bilder* (Green Tendrils around old Pictures, 1937) appearing when Reuter was seventy-eight years old. Many critics argue that she never again achieved the artistic and intellectual level of *From a Good Family*. In 1904, however, a young Thomas Mann judged her *Liselotte von Reckling* (1903) to be a profound work equal to *From a Good Family* and expressed admiration for *Frau Bürgerlin und ihre Söhne* (Frau Bürgerlin and her Sons, 1899).[18] Moreover, if the number of reprints is a reliable indication, her *Frauenseelen* (Women's Souls, 1902) — forty-eight — and her *Ellen von der Weiden* (1900) — sixty-five — enjoyed an even greater, albeit quieter, success than *From a Good Family*.[19] Of her remaining novels, only *Das Tränenhaus* (House of Tears, 1908) had anything like the political impact on the reading public of *From a Good Family*. Set in a home for unwed mothers in Southwest Germany, *House of Tears* explored the treatment of unwed mothers in turn-of-the-century Germany, insisting on women's right to motherhood. While negative contemporary reviews regarded

Reuter's novel as yet another threat to the German family, favorable ones believed it struck a blow for the League for the Protection of Mothers. Nevertheless, in a lengthy review of *House of Tears* Hedwig Dohm expressed reservations about a book that, she thought, tended to portray women's suffering as eternal rather than historically determined.[20] *Die Töchter. Roman zweier Generationen* (1927), translated into English in 1930 as *Daughters*, evoked a changed, postwar Germany, a Germany worlds apart from the Imperial Germany presented in *From a Good Family*. In this ostensibly altered world Reuter returned to some of her earliest themes — marriage, pregnancy, the family, the mother-daughter relationship, female desire and sexuality — to produce a psychologically perceptive novel, a good read, what might appropriately and respectfully be called good middlebrow literature.

Reuter had begun her career as a writer with vignettes from Egypt for a local newspaper, and she continued throughout her life to write book reviews, sketches, and journalistic essays published separately or in newspapers and magazines, both in Germany and Austria. Notably, she wrote lengthy essays on two of the very few women writers who at the time had been canonized in German literature: one in 1904 on the Austrian fiction-writer Marie von Ebner-Eschenbach (1830–1916) and one in 1905 on the poet Annette von Droste-Hülshoff (1797–1848). Ebner, the first woman to receive an honorary doctorate from the University of Vienna, thanked Reuter warmly for her generous portrait: "You have treated me with great affection. You have given me the best thing that one person can give another. Of course I would like to contradict you now and again. I know a much more subtle psychologist than Marie Ebner; her name is Gabriele Reuter."[21] An essay on marriage, *Das Problem der Ehe* (The Problem of Marriage, 1907) and an essay entitled *Liebe und Stimmrecht* (Love and Suffrage, 1914) manifest Reuter's "non-ideological commitment to the women's movement."[22] From 1916–24 Reuter also contributed regularly to the bourgeois newspaper, *Neue Freie Presse* (New Free Press) in Vienna. In 1919, for example, she wrote a series of articles chronicling political events in Berlin, including the collapse of the Spartacist Revolt and the deaths of the radical leaders Karl Liebknecht and Rosa Luxemburg.

During the inflation of 1922–23 Reuter, like many Germans, lost her savings and apparently began seeking new sources of income, a search that led her to the *New York Times Book Review*. Her first article for the *Book Review* appeared on 7 October 1923, marking the beginning of what was to be a sixteen-year association with the American newspaper, during which she reviewed close to 700 German books. The typescripts of her reviews evidence meticulous tallying, suggesting that she was paid by the word, and a tribute on the occasion of her eightieth birthday confirms that the *Times* had constituted an important source of income in her old age.[23]

Tracing the course of Reuter's work for the *Book Review* where books were news[24] tells a bleak story of the decline of literary culture in Germany under the National Socialists. In the 1920s Reuter reviewed for her American audience books published in Germany by the likes of Vicki Baum, Bertolt Brecht, Max Brod, Carl Einstein, Hermann Hesse, Alfred Kerr, Annette Kolb, Thomas Mann, Emil Ludwig, Alfred Polgar, Arthur Schnitzler, Frank Thiess, Ernst Toller, Fritz von Unruh, and Jakob Wassermann, to name a few. After 1933 most of these authors were banned and/or in exile. Although there were notable exceptions, we find her increasingly reviewing travelogues, biographies, history books, picture books, and other non-fiction works that focus on countries besides Germany — the United States, Great Britain, and China. Her last review for the *Times*, published on 8 October 1939, shortly after the outbreak of the Second World War in Europe, treats German books on Shakespeare. Meanwhile in January of 1938 the exiled German-Jewish writer Heinz Liepman (1905–66), recently arrived in New York, began offering readers an alternative view of German literary life by contributing reviews of works by exiled German authors like himself. His articles contrast starkly with Reuter's bland assessments of the trivial German fiction produced under National Socialism. The *Book Review*, however, recognized Reuter's difficulty and offered a tactful tribute on her eightieth birthday: "In the last six years we have admired the consummate tact and diplomacy with which Frau Reuter has avoided controversial political subjects and has concentrated on the novels, poetry, art and philosophical books appearing contemporaneously, which express permanently the true German Geist."[25]

In 1941, at age eighty-two and nearly blind, Reuter died in Weimar, where she had lived since 1924. During her last years she had not exactly been forgotten but rather contained as a representative of the battles of a bygone era. The struggle for women's rights and freedom, we read with astonishment in articles on Reuter from the 1920s and 1930s, was a dead issue; these rights and this freedom had been achieved. And to some extent Reuter seemed to think so herself. In 1928 her recollections of *From a Good Family* assumed an almost apologetic tone: "Today young women laugh about [my book] like something that's very funny, dusty with age, inconceivably old-fashioned. The way to higher and further intellectual development is now open to every girl .... " Nevertheless, she concluded her remarks with the admonition that families like Agathe's still existed in Germany.[26] In 1929 she spoke somewhat wistfully of the present generation of women who had no idea of how much they owed their freedom to the previous generation.[27] Ten years later in Nazi Germany a commemorative article on *From a Good Family* referred to prejudices to which Reuter's Agathe Heidling was subjected, "prejudices that we can hardly comprehend nowadays, since the way to joyous work is wide open to woman as well as man."[28] Nearly forty years would pass before such views would be systematically interrogated in Germany.

The Historical Background: Imperial Germany

From a Good Family opens with Agathe's confirmation at age sixteen. Some months thereafter, we learn, German unification has taken place. At the conclusion of the novel Agathe is not yet forty. Her coming of age thus coincides with the first two decades of the Second Empire and the reign of Wilhelm I as German Emperor (1871–88). While in 1871 most Germans — including Reuter's own family[29] — celebrated the German victory over Napoleon III and the long-anticipated unification of Germany under Prussian aegis, the following decades were fraught with insecurity and conflict.

In the early 1870s wild speculation in the newly formed empire was followed by a stock crash in 1873 and subsequent years of economic recession, a recession that, some scholars argue, lasted until 1896. These vicissitudes coupled with stepped-up industrialization and concomitant urbanization generated an urban population whose extreme poverty could not be ignored, especially as that population was becoming increasingly vocal. The Social Democratic Workers' Party had been founded in Eisenach shortly before unification in 1869 and steadily gained in power during the early years of the Empire. Increasingly alarmed by this so-called "red tide," the German government began taking the first harsh measures against the socialists in 1874; in 1878 the German chancellor Otto von Bismarck seized the occasion of two assassination attempts against Kaiser Wilhelm I to urge the passage of the so-called Socialist Laws, laws that empowered the government, among other things, to dissolve social democratic organizations, to ban social democratic agitators and to suppress social democratic publications. The years 1878–80 also saw the defeat of the National Liberal Party and the decisive victory of the Conservatives in the Reichstag.

Soon after unification Bismarck initiated a struggle between church and state, aimed largely at the Catholic minority in the new Reich, a minority that Bismarck characterized as the enemy within. This campaign, known as the Kulturkampf (1872–87), led to a series of legislative measures, the most important being the so-called May Laws of 1873, laws pertaining principally to the Catholic Church but also affecting the Lutheran Church. These laws sought to establish state control over the education and appointment of clergy. By the end of the Kulturkampf nearly 2,000 priests had been jailed or exiled and millions of marks of church property seized.

Meanwhile German unification facilitated the implementation of technological innovations that improved transportation and communication within the Reich, and these improvements further supported Germany's rapid industrialization. German know-how made significant advances in technology, science, and medicine, proclaiming to the modern world that Imperial Germany was a force to be reckoned with. In the 1880s Germany belatedly entered the arena of nineteenth-century European colonialism by taking under protection German Southwest Africa, Togoland, Cameroon, and German East Africa, as well as the Marshall Islands and German New Guinea.

In this new and aggressive nation a culture of individualistic careerism and advancement began to replace the genial sociability that Germans had once seen as central to German middle-class life. During the last quarter of the century, German medicine was also treating a new ailment, neurasthenia, nervous exhaustion, a disease labeled the "characteristic sign of our cultural period."[30] This sickness, reputed to be widespread in capitalist America, was thought to result from precisely the new high-pressure society of Imperial Germany.[31] In a medical handbook on neurasthenia the medical doctor

Rudolph von Hösslin claimed, "Our cultural situation and civilization are not without influence on the genesis of neurasthenia . . . the harsh struggle for survival in particular requires a greater harnessing of all our intellectual, moral, and physical powers."[32] Hösslin further noted that both men and women suffered from the disease; often it was misdiagnosed in women as hysteria. It was perhaps observed more often in men, he explained, simply because men as breadwinners carried the heavier load in the struggle for survival. Those men involved in high-pressure occupations, especially those demanding mental exertion like speculators, entrepreneurs, bureaucrats, and teachers, he explained, were most vulnerable of all.[33]

Public life and politics do not stand at the center of Reuter's vision in *From a Good Family*, nevertheless throughout her examination of middle-class domestic life Reuter alludes to the larger world of Imperial Germany and also to the particular situation in Prussia.[34] Young women celebrate Germany's victory by wearing clothing patterned after military uniforms. Agathe's cousin Martin must leave M. on account of his radical politics when the first harsh measures are taken against the socialists. An unorthodox Lutheran pastor is forced out of office as a result of the May Laws, and Agathe's father must retire from government service during a shift in climate in the German parliament. Moreover, Reuter uses the subplot of Wiesing, the Pomeranian country girl who is confirmed with Agathe and brought to the city to work for the Heidlings, to point to the ills of urbanization, the precariousness of the lives of servants, and the complicity in, indeed, responsibility of the bourgeoisie for their misery.

If readers have not realized by the end of the novel that Agathe's personal tragedy is tied to the formation of the new German nation, Reuter makes this connection explicit when she describes the gathering of women at an iron spring where they attempt to replenish the blood and iron that has been leeched from their bodies in the name of empire. Reuter thus forges an ironic link between the iron-poor blood that contemporary physicians saw at the root of nearly every female complaint and Bismarck's famous characterization of the empire wrought from blood and iron.

The Ideology of Gender and the Education of Middle-Class Girls

Reuter's harrowing anatomy of a middle-class girl's failed life seeks the origins of arrested development in the prevailing gender ideology of the economically powerful middle class, an ideology that understood the patriarchal and distinctly middle-class family to form the basis of the state. According to this ideology the husband and father functioned as sovereign in the family unit, breadwinner, and representative in public affairs. Male honor was of supreme importance in this public life, and every person in the family reflected upon that honor. Fathers were therefore obliged to keep a firm hold on money matters and to watch over the sexual behavior of family members. Women's role, on the other hand, was to oversee the domestic sphere, to bear and raise children, to create a harmonious home that in its decor and decorum appropriately displayed family prestige, honor, and wealth. Women were seen as naturally submissive, self-sacrificing, and intellectually inferior, but also as in need of being taught to conform to these stereotypes. The highest destiny or vocation of woman was motherhood, so the reigning ideology of gender had it: women contributed to the state by bearing and raising its future (male) citizens. In a manual for girls from 1878, Caroline S. J. Milde upheld precisely this view: "The highest and most rewarding female profession . . . is as wife and mother; and if it's true that the well-being of the state rests on the well-being of the family, and in turn that the center of the family is to be sought in the woman as wife and mother, then this must be the goal of education."[35] Lutheran Protestantism, the official state religion, and German schools for girls colluded to enforce such understanding of woman's vocation as wife and mother.

As social reformers of the time frequently noted, in the uncertain financial climate of Imperial Germany strikingly few middle-class women actually had the financial wherewithal, that is, the necessary dowry, to marry and live the domestic life to which they had been bred.[36] Other options needed to be open to women who might well be forced to support themselves. Despite these hard facts, German feminists, such as Luise Otto-Peters (1819–95) and Fanny Lewald (1811–89), still felt compelled to couch arguments in favor of women's education precisely in terms of the sacred duty women had to the state as educators of their children.[37]

In the late nineteenth century few members of the bourgeois women's movement would have contradicted the notions of a natural difference between the sexes and of woman's natural vocation as mother. Many moderate feminists like Helene Lange (1848–1930) — and indeed Reuter herself — tended at bottom to see other occupations largely as a matter of economic necessity and an unfortunate deterrent to motherhood, woman's primary vocation.[38] There were in fact few paid occupations, Reuter pointed out on one occasion, that were spiritually fulfilling.[39] Furthermore, at the turn of the century much of women's political activism centered precisely on motherhood and particularly on the rights of unwed mothers, the obligation of the state to provide support to single mothers, the necessity of protecting unwed mothers from moral censure, and generally the need to change the prevailing mores regarding the relations between the sexes. Fundamental to this activism was the assumption that motherhood was women's natural right and that no woman would fail to have children if given the choice. Moreover, when feminists did argue for women's right to paid work, they often recommended occupations that required woman's allegedly natural propensity to nurture — health care and education.

If the quantity and number of editions and reprints of confirmation books, educational manuals, etiquette books, and instructive fiction for girls is an indication, the cultural task of conditioning middle-class girls for their vocation as wives and mothers was not an easy one. Be that as it may, the proliferation of these books provides palpable evidence of the purchasing power of the middle class and its eagerness to secure its place in the new German Empire by properly educating its young women. The first six chapters of Reuter's novel — confirmation, boarding school, the first ball — will have resonated with middle-class female readers. Indeed, these chapters reproduce precisely those events, those scenes, and those views that these readers would have known first-hand as well as from their reading both of fiction for girls and of religious and secular handbooks. Beginning on the first page, however, when Agathe is unable to keep her mind on divine things as she partakes in Communion, Reuter departs markedly from the affirmative light in which this educational literature customarily presented the holy rituals of a young woman's life.

The middle-class girl's confirmation at age fifteen or sixteen was seen as a significant rite of passage into womanhood. Thereafter she would join a larger social world and often find herself engaged within a few short years. Much of what Agathe Heidling experiences on her confirmation day can be found previewed, for example, in the widely circulating *Heilige Stunden einer Jungfrau. Eine Konfirmationsgabe* (Holy Hours of a Maiden. A Confirmation Gift), a book that in 1893 when Reuter was writing *From a Good Family* appeared in its thirteenth edition.[40] This book prepares the confirmand not only for her spiritual life as a Christian but also for her social life, a life "in which young men also take part," the author delicately notes.[41]

In addition to such religious manuals, girls and their mothers could consult a plethora of secular manuals and etiquette books for help in navigating a safe course through puberty to life as wife and mother. These guides not only offer practical advice about dress, table manners, deportment in various social situations, letter writing, and proper reading material, to name but a few of their subjects, but preach the ideology of gender that dictates submissiveness and self-control and that enshrines love as woman's special purview. Reuter's description of Agathe's preparations for her first ball sounds remarkably like a parody of Julie Burow's idealized depiction in *Das Glück eines Weibes* (A Woman's Happiness, 1860) of the rituals preceding a young woman's first ball.[42] Burow (1806–1868), a frequent contributor to the nineteenth-century German fashion magazine, *Der Bazar*, also writes in her manual in glowing terms of woman's ability to love and maintains that the superiority of men resides precisely in the nature of female love: woman's love must revere its object.[43]

In 1892 young women could read in the seventh edition of *Aus der Töchterschule ins Leben. Ein allseitiger Berater für Deutschlands Jungfrauen* (From the Girls' School into Life. An all around Guide for Germany's Maidens, 1892), for example, that the affianced girl had to learn to control herself and that the wife had the duty to make the home as appealing as possible so that her husband, exhausted from the day's work, could recover there.[44] Franz Ebhardt reminded his readers in 1885, "The man is the head of the house;

the woman is, however, its soul, the center around which the domestic sphere turns. Her deeds and nature make the man's house
into his castle."[45]

Books and magazines for girls similarly took on the task of shap-
ing their readers for lives as wives and mothers. The widely circulating *Backfischchen's Leiden und Freuden* (The Sorrows and Joys of an
Adolescent Girl, 1872) by Clementine Helm (1825–96) — the fifti-
eth edition appeared in 1896, a year after the publication of *From a
Good Family* — tells the story of teenaged Grete who is sent to her
aunt to learn proper behavior. Predictably, by the time she returns
home she has become a lady and also captured a male heart. Emmy
von Rhoden's *Der Trotzkopf* (1885; translated as *Taming a Tomboy*,
1898), which is still in print in Germany in a slightly revised version,
offers its readers a more lively heroine. In the end, however, Ilse, the
sassy and untutored tomboy, returns to her parents a well-behaved
young lady, having learned much from her charming circle of friends
at boarding school and having acquired a fiancé over the course of
her homeward journey. Rhoden (1832–85) represents boarding
school here as a happy, familiar place where girls form loving friend-
ships and learn from the good examples of these friends and where
occasional teasing or pranks never get out of hand. Reuter, by contrast, offers a harrowing counter-version in which Agathe Heidling
finds herself subjected to yet another kind of social pressure from an
alien "girl culture" and who, when she shows herself unequal to her
social task, is ostracized. These books and their many imitations present the taming of girls' impulses as a benignly constructive and
relatively painless process; in the end only the girls who do not learn
womanly submissiveness and unselfishness lead unhappy lives. The
books do not even hint that "good girls" might suffer as a result of
their conforming.

Hysteria and Women's Social Conditioning

Central to the defeat of Reuter's heroine is the fact that despite an
incipient high-spiritedness and independence of mind Agathe eventually internalizes the attitudes of her class and her culture to the
point that she censors her own thoughts and actions, almost before
they cross the threshold of consciousness. Forbidden knowledge is
laboriously repressed so that it returns only occasionally "like a bad

smell." When punished after a minor rebellion upon being initiated into the facts of life, Agathe has a temper tantrum, gives in and becomes hoarse; when at last the man she loves comes to call, she can't speak; when she is torn between her feelings of envy of Fräulein Daniel's love affair with Lutz and her bourgeois horror at the actress's Bohemian life, a blood vessel bursts in her lungs; her final flirtation with freedom ends with a nervous breakdown. Airing such conflicts, discussing them frankly with friends, hardly comes into question, and Agathe, like all her friends, jealously guards her secrets.

One common reaction to dilemmas arising from the pressure to adhere to strict social codes has been well-documented for late nineteenth-century western culture. Women took sick; they became — in the language of the time — hysterical, displaying an array of bizarre symptoms, from obsessive-compulsive behaviors to hoarseness to coughing to unexplained lameness to, in extreme cases, trance-like states in which their entire bodies became rigid. While feminist scholars have suggested that hysteria could be read as a form of rebellion, Elaine Showalter has observed that in its historical context "hysteria was at best a private, ineffectual response to the frustrations of women's lives. Its immediate gratifications — the sympathy of family, the attention of the physician — were slight in relation to its costs in powerlessness and silence."[46]

The treatment of hysterics proved an absorbing challenge for late-century medicine. Uncertain as to the etiology of hysteria, the doctors combatted its symptoms with every possible means — from shock treatments to doses of iron to mineral baths to hypnosis. It should not surprise us, then, to note that Freud and Breuer's path-breaking *Studies in Hysteria*, in which the two doctors outline the now famous "talking cure," appeared the same year as *From a Good Family*. Many of Freud and Breuer's female patients were, like Reuter's Agathe Heidling, proper middle-class young women of striking intelligence and sensitivity often in their late teens to early twenties. The infamous case of Anna O., that is, Bertha Pappenheim (1859–1936), especially invites comparison. Born in the same year as Reuter and from a well-to-do middle-class Jewish family, Pappenheim eventually recovered — although apparently no thanks to Breuer and Freud — to become a feminist and philanthropist.[47]

Reuter could not have known the *Studies in Hysteria*, but her story of a middle-class girl exhibits striking points of coincidence with Freud and Breuer's case studies, including the appearance of so-called hysterical symptoms following disappointment in love and/or sexual frustration, the importance of daydreaming, the repression of sexual knowledge, the need of women to break the silence about their psychosexual lives in order to be cured.[48] Freud in fact praised Reuter in an aside for her psychological acuity in *From a Good Family*.[49] While Freud eventually sought the pathology of his female patients largely in their sexuality and thus mistakenly dismissed other contributing factors as in the now infamous Dora case of 1905, Reuter repeatedly and emphatically linked psychosexual development to intellectual development, and moreover, made explicit the role of the larger cultural context in that development. In her autobiography she records her dismay when her male friends appeared primarily interested in the novel as revelations about women's sexuality, having missed her larger point.[50]

For Agathe every lover, real or imagined, promotes growth, each time expanding not only her experiential world, but also firing her imagination and broadening her intellectual horizons. Agathe's desire is not only sexual but also spiritual and intellectual. Indeed, the most erotically charged moment of the novel pertains not to physical love but to social ideas: when Agathe reads her cousin Martin's radical social tracts in chapter 14 of part 1: "The girl threw herself down full length upon the little sofa, her arms spread wide in helpless desire for something that she could embrace, in the desire to be impregnated with strength, to receive the fructifying breath of spirit and intellect that streams over the earth in a spring storm." When Agathe is finally cured as it were, she is devoid not only of sexual desire but also of intellectual and spiritual longing. What she really wants is not sexual experience alone, but a meaningful life, a project, a child, something to live for. And this is where Reuter differs from Freud in construing women's nervous pathologies. If Agathe must be construed as neurotic, it is not because she, like Sue Bridehead in Thomas Hardy's *Jude, the Obscure* (1895), gives the intellect precedence over the body, but because the spirit goes hungry.[51]

From a Good Family as Milieu Study

From a Good Family constitutes, like the naturalist fiction that served as Reuter's inspiration, a milieu study, that is, it examines how an individual organism interacts with its environment. In keeping with this outlook Reuter focuses not only on Agathe's individual sufferings but depicts them in their habitat, the middle-class family, and in their age, the Second German Empire. Reuter read both Charles Darwin and his German popularizer, Ernst Haeckel, and like many of her contemporaries, including Thomas Mann in *Buddenbrooks* (1901), her outlook is influenced by the notion of a struggle to survive in which those individuals less well equipped and less adaptable will ultimately perish. She presents on the one hand Agathe, who becomes increasingly exhausted by her inability to fulfill her so-called destiny of marrying and producing a family, and on the other, Eugenie, who is not only a stunning physical specimen and naturally buoyant but a masterful manipulator of society and its rules. Eugenie herself quips that eating for the sake of her splendid figure prepares her for life's struggle. While Agathe's physical attack on Eugenie may seem overdrawn, it corresponds to the vision of a world in which the struggle to survive becomes ever more vicious and the wounded individual persists as long as is physically possible and with whatever means available.

To some extent Agathe's vulnerability seems inherited, especially as she eventually suffers the same attacks of neuralgia that had plagued her mother. Agathe's father, too, seems inadequate to his work and social role as Prussian bureaucrat. He too suffers from nervous exhaustion and displays a rigidity that reveals the very fragility of his social position and of his self-image. Even Agathe's brother, whose lack of sympathy for Agathe and brutish exploitation of the housemaid dispose readers to overlook his vulnerability, reveals himself to be barely adequate to the social roles prescribed for him. Not only does his life as an officer appear to be getting the better of him, in the end he succumbs to Eugenie's superior vitality; indeed, Eugenie completely dominates this fatuous man who had thought to marry her for her money. In this respect Reuter's portrait of a declining middle-class family anticipates Thomas Mann's best-selling novel *Buddenbrooks* in which the Buddenbrooks, a North German merchant family, prove inadequate to modern times only to be displaced by the more vigorous and more ruthless Hagenströms. Both Reuter and Mann partake of the general cultural pessimism of the fin-de-siècle, in which individuals appear as hollow shells exhausted by the strain of living, a pessimism shaped in part by their reading of Schopenhauer.

On the other hand, to read Reuter's tragedy of a girl from a good family solely in the pessimistic determinist vein of late-century literary culture is to miss the strong implication that in a changed world Agathe Heidling might have survived, a view fully in keeping with a Darwinist vision. Certainly many of Reuter's contemporary reviewers recognized precisely this point, understanding *Aus guter Familie* as a cry for change.

In the end it is not merely Agathe's sensitive nature that is lethal, but rather the combination of it with the relentless enforcing of codes of gender in her milieu. Indeed, while Thomas Mann aptly characterized her as a "sensitive bourgeoise" — and thus likely to be defeated by the pain of living — she in fact proves startlingly hardy. She bounces back from repeated setbacks, tries new avenues of self-fulfillment only to be repeatedly thwarted, sometimes by outward circumstances and convention and sometimes by her own longings, illusions, prejudices, and cowardice. This unexpected toughness suggests that under different conditions Agathe might have grown into a strong, intellectually independent person.

Reuter's use of plant imagery at key points in Agathe's story betrays traces of nostalgia for the organic development inherent in the idea of *Bildung*[52] that had been central in German thought and that continued to inform middle-class reform movements in Imperial Germany. Central to *Bildung* is the notion that every person harbors innate talents and powers of development that will come to fruition through careful cultivation and productive interaction with his or her culture. In Agathe Heidling Reuter presents a case of stunted growth, of development that fails to take place because the culture around her does not foster it. What happens, Reuter asks, when every awakening leads to nothing? One possibility, she suggests, is to relinquish the idea of reciprocity native to *Bildung* and to work instead to break with, even destroy, the existing culture. With the reappearance of the former Social Democrat, Martin, as a free individual Reuter introduces Agathe to a radical individualism pitted against the culture.

In the early 1890s "we had all read our Max Stirner," Reuter writes in her autobiography.[53] Indeed, Stirner's *Der Einzige und sein Eigentum* (The Ego and Its Own, 1845) with its advocacy of a substantive individual autonomy was generally taken up in the late nineteenth century as a founding text of individualist anarchism.[54] While Reuter's friend, the anarchist John Henry Mackay, became one of Stirner's principal advocates in Germany, she herself found Stirner's thought to be a dead end and moved on.[55] Thus while writing *From a Good Family*, she, like many German intellectuals of the 1890s, was also reading Nietzsche. In her autobiography she describes how she frequently met to discuss the philosopher's works with a small circle of friends in Weimar, a circle that included Rudolf Steiner (1861–1925), the founder of anthroposophy. This group of friends prided themselves on having put their bourgeois origins behind them, on having landed in a place "beyond good and evil." Nevertheless, Reuter recalled, "setting up house there was not as easy as it appeared; we women were often sorely conflicted."[56]

In *From a Good Family* Martin reenters Agathe's life as the author of a *Book of Freedom* and the proponent of a program of radical individualism that, he believes, will enable Agathe to liberate herself at last. In his insistence on individual freedom, Martin embodies a type of his era, one that, Reuter elsewhere asserts, just as surely originated in the middle class as did the female hysteric. "A number of the men who presently are undermining the bourgeoisie with pen and pencil . . . are the truculent and vigorous children of that fat, aged bourgeoisie," she remarks in a review of Mackay. "It's the nemesis of history."[57] Despite sympathy of understanding Reuter distances herself in this essay from these angry young men so eager to slay their fathers; their ways are not hers even if she, too, attempts to overcome her upbringing. Nor are they Agathe's. Although Martin's plan raises hope, such a break is hardly a viable option. In the end, she cannot give up the lifelong habit of pleasing others and does want to be loved as she had been told she would be. Despite the noxious effects of her immediate environment her well-being remains grounded in the social; she cannot live for herself alone. While we might understand Martin's scorn for Agathe, Reuter also suggests that he has only a limited understanding of her situation because he has been socialized as a man.[58]

Agathe's confrontation with Martin also brings to a climax the theme of male sexuality that has haunted the novel, a sexuality that matches imperfectly with the delicate sensibilities of this refined and coddled middle-class girl. While Agathe passionately longs in the final pages of the novel for the one kiss that has been denied her, the text has in the meantime slowly constructed a different picture of male sexuality, a sexuality that at times seems brutal, chaotic, and menacing. Agathe's brother exploits the housemaid, a soldier gets the housemaid pregnant, Agathe recoils at the barely disguised sexual desire of her dance partners, Lutz fathers an illegitimate child with Fräulein Daniel while flirting promiscuously with other women and ever in search of a rich wife, Raikendorf entertains liaisons with various married women and wonders in passing what Agathe might be like in bed, a fat vulgarian harasses a Swiss waitress, and at the very moment when Agathe idealistically contemplates a new life with Martin in Zurich, he makes clear that for him freedom also means sexual license. Even the doctor charged with curing the women at the spa does not hesitate to take advantage of his position to flirt with his patients.

Although Agathe's foil, Eugenie, in fact proves equal to this male sexual world, Reuter's text constructs and criticizes a society that favors such male sexuality. In this respect Reuter's novel resembles the English feminist literature of the 1880s and 1890s that, as Elaine Showalter asserts, "represented a reaction to a male sexual force that struck even the most passionate women as alien — indiscriminate, incessant and injurious."[59] While Reuter's novel by no means invites us to identify indiscriminately with Agathe's point of view here, it nevertheless does suggest that sexual mores must be altered; women's freedom and happiness will not be attained, however, simply by emulating the male sexual behavior condoned by the double standard that Eugenie so adroitly exploits.

From a Good Family and Progressive Nineteenth-Century German Fiction by Women

"Never was the dominant idea of woman, the 'ideal' of woman rendered so childish as in the nineteenth century," the Austrian feminist activist, essayist, and fiction writer Rosa Mayreder (1858–1938) argued in 1905 — and in this she was certainly of one mind with

Reuter. "To grasp this process fully one must seek the picture of femininity in that literature written specifically for women."[60] "[Its] principal content . . . ," she continued, "is . . . the relationship between man and woman. But its theme is not perchance marriage, that difficult and complicated relationship that is so full of conflict and so definitive for women's lives, but rather loving and becoming engaged."[61] Mayreder aimed her polemic at what she called "family literature," fiction written for popular magazines designed to appeal to a middle-class audience, particularly women. The magazines prescribed a format, she pointed out, that dictated a happy ending. They frowned on political content of any kind and certainly on plots that in any respect endangered the patriarchal middle-class family.

Mayreder's point is well-taken for the vast popular literature that circulated in the German-speaking world in the nineteenth century — the literature for girls described above constitutes but one of many such genres. Nevertheless, Mayreder's bleak assessment does not acknowledge that the nineteenth century did in fact produce a number of counter-examples, that is, writing that tested precisely these cultural stereotypes and deviated from or at least pushed the limits of the conventions of genre.[62]

The 1830s and 1840s, the two decades preceding the March Revolution of 1848, saw an important upswing in women's literary production, and in particular that of the progressive kind. Writing by women, such as the feminists Fanny Lewald and Luise Otto-Peters, the unconventional Bettina von Arnim (1785–1859), Luise Mühlbach (pseud. for Clara Mundt, 1814–1873), and even the archaristocrat Ida von Hahn-Hahn (1805–80), painted striking portraits of outspoken women who confronted new kinds of problems, even if ostensibly operating largely within the conventional literary boundaries of courtship and marriage. Later in the century even best-selling author E. Marlitt (pseud. for Eugenie John, 1825–1887), against whom Mayreder's polemic was surely directed in part, supplied her readership with stories of upward mobility. Despite their conventionality they insist on the importance of women's education and the cultivation of women's talents, even if, as in *Das Geheimnis der alten Mamsell* (The Secret of the Old Mamsell, 1868), the ultimate reward is merely becoming the wealthy doctor's wife.[63] And a few years before the appearance of *From a Good Family* Marie von Ebner-Eschenbach had published her controversial novel of adultery *Un-*

sühnbar (Beyond Atonement, 1889), which portrays the fragility of
the social mores that constituted the very foundation of the Austrian
nobility.[64] During most of the nineteenth century these counter-
narratives and counter-images constituted but a small part of the literature written and read by women; toward the end of the century,
however, they began to multiply.

Mayreder's condemnation in 1905 of nineteenth-century images
of women, itself belonged to a trend in women's writing that had
been well underway for over a decade. Indeed, precisely the decade
between *From a Good Family* and Mayreder's essay yielded an abundance of German and Austrian novels and short stories that depict
and challenge the constraints placed on women's lives. Reuter's
novel just preceded the wave, in fact helped to shape it.[65]

Between 1896 and 1905, for example, Mayreder herself published works of fiction that question contemporary middle-class social practices and especially codes of gender: two novels, *Idole.
Geschichte einer Liebe* (Idols. The Story of a Love, 1899) and *Pipin.
Ein Sommererlebnis* (Pipin. A Summer Experience, 1903), and two
collections of shorter pieces, *Aus meiner Jugend: Drei Novellen*
(From my Youth: Three Novellas, 1896) and *Übergänge* (Transi-
tions, 1897).[66] In the short story "Sein Ideal" (His Ideal, 1897) she
sketches an ironic portrait of a marriage in which a husband discov-
ers that his charming but ignorant bride, who corresponded in every
respect to his ideal, makes a singularly uninteresting and irritating
life partner.

Helene Böhlau (1856–1940) — whom Reuter knew from Weimar — similarly questioned nineteenth-century images of femininity
in her provocative novel *Halbtier!* (Half-Animal!, 1899), a work that
recalls many of the themes of *From a Good Family*.[67] Between 1894
and 1909 Hedwig Dohm, best known for her feminist essays, published four novels and a number of shorter pieces of fiction that treat
women in search of identity and freedom. The female protagonists
of these four novels — *Werde, die du bist* (Become Who You Are,
1894), *Sibilla Dalmar* (1899), *Schicksale einer Seele* (Fates of a Soul,
1899), and *Christa Ruland* (1902) — come to a broadly feminist
perspective on their lives and in the last three manage to change
their lives accordingly.[68] Although not politically feminist in outlook,
Franziska zu Reventlow's (1871–1918) autobiographical novel *Ellen
Olestjerne* (1903) told the story of a protagonist who deviated wildly

from nineteenth-century conventions of womanhood, shocking contemporaries with its frank rendering of erotic liberation from family and moral strictures.[69] Between 1897 and 1899, the internationally acclaimed Clara Viebig (1860–1952) wrote three novels in which the heroines struggle for independence in the face of convention. In *Es lebe die Kunst* (Long Live Art!, 1899) the heroine, who is an artist, manages to combine successfully the demands of family and career.[70] In a series of literary works, beginning with *Florentiner Novellen* (Florentine Novellas, 1890), Isolde Kurz (1853–1944) portrayed strong women struggling against contemporary ideals of femininity.[71] Furthermore, in novels and short stories written in the years 1893–1904 and in some cases published over a decade later, Lou Andreas-Salomé (1861–1937) created a series of extraordinary women who "discover their freer self."[72] Her *Fenitschka* (1899), for example, treats the conflict that an independently minded woman encounters when she falls in love.[73]

Reuter's novel, by contrast with Salomé's and those of many other women authors from this period, does not promote positive identification with an exceptional heroine; rather it offers a systematic and relentless examination of an ordinary young woman's socialization into her gender and class, an everyday story. Moments of identification with the female protagonist are just as likely to produce embarrassment as sympathy in the reader. While Reuter's story of arrested development is most certainly of its age, few of the novels by female contemporaries in Germany and Austria can approach *From a Good Family* in impact, literary finesse, psychological acuity, and social analysis.

From a Good Family in the English and American Literary Context

From a Good Family delineates the perils of being born female into a particular class in a particular time and place. Nevertheless the appeal and pertinence of this book is not confined to that particular historical context. In fact this novel evinces many points of contact with late nineteenth and early twentieth-century American and British fiction, and also with our own late twentieth-century fiction. In its portrayal of a nervous breakdown, for example, it invites comparison with "The Yellow Wallpaper" (1892), Charlotte Perkins Gilman's first-person account of a woman undergoing the infamous rest cure. Its astute depiction of gendered codes of propriety in the "better" classes recalls Edith Wharton's *House of Mirth* (1905), Henry James's *The Awkward Age* (1898), and Kate Chopin's *The Awakening* (1899). Like these novels, it paints a world in which the interests of men and women increasingly diverge to the detriment of both, what Henry James described in 1892 in the American context as "the growing divorce between the American woman (with her comparative leisure, culture, grace, social instincts, artistic ambition) and the male American immersed in the ferocity of business with no time for any but the most sordid interests, purely commercial, professional, democratic and political."[74]

From a Good Family also demands to be read alongside nineteenth and early twentieth-century English and American novels that trace their heroines' transition from girlhood to adulthood and social integration and typically end in marriage, works that Patricia Meyer Spacks has termed novels of female adolescence:[75] Fanny Burney's *Camilla* (1796), Jane Austen's *Pride and Prejudice* (1813), Charlotte Brontë's *Jane Eyre* (1847), Emily Brontë's *Wuthering Heights* (1847), Louisa May Alcott's *Little Women* (1868), George Eliot's *Mill on the Floss* (1860), and Henry James's *Washington Square* (1881), to name a few of the better-known examples. Reuter, born one to three generations after many of these English and American authors, appears more skeptical of the possibility of a triumphant passage in the absence of social change. She is of course by no means alone in allowing her heroine to be defeated, but her portrait of Agathe Heidling frustrates many of the genre expectations set up by precisely this English and American writing. Although manifestly sensitive and intelligent, Agathe is not an exceptional person and certainly not an artist like Chopin's Edna Pontellier.[76] Furthermore, Agathe's story does not find closure in a typical manner: neither does she marry nor does she drown morally triumphant like Eliot's Maggie Tulliver or sensually alive like Edna. Nor does she in any sense escape in the end, not even into the conventional madness that Sandra Gilbert and Susan Gubar have identified as typical of nineteenth-century literature by women.[77] Although Agathe fantasizes her own death by drowning and does go mad for a time, her society forces her into a bleak recovery of sorts.

Finally — to name only a few a recent examples — the success of Margaret Atwood's historical novel *Alias Grace* (1996) and that of Mary Bray Pipher's non-fiction study of adolescent girls, *Reviving Ophelia: Saving the Selves of Adolescent Girls* (1994), as well as the recent spate of film versions of nineteenth-century novels depicting the limitations of gender and class strongly suggests that the kinds of social restrictions and cultural ills outlined in *From a Good Family* continue to interest us, indeed, still haunt us, albeit in new forms keyed to our historical moment and our culture. Reading *From a Good Family* offers both moments of recognition and of instructive alienation.

Lynne Tatlock
St. Louis, Missouri, January 1999

Notes

*All translations are my own.

[1] [Helene Lange?], "Bücherschau. 'Aus guter Familie,'" *Die Frau* 3 (1895–96): 317.

[2] Hedwig Dohm, "Gabriele Reuter: 'Das Tränenhaus,'" *Der Tag* 23 December 1908, Call No.: GSA 112/25. This is one of several articles held in the *Goethe- und Schiller-Archiv* in Weimar, Germany, that will be cited here. This archive holds many newspaper clippings from Reuter's own collection. Unfortunately the requisite bibliographical information has frequently been cut off these articles. References to these clippings therefore include all available bibliographical information as well as the call number of the folders in which they are held in the archive.

[3] Helene Stöcker, "Gabriele Reuter. Zu ihrem siebzigsten Geburtstag," *Neue Rundschau* 40 (1929): 270.

[4] Gabriele Reuter, no title, *Beilage der Neuen Freien Presse*, 28 October 1928, Call No.: GSA 112/11.

[5] Hans Olden, "Die Leiden der jungen Agathe," [1896], Call No.: GSA 112/12. Olden knew Reuter personally from Weimar and no doubt also knew that her novel, like *The Sufferings of Young Werther*, had an autobiographical basis. Franz Servaes refers to Olden's review in his own and suggests that *From a Good Family* was in fact modeled after Goethe's novel. While he expresses some skepticism about Olden's comparison, he nevertheless concedes that the book has had an unusually large cultural

impact (Franz Servaes, "Feuilleton. Leidensbekenntnisse eines Mädchens," [*Neue Freie Presse*], n.d., Call No.: GSA 112/12).

[6] See Gabriele Reuter, *Vom Kinde zum Menschen. Die Geschichte meiner Jugend* (Berlin: S. Fischer: 1921), 474.

[7] Thomas Mann, "Gabriele Reuter," *Aufsätze, Reden, Essays*, ed. Harry Matter, 8 vols. (Berlin: Aufbau-Verlag, 1983), 1: 42.

[8] *Encyclopedia Britannica*, 11th ed., s.v. "German literature."

[9] Victor Klemperer, "Gabriele Reuter," *Westermann's Monatshefte* 52 (1908): 871.

[10] Heinrich Meyer-Benfey, "Gabriele Reuter," *Zeitung für Literatur, Kunst und Wissenschaft. Beilage des Hamburgischen Correspondenten*, 28 May 1905, Call No.: GSA 112/225.

[11] "Feuilleton. Ein neues Buch," *Zweite Beilage zu Nr. 569 der Breslauer Morgen-Zeitung*, 5 December 1895, Call No.: GSA 112/12.

[12] Peter de Mendelssohn, *S. Fischer und sein Verlag* (Frankfurt a. M.: S. Fischer, 1970), 148.

[13] Richard Johnson has noted concerning the fact that academics, too, seem to have forgotten her that "a man who wrote as much and as well as Reuter would not be a nonentity among Germanists" (Richard Johnson, "Gabriele Reuter: Romantic and Realist," *Beyond the Eternal Feminine. Critical Essays on Women and German Literature*, eds. Susan Cocalis and Kay Goodman [Stuttgart: Akademischer Verlag Hans-Dieter Heinz, 1982], 226).

[14] The following biographical sketch has benefited from Gabriele Reuter's autobiography *Vom Kinde zum Menschen*; Faranak Alimadad-Mensch, *Gabriele Reuter. Porträt einer Schriftstellerin* (Bern: Peter Lang, 1984); Katherine R. Goodman, "Gabriele Reuter," *German Fiction Writers, 1885–1913*, vol. 66, pt. 2 of *Dictionary of Literary Biography* (Detroit: Bruccoli Clark Layman, 1988), 411–17; Linda Kraus Worley, "Gabriele Reuter: Reading Women in the 'Kaiserreich,'" *Autoren damals und heute. Literaturgeschichtliche Beispiele veränderter Wirkungshorizonte*, ed. Gerhard P. Knapp (Amsterdam: Rodopi, 1991), 419–39; and newspaper clippings and papers held in the *Goethe- und Schiller Archiv* in Weimar, Germany. I agree with Worley's astute caveat that we must read Reuter's autobiography critically as "she also may have allowed her early fictional narratives to influence the portrayals in her autobiography . . . " (Worley, 419); the points of coincidence between the novel and the autobiography do indeed suggest a degree of reconstruction after the fact. Nevertheless, Reuter's autobiography remains our most detailed source of information on the first thirty-six years of her life.

[15] This title, which was not Reuter's own and was given the novel by the publisher, in fact duplicates that of a novel from 1842 by the prolific novelist Luise Mühlbach (1814–1873). Reuter apparently was not aware of this.

[16] Reuter, *Vom Kinde zum Menschen*, 462.

[17] Alimadad-Mensch, *Gabriele Reuter*, 184.

[18] Mann, "Gabriele Reuter," 42.

[19] Mendelssohn, *Fischer*, 149.

[20] Dohm, "Gabriele Reuter."

[21] Marie von Ebner Eschenbach, Letter to Gabriele Reuter, 10 December 1904, *Goethe- und Schiller-Archiv*, Weimar, Germany, Call No.: GSA 112/218b.

[22] Goodman, "Gabriele Reuter," 416.

[23] Paul F. C. Vaka, "Gabriele Reuter at Eighty," *The New York Times Book Review* 5 February 1939.

[24] See Francis Brown, *The Story of The New York Times Book Review* (New York: The New York Times Company, 1969), 3, 10.

[25] Vaka, "Gabriele Reuter at 80."

[26] Reuter, *Beilage der Neuen Freien Presse*, 28 October 1928.

[27] Qtd. by Else Gießmann, "Die Reuter." *DGA*, 13 February 1929, Call No.: 112/321.

[28] Helene Busch-Elsner, "'Aus guter Familie' im Lichte von heute. Zum 80. Geburtstag von Gabriele Reuter am 8. Februar," [1939], Call No.: GSA 112/223.

[29] Reuter's mother gave birth to a daughter whom the family proudly named Viktoria Germania and who died in infancy (Reuter, *Vom Kinde zum Menschen*, 134, 147).

[30] Franz Carl Müller, introduction to *Handbuch der Neurasthenie*, ed. Franz Carl Müller (Leipzig: F. C. W. Vogel, 1893), v.

[31] Elaine Showalter observes that neurasthenia was originally an American disorder, described in the 1860s by George Miller Beard as the "American nervousness." Beard believed that the illness was "the price exacted by industrialized urban societies, competitive business and social environments, and the luxuries, vices, and excesses of modern life" (Elaine Showalter, *The Female Malady. Women, Madness, and English Culture, 1830–1980* [New York: Pantheon Books, 1985], 135).

[32] Rudolph von Hösslin, "Aetiologie," *Handbuch der Neurasthenie*, ed. Franz Carl Müller (Leipzig: F. C. W. Vogel, 1893), 65.

[33] Hösslin, "Aetiologie," 67–68.

[34] For an examination of *From a Good Family* as a critique of Prussia in particular, see Elke Frederiksen, "Der literarische Text im späten 19. Jahrhundert als Schnittpunkt von regionalen, überregionalen und Geschlechts-Aspekten: Gabriele Reuters Roman *Aus guter Familie* zum Beispiel," *Literatur und Regionalität*, ed. Anselm Maler (Bern: Peter Lang, 1997), 157–66.

[35] Caroline S. J. Milde, *Der deutschen Jungfrau Wesen und Wirken. Winke für das geistige und praktische Leben* (Leipzig: C. F. Amelang, 1878), 333.

[36] On the subject of the dowry, Reuter noted in an essay on marriage that "the young man who would find it outrageous if his wife were to contribute to household expenses by means of her work in some sort of occupation often lays claims to her inheritance as if it were his sole property to manage as he likes" (Gabriele Reuter, *Das Problem der Ehe* [Berlin: E. Kantorowicz, 1907], 40).

[37] Luise Otto-Peters, *Das Recht der Frauen auf Erwerb* (Hamburg: Hoffman and Campe, 1866), 69; Fanny Lewald, "Meine Tochter ist noch ein völliges Kind" [1861] in *Frauenemanzipation im deutschen Vormärz. Texte und Dokumente*, ed. Renate Möhrmann (Stuttgart: Philipp Reclam, 1978), 17–22, esp. 18–19.

[38] See Helene Lange, "Die Stellung der Frauenbewegung zu Ehe und Familie" [1908] and "Die wirtschaftlichen Ursachen der Frauenbewegung" [1908] in *Die Frauenfrage in Deutschland 1865–1915. Texte und Dokumente*, ed. Elke Frederiksen (Stuttgart: Reclam, 1981), 127–48 and 311–20 respectively. On the role of maternalist thinking in German bourgeois feminism, see Ann Taylor Allen, *Feminism and Motherhood in Germany, 1800–1914* (New Brunswick, NJ: Rutgers UP, 1991).

[39] Reuter, *Beilage der Neuen Freien Presse*, 28 October 1928.

[40] Friedrich Wilhelm Opitz, *Heilige Stunden einer Jungfrau. Eine Konfirmationsgabe*, 13th ed. (Emden: Verlag von W. Haynel, 1893).

[41] *Ibid.*, 212.

[42] Julie Burow, *Das Glück eines Weibes* (Bromberg: Louis Lebit, Königl. Hofbuchhändler, 1860), 73.

[43] *Ibid.*, ix.

[44] *Aus der Töchterschule ins Leben. Ein allseitiger Berater für Deutschlands Jungfrauen*, ed. Amalie Baisch, 7th ed. (Stuttgart: Deutsche Verlags-Anstalt, 1892), 185 and 191 respectively.

[45] Franz Ebhardt, *Der gute Ton in allen Lebenslagen. Ein Handbuch für den Verkehr in der Familie, in der Gesellschaft und im öffentlichen Leben*, 9th ed. (Leipzig: Julius Klinkhardt, 1885), 43.

[46] Showalter, *The Female Malady*, 161.

[47] Inge Stephan, *Die Gründerinnen der Psychoanalyse. Eine Entmythologisierung Sigmund Freuds in zwölf Frauenporträts* (Stuttgart: Kreuz Verlag, 1992), 41–42. See also Marion A. Kaplan, "Anna O. and Bertha Pappenheim: An Historical Perspective," *Anna O. Fourteen Contemporary Reinterpretations*, eds. Max Rosenbaum and Melvin Muroff (New York: The Free Press, 1984), 101–19.

[48] Elaine Showalter reminds us that Freud's case studies in fact read like Victorian novels (Elaine Showalter, *Hystories. Hysterical Epidemics and Modern Culture* [New York: Columbia UP, 1997], 85–86).

[49] Qtd. by Worley, "Reading Women in the 'Kaiserreich,'" 423.

[50] Reuter, *Vom Kinde zum Menschen*, 470.

[51] Notably precisely a German reviewer thought that Sue Bridehead embodied a new type. Hardy reported in his preface to the second edition of 1912 that a German reviewer had informed him that Sue Bridehead was "the first delineation in fiction of the woman who was coming into notice in her thousands every year — the woman of the feminist movement — the slight, pale 'bachelor' girl — the intellectualized, emancipated bundle of nerves that modern conditions were producing, mainly in cities as yet . . . " (Thomas Hardy, *Jude the Obscure* [New York: Random House, 1967], xxxiv–xxxv).

[52] Jeannine Blackwell in fact argued in 1982 for *From a Good Family* as a new kind of Bildungsroman (Jeannine L. Blackwell, *"Bildungsroman mit Dame*: The Heroine in the German Bildungsroman from 1770 to 1900" [Ph.D. diss., Indiana University, 1982]).

[53] Reuter, *Vom Kinde zum Menschen*, 448.

[54] See David Leopold, introduction to *The Ego and Its Own*, by Max Stirner (Cambridge: Cambridge UP, 1995), xi.

[55] Reuter, *Vom Kinde zum Menschen*, 448.

[56] Reuter, *Vom Kinde zum Menschen*, 451.

[57] Gabriele Reuter, "John Henry Mackay. Eine litterarische Studie," *Die Gesellschaft. Monatsschrift für Litteratur, Kunst und Sozialpolitik* 7.10 (1891), 1309–10.

[58] Worley, "Reading Women in the 'Kaiserreich,'" 435.

[59] Elaine Showalter, *A Literature of Their Own. British Women Novelists from Brontë to Lessing* (Princeton: Princeton UP, 1977), 189.

[60] Rosa Mayreder, "Familienliteratur" [1905] in Rosa Mayreder, *Zur Kritik der Weiblichkeit. Essays*, ed. Hanna Schnedl (Munich: Verlag Frauenoffensive, 1981), 126.

[61] Mayreder, "Familienliteratur," 129.

[62] A recent anthology of thirty-one women's short fiction in German produced in the years 1850–1907 offers insight into the vast literary production by women and suggests that there is much more to be known about the narratives produced in this tense transitional era: Michelle Stott and Joseph O. Baker, eds., *Im Nonnengarten: An Anthology of German Women's Writing 1850–1907* (Prospect Heights, IL: Waveland Press, Inc., 1997).

[63] For a concise treatment in English of Marlitt's life and works, see Brent O. Peterson, "E. Marlitt (Eugenie John)," *Nineteenth-Century German Writing, 1841–1900*, vol. 29 of *Dictionary of Literary Biography* (Detroit: Bruccoli Clark Layman, 1993), 223–28.

[64] See Vanessa Van Ornam, introduction to *Beyond Atonement* (Columbia, SC: Camden House), 1997. vii-xi.

[65] Reuter, *Vom Kinde zum Menschen*, 434–35. Klemperer notes, "Few books have been accorded the honor of as many imitations as has the novel *From a Good Family*" (Klemperer, "Gabriele Reuter," 871).

[66] For an English treatment of Mayreder's fiction, see Jane Sokolosky, "Rosa Mayreder: The Theory in her Fiction" (Ph.D. diss., Washington University, 1997).

[67] Alyth F. Grant, "From 'Halbtier' to 'Übermensch': Helene Böhlau's Iconoclastic Reversal of Cultural Images," *Women in German Yearbook* 11 (1995): 131–50.

[68] Chris Weedon, "The Struggle for Women's Emancipation in the Work of Hedwig Dohm," *German Life and Letters* 47.2 (April 1994): 182–92.

[69] For a concise treatment in English of Reventlow's life and works, see George C. Schoolfield, "Franziska Gräfin zu Reventlow," *German Fiction Writers, 1885–1913*, vol. 66, pt. 2 of *Dictionary of Literary Biography* (Detroit: Bruccoli Clark Layman, 1988), 418–25.

[70] For a concise treatment in English of Viebig's life and works, see Erich P. Hofacker, Jr., "Clara Viebig," *German Fiction Writers, 1885–1913*, vol. 66, pt. 2 of *Dictionary of Literary Biography* (Detroit: Bruccoli Clark Layman, 1988), 470–79.

[71] For a concise treatment in English of Kurz's life and works, see Timothy A. Bennett, "Isolde Kurz," *German Fiction Writers, 1885–1913*, vol. 66, pt. 1 of *Dictionary of Literary Biography* (Detroit: Bruccoli Clark Layman, 1988), 280–84.

[72] Angela Livingstone, *Lou Andreas-Salomé* (London and Bedford: The Gordon Fraser Gallery, Ltd., 1984), 212; for Livingstone's summary of Salomé's fiction writing in this period, see 204–20. See also Margit Resch, "Lou Andreas-Salomé," *German Fiction Writers, 1885–1913*, vol. 66, pt. 1

of *Dictionary of Literary Biography* (Detroit: Bruccoli Clark Layman, 1988), 3–17 and Biddy Martin, *The (Life)Styles of Lou Andreas-Salomé* (Ithaca: Cornell UP, 1991).

[73] See Gisela Brinker-Gabler, "Selbständigkeit oder/und Liebe. Über die Entwicklung eines 'Frauenproblems' in drei Romanen aus dem Anfang des 20. Jahrhunderts," *"Frauen sehen ihre Zeit": Katalog zur Literaturausstellung des Landesfrauenbeirates Rheinland-Pfalz* (Mainz: Ministerium für Soziales, Gesundheit und Umwelt Rheinland-Pfalz, 1984), 41–53. Although Brinker-Gabler does not draw explicit comparisons, she implies commonality by examining both *Fenitschka* and *From a Good Family* in this piece.

[74] Qtd. by Elaine Showalter, introduction to *The Awakening. A Solitary Soul*, Everyman's Library, no. 132 (New York: Alfred A. Knopf, 1992), xvi.

[75] See Patricia Meyer Spacks, *The Female Imagination* (New York: Alfred A. Knopf, 1975) and Patricia Meyer Spacks, *The Adolescent Idea. Myths of Youth and the Adult Imagination* (New York: Basic Books, 1981).

[76] As Showalter maintains, although a twenty-nine-year-old woman, Edna experiences the adolescent emotions of a belated awakening, and in this sense Chopin's novel might be seen as another novel of female adolescence (Showalter, introduction to *The Awakening*, xxi).

[77] Sandra M. Gilbert and Susan Gubar, *The Madwoman in the Attic. The Woman Writer and the Nineteenth-Century Literary Imagination* (New Haven: Yale UP, 1979). Gilbert and Gubar note that "dramatizations of imprisonment and escape are so all-pervasive in nineteenth-century literature by women that we believe they represent a uniquely female tradition in this period" (Gilbert and Gubar, *Madwoman*, 86). The escapes can, however, be perverse: lunacy, suicide, anorexia, and bulimia.

Works Cited

Newspaper articles consulted in the *Goethe- und Schiller-Archiv* in Weimar, Germany, are cited with all available bibliographical information and by the call number of the file in which they are held.

Allen, Ann Taylor. *Feminism and Motherhood in Germany, 1800–1914.* New Brunswick, NJ: Rutgers UP, 1991.

Alimadad-Mensch, Faranak. *Gabriele Reuter. Porträt einer Schriftstellerin.* Bern: Peter Lang, 1984.

Baisch, Amalie, ed. *Aus der Töchterschule ins Leben. Ein allseitiger Berater für Deutschlands Jungfrauen.* 7th ed. Stuttgart: Deutsche Verlags-Anstalt, 1892.

Bennett, Timothy A. "Isolde Kurz." In *German Fiction Writers, 1885–1913.* Vol. 66, pt. 1 of *Dictionary of Literary Biography.* Detroit: Bruccoli Clark Layman, 1988.

Blackwell, Jeannine L. *"Bildungsroman mit Dame:* The Heroine in the German Bildungsroman from 1770 to 1900." Ph.D. diss., Indiana University, 1982.

Brown, Francis. *The Story of The New York Times Book Review.* New York: The New York Times Company, 1969.

Brinker-Gabler, Gisela. "Selbständigkeit oder/ und Liebe. Über die Entwicklung eines 'Frauenproblems' in drei Romanen aus dem Anfang des 20. Jahrhunderts." In *"Frauen sehen ihre Zeit": Katalog zur Literaturausstellung des Landesfrauenbeirates Rheinland-Pfalz.* Mainz: Ministerium für Soziales, Gesundheit und Umwelt Rheinland-Pfalz, 1984.

Burow, Julie. *Das Glück eines Weibes.* Bromberg: Louis Lebit, Königl. Hofbuchhändler, 1860.

Busch-Elsner, Helene. "'Aus guter Familie' im Lichte von heute. Zum 80. Geburtstag von Gabriele Reuter am 8. Februar." [1939]. Call No.: GSA 112/223.

Dohm, Hedwig. "Gabriele Reuter: 'Das Tränenhaus.'" *Der Tag,* 23 December 1908. Call No.: GSA 112/25.

Ebhardt, Franz. *Der gute Ton in allen Lebenslagen. Ein Handbuch für den Verkehr in der Familie, in der Gesellschaft und im öffentlichen Leben.* 9th ed. Leipzig: Julius Klinkhardt, 1885.

Ebner Eschenbach, Marie von. Letter to Gabriele Reuter. 10 December 1904. *Goethe- und Schiller-Archiv*, Weimar, Germany. Call No.: GSA 112/218b.

Encyclopedia Britannica. 11th ed. s.v. "German literature."

"Feuilleton. Ein neues Buch." *Zweite Beilage zu Nr. 569 der Breslauer Morgen-Zeitung*, 5 December 1895. Call No.: GSA 112/12.

Frederiksen, Elke. "Der literarische Text im späten 19. Jahrhundert als Schnittpunkt von regionalen, überregionalen und Geschlechts-Aspekten: Gabriele Reuters Roman *Aus guter Familie* zum Beispiel." In *Literatur und Regionalität*, edited by Anselm Maler. Bern: Peter Lang, 1997.

Gießmann, Else. "Die Reuter." *DGA*, 13 February 1929. Call No.: 112/321.

Gilbert, Sandra M. and Susan Gubar. *The Madwoman in the Attic. The Woman Writer and the Nineteenth-Century Literary Imagination.* New Haven: Yale UP, 1979.

Goodman, Katherine R. "Gabriele Reuter." In *German Fiction Writers, 1885–1913.* Vol. 66, pt. 2 of *Dictionary of Literary Biography*. Detroit: Bruccoli Clark Layman, 1988.

Grant, Alyth F. "From 'Halbtier' to 'Übermensch': Helene Böhlau's Iconoclastic Reversal of Cultural Images." *Women in German Yearbook* 11 (1995): 131–50.

Hardy, Thomas. *Jude the Obscure.* New York: Random House, 1967.

Hofacker, Erich P., Jr. "Clara Viebig." In *German Fiction Writers, 1885–1913.* Vol. 66, pt. 2 of *Dictionary of Literary Biography*. Detroit: Bruccoli Clark Layman, 1988.

Hösslin, Rudolph von. "Aetiologie." In *Handbuch der Neurasthenie*, edited by Franz Carl Müller. Leipzig: F. C. W. Vogel, 1893.

Johnson, Richard. "Gabriele Reuter: Romantic and Realist." *Beyond the Eternal Feminine. Critical Essays on Women and German Literature*, edited by Susan Cocalis and Kay Goodman. Stuttgart: Akademischer Verlag Hans-Dieter Heinz, 1982.

Kaplan, Marion A. "Anna O. and Bertha Pappenheim: An Historical Perspective." In *Anna O. Fourteen Contemporary Reinterpretations*, edited by Max Rosenbaum and Melvin Muroff. New York: The Free Press, 1984.

Klemperer, Victor. "Gabriele Reuter." *Westermann's Monatshefte* 52 (1908): 866–74.

[Lange, Helene?]. "Bücherschau. 'Aus guter Familie.'" *Die Frau* 3 (1895–96): 317.

Lange, Helene. "Die Stellung der Frauenbewegung zu Ehe und Familie" [1908]. In *Die Frauenfrage in Deutschland 1865–1915. Texte und Dokumente*, edited by Elke Frederiksen. Stuttgart: Reclam, 1981.

——. "Die wirtschaftlichen Ursachen der Frauenbewegung" [1908]. In *Die Frauenfrage in Deutschland 1865–1915. Texte und Dokumente*, edited by Elke Frederiksen. Stuttgart: Reclam, 1981.

Leopold, David. Introduction to *The Ego and Its Own*, by Max Stirner. Cambridge: Cambridge UP, 1995.

Lewald, Fanny. "Meine Tochter ist noch ein völliges Kind" [1861]. In *Frauenemanzipation im deutschen Vormärz. Texte und Dokumente*, edited by Renate Möhrmann. Stuttgart: Philipp Reclam, 1978.

Livingstone, Angela. *Lou Andreas-Salomé*. London and Bedford: The Gordon Fraser Gallery, Ltd., 1984.

Mann, Thomas. "Gabriele Reuter." In vol. 1 of *Aufsätze, Reden, Essays*, edited by Harry Matter. Berlin: Aufbau-Verlag, 1983.

Mendelssohn, Peter de. *S. Fischer und sein Verlag*. Frankfurt a. M.: S. Fischer, 1970.

Martin, Biddy. *The (Life)Styles of Lou Andreas-Salomé*. Ithaca: Cornell UP, 1991.

Meyer-Benfey, Heinrich. "Gabriele Reuter." *Zeitung für Literatur, Kunst und Wissenschaft. Beilage des Hamburgischen Correspondenten*, 28 May 1905. Call No.: GSA 112/225.

Mayreder, Rosa. "Familienliteratur" [1905]. In *Zur Kritik der Weiblichkeit. Essays*, edited by Hanna Schnedl. Munich: Verlag Frauenoffensive, 1981.

Milde, Caroline S. J. *Der deutschen Jungfrau Wesen und Wirken. Winke für das geistige und praktische Leben*. Leipzig: C. F. Amelang, 1878.

Müller, Franz Carl. Introduction to *Handbuch der Neurasthenie*, edited by Franz Carl Müller. Leipzig: F. C. W. Vogel, 1893.

Olden, Hans. "Die Leiden der jungen Agathe." [1896]. Call No.: GSA 112/12.

Opitz, Friedrich Wilhelm. *Heilige Stunden einer Jungfrau. Eine Konfirmationsgabe*. 13th ed. Emden: Verlag von W. Haynel, 1893.

Otto-Peters, Luise. *Das Recht der Frauen auf Erwerb*. Hamburg: Hoffman and Campe, 1866.

Peterson, Brent O. "E. Marlitt (Eugenie John)." In *Nineteenth-Century German Writing, 1841–1900*. Vol. 29 of *Dictionary of Literary Biography*. Detroit: Bruccoli Clark Layman, 1993.

Resch, Margit. "Lou Andreas-Salomé." In *German Fiction Writers, 1885–1913*. Vol. 66, pt. 1 of *Dictionary of Literary Biography*. Detroit: Bruccoli Clark Layman, 1988.

Reuter, Gabriele. No title. *Beilage der Neuen Freien Presse*, 28 October 1928. Call No.: GSA 112/11.

——. "John Henry Mackay. Eine litterarische Studie." *Die Gesellschaft. Monatsschrift für Litteratur, Kunst und Sozialpolitik* 7.10 (1891): 1304–14.

——. *Das Problem der Ehe*. Berlin: E. Kantorowicz, 1907.

——. *Vom Kinde zum Menschen. Die Geschichte meiner Jugend*. Berlin: S. Fischer: 1921.

Schoolfield, George C. "Franziska Gräfin zu Reventlow." In *German Fiction Writers, 1885–1913*. Vol. 66, pt. 2 of *Dictionary of Literary Biography*. Detroit: Bruccoli Clark Layman, 1988.

Servaes, Franz. "Feuilleton. Leidensbekenntnisse eines Mädchens." [*Neue Freie Presse*], n.d. Call No.: GSA 112/12.

Showalter, Elaine. *The Female Malady. Women, Madness, and English Culture, 1830–1980*. New York: Pantheon Books, 1985.

——. *Hystories. Hysterical Epidemics and Modern Culture*. New York: Columbia UP, 1997.

——. Introduction to *The Awakening. A Solitary Soul*, by Kate Chopin. Everyman's Library, no. 132. New York: Alfred A. Knopf, 1992.

——. *A Literature of Their Own. British Women Novelists from Brontë to Lessing*. Princeton: Princeton UP, 1977.

Sokolosky, Jane. "Rosa Mayreder: The Theory in her Fiction." Ph.D. diss., Washington University, 1997.

Spacks, Patricia Meyer. *The Adolescent Idea. Myths of Youth and the Adult Imagination*. New York: Basic Books, 1981.

——. *The Female Imagination*. New York: Alfred A. Knopf, 1975.

Stephan, Inge. *Die Gründerinnen der Psychoanalyse. Eine Entmythologisierung Sigmund Freuds in zwölf Frauenporträts*. Stuttgart: Kreuz Verlag, 1992.

Stöcker, Helene. "Gabriele Reuter. Zu ihrem siebzigsten Geburtstag." *Neue Rundschau* 40 (1929): 268–72.

Stott, Michelle and Joseph O. Baker, eds. *Im Nonnengarten: An Anthology of German Women's Writing 1850–1907.* Prospect Heights, IL: Waveland Press, Inc., 1997.

Vaka, Paul F. C. "Gabriele Reuter at Eighty." *The New York Times Book Review,* 5 February 1939.

Van Ornam, Vanessa. Introduction to *Beyond Atonement.* Columbia, SC: Camden House, 1997.

Weedon, Chris. "The Struggle for Women's Emancipation in the Work of Hedwig Dohm." *German Life and Letters* 47.2 (April 1994): 182–92.

Worley, Linda Kraus. "Gabriele Reuter: Reading Women in the 'Kaiserreich.'" *Autoren damals und heute. Literaturgeschichtliche Beispiele veränderter Wirkungshorizonte,* edited by Gerhard P. Knapp. Amsterdam: Rodopi, 1991.

Translator's Note

Gabriele Reuter's *Aus guter Familie. Leidensgeschichte eines Mädchens* was reprinted twenty-seven times in two distinct impressions that exhibit only slight differences: variant typographical errors and omissions so minor as to be accidental, that is, the result of imperfect editing. The current translation relies on both editions to reproduce a corrected text as Reuter would surely have done had she edited it for a third impression.

This translation does not aspire to reproduce the English language of the late nineteenth century. It does, however, avoid obvious anachronisms and strives for a standard, slightly antiquated but nevertheless spoken English. Such English at least suggests Reuter's High German, the language spoken by the educated middle classes in Prussia, an idiom that differs from the dialects spoken by the lower classes and in circles more closely allied with regional culture. Reuter writes in a highly oral, ostensibly spontaneous and impressionistic style, making liberal use of dialogue as well as paraphrases of speech as reflected in the consciousness of her principal character. In its frequent use of the technique of *style indirect libre* the translation faithfully reproduces the original in order to recreate the subtle shifting of the narrative between the objective rendering of the milieu and the milieu as experienced by Agathe.

While an argument can be made for the universality of Reuter's story of arrested development, the text does focus on a specific time and place. In order, therefore, to retain a trace of the Germanness of the setting, the translation retains German street names and the use of *Herr*, *Frau*, and *Fräulein*, forms of address familiar to most educated North Americans. The professional and honorific titles, characteristic of Imperial Germany, presented a thorny problem, however. Not only were men typically addressed as *Herr* followed by their title, their wives were addressed and identified by their husbands' title, sometimes in the feminine form and sometimes in the masculine form, preceded by *Frau*. Most of these titles are not only unfamiliar to North Americans but also unpronounceable for those who do not speak German. The translation therefore strikes a compromise by rendering these titles in English forms but combining them with *Herr* and *Frau*, and thus producing such combinations as "Herr Privy Councillor" and "Frau President." In the nineteenth century there was an analogous, albeit not widespread, English reference to women by their husband's titles, as in the example of Mrs. Alderman Parkinson in Margaret Atwood's *Alias Grace*. In cases that are not a matter of direct address, however, such female titles as *Regierungsrätin* are most often rendered in this translation as the "privy councillor's wife."

Some of the names used in the novel have also been anglicized in order to make them pronounceable; *Dorte* becomes Dottie and *Mariechen*, Marietta. Similarly, the spellings of some German names have been slightly altered so that English-speaking readers will pronounce them more like German, as in *Malwine*/Malvina and *Luise*/Luisa. The spellings "Eugenie" and "Agathe" have, however, been retained; in both cases the original German corresponds to the French spelling that might have been used in a British or North American context for women of this social class. Especially in the case of "Eugenie," a name made popular by Empress Eugenie of France (1826–1920), it is even possible that some Germans would have used the French pronunciation.

Reuter's use of the word *Mädchen* (girl) throughout her novel for characters well beyond adolescence presented an additional problem. In nineteenth-century Germany *Mädchen* could refer to single women like the cognate in the now seldom-used English expression "maiden aunt." Hence designations like *ältere Mädchen* (literally, "oldish girls") were in fact polite, although perhaps subtly condescending, terms for unmarried women of a certain age. Reuter makes explicit the irony of such usage, its symbolic weight in a society that does not allow single women to become adults. Despite the fact that the use of the designation "girl" for adult women is now currently considered offensive in some circles, the translation for the most part reproduces Reuter's use of *Mädchen* as "girl"; to do otherwise is to obscure her point.

The pronounced differences in German and English syntax and punctuation necessitated deviation from Reuter's original. Nevertheless, the translation seeks, within the boundaries of English, to recreate the same effects, as for example in the case of the staccato prose in which Reuter records Agathe's nervous breakdown or that of the fulsome style that characterizes the sententiae that the pastor and the privy councillor utter on the occasion of Agathe's confirmation. The goal of this translation was ultimately to produce a text domesticated enough to be easily readable by a contemporary English-speaker, but with a trace of the foreign ample enough to suggest another era and another place.

From a Good Family

Part 1

I.

A beam of springtime sun fell broad and bright through the dusty arched window of a village church. Cutting a warm, shining swath through the gray twilight, it vanished behind a white lattice in the damp, shadowy depths of the chancel which a number of ladies and gentlemen occupied, dressed in their Sunday best. The girl who was to be confirmed stood squarely in the path of light before the altar, the little cross on her breast glowing like a celestial symbol. Above her solemn rosy child's face, which was bathed in tears, her brown hair glimmered like a wreath of worldly delights sprinkled through and through with a thousand golden glints.

She stood entirely alone on the holy spot, filled with awe by the meaning of the moment, afraid to utter the vow that hovered on her lips and that was to oblige her irrevocably to lead a life of truth and sanctification.

Among the narrow wooden benches behind her she heard the din of a few kneeling day laborers' children who had already been confirmed. Agathe suddenly felt a morbidly vehement desire to hide herself there among those children with their meticulously slicked down hair, their faces reddened with scrubbing, and their ungainly figures. She wished she could fortify herself in fellowship with them.

Her heart nearly ceased beating, a fear seized her, a dizziness, as she sank to her knees and bowed her head, feeling as if in the next minute her existence — the existence she rejoiced in — would have to be exchanged for a condition of alien awe full of sublime suffering and oppressive rapture.

Above her Agathe heard the gentle, seriously solemn voice of the pastor directing the question to her: Would she forsake the Devil, the world, and all its pleasures, would she belong to Christ and would she follow Him? In sweet melancholy she breathed a "yes," felt the touch upon her head of the hands that blessed and made a wrenching effort to submerge all her senses in the worship of the eternal Divinity, of the Lord who hovered over her.

But she heard the rustling of her own silk dress; an emotional whispering and a suppressed sob from the chancel where her parents were sitting reached her ears. Somewhere she heard a hymnal tumble noisily to the floor followed by a mumbled apology. She attended to the false notes of the sexton's soft organ accompaniment. Involuntarily she thought of a book, of an indecent passage that dogged her . . . . Tears welled up beneath her lowered eyelids. She folded her hands convulsively; she watched her teardrops form damp stains on her black gloves; she could not pray . . . .

Not in this hour? She couldn't belong only to God even for a few seconds? And she had sworn to renounce the world her whole life long! She had sworn a false oath, had committed an inexpiable sin! My God, my God, what anguish!

Was the Devil tempting her? There really *was* a devil. She felt quite clearly that he was close by, gloating over her inability to pray. Dear Lord, don't abandon me! Perhaps she was being tested because she hadn't been honest in the confession she had had to write down and give the pastor. Should she have humbled herself so terribly . . . confess that? No, no, no! That was quite impossible. She'd rather go to hell!

She broke out in a sweat; the shame of it tortured her so! She certainly couldn't write that down. A thousand times better to go to hell!

. . . Don't think about it now . . . just don't think. What could one do to get control over one's thoughts? She was always thinking . . . . Everything was so mysteriously terrible in this Christian religious life. She did want to accept it . . . . And she had promised to. Now she had to. She had no choice!

Her knees shaking unbearably, the girl returned to her seat. The song of the congregation and the sound of the organ swelled while the pastor made preparations for Communion, poured wine from the graceful pitcher into the silver chalice and lifted the embroidered linen cloth from the plate with the holy wafers.

The light of the tall wax candles flickered restlessly. Agathe closed her eyes, blinded by the bright sunshine that flooded the church where billions of dust particles swirled. Was the heavenly sun there only to bring all that was hidden to a terrifying clarity?

In dull astonishment she heard her fellow confirmands whispering in Low German[1] next to her — towheaded girls who emanated a scent of cheap pomade.

"Wiesing, where's your mother?"

"She has ta take care of our little calf."

"I'll be! Has it come already? That's great! I wanna hear all about it!"

"Star had it at twelve on the button. We were in that stable all night long!"

How could they talk about something like that in church, thought Agathe. A trace of arrogant disdain stirred at the corners of her mouth. She became calmer, more certain in the feeling of her ardent intention. A fatigue, a kind of blissful exhaustion stole over her during the singing of that old mystical communion song:

> Soul, adorn yourself with gladness,
> Leave the gloomy haunts of sadness,
> Come into the daylight's splendor,
> There with joy your praises render.
>
> Bless the one whose grace unbounded,
> His amazing banquet founded;
> He, though heavenly, high, and holy,
> Deigns to dwell with you most lowly.
>
> Hasten as a bride to meet him,
> Eagerly and gladly greet him.
> There he stands already knocking;
> Quickly, now, your gates unlocking.
>
> Open wide the fast-closed portal,
> Saying to the Lord immortal;
> "Come and leave your loved one never;
> Dwell within my heart forever."[2]

Now it was not the sublime God-Father, who demanded sacrifice, no longer the Holy Spirit, the inconceivable terrible one, who menaced those who offended Him with the flames of the eternal fire, who never forgave; no, now the Heavenly Bridegroom approached with comfort and love.

5

"Whoever eats and drinks there when he is not worthy be damned"[3] — it does say that there too. But a glad conviction came over the girl. Before her mind's eye appeared the image of Jesus of Nazareth, as art, as Titian has fashioned Him, in His beautiful, youthful humanity — *He* was the one she loved . . . . A thirsting and yearning for the mystical union with Him made the young woman's every nerve ending tingle. The strong wine ran a fiery course through her exhausted body. A gentle, tender happiness that was nevertheless full of renunciation thrilled through her inmost soul. She had been found worthy to experience His presence.

* * *

Agathe's parents, her brother, her uncle, and the wife of the preacher in whose house she had been living for several months also took Communion so that they might bind themselves in love to the child. That's why the pastor had taken care of his rustic confirmands and their relatives first and then called the daughter of the privy councillor[4] and her family to approach the Lord's table. So Agathe stood there surrounded by all of those who were closest to her in this world.

The grumpy old peasants and the sleepy hired hands watched the deportment of the strangers with indifference; the wives of the tenant farmers and the day laborers, however, were full of curiosity. Despite his dignified bearing the stately gentleman with the decoration who carried his tall hat on his arm couldn't hide the emotion that flickered over his features. Turning his head to one side, he removed a slight dampness from his eyelash with the tip of his finger. The women took note of it with satisfaction. And then the mother's black satin dress and her lace wrap excited a softly whispered admiration. The privy councillor's wife herself had the feeling that her dress was obtrusive in these humble surroundings, and when she approached the altar, she pressed her train to her, anxiously and with embarrassment, crying and sighing deeply and painfully from time to time. When the congregation sang the last verse, her fingers stole toward Agathe's hand and pressed it convulsively. Hardly had the worship service ended when Frau Heidling embraced her daughter with a kind of troubled passion that seemed little suited to the occasion, murmuring several times through her tears, "My child, my sweet, beloved child!" without being able to get to the end of her blessing.

But the tearful mother was not permitted to keep her child pressed to her heart. Father also wanted his turn, Uncle Gustav, Brother Walter, Pastor Kandler's wife — everyone wanted to wish her well. While still at the church door, each one offered the girl a few words of advice as to how she should face her imminent life as a grownup.

With a radiant smile on her little tearstained face she listened to all the golden words of love, to the wisdom of her elders. She felt herself so weak, so in need of help, and so ready to do what everyone wanted her to, to make everyone around her happy. She was herself so happy now!

Her brother, who was soon to take his school-leaving examination, considerately ran back into the church to retrieve the bouquet she had forgotten while the others made their way to the parsonage. Agathe waited for him, looked at him gratefully and placed her arm in his. And so they followed their parents.

"Forgive me for all my unkindnesses," Agathe murmured humbly to the boy who would soon graduate from school. Walter flushed with embarrassment and grumbled something unintelligible as he disengaged himself from his sister.

"So, Jochen, how's the bay?" he cried out to the pastor's coachman. With a short run and the agile leap of the gymnast he sailed over a plow that stood in the sun-drenched courtyard and disappeared with Jochen through the stable door. Agathe went into the house alone. Several packages had arrived for her. They had been kept from her in order not to distract her on the morning before the religious observance. At breakfast she had received only the pretty cross, which Papa had fastened by its fine gold chain around her neck. Now it was presumably permissible to give herself over a little to curiosity about the presents from relatives and girlfriends.

On this spring day the parlor of the parsonage with its low ceiling still exuded the coolness of a cellar. The grownups were refreshing themselves with wine and little open-faced sandwiches. Agathe was not hungry. She sat down on the rug with her packages, tugged at the seals, pulled the wrapping paper this way and that. Her cheeks burned fiery red. Her fingers trembled.

"Now, Agathe, don't cut all that good string to pieces," her mother reprimanded her. "You're always so impetuous!"

"If a girl unties knots patiently / she'll get a good husband surely," the pastor's wife chimed in from the adjoining room where the dining room table was being set.

"Oh, I don't want a husband!" Agathe cried gaily, and rip, tear, the wrappings flew to the floor.

"Well, don't forswear it, little girl," said fat Uncle Gustav and looked at her with a sly smile out from behind his little glass of marsala. "From now on you've got to think seriously about such things."

"I won't hear of it," interrupted the privy councillor's wife. In her tone of voice one could hear the certain knowledge of victory that belongs to mothers of very young daughters. Just come, you suitors . . . my daughter will certainly marry, but which of you is really good enough for her?

"Rückert's *Springtime of Love*!"[5] Agathe suddenly squealed loudly and waved a tiny red book in the air with such delight that everybody around her burst out laughing.

"For her confirmation? A little premature!" Papa noted with surprise and disapproval.

"From Eugenie I assume?" the privy councillor's wife inquired. She answered her own question: "Naturally, that's just like Eugenie."

In the meantime the content of a second package came to light.

"Gerok's *Palm Leaves*[6] — from dear Aunt Malvina," Agathe reported, this time more calmly and with devout piety.

"Oh, what a darling bracelet! It's exactly what I wanted! A pearl in the middle! Right, Mama, it's real gold, isn't it?" She fastened it around her wrist. Snap! The little clasp sprang shut.

" — and here's another book! A deluxe binding! *Woman's Life and Deeds as Maiden, Wife and Mother*.[7] Whoever is it from? Frau President Dürnheim. How kind! No, how very kind! Just look, Mama! *Woman as Maiden, Wife and Mother with Illustrations by Paul Thumann and other German Artists*!"[8]

"No, no, how very happy I am!"

Agathe jumped up suddenly from the rug and danced for pure joy around the room among the yellow and brown pieces of wrapping paper. The unruly little curls upon her forehead; the chain and the cross on her breast; the *Springtime of Love* and the *Woman as Maiden, Wife and Mother*, both pressed tenderly to her — all these things hopped and danced with her.

The grownups on the sofa and in the armchairs smiled again. How charming she was! Oh, yes, youth is beautiful!

Finally Agathe tumbled down completely out of breath next to her mother, threw all her treasures into her mother's lap and rubbed her brown tresses against her mother's dress like a happy little dog.

"Oh, I'm completely mad," she said abashedly when her mother shook her head slightly. Agathe felt a prick of conscience because Pastor Kandler entered just at that moment. He had removed his robe and was carrying his everyday hat in his hand.

"You're going out again?" his wife asked startled.

"Yes, don't wait dinner for me. I've got to congratulate the Groterjahns, you know. I hear their family has been increased by a little calf," he said with the good-natured irony of the resigned country parson who has learned long ago that village people can only be made to listen obediently to the Christian gospel of redemption if one shows a personal interest in their material woes. "So I'll invite Wiesing over this evening. You wanted to speak with her yourself, didn't you, dear Cousin?" he asked the privy councillor's wife.

"Yes, if the girl would like to move to the city, I wouldn't mind giving her a try," she answered.

At table Agathe sat between Father and Mother before a place setting wreathed with yellow cowslip primroses. Pastor Kandler was seated across from the newly confirmed girl. Next to him Uncle Gustav's rosy face shone out from between his blonde mutton chops above the white napkin he had tucked under his chin. The pastor's wife had been escorted to the table by the privy councillor. At the far end of the table, amidst the younger set, sat an old seamstress who was in the habit of spending Easter at the parsonage. After each course she drew her knife between her lips in order not to lose one little bit of the splendid food and the nourishing gravy. As a young man in his last year at school, Walter felt his dignity injured because they had given him this gap-toothed creature as dinner companion, and he found it terribly annoying not quite knowing whether it was more appropriate for him to speak to her or simply to ignore her presence. The privy councillor's wife also cast disconcerted glances at the old mending woman; she thought her husband might be offended by her presence.

But Privy Councillor Heidling merely found the woman mildly amusing. He was fully aware that he was among naive, gauche little people. It had been his well-considered intention not to have his daughter confirmed in the circle of her friends with the fashionable preacher in M.,[9] but instead under the guidance of his spouse's modest cousin. He valued a straightforward piety in the female sex. For the German man, duty; for the German woman, religious faith and fidelity.

Given his position and circumstances in the city, it went without saying that the religious foundation he had instilled in Agathe ought never to obtrude into the foreground of life, just as it went without saying that prayers at table and the old mending woman had their place here in this Pomeranian village. Voss's *Louisa*[10] came to mind — in his younger years he had thumbed through it once. It had done his daughter good to enjoy this idyllic retreat. Agathe had become strong and healthy and rosy during the quiet winter — on sleigh rides over the snowy fields in the clear, crisp country air. His child hadn't pleased him when she returned from boarding school. He had noted in her vanity, garrulousness, and a certain scatterbrained quality. Of all things not that! He demanded that women live up to his ideals.

Involuntarily these thoughts fashioned themselves into the phrases of a speech. He remained silent in the face of the pastor's wife's attempts to make conversation, and his manicured hand played with his grayish blonde beard.

Meanwhile Pastor Kandler was tinkling his glass. As soon as he cleared his throat, the privy councillor's wife pulled out her damp batiste handkerchief — her bridal handkerchief — as a precaution. And it was a good thing too, for as he spoke tears rolled continuously down the dull and faded visage whose cheeks had taken on a fleeting nervous reddishness. He spoke so movingly! He touched her in so many ways!

The Bible verse "For all things are yours; and you are Christ's"[11] provided the basis for his speech. Pastor Kandler searched his imagination for a true-to-life description of the joys that life offered a modern young woman who belonged to elegant bourgeois society: in the family, in association with girls her own age, in nature, artistic endeavors, and reading. He alluded also to other joys that awaited her — for it was the way of the world. Beautiful, innocent as she sat before him in her little black silk dress, her brown eyes looking at him attentively from out of the soft, bright little face — how soon might the dear child be a bride. "All things are yours!"

But how ought "all things" be exploited? Possess as if you possessed nothing, enjoy as if you did not enjoy! You are even allowed dancing, even going to the theater, but you should dance in a respectable manner. Pleasure in art should be confined to pure art devoted to God. You should not despise education. But beware, my child, of modern learning which leads to doubt and skepticism. Rein in your imagination so that it does not dangle unchaste images before you. Love, love, love should be your entire life. But this love should remain free of selfishness. Covet not what is theirs.[12] You may desire happiness. You may even be happy, but in a righteous manner . . . for you are Christ's disciple, and Christ died on the cross! Only he who has completely overcome the world will pass through the thorn-braced gates to eternal joy, to the wedding of the lamb!

Agathe was compelled to weep once more. She was seized anew with the alarming awareness that had accompanied her in all the hours of catechism without her daring to confess it to her spiritual advisor. She didn't understand at all what she was supposed to do in order to enjoy as if she did not enjoy. She had tried often enough to follow his words. When she had snowball fights in the garden with the pastor's boys, she tried to think of Jesus. But if the boys pressed her hard and she had to defend herself all around and the fun became quite crazy, then she forgot her Savior completely. If her food tasted quite good to her — and nowadays she always had an excellent appetite — was she supposed to act as if it didn't taste good to her? But that would have been a lie.

Probably she hadn't yet understood the secret of this Bible verse. Oh, she felt quite unworthy of the fellowship of mature Christians! But it was just lovely to be confirmed now — and it was high time; after all, she was about to turn seventeen.

If the pastor had made it clear to the child what her responsibilities were as a citizen of heaven, Father now began to outline to Agathe the duties of a citizen of the state.

The woman, the mother of future generations, the mainstay of the family, is an important unit of society when she is conscious of her place as the unpretentious, hidden root.

Privy Councillor Heidling liked making sententious statements. He was pleased with his metaphor.

"The root, the mute, patient, immovable root that appears not to have a life of its own and yet bears the tree of humankind . . . . "

At that moment a present for Agathe arrived. The country postman, to show his thanks for the generous tip he had received that morning, had brought it over from the little train station despite the holiday.

"O my! Mani sent that!" said Agathe and blushed. "He promised, but I thought he'd forget."

"Your cousin Martin you've told us so much about?" the pastor's wife asked inquisitively.

Agathe nodded, falling silent, lost in happy memories.

Herwegh's poems[13] . . . . And the summer vacation at Uncle August's in Bornau . . . the sun-drenched lawn where she had lain and reveled in the glowing verses that Martin could declaim so splendidly . . . . How she shared his raptures over freedom and fights on the barricades and red caps, over Danton and Robert Blum . . . . In between times Agathe also raved about Barbarossa and his long-awaited awakening.[14]

She hadn't seen Martin since then. He was doing his year of military service now. Oh, the dear, good boy.

Agathe was too busy opening the book and reading her favorite passages to notice that an embarrassed silence had fallen over the table.

When she looked up, her gaze met Uncle Gustav's as he zealously busied himself with the opening of a champagne bottle. His face widened with a suppressed grin. Pastor Kandler stood up, went silently around the table and took the Herwegh from her hand. He went up to the privy councillor and showed him a passage here and there. Both gentlemen looked serious. There was something unpleasant in the air.

"I really wouldn't have thought the rascal could be so stupid," the privy councillor burst out in annoyance.

"My dear child," said Pastor Kandler trying to placate Agathe, "I think we'll send the book back and ask your cousin Martin to exchange it for another. There are so many lovely poems that are more appropriate for a young girl and that you'll like better."

Agathe had blanched.

"I wanted Herwegh's poems!" she finally exclaimed.

"You probably didn't know the book?" her father asked with the same unsettling gentleness that had accompanied the pastor's suggestion. They wanted to spare her on her confirmation day, but it was certain — she had done something terrible!

"Yes I did!" she said hurriedly and softly and added even more shyly, "I thought they were beautiful!"

"Presumably you were familiar with some of them," Pastor Kandler apologized for her. His gaze fastened upon her imposingly. Could it be that the gentle child had deceived him in her ardent devotion to Christianity? Where did this sudden spirit of rebellion come from?

"What was it you particularly liked about these poems?" he probed cautiously.

"The language was so beautiful," the girl whispered disconcertedly.

"Didn't you ever realize that these verses contradict certain things that I have tried to teach you?"

"No, I thought you were supposed to fight and die for your convictions!"

"Certainly, my child, for a good conviction. But presumably one really shouldn't fight for a foolish and pernicious conviction?"

Agathe remained silent and covered with confusion.

Father and spiritual advisor conferred.

"These really are worrisome symptoms," said the privy councillor. "I don't understand my nephew at all! Wearing the King's uniform! Downright shocking!"

"I don't think we need to take the matter so seriously," ventured Pastor Kandler contemplating the privy councillor with a quiet, ironic smile. "Youth has, as you know, its weak moments when an intoxicating poison has effects that soon pass if one has a healthy disposition. We all know this from our own experiences!" He put the offensive book aside and returned to his seat.

"Wouldn't the ladies and gentlemen like a piece of cake?" asked the pastor's wife amicably.

Uncle Gustav popped the cork of a champagne bottle into the fork that he held over it. He performed the task with grandiose ceremony; the champagne was his contribution to the celebration. The pastor's two sons whooped at the trick. The bubbling wine flowed into the glasses. They raised their glasses and clinked them together. The pall that the newly confirmed girl's bloodthirsty desire for revolution had cast upon the assemblage gave way to that old quietly emotional cheerful contentment. Agathe's brown eyes, however, retained a sort of brooding.

Uncle Gustav patted his little niece kindly on one round cheek and cried out with his jovial laugh, "For the time being, however, more blossom than root!" Then he whispered in her ear, "Stupid little thing, you don't unwrap presents from charming cousins in front of all the dinner guests!"

Unfortunately Uncle Gustav himself was a bit of an embarrassment for the family. He had no principles, and for this reason he never accomplished anything worthwhile in the world. So he married, for example, a woman who had all kinds of questionable adventures behind her and who in the end ran off with a count. The relatives couldn't excuse him for that. Agathe liked him despite everything. He was so kind; if the opportunity presented itself to help someone in small ways or large ones, you could always count on him to be ready to lend a hand. Of course the things he said didn't carry much weight. Agathe continued to reflect.

"All things are yours," she had just been reassured, and right afterwards they took away the gift from her dearest cousin without even asking her. Naturally she didn't dare to offer opposition. She had, after all, promised obedience and humble submissiveness for her entire life.

* * *

Later when the grownups were taking a postprandial nap in various comfortable corners of the parsonage — they had become a little hot and tired from the rich noon meal and the champagne — Agathe strode up and down the wide garden path behind the house. The boys had been ordered not to bother her today and not to take her off to play as they usually did. They were taking a walk with Walter. The pastor's wife, unseen by her guests, was helping the maid wash the dishes in the kitchen; now and again a clatter resounded from that direction; otherwise silence reigned in the house and garden.

With secret pleasure Agathe listened to her silk train rustling over the gravel, folded her hands and asked our dear Lord please to take away the anger from her heart. It was simply too horrible that today, the day of her confirmation, she was mad at her pastor and her father! Surely this was where conquering the self and renunciation began. She really was still quite stupid! To find such a dangerous poison beautiful . . . . The beginning of Martin's favorite poem came to mind:

> Tear the crosses from the earth.
> They shall all become swords —
> God in Heaven will pardon it.[15]

Yes, that was indeed a frightening verse and was certainly the one Uncle Kandler had just come across. But still, there was such boldness in it, and then our dear Lord was in fact specifically asked for forgiveness. Agathe had always really liked that about the poem.

But it was always that way: you had to distrust the things you liked.

She looked up into the bright blue spring sky, questioning and doubting. Not a single cloud could be seen; it was infinitely clear, and the sun beamed warmly. There was still hardly a shadow in the garden. The golden rays could dance through the branches of the trees down to the ground. And the singing and rejoicing of the birds would not quit.

It was a pity she had to return to the city tomorrow, just now when it was becoming so charming here, more beautiful day by day! Even since yesterday everything had changed again. Bushes and shrubs no longer wore winter's gray. The branches bore a transparent colored veil. If you stepped closer and bent down to them, you saw that the veil of color was comprised of thousands upon thousands of tiny little buds. Oh, but how sweet! Agathe went from one to the other. The knotty branches of the apple trees stretched over the path, shimmering dark red. High up on the tall pear tree, greenish white; the airy branches of the sour cherry, snowy white. On the chestnut trees tiny inquisitive woolly green hands stretched forth out of shiny brown capsules, and the Cornelian cherry was completely

15

coated with bright yellow. The lilac, the hornbeam, each had its own shape, its special color. And here in sun and rain each quietly and joyfully became what it was meant to be.

Plants have it much, much better than people, thought Agathe with a sigh. No one scolded them; no one was dissatisfied with them; no one gave them good advice. Utterly serene, the old tree trunks watched their little brown, red, and green bud children grow. Did it distress them when the snails, the caterpillars, and the insects ate a number of them?

Agathe stroked the scabby bark of the old apple tree.

Might the birds have taken on the task of scolding? What a strange notion. Agathe giggled about it to herself. Oh, God forbid! The birds had an awful lot to do at this time of year, what with all their billing and cooing. Were there perhaps also birds that loved unhappily? Hm, well — naturally, the nightingale! By the way, poets really couldn't be absolutely certain of that.

Oh, if only she had been born a little bird or a flower!

Agathe walked down a narrow path to the mill pond. It lay at the end of the garden which gently sloped down to it from the house. Because the pastor's sons were always falling in the water they had let the path grow up with weeds. Agathe had to part the brush in order to get through. She wanted to say goodbye to the little bench that stood down beside the pond, secluded and intimate. The previous fall — and now again this spring — she had often sat there and read or dreamed in the warm hours at midday.

On the left bank of the quiet lake that extended out to a swampy field of reeds stood the mill with its overhanging thatched roof and the large wheel. In the bay at the parsonage garden small lily pads floated on the surface of the water. In the fall it had been completely covered here with the green platters, and dragon flies had whirred above it. The slimy stems of the plants had even pushed through the gray planks of the dilapidated boat that was rotting there in the water.

At first Agathe had cherished romantic dreams of the old skiff: how it had served out there in the storm and the waves, how it had seen the sea and had foundered on rocky cliffs. The pastor's sons had made fun of her with this story. The boat had always been on the mill pond, but what with the many aquatic plants and the reeds you couldn't go anywhere with it; so on account of its motionlessness, it had gradually become this miserable, worthless wreck. Now Agathe couldn't stand the boat. It made her sad. Her young girl's imagination was stirred by vague desires for greatness and sublimity. She liked to think about distant places, open spaces, and boundless freedom while she sat on the tiny bench by the little pond where she had to be very still so she wouldn't tip over and so the bench wouldn't break into pieces; it, too, was certainly quite rotten.

Suddenly Agathe recalled the confession she had had to write down and give to her spiritual advisor. Its superficiality and dishonesty . . . and now it became a certainty for her: she herself was to blame for the discord that had disturbed this holy day. Troubled and filled with shame, she stared into the water that on the surface appeared so clear with happy little golden flashes of sunshine and that deep down below was filled with rotten vestiges of the vegetation of years past.

II.

Agathe Heidling and Eugenie Wutrow had been friends for a very long time — since that morning when they had both been taken to school for the first time with little white pinafores and new slates and primers and had been assigned seats next to one another. They had exchanged candies from the cornucopias[16] they had received for the first day of school, and so they had become friends. Their mamas had sent them to this small, elegant private school; in the public higher girls' schools children from all sorts of families were brought together, and the girls could very easily bring home a nasty word or vulgar manners.

Either Agathe picked up the little Wutrow girl on her way to school or Eugenie rang the Heidlings' bell at 7:45. To do so she had to stand on her tiptoes until one day when Mama Heidling tied a little rope to the yellow brass ring of the bell pull. The girls always stuck together in their free time as well. Agathe loved to be at Eugenie's. There they were left more in peace with their dolls and little pictures and patches of silk, with their secrets and their endless chattering and giggling.[17]

The large, old merchant house that belonged to Eugenie's parents concealed any number of nooks and crannies, delightful for playing and hiding. There were dark corridors here in which even during the day solitary gas lamps burned and skinny-legged clerks brushed hurriedly past the little girls. Behind latticed dusty windows, the office, and there on a high swivel chair sat Herr Wutrow, a shriveled, deaf, coarse little man. A courtyard with huge empty crates and a dirty, gray building to the rear filled with a troop of men and women workers who rolled cigars in barren rooms. The factory, the office, the corridors — everything smelled of tobacco. The sweetish-acrid smell even penetrated the large living room of the main house out in front. Here Frau Wutrow was constantly having the parquet waxed and the windowpanes washed. That's why it was always cold and drafty. Despite these efforts, however, the smell of tobacco lingered.

The house — where everything was quite different from what it was at her parents' house — had a mysterious attraction for Agathe. She was afraid of the clerks and the women workers and even more of Herr Wutrow himself. She had an instinctive dislike of Frau Wutrow, and she very often quarreled with Eugenie, ran home crying then and hated her girlfriend. But Eugenie always came for her again, and things were as before. Eugenie could never play properly. She didn't really love her dolls and didn't believe there was a doll language that Holdewina, the big doll with the porcelain head, and Katy, the baby doll, set to chattering brightly as soon as their little mothers were out of earshot.

Agathe had her friend to thank for a number of talkings-to as Eugenie persuaded her to stroll down all kinds of side streets in the city, to ring doorbells and run away, to stick out her tongue at old ladies who sat behind flowerpots at ground floor windows and to talk to schoolboys.

Most of all Eugenie liked spending time in the factory. She sneaked up on the men and stroked the dirty skirts of the women workers and slipped them cakes and apples fetched in secret from her mother's pantry to make them tell her little stories in exchange. The foremen had to chase her away constantly. In the blink of an eye she was back again.

Yes, and Eugenie also knew that Walter had a girlfriend whom he kissed, and if his teachers were to hear of it, he would be sent to the principal's office. Meta Hille from the ninth grade was his sweetie, she said. Come now, someone like that! Yes, yes, yes, quite certainly, truly!

Whenever Eugenie had ferreted out things like that, her slim little body would shake with pleasure. She would squint her gray eyes shut and blink triumphantly over her pretty little nose.

Hooray! That was just great!

One Sunday afternoon the two little friends were sitting on the lowest branch of the low-hanging old yew tree in the Wutrows' garden. They held their batiste skirts with their fingertips and waved them back and forth; they had been turned into two birds by a wicked fairy and were shaking their pink and white plumage. Agathe had made up the game. She wanted so much to learn to fly.

Then they no longer knew what to do to get through Sunday afternoon.

Arm in arm they strolled along the beds of blooming bear's ears or pansies, along their stiff boxwood borders. Between the walls of the rear buildings that framed the old-fashioned, gracefully manicured urban garden, it was already getting gray and dusky while high above the children a pink cloud slowly paled against the greenish April sky.

"Hey," Agathe whispered very softly. "It's not true, after all — that thing about babies . . . . My mama — "

"Shame! You told! You tattletale!"

"No, I just asked!"

"Oh, your mama . . . . Mothers always lie to us!"

"My mother doesn't tell lies!" cried Agathe in an injured tone of voice.

The quarrel turned into a secretive murmuring and whispering between the little friends. A couple of times Agathe cried out, "Shame, Eugenie, oh, no, I don't believe that . . . . "

Cries for help like frightened bird calls when a cat steals toward the nest sounded forth from the evening shadows beneath the old yew tree where the little girls huddled together. And shivering and burning with excitement and shame, Agathe did listen and listen and softly asked, pressing herself close to Eugenie and finally lapsing into an endless giggling.

That was just too funny, too funny . . . .

But Mama had lied, after all, when she told her that an angel brought little babies.

Eugenie was much better informed.

How the two started and sprang to their feet when Frau Wu-trow's sharp voice called them in! Agathe's heart beat furiously; she could hardly bear it. She didn't dare enter the room with the bright lamp, hurriedly fetched her hat from the foyer and ran out without saying goodbye.

Those other things Eugenie had told her — no, they were disgusting. Shame! Shame! Completely dreadful. No, it simply couldn't be true. But — What if it were?

And her Mama and her Papa . . . . She was completely mortified.

When Mama came to give her a good night kiss, she hastily turned her burning face to the wall and buried it in the pillows. No! She could never again ask her mother such a thing. Never.

The next morning Agathe dallied until the very last moment before she had to leave for school. Now it was far too late to stop by for Eugenie. When she heard at school that Eugenie had caught a cold and had to stay home, she was relieved. With real pangs of conscience she continuously entertained the thought that Eugenie might die . . . . And then no one in the world would find out what they had talked about yesterday. That would be just too awful — Oh, if only Eugenie would die instead!

"Frau Wutrow has already sent for you twice to come over," said Frau Heidling to her daughter. "Why don't you go on over? Did you two quarrel?"

"I don't like Eugenie any more."

"Oh, who drops friends so quickly!" said Frau Heidling censoriously. "What did Eugenie do to you?"

"Nothing!"

"Well then, it's not nice of my little girl to neglect her sick friend. Take Eugenie the forget-me-nots I bought at the market. Eugenie is sometimes a little sarcastic, but my little Agathe is also sometimes a little touchy. You can learn a lot from Eugenie. She curtsies so nicely and is always ready with a friendly answer and never sulks like my little dreamer!"

Agathe didn't look at her mother. Grumpily she unloaded her books. Her throat hurt terribly as though it were completely raw. She felt like throwing herself to the floor and screaming and crying loudly. But without saying another word she obediently took the bunch of flowers and left. On the way she ran into a girl she knew

20

who attended the municipal public school. So she threw away the flowers and went strolling with the girl.

When their ramblings brought her back to her parents' house, Mama looked out the window and called her to dinner.

Agathe didn't answer and kept on going. She heard her mother calling behind her and walked on and on. She didn't want to go home ever again.

In an open square with flower beds she sat down on one of the iron chains hung between stone pillars to protect the grounds. She held on with both hands and dangled her legs. Only the most vulgar children did that! The public schoolgirl sat on another one of the chains. They chatted like that. About America. How far it was to get there. The teacher had told them that America lay exactly on the other side of the earth. You only needed to dig a hole, terribly deep, deeper and deeper, and then at last you'd get to America.

"But first there's water and then fire," Agathe mused. The teacher hadn't said that. But Agathe believed it — most definitely. She was seized with a terrible desire to try digging that hole sometime.

At that moment Eugenie came walking with her mother down the opposite sidewalk in the bright sunshine. She was wearing her new lilac velvet paletot and the beret with the feather trim.[18] Wasn't she putting on airs! She walked decorously between her mother and an officer. Suddenly she saw Agathe and stopped in amazement. She waved and called her name. But Agathe dangled her legs and did not come. Frau Wutrow said something to Eugenie. It seemed to Agathe that all three of them looked at her angrily and then strolled on.

Agathe laughed disdainfully. Then she went home with the public schoolgirl who had already eaten her midday meal at twelve o'clock, had coffee with her and in the courtyard tried to dig the hole that would lead to America. Oh, if it were only really true! They worked terribly hard just to remove the gravel and the dirt. Then to their boundless amazement they ran into red bricks. Agathe felt quite odd as if a miracle were about to occur — God knew what she would see now. Sweating and groaning, they tried to remove the bricks forcibly. And just as one of them had moved just a little bit, someone came along. The other girl screamed loudly in terror: "Ack! Black Julie! Black Julie!"

She chased Heidi away and Agathe right behind. While the mistress of the house scolded into the void about her ruined courtyard, the two little girls hid in the woodshed and didn't move a muscle for fear.

But going home — She had to sometime, after all; it was already getting dark. She would have been scared to death out on the street at night. There were murderers out there. She had to. "O God! O dear God, let Mama have company!"

God was so kind. Perhaps He would do her this favor.

Frau Heidling had in the meantime sent someone over to the Wutrows' to see if Agathe was there.

No, but they'd seen her sitting there on Kasernenplatz, dangling her legs.

Now Agathe had forgotten everything that had plagued her so that morning. She only felt a monstrous fear of her mother, like that of a tiny little worm in the face of an awe-inspiring sublime being. And a kind of vague longing was also mixed in with her monstrous fear. Perhaps her mother thought she had been playing at the Wutrows' and everything was all right.

Faint of heart, she softly rang the bell. Walter tore open the door, laughed loudly and shouted, "So here she is, the brat!"

Her mother took her by the hand, led her into the guest room and left her standing in the dark.

Mama wouldn't, would she? No, she was already a big girl, thought Agathe and shivered with fear. No, Mama couldn't do that, could she? She was already in school.

Frau Heidling came back with a lamp and the rod.

"No! No! Oh, please, please, don't!" screamed Agathe and struck out furiously. It was a wild struggle between mother and daughter. Agathe tore the lace off Mama's dress and kicked at her. But she got her blows — like a tiny little child.

When the terrible punishment was at an end, an exhausted Frau Heidling tottered to her bedroom and sank gasping and weeping onto her bed. She knew she was not supposed to let herself get upset and that she would have to suffer terrible neuralgia. Up to the last, while she was still filled with anxiety and worry about Agathe, she had struggled with herself: did she really have to do it? Yes, it was her duty. The child couldn't be permitted to disregard all authority.

Then when she saw Agathe, her anger had simply gotten the better of her.

The girl lay in the guest room on the plank floor and was still crying, sobbing and sobbing. She could only croak the sobs, her entire little body shaking convulsively all the while. She wanted to scream herself to death. She couldn't live any longer with such shame . . . . What would Papa say? He would be sorry when he didn't have his little girl any more. But Mama — it was all right with her, just fine . . . .

Finally she became so tired that everything around her and everything in her blurred. Her head muddled, she stood up and crept, reeling, into bed.

* * *

Agathe didn't love her mother anymore. She concealed her anguish and pangs of conscience about this, concealed a burden too heavy for her young shoulders. Her bearing became slack; her face acquired a trace of peevishness and fatigue. But the doctor, whom they consulted, said it came from her slumping on the schoolbench.

A while later Agathe's father was transferred to a smaller city as the deputy of the district magistrate. There was no higher girls' school here and Agathe acquired a governess.

She gradually recovered and brightened up again. Probably it wasn't at all like what Eugenie had said, she thought then. Because it seemed just too impossible, in the end she more or less forgot her confused knowledge. Only now and then, prompted by a word from the grownups, a passage in a book, a picture, sometimes by nothing at all, the memory of the hours in the Wutrows' garden awakened in the dark corridors of her mind and tortured her like a bad smell one can't get rid of or like the knowledge of a dreary, ominous secret.

III.

Frau Heidling cherished the vague ideal of a close relationship between a mother and her only daughter. However, she had no idea how to go about cementing one like that between herself and Agathe. She scrupulously tended to Agathe's clothes, her toothbrushes, boots, and corsets. But whenever Agathe came to her with one of her explosions of burning interest in each and every thing in the world — in the mysteries of Nero's character and in Bürger's love for Molly,[19] in the rings of Saturn and the resurrection of the dead — she always saw the same half-embarrassed, half-placating smile on her mother's pale, sickly face. And precisely at that moment her mother would cut her off with one of those endless remonstrances: "Stand up straight, Agathe; you've lost the ribbon from your pigtail again! Are you never going to become a proper girl?" That provoked tears and impudent retorts.

Frau Heidling often wondered in amazement whether it was possible that she herself had ever been so lively and high strung; nowadays everything that happened outside her family and her household was a matter of complete indifference to her. Her husband especially valued an intellectual modesty clothed in refined form in a woman, and surely if a woman loves a man she will automatically strive to be exactly what he likes. Yes, and all the confinements and the deaths of little children — that makes a woman's brain quite tired. But then one has done one's duty in life. Frau Heidling could often become quite worried that Agathe, what with all the restless roving of her thoughts, could go astray someday.

Every day there were violent scenes with the governess. Fräulein was obsessed with her scheme to get the little town's well-to-do apothecary or an elderly justice to marry her. Agathe despised her with all her heart for this. With bitter feelings she came to the realization that there was an unbridgeable gap not only between Fräulein and her, but also between parents and children. Alone and completely misunderstood, she would have to die of this grief. Truly reveling in feelings of revenge, she could imagine her mother's tears of remorse, her father's despair. And she loved Papa more than her mother. It was true that he usually laughed when she expressed an opinion, but at least he didn't scold her so much. Actually it was a comfort to cling to the idea that she was perhaps not her parents' real child and that this was why she couldn't love them as passionately as she most ardently wished she could. Otherwise — otherwise she was nothing but a completely rotten, spoiled child.

Frau Heidling inquired of other reliable women how one was to deal with adolescent girls. "Of course one shouldn't grumble," she said with a sigh, "but our dear Lord really arranged things oddly when he left the mother who bore the children no strength to rear them as well. Agathe takes a terrible toll on me."

Everyone advised her to send her to boarding school. She realized then that the evil that was torturing her was a widespread one, and that put her mind completely at ease.

Since she had many connections in her previous place of residence, the capital city of the province, she turned to them to inquire about an appropriate institution. So that her daughter wouldn't feel abandoned in a strange place away from home, she selected the institution attended by many of Agathe's former friends, among them Eugenie Wutrow.

* * *

"Hey, come on, 'fess up! Who's your 'sweetheart'?"

This was one of the first questions Agathe was asked by her schoolmates after the headmistress had led her into the study where the young girls sat around a big table with notebooks, books, and needlework.

Agathe had started learning English a year ago, but the word "sweetheart" hadn't come up yet in the grammar. She said so shyly, and they ridiculed her mercilessly.

Agathe occupied the same dormitory as Eugenie. At first she was troubled by the childish fear that Eugenie might make some kind of allusion to the conversations they had had as little girls. But Eugenie appeared to have completely forgotten them. She had turned into a pretty girl and was already quite elegant. Agathe, to her own amazement, immediately got a violent crush on her. There was no greater pleasure than being with Eugenie Wutrow, nestling against her and kissing her. Eugenie treated her childhood playmate's attachment like the adoration of a man. Sometimes she was cold and coy and harshly rejected Agathe's caresses. Agathe could soften her neither by offering to do her arithmetic homework nor with the rapturous letters she laid on her friend's pillow. Suddenly Eugenie was charmingly nice again.

Lately Agathe had suffered frequently from toothache and swollen cheeks. When she moaned at night in her bed behind the screen — the room was partitioned in this way into various little private compartments — Eugenie would slip over in her bare feet with eau de cologne or chloroform, sit on the edge of her bed and stroke her forehead slowly and evenly until the pain abated and Agathe fell asleep under the hypnotic effect of the soft girlish hand.

Eugenie was possessed of a practical nature. Without much deliberation she knew what to do in every situation. She was generally well liked by the other adolescent girls. Agathe was plagued a good deal by jealousy whenever Eugenie went off with other girls or if she even put her arm around the waist of another girl.

That's why it made her terribly sad that she couldn't support her beloved friend when a matter arose that violently upset the hearts and minds of the boarding school's students. Around ten of the younger girls who were not yet confirmed took religious instruction from the principal of the school, a doctor of theology and philology by the name of Engelbert.[20] He belonged to the Protestant Union,[21] hadn't become a pastor as a matter of conscience and expressed openly to his pupils his opinion that Jesus Christ was only a man, the real son of Mary and Joseph. A huge rebellion broke out among the girls on this account. The daughter of an English pastor announced that her parents would take her out of the school immediately if they heard anything of the sort from Dr. Engelbert. Agathe's pious belief in miracles rebelled at such a prosaic view of the gospel. But Dr. Engelbert tried especially hard to convert her of all people to his views. There were not many among the young girls who grasped historical questions with such a personal interest as did Agathe. For the first time ever she had to make an independent decision; Dr. Engelbert always demanded independence of his pupils. Agathe remained stubbornly faithful to her God-Redeemer: without miracles and without the sway of supernatural powers the world seemed to her barren and monotonous. Wherever she looked, all life, birth, and death seemed to her a miracle; she felt herself surrounded by incomprehensible mysteries that one dare not touch.

In religion class there were passionate disputes, vague, but all the more violent arguments until Agathe was sobbing and even Dr. Engelbert, a soft-hearted idealist, had bright tears flowing into his large full beard. The religious dispute continued during leisure hours and on into the dormitories. Eugenie immediately sided with Dr. Engelbert. She maintained that only a person with limited understanding could believe in miracles. Agathe lived in fear that Eugenie thought her stupid and would break off their friendship. But she couldn't sacrifice to her friend the prospect of eternal life filled with the song of angels and heavenly glory.

What bliss one day, then, for Agathe to be invited over to Eugenie's little compartment and fed with chocolates. An older Englishwoman who was rather tolerant because of her indifference to everything German was in charge of the dormitory. Besides Agathe and Eugenie only a few recently arrived countrywomen of the "Miss" slept there.

"Agathe, have you ever been fond of a man?" Eugenie asked softly.

"Why, Eugenie, how can you think such a thing?" whispered Agathe, startled and blushing deep red.

"You don't trust me," said Eugenie in an injured tone of voice and put the box of chocolates back into her dresser. "Just go. I'm tired." She blew out the lamp and got into bed. "If you were candid, I'd have told you something too. But you're always so secretive. You're a goody-goody. Yes, that's what you are."

Eugenie rolled over and faced the wall. Agathe sat irresolutely on the edge of the bed in her corset and chemise. From the other compartments she heard peaceful breathing and the contented murmur that the Englishwoman was wont to emit while she slept. It was comfortably warm in the room and smelled of ground almonds and fine soap.

Agathe finally resolved to confess that she was fond of her cousin Martin. She wanted to show herself worthy of the confidence of her adored Eugenie.

Eugenie raised her head. "Have you kissed?"

Agathe protested that it wasn't "like that"; she simply liked her cousin better than the other boys.

Eugenie stretched out on her bed, her head on her arm.

"Agathe, I've loved!" she said after a while in a hollow, solemn voice.

Agathe's heart beat in her breast like a hammer.

"And — and — have you — "

"Kissed? Oh, to the point of suffocation! And he kissed me!"

Eugenie had raised herself up, thrown both arms around her friend and pulled her impetuously to her. Agathe felt the girl's entire body tremble.

27

"That's why they sent me to boarding school! But it would have been over anyway. The wretch! He was unfaithful to me!"

She flung herself back into her pillows. Her muffled sobbing emerged from the pillow feathers.

"Who was it?"

"Someone from our office . . . . You know, the little room where the crates with the cigar samples are, where it's so dark — that's where we always met. Oh, how he could flatter a girl, how sweet he was and took me on his knee when I didn't want him to — "

Eugenie kissed Agathe passionately and then pushed her away. "Go away. You're a child. I shouldn't have told you that."

Agathe protested that she was not a child.

"Swear that you won't tell anyone! Not even your mother. Raise your hand! Swear it by God!"

Agathe swore. She was completely dumb with amazement.

"He wanted to follow me," Eugenie burst out excitedly.

"Here?"

"Just let him come! I'll throw him out. He was unfaithful to me! The scoundrel! He had something going with Rosa at the same time, and she told everything to get revenge! I hate him!"

"Eugenie, oh, poor Eugenie! I had no idea how unhappy you were," whispered Agathe in shy admiration.

"No, you can't tell by looking at me," said Eugenie. "During the day I hide it. But at night — ! Then I often want to kill myself. If I drink all this chloroform, I'm dead. I always carry it with me!"

Horrified, Agathe tore the little bottle with the tooth medicine from her friend's hand and tearfully implored her, for the sake of her parents and their friendship, to bear the burden of her existence.

She stood under the spell of the great classic passions. Memories of Egmont, of Amalia and Thekla tumbled through her imagination.[22] Her friend acquired an unprecedented greatness through her confession that she too had "lived and loved."

The vengeful factory girl was the only disturbing element in this holy affair. And besides, she didn't believe that the clerk had been unfaithful. He would certainly come soon and explain everything. But what if Eugenie threw him out? What if he were to shoot himself in despair? Agathe had a presentiment of tragic scenes and lay awake in her own bed for hours with flaming cheeks and aroused senses. She felt as if ants were running softly and hurriedly over her entire body. All the while she heard Eugenie's restless movements, her deep sighing.

As a result of her mooning over her friend's confession the question occurred to her whether she herself didn't love her cousin Martin . . . like that . . . like that . . . the way Eugenie meant. But it wasn't so; no, it was completely different, completely different.

Finally she dozed off.

Suddenly, after a short time, she woke up, awakened by a great, burning longing that was completely alien to her, completely new and horrifying and yet enchantingly blissful, so that she surrendered to it completely for a moment.

"Mani!" she murmured tenderly and in bewilderment and clasped her hands fearfully. "O dear God!"

She began to calculate how many days it was until summer vacation when she would see her cousin again.

She fell asleep over this, and this time she slept a fast and dreamless sleep until morning.

* * *

Agathe was amazed again and again how firmly and securely Eugenie locked her great passion in her heart and how actively she participated in all the foolishness that went on during the day. Besides the religious battles the young ladies occupied themselves mainly with the question of who among them had the longest eyelashes. To put an end to doubt they went about taking the most difficult measurements. Really you had to be very interested in the matter to slide a piece of paper under your eyelid and to let someone wave a pencil around right in front of your eyeball.

In the middle of the quarter a new pupil came, the daughter of a famous writer from Berlin. She was received with the greatest anticipation. A completely colorless ivory face and pale green eyes beneath black eyebrows that grew together over her nose made this girl's exterior singular enough. In addition the ability to tickle her nose with her big toe and to bend and dislocate her fingers effortlessly in all possible directions — all that had to surpass even the boldest expectations of something extraordinary. As soon as she saw the new girl, Agathe had a bad feeling.

Since Klotilde announced that her father had always corrected her essays, Dr. Engelbert naturally put her in the highest class without further testing. He believed he owed it to the glory of a leading German literary light to do her this honor. The young lady, however, so little fulfilled the hopes they had for her that Dr. Engelbert was forced to send her back to the second class, which his wife taught. It turned out that Klotilde was only the stepdaughter of the poet and thus couldn't have inherited his talents.

Already on the first evening Eugenie took a walk with the new girl and let her teach her the art of making her nose look Grecian. Agathe ventured a shy objection. But it was poorly received. Eugenie neglected her during the next few days in truly brutal fashion.

A fierce correspondence ensued between the two dormitory mates. In lofty phrases they wrote one another the most insulting things. Agathe spent night after night weeping with anger and jealousy. In the end Eugenie told her straight out: she loved Klotilde; she had felt it from the first moment on. One couldn't do anything about love, and Agathe should find herself another friend. They didn't talk with one another anymore; they passed by without looking at one another.

It was only a small comfort that an ugly little Jewish girl seized the opportunity to impose herself upon the abandoned girl.[23] Agathe began to see Eugenie's love affair with the clerk in a different light and to see something forbidden and ugly in it. Who knew — she might even be in the wrong; she was a faithless sort.

In the meantime Eugenie seemed to be having a good time with the new girl. During the day the young girls read Ottilie Wildermuth and Polko; at night they read Eugène Sue in bed.[24] In addition a grimy volume from a lending library, its title page torn out, secretly made the rounds. It recounted the vicissitudes of a woman who is suddenly afflicted with the body of a mouse, which fact she carefully tries to hide while malicious chance constantly reveals the secret. Agathe found this story stupid and repulsive.

So they said she was prudish and they were on their guard against her. Klotilde had brought along some of her father's works, which she lent to her favorite girlfriends, always with the insulting admonition not to show them to that pious Agathe.

And how the girls blushed when they read the books in concealed bowers! It was just too horribly exciting to imagine that such a fine, elegant gentleman like the poet, toward whom Dr. Engelbert had been obsequiousness itself, wrote such terrible things. If only the girls wouldn't always interrupt their whispering whenever Agathe approached! She was dying of curiosity to find out what it was that everyone was so terribly preoccupied with. But pride kept her from asking a single question. It was awful being shut out and despised when one longed so boundlessly for intimacy and love.

Finally she learned the mystery from the Jewish girl who, to her secret annoyance, ran after her with the loyalty of a little dog. Dr. Engelbert's wife was probably going to have a baby.[25] The young ladies were united in their outrage that such an offensive sight should be forced upon them, daughters from the best families!

Why ever were they so incensed, thought Agathe. After all, they all had little brothers and sisters. She was moved and a little confused. When Frau Engelbert came into the room, she tried unobtrusively to do her a kindness and eagerly did her lessons in order not to try her patience in class.

Frau Engelbert tried to set her own mind at ease with the prospect that the blessed event would take place during the summer vacation. Nevertheless she felt with growing uneasiness how twenty-five pairs of young eyes observed with greedy pleasure every change in her outward appearance and how twenty-five merciless girl's tongues muttered and whispered about it.

Her husband found her anxiety excessive, and with his lovely idealism he made the case to her that German girls were far too innocent and well-bred even to notice the matter.

Then the girls were distracted in quite a sad fashion. One of the schoolgirls, a bright, friendly creature, came down with typhoid fever[26] and within a few days was a corpse. They had cared for her in the remote sick room, and none of the children was allowed to see her in her coffin. Unpleasant, sad things were to be kept as far away as possible from these young things. Despite this precaution several of the schoolgirls suffered fits of crying. They had to leave the lamps on in the dormitories because most of the girls were afraid to sleep in the dark.

Agathe, too, was boundlessly upset. She was plagued by an unnaturally heightened desire to see the corpse, indeed to touch it.

She was ashamed of herself, sought to control herself and read the ninetieth psalm in her Bible.

It was late in the evening. Eugenie was talking to the English-woman and telling her that she had left her vocabulary book with Klotilde and wanted to go over and get it because she had to study it early tomorrow morning. After a bit of talking back and forth Eugenie vanished. A quarter of an hour passed. Then she came back and slipped into Agathe's compartment.

"Agathe," she whispered crying, "we saw Elisabeth's corpse. I had to. Otherwise I would've gotten sick too."

"How do you get to see her?" asked Agathe raising herself up.

"The sick room has a window onto the corridor, you know. It's open behind the curtain. There's a light on. She was so beautiful, but so gruesome! Oh, Agathe, it's terrible to die so young!"

The estranged friends embraced and cried together. Then Agathe put on her stockings and threw on her petticoats and her raincoat.

"I want to go there too!"

"Yes, there's a chair in a corner of the corridor. You have to get up on it. Just wait a bit so that Miss doesn't notice anything."

In fear and dread Agathe slipped through the dark corridors of the great house, down a staircase, up another until she came to the remote room of the side wing where young Elisabeth lay in her cof-fin.

A cool breeze blew through the window and ruffled her hair when she lifted the curtain. A strange, ghastly smell wafted toward her. The lamp that burned on the table to one side threw a clear light right onto the face of the dead girl and onto the waxen hands that lay folded on her breast.

When Agathe spied the peaceful white countenance with its closed eyes beneath the adorning green wreath of myrtle, her sick excitement receded and she became very peaceful inside. She low-ered the curtain and climbed down again with beautiful, solemn feelings. She folded her hands and leaned against the wall.

"Dear God, let me die too," she prayed. The life she so antici-pated seemed worthless in comparison with this peace. She was not thinking of resurrection. She would have liked to cease to be in this moment, to be melted into nothingness, but without being con-scious of it.

The sadness and the longing for death remained with her for a long time. When Eugenie tried to get close to her again, it no longer made her happy.

IV.

Summer vacation in the country . . . . Doesn't a scent of roses and strawberries waft by? Foaming milk, fresh from the barn! Baskets full of cherries, shiny black and yellowish red! A tart half as big as the table with a thick butter and sugar crust. Slabs of honey removed from the hive right before curious eyes . . . . And sun, sun, sun!

Trips through fields that exude a powerful smell of ripening grain, through forests where little brown does peer quickly and anxiously out from behind distant tree trunks. Boy cousins and girl cousins rattled and shaken together in open pony carts and drenched by the rushing rain of an unexpected thunderstorm. Dripping bunches of hair and ruined summer hats and blissful, joyful, glowing young faces!

And delightful, snug sitting together on little corner sofas in the shadow of old-fashioned cupboards with wood carvings, so like brother and sister — and yet not exactly brother and sister . . . .

Fanatic playing of croquet on the broad lawn in front of the house . . . often in pitch dark a final game to get revenge, inadequately illuminated by the stable lantern which gallant boy cousins carry from wicket to wicket.

Dancing to the accompaniment of a whistled polka through the expansive, empty banquet hall with family portraits from the Empire and Biedermeier periods.[27] Uncles and aunts as oddly dressed up children who hold rabbits and white doves in their hands and who smile down from the walls at the antics of the youth of a new generation.

And above all the huge noon meal where Uncle August finally had to lay down the law: "People will *eat* here; no laughing."

But then you would have had to forbid the boy cousins and the girl cousins to speak, to look, to move. What was it then that was always so incredibly funny? Agathe and Martin's shared enthusiasms and the dry remarks that Cousin Mimi interspersed? The smart turns of phrase of the cadets, the sons of Uncle August Bär, or the unnaturally deep and pathetic voice that Agathe's brother had recently begun to affect?

You just had to laugh about everything and about nothing, laugh the whole day long until you were practically falling off your chair, until the girls reeled toward one another, oddly gasping with laughter, their faces covered with tears, and the big boys roared with pleasure, slapped their thighs and leaped around the room as if seized with St. Vitus's dance.

Aimless roaming in the beautiful park, radiant dreaming under shady trees in the heat of midday, wise conversations, serious and eager arguments about all the big questions in the world you know nothing about! Wasn't that foolish! Oh, wasn't it all healthy and good and beautiful! Youth, life, an abundance of energy and cheer.

One day Agathe wrote a long letter to Eugenie in which she sketched in glowing terms her delightful vacation in Bornau at Uncle August Bär's. Martin's name appeared in practically every sentence, but only in the most harmless connections.

She didn't write that the insufferable, funny boy had stolen a little strand of green yarn that she desperately needed for her needlework. She was also silent about how terribly he had upset little Agathe when in the presence of their most dignified aunts, their most sarcastic uncles, of Mama and Grandmama, he had pulled the little strand of yarn out of the pocket of his gray summer jacket with impudent deliberateness, wrapped it around his fingers, waved it back and fourth and increased Agathe's embarrassment and anger to the highest degree by pressing it to his heart and lips — to be sure with the necessary precaution; he went into the window niche to do it. And she could never have made up her mind to tell Eugenie that one day when they were both alone in the room the bold fellow had knelt down next to the chair she was sitting in and said he would stay there until she gave him a kiss and he didn't care a bit if someone came in and saw it. If she intended to demur that long, it would be her own fault!

Agathe had immediately pushed him away. She jumped up and ran down the stairs. She heard Martin behind her taking three steps at a time and fled through the iron gate, which she slammed with a bang. So for a quarter of an hour they chased around the linden tree, through the courtyard and round the stables until the noonday bell rang. He didn't catch her; she had never been so fleet of foot. Perhaps Martin also saw her genuine fright and didn't even want to catch up with her.

As Agathe, flushed and out of breath, redid and pinned up her braids which had come undone, she felt very virtuous and noble. Actually she was a quite different being from Eugenie who had sat on a clerk's knee in a dark room. And she wanted always to remain stern and forbidding until — yes, until He came, the most magnificent one of all! Visions of white clouds of veil and burning candles on an altar floated through her imagination.

Or dead, quiet, in the black coffin with the crown of myrtle above her pure brow. Oh, how sad. Oh, how beautiful! Ready tears flowed from Agathe's eyes at the mere thought.

Feeling a cordial sympathy toward her poor cousin, the demure young girl came to the table a little late. Martin was just filling his plate with macaroni pudding.[28] He tucked into it immediately and didn't look at her at all. Agathe was a little disappointed. The noble, unrelenting girl acquired a touch of pique.

During the following days Martin didn't behave like an unhappy suitor; he was not importunate either, but boorish, crude, and impudent. Then on the following Sunday he brought Agathe a flower for church, one of the singular brown sweetshrub blossoms that could be found only in the old-fashioned garden at Bornau. He knew that she especially loved its strong, heavy, spicy scent. The two were good friends again. He did not, however, try to kiss her again. The little green strand of yarn had never resurfaced since.

V.

Herr Heidling had been transferred back to the provincial capital as privy councillor while at Pastor Kandler's his daughter's education was receiving, as it were, its final consecration after boarding school. The family moved into the third floor of an elegant building in the new district that was to link the narrow, musty, crowded streets of the old town to the mighty central train station, which was still under construction.[29]

Every gust of wind from the fields could still blow unimpeded through the streets, which were only half finished. It was not exactly pleasant: the wind always found limestone dust and clouds of sand from the many construction sites to swirl up into the air and it was always blowing the steam first this way and then that, as well as the pungent, repulsive smell of the asphalt, which was heated up in large black vats over open fires and made ready for paving the sidewalks. Unprotected by equally tall neighbors, the buildings that were already finished stretched up to frightening heights with their heavy carved front doors, their facades which were overloaded with stucco work, caryatids, and balconies, and their naked, windowless sides.

Nevertheless people did realize that this new district would shortly become the jewel of M. Everyone understood that progress would have to be bought at the cost of an unpleasant transitional period. The apartments were in demand and very expensive.

Agathe was to begin her life as a grownup here. She intended to shape it according to her own lights. To be sure, she had to be considerate of her parents, but Papa and Mama loved her so much that they would certainly go along with her in everything, especially since she wanted only the Good and pursued the most lovely ideals.

Confession and Communion had such power to expiate sin! She felt free and easy; her soul felt as if it had been washed clean. And actually, now that she was grownup, it really couldn't be so bad if she knew some things that people shouldn't even know she thought about.

Agathe solemnly laid out her confirmation presents in the room with the pretty bay filled with flower pots — her parents had redecorated this room and given it to her for her very own.

Herwegh's evil songs of revolution and protest had been exchanged at the bookstore for a collection of poems entitled *Pearls of Pious Love*.[30] Martin disdainfully termed it simply "Pious Pearl."

After doing his year of military service he had visited the Heidlings on his way to the university. But Agathe no longer got on with him. He had acquired a crude manner of scorning everything she considered beautiful and of breaking into loud, wild laughter at every opportunity. As a result of his unendearing demeanor Agathe began to doubt even more that revolution and Christianity could be combined. She studied the newspapers avidly, but put off making a definitive choice of a political party. She wanted to inform herself thoroughly first.

. . . How drolly the little red *Springtime of Love* peered out from the array of dried bouquets and leather jewelry boxes on the little table where she had placed her gifts. But the deluxe volume *Woman's Life as Maiden, Wife, and Mother* occupied the center, reigning supreme. Its rich gilt radiated a soft, mystical splendor.

Her present circumstances constituted a novitiate that preceded her initiation into the holy mysteries of life. The simplest domestic chores inducted Agathe into that profession of German housewife which was mandated by God and which was at the same time so very sweet and delightful. If on Sunday she was allowed to take a table-cloth from her mother's beautiful linen closet and to distribute the comforter covers and the sheets for the household she did so with joyful devotion, as one performs a symbolic act.

* * *

In the attic room beneath the roof a delicate sunbeam wandered through the little dormer window over cobwebs and dust balls. It boldly and merrily gilded a little corner here and a little tip there of the superfluous junk that had been reverently stored here: pictures from her grandparents' home and faded cushions, Walter's rocking horse, and the slippers the privy councillor's wife had danced in as a bride. Frau Heidling could never resolve to part with anything that had once been dear to her, and so the contents of the attic faithfully accompanied the Heidlings' every change of residence.

So Agathe buried her toys among the most precious memories of times past in a crate packed carefully with little camphor bags. Thus once again a miniature version of an entire nursery passed through her fingers — the many dainty objects necessary for taking care of the tiniest of beings right down to the swaddling bands and diapers, the bathtub, and the hot water bottle. By using them to play and pretend, the most secret nerve endings of the future wife and mother are set to tingling in trembling anticipation.

As she bade her favorite doll farewell with a soft kiss on the fore-head, Agathe dreamily recalled the breathless delight with which she had unbuttoned her dress and put the cold, hard little wax head to the tiny buds of her child's breast to nurse. Smiling with embarrass-ment, she touched the soft rounding of her bosom. The dressmaker could never make her bodice tight enough to suit her; she was ashamed of the unaccustomed fullness of her contours.

At the bottom of the crate beneath a faded pink blanket lay the little things that she herself and her deceased baby brothers and sisters had once worn. These things were all stored away until the day when Agathe could get them out to use for her own living little children. Curious, she lifted the pink blanket a little and pulled out a tiny, delicate little shirt trimmed with lace. Oh, how sweet! How sweet!

She stuck her fingers into its little arms and smiled at it.

Wasn't it all mysterious, strange? A profound miracle . . . . And everything she heard, everything she dreamed made it all the more incomprehensible . . . . Oh, the silent blissful expectation inside her — day and night — day and night —

* * *

In contrast to the lassitude and lethargy she had had to combat while at boarding school, she was filled now with a constant desire for movement and activity. She often felt infinitely happy — and for no particular reason. While she dusted the furniture, her high soprano voice could suddenly ring out in loud rejoicing. Countless things were begun all at the same time: art history, dressmaking, music and visits to girlfriends and to poor people to whom the savings from her clothing allowance flowed. Oh, yes, so very practical, loving, self-sacrificing, and at the same time clever and highly refined! To achieve all that one did have to hustle! Everything, everything for Him — her beloved, glorious, future, as yet unknown husband! For oneself alone, only for the pure love of it — no, that would have been selfishness. And it was of course really so lovely, so sweet to live for others.

Agathe attached herself to her mother with a newly awakened tenderness. She found charming little ways of showing her father consideration. The privy councillor began to contemplate his daughter with quiet affection. He experienced that heartfelt joy in the constant proximity of a fresh young girl that for older men transfigures home with a new, sunny charm, a charm untroubled by sensual storms, hardly less pleasing, but more peaceful than that of the first years of marriage — a charm that plays around parents like a gentle breath of spring air, that fills fossilized ardor and dried-up habit with warm, pulsating life.

* * *

Agathe celebrated her seventeenth birthday in her snug, well-heated room with the bay, surrounded by roses in full bloom and rosy girlfriends.

The girls were in the exalted mood in which they found themselves daily, most especially, however, whenever they got together,
and that, too, happened daily — at least once. Their conversations
had as a result of this daily contact also gradually taken on a certain
free and easy familiarity.

"Aren't you getting big, Eugenie! Come on, show us! Truly,
girls, it's all real!" The young lady with the enviable breasts sat down
on Agathe's cretonne sofa with the calm certainty of victory.[31]

"Ryemeal gruel with eggs for breakfast; in the afternoon a bowl
of semolina porridge. So there. Now you know."

"I wouldn't want to eat that," cried pale Lisbeth Wendhagen,
nibbling a bit of macaroon.

"But you have to prepare for life's struggle," Eugenie remarked
sagely.[32]

"Shame, Genie!"

"Our chaste Agathe's turning red," Eugenie said helping herself
to some cake. "The dear child still hasn't managed to shake that
habit!"

"Oh, it's terrible!" Agathe's cheeks flamed even redder at this
annoying apology.

"I suppose you never turn red anymore?" snapped an older girl
from their set.

"Oh, but of course, but only when I want to! You hold your
breath! Watch me!"

They observed the trick with admiration and much laughter.

"I'll have them make semolina porridge for me too," mused Fräulein von Henning who had stood the entire time gravely contemplating herself in the mirror. Even as she said it, she considered whether
her mother would likely authorize the extra expense. It really was
abominable to have to economize like that!

"Excellency Wimpffen said semolina is very bad for the complexion!"

"How so?"

"Well, I think the semolina grains aren't so digestible and somehow creep around in your body."

"Oh, what nonsense!" Eugenie countered.

"Oh, yes! Excellency Wimpffen told Mama: In Russia young girls
never eat semolina because the semolina grains get lodged under the

skin and fester. Goose bumps and pimples and all sorts of things come from that!"

The girls went silent. That sounded serious!

"I don't believe that," said Agathe in a calm voice. "Nowadays everybody claims to know something! Peacock feathers are also supposed to be bad for you!"

"I suppose you don't believe that either?" asked Lisbeth Wendhagen importantly. "My old uncle — "

"I don't know about peacock feathers," cried the daughter of the supreme magistrate,[33] "but water lilies . . . . I've experienced it myself; no one can make me think otherwise! Last year when I was at my aunt's in Potsdam, my cousin brought in an entire armful from a boating excursion. Several ladies did try to warn her that those things bring bad luck, but she wouldn't hear of it! Right! The next day she got diphtheria; she practically died of it! Oh, yes, I've learned to be wary of water lilies!"

Despite the dangers that mysteriously menaced their lives and beauty from all sides, the young creatures were frivolous enough to engage in an avid discussion about the upcoming prospects for balls. The Wutrows wanted to put on a dance! And then the big lawyers' ball! Agathe had gotten a charming ballgown: real Parisian dog roses — terribly expensive — from Uncle Gustav.

"Say, your Uncle Gustav must have money if he can live like that and do nothing. In the end he'd be a good catch, wouldn't he?"

"Oh, no. He hasn't got any money! That is, he always says if his invention succeeds he could become a millionaire!"

"Oh, *Fountain of Youth*!" An endless giggling sounded around the coffee table. They seemed not to take Uncle Gustav's invention very seriously despite its poetic name.

"Your uncle is precious! We call him the cherry blossom on account of his beautiful white summer suits! Agathe, in the end you'll marry him, after all!"

Agathe laughed loudly and merrily, and all of them joined in with renewed laughter.

"Hey, 'fess up! Has he ever kissed you?"

"Oh, what nonsense — only on my birthday."

"I always kiss my uncles and boy cousins," piped the high little voice of a cute black-haired girl. "What else are they good for?"

"It's not the custom in our family," said Agathe haughtily.

"That's true!" cried Eugenie. "You're all so horribly respectable! But your father quite likes to put his arms around a person's waist now and again!"

"Shame, Eugenie!"

"Goodness, don't be like that! He's an old man. What does it hurt?"

"Picture this! The other day someone spoke to me on the street," Lisbeth Wendhagen began. Her little freckled face with its pale eyelashes became quite animated. "It was frightful!"

"Would you like some more coffee, Lisbeth?"

"No, thank you. One, two, three . . . now I've lost count again! This blasted pattern! There. So naturally I walk faster and faster; he's right behind me . . . . "

"How horrible!"

"What did he say to you?"

"Oh, I simply can't repeat it. Finally I get up the courage and say, 'Sir, you are mistaken!'"

"One shouldn't even respond!"

"I'm not allowed to go out alone in the evening!"

"Oh, sometimes it's quite amusing. Do you remember how when we were still in school we used to stroll down Breitenstrasse[34] and the boys from the Gymnasium[35] would come along?"

"But what happened? Go on with your story," cried impatient voices.

"I got home, rang the doorbell bathed in sweat! What do you think! That fellow! He replies to me, 'No, Fräulein, I'm not mistaken!' What do you say to that?"

"Once a fellow spoke to me out on the Glacis,"[36] cried Eugenie. "He was a gentleman; I recognized it immediately. Do you know what I replied? I said I'd be grateful for his escort! I had quite a pleasant conversation with him, and he brought me right to our front door! The next day he sent me a bouquet anonymously!"

"Wow, that Eugenie! You really are a shameless creature! Oh, whipped cream! I could eat myself to death with it!"

"Well, God bless your attempts!"

"Just don't stuff yourself before the lawyers' ball!"

"Our dance party will be right after it," cried Eugenie. "Girls, I'm just as happy as I can be! We've invited your cousin Martin too, Agathe! See how blissfully happy she is!"

"That's not true. I'm not at all interested in him!"

"Come now, dear child, don't act like that! I can't stand it!"

"Oh, heavens, do you think Junior Barrister Sonnenstrahl will engage me for the cotillion?"[37] Lisbeth sighed. "He has such a heavenly mustache!"

"I think Lieutenant Bieberitz's is much handsomer. Your Sonnenstrahl has bandy legs."

"And your Lieutenant Bieberitz wears a corset!"

"How can you say something like that?"

"Our dressmaker told me for certain. He lodges with her mother."

"Do you use Trine?"

"She's not allowed to work for us anymore! She's a horrible gossip! You should hear the stories she tells! Disgusting!"

"Tell, tell!"

"No, I'm too ashamed."

"Out with it, out with it, talk! Well — "

"Just imagine! Old Tademir who's married — Oh, Frau Privy Councillor . . . . "

"Well, my dear girls, are you having a good time? Agathe, are you being an attentive hostess? How are things at home?"

"Very well, thank you, Frau Privy Councillor!"

"Dear Agathe is allowed to come to our hop, isn't she, Frau Privy Councillor?"

"Oh, Frau Privy Councillor, how can you even say such a thing; you're certainly not bothering us . . . . "

Different voices. Different movements. Well-bred curtsies. Smiling, composed faces even if they were still glowing a vivid pink from the boisterous and confused shouting. It went well with their eyes, which were quietly and peacefully lowered over their needlework.

They spoke of painting on wood,[38] of the latest book of a popular woman writer of books for adolescents.

After all, these were nice girls, Agathe's girlfriends. Only Eugenie aroused Frau Heidling's suspicion. Vague rumors were circulating about a silly love affair on account of which she had been sent away. Surely merely one of those nasty bits of gossip that so readily dog pretty girls. The privy councillor's wife had to confess to herself that she had never been able to detect anything questionable in Eugenie.

42

The girl had much better manners than her mother, not to mention old Wutrow.

VI.

In the manual *Woman's Life and Deeds as Maiden, Wife and Mother* it said the first ball was one of the most beautiful days in a young girl's life. All the emotions that the little heart beating under the tarlatan bodice was to feel at the sound of the dance music were described in detail there. Yes, in her description of these most important joys of youth, the author waxed truly rhapsodic.

And not only the voice of the oracle that intoned from the temple of poetry, but also President Dürnheim's wife and Mama's other acquaintances — thin-faced, haggard wives of councillors and heavy-set wives of councillors; kind, witty wives of councillors and simple wives of councillors; wives of councillors of the court and of the government; and unmarried ones who had only managed to achieve the rank of member of a councillor's family — they all patted the little Heidling girl's cheek or nodded at her. Your first ball! Such a lucky child! Oh, yes, your first ball! They, too, slim and happy and fresh as the morning dew, had once looked forward to their first ball.

So it's true! One's first ball must be an unprecedented enchantment.

And Agathe had received a gorgeous dress too. But Mama was unwilling to pay for long gloves — in her day young girls never wore long gloves like those that were now the fashion. Recently Mama had begun anxiously saving money — since Walter had resolved to become an officer. Her parents were always having to send him 300 marks — that certainly *was* bad! But Eugenie had wonderful gloves, up to her elbows, and she immediately bought herself several pairs in case one of them ripped. Agathe found it truly agonizing that she kept on thinking about her gloves. There were, after all, so many other things that should have occupied her more, for example, whether she would fall in love. According to the deluxe volume this mostly happened at the first ball. She'd already been a grownup girl for eight months, so it really was high time!

Martin Greffinger came over from the university town, which was not far away, to go to the lawyers' ball.

"He'll certainly give you a bouquet, won't he?" Agathe's girl-friends conjectured, and for this reason Agathe showed him a sample of her dress. A bouquet in the color of the ballgown. What bliss!

"Three proletarian families could live for four weeks on all the nonsense you're draping on yourself," said Martin disdainfully. "I guess I'm supposed to get you a bouquet too, now that I've let my-self in for playing the fool here among you geese today! Well, Agathe, I wouldn't have thought you'd become just like all the rest."

Agathe sulked, and the privy councillor took Martin to task for his improper manner of expression. Agathe was severely punished for her touchiness: as a result of it a dispute arose between Father and Martin, a dispute that began during afternoon coffee, that embit-tered the cozy festivities before the ball, and that continued, accom-panied by countless cigars, on into evening.

Martin's predilection for Herwegh's poems was severely criti-cized.

Now and again Agathe heard angry outbursts as she went about getting ready for the ball.

"How can someone with such views intend to enter the civil service?"

"The suffering of millions . . . . The capitalist economy . . . . "

"Pure socialism . . . . Empty talk . . . . "

"Ossified creatures of habit . . . . Rotten bourgeoisie . . . . "

Martin's eyes took on a wild, frightful expression, and the scorn-ful lines that now always framed those pouting lips, which still scarcely evidenced a trace of a beard, sharpened to a grimace. The privy councillor strode up and down in the parlor as he was wont to do when he was in a very bad mood.

Mama, who had lived the entire day in fear of an attack of her neuralgia — she had had to run around so much, and that never agreed with her, but Agathe certainly couldn't take care of her clothes herself — poor Mama really did have to lie down on the sofa in the adjoining room. Meanwhile the hairdresser arrived, much later than expected, naturally. There was a chasing and scrambling until they were ready, and everything smelled of Hoffmann's drops and valerian tea, remedies that the privy councillor's wife took to revive herself.[39] The men could hardly be separated. Agathe was to dress in ▾

the parlor in front of the large mirror. Oh, how unpleasant and horrible it all was!

When she had finished primping, she had to turn slowly, as if she were on a turntable, in front of her assembled family and the servants. The chandelier was lighted for the occasion.

She was seized with an oppressive joy at the flattering remarks of her father, at the grumbling enthusiasm of Dottie, the old cook, at the excited oohing and aahing of the little housemaid, and at the quiet triumph on her mother's suffering face. The person in the mirror was so alien to her. In the airy white ruching[40] and flounces, entwined, as it were, by the long rose tendrils, with her hair piled up and curled, she almost seemed to herself a beauty! What if she of all the hundred girls at the lawyers' ball were to be declared the queen! Mama brought her a glass of red wine because she suddenly looked so pale.

They hadn't wanted to take a carriage; it really wasn't so far. Agathe found it quite miserable having to slog through rain and snow in huge galoshes with her skirts pinned up, muffled up like a veritable monster, and on top of that in Martin's presence. She looked enviously at every coach that thundered past them. The dispute between uncle and nephew over the latter's views nearly broke out again, and thereafter they strode onward in obscure silence, one of them out in front, the other right behind.

Agathe choked on her tears.

In thinking about the suffering of millions Martin had forgotten about her bouquet for the ball.

* * *

The young girls stood there in long rows and in small groups — like a gigantic bed of delicately toned spring hyacinths — pink, bluish, maize, white, pale green. Hands crossed over fans, elbows of bare shivering arms pressed tightly to hips, carefully whispering to one another and nodding shy greetings with flower-bedecked blonde and brown coiffures. Only a few of them who had been going to balls for a while dared to smile; most of them, however, managed only an expression of strained excitement.

Separated from the airy rainbow-hued clouds of dresses, from the anxious, bare white shoulders, separated by a wide, empty space that was enclosed above by a richly ornamented stucco ceiling and below by a parquet floor that was as smooth as glass, there stood a wall of black frock coats and white shirt fronts that shone as hard and glossily as the parquet, and short, meticulously parted hair, little mustaches that had been carefully curled. On the male side one noticed principally the effort of smoothing on white gloves, and besides that, whispering in undertones as on the opposite side of the room, a stiff bow, a solemn shaking of hands. A small circle of flashing epaulets and uniforms separated itself off from the black phalanx. Here there was loud talking; the comrades inspected the ballroom with the scornful look of the victor and with a light, dancing step ventured across the frightfully empty room to the bed of hyacinths, each time setting off a soft trembling and a slight stirring there.

In twos and threes the black figures now also freed themselves from the crowd and went diving for dance partners among the luminous, colorful clouds of dresses. But from the perimeter of the ballroom many maternal eyes peered and peered at the army troops that had positioned themselves opposite one another in combat position. Many a mouth would have loved to shout commands and instructions from the sidelines! The fathers stationed themselves in the adjoining rooms and in the doors to the ballroom as the service corps and supply officers, so to speak, who are of course indispensable to an army.

And now the fanfare sounded loudly for the attack, and the black ones threw themselves upon the light ones; everyone whirled together in mingled confusion, and the battle could begin. Whew! That made for hard work! How the drops of sweat ran down the manly faces and were dried in vain with white handkerchiefs! How the shreds of tarlatan flew from the thin dresses, the strands of coifed hair freed themselves, the shoulders warmed, and the eyes brightened!

And the mothers' conversations went completely silent, and they pursued the individual pairs in the waves, with craned necks and lorgnettes and pince-nez — one myopic woman even used opera glasses.

And the fathers settled comfortably into beer and skat and long political disputes, which in fact were not very exciting because as a Prussian bureaucrat one could have only one opinion and was always loyal to kaiser and empire.

Yes, now the joys of the ball had reached their zenith!

* * *

Agathe was amazed at the simplicity of Eugenie's outfit which, despite much pleading, not a single friend had been allowed to see ahead of time. To go to Berlin twice and to spend so much money for this little dress!

No trim, no ruching, no flowers. It looked fabulous; there was no denying it. Whereas most of the young ladies' trains formed a splendid edifice that offered a stiff and steady resistance of tulle to their owner's turns and could be brought into line only with a kick to one side, Eugenie's train conformed to the slightest turning of her body. The bodice, moreover, appeared to be a pale pink membrane stretched tightly around her proud bosom.

This winter it was the fashion to wear small oval wreaths. Eugenie had eschewed this ornament as well. Her hair was not even done up in an artful manner; her finely shaped head with its blonde hair and its piercing gray eyes and its coloring, which by day was rather ruddy, was veiled in a dusting of powder that lent it a softened, faded appearance. But her exquisitely formed shoulders and arms emitted, as it were, a radiance, a soft white light. Instead of a gold chain, around her neck she wore a little band of tulle that had been tied in a childish bow next to one ear. A bit of whimsy — Agathe knew that her friend had an ugly scar on that spot beneath her ear.

"She knows what she's doing . . . . Well, youngsters, my hat's off! She knows what she's doing!" said Uncle Gustav with a reverent expression. He was considered to be the finest connoisseur of feminine beauty in the city. His ex-spouse was said to have been an enchanting woman — a veritable demon of charm, they said.

When Agathe saw the abundance of elegant figures, she suddenly lost all hope of success. She lost her confidence, didn't know how to stand, what to do with her hands, where she should look. Her mother came over to her and removed the collar trimmed with swan, which in her confusion she had left on. The privy councillor's wife whispered to her not to look so serious; otherwise no gentleman would ask her to dance.

Heavens! That would be terrible! Agathe began to feel a fear such as she had never known in her young life. Driven by this fear —

she really was ashamed of it — she shrank behind her friends and fled to a corner of the ballroom.

It would have been such a disgrace to be a wallflower at her first ball! She regretted not having accepted Martin's offer to dance the opening waltz with her. This morning it had seemed to her a pitiful last resort. Now she would have been glad of this last resort. She watched Eugenie in the foremost row, surrounded by five or six gentlemen who passed her dance card from hand to hand, eagerly deliberating over it. And no one had approached her yet . . . .

Next to her stood an ugly, oldish creature with gentle, resigned eyes who said to her comfortingly: "There are always so many more ladies than gentlemen." Large groups of young men spoke freely and easily with one another; it didn't occur to them that people expected them to dance.

A bald assessor,[41] who had the reputation of being very clever and amiable, slowly strolled past the ranks of the ladies. He looked at each one through his pince-nez, examined each from the little curls on her forehead down to her white satin slippers. He also went up to the shy ones in the back. He greeted Agathe since he knew her father and remained standing in front of her for a second. She held her dance card in trembling fingers and made an involuntary motion to hand it to him.

"Doesn't the lady care to dance? Is that why she has withdrawn to the back like this?" he asked and strolled on past.

Agathe bit her lip. Something loathsome welled up in her: a hate, a bitterness, an anguish . . . . She would have liked to run to her mother and cry: Why did you bring me here? Why did you do this to me? Why this . . . this . . . this insult that she could never wash off?

The dance began. A little blonde fellow threaded his way through the whirling pairs toward the corner where Agathe had been left standing with the oldish creature. His eyes looked at Agathe in astonished admiration; he flushed for pure rapture at the thought of holding her in his arms, but he hadn't been introduced to her and — No, before he would have dared to introduce himself to her, he had sooner fetched his sister's friend who stood right beside her. Gratefully the oldish creature skipped off with the little fellow, and Agathe was left standing alone.

Suddenly people noticed her, and everyone was surprised that she was not dancing. After all, she was indisputably one of the prettiest girls. The mothers exchanged their observations; they went over to Privy Councillor Heidling's wife who smiled with her pitiful mouth, which was crooked from raging neuralgia, and said amicably, "Yes, these are the sorts of experiences one has at balls." The mothers all agreed: young girls couldn't avoid experiencing such things. But several thought privately that it was quite maladroit of the privy councillor's wife not to have given a little party with a good supper before the ball at which her daughter's dance card would have been filled. The privy councillor's wife had relied too much on the tender, innocent charm of Agathe's seventeen years.

As if every gentleman became mindful of an unpardonable of-, fense, Agathe was from then on engaged for the extra dances.[42] She tried to be happy, but the vain waiting had spoiled her mood. The strong smell of pomade in her partners' hair and a certain other inexplicable something that emanated from those men with whom she was suddenly in such close proximity made her uneasy. She found it excruciating the way the first of them put his arms round her and as they danced pressed her close and then closer to him. The second one stretched her arm out horizontally as if it were a spear for carving a path through the crowd; the third pressed her hand convulsively in his and moaned and panted. A fourth swung his arm and hers wildly up and down to the beat and kept stepping on her toes.

She had whirled around with her brother and her cousins, confidently and happily; here she forgot all she had learned, stiffly and fearfully resisted her partners' lead and made the stupidest mistakes. It was a release for her when Uncle Gustav asked her to dance.

Uncle Gustav had given each of Agathe's girlfriends a little bottle of *Fountain of Youth* and now he asked all of the young ladies to dance in order to convince himself of the effect of his beauty wash. He danced for business reasons. While he held his niece in his arms with studied chivalry, she heard him saying in an undertone, "Too much benzoin.[43] A little more lavender couldn't hurt. What do you think, Agathe?"

But even so, he danced much, much better than the young gentlemen; that was generally acknowledged. He also dressed with impeccable taste. No one knew how he managed it on his meager income. Occasionally and with a condescending expression as if he were communicating an important diplomatic secret, he gave the rich young merchants or the ambitious ones among the lawyers the address of his tailor in the capital. Uncle Gustav lived on the perquisites available to cultivated gentlemen with wide circles of acquaintances. Nevertheless he glossed over this fact with cheerful idealism. He aspired to disseminate beauty. For him "beauty" was a coat that didn't ripple, a perfume that was both pleasing to refined noses and good for your health.

When the supper commenced, Agathe's dinner escort asked her whether she would like to make a cozy foursome with her friend Eugenie. Agathe assented. Martin was Eugenie's escort; Lisbeth Wendhagen also joined the group. She did not, however, add much to the merriment because she tried constantly to keep her eye on a second table behind her where Junior Barrister Sonnenstrahl was paying court to one of her girlfriends. She also complained to Agathe that her shoes were too tight and that she was thus forced to spend the whole evening standing on one foot in order to rest the other one. Eugenie, in contrast, was in the best of spirits, and the two gentlemen also made their best effort to keep the conversation lively. They exchanged all kinds of witty jokes and wagers, nibbled the dessert prematurely and taught one another the proper way of toasting whereby you gazed into one another's eyes. Agathe noted that this was not the kind of harmless jollity that had characterized her previous intercourse with young people. They all appeared to have donned a peculiar ceremoniousness along with their ball attire. A couple of times Agathe had to burst into loud giggling because she recalled that her dinner partner, who was now calling her Fräulein Heidling and who presented each dish to her with incredible politeness, had once in her presence gotten into a terrible fist fight with Walter, during which she herself had gotten hit a few times. In the end the boys had rolled around on the ground, disheveled and scratched up.

Martin and Eugenie also seemed like strangers to her. In place of the rudeness he had flaunted but two hours earlier Martin had acquired a strange sentimentality, and Eugenie was saying everything with affected little gibes and deliberate gestures and glances whose meaning Agathe did not yet comprehend. At the same time she felt, however, that she, too, increasingly lost herself in a completely unnatural demeanor. When the noise at the large tables became louder and louder and the gentlemen were partaking of the champagne in a lively fashion, either leaning far back in their chairs or leaning far forward over the table, and everybody around her was laughing, shouting and whispering, Agathe became very sad for no reason. The behavior of the people around her no longer amused her and instead seemed to her meaningless and incomprehensible. On the face of the friend of her youth, Martin, she saw an expression of tense excitement, an expression of agony combined with an odd smile. His gaze did not stray from Eugenie, but he appeared hardly to hear what she was saying; he kept staring at her neck, at her bosom. Her dress was so low cut; how could she stand it without dying of shame, thought Agathe indignantly. At the same time something in her own chest hurt. It was like a disappointment, as if she were now forever estranged from Martin . . . as if something were slipping away from her that she had regarded as her un-contested property . . . . What was it? Surely she didn't love him? She wouldn't think of it!

Obscure instincts drove her to look at young Dürnheim at her side just as Eugenie did Martin — with this mysterious meaning in her gaze. But when he responded in kind, she found it unpleasant; she became annoyed with herself and also with the young man who seemed to her insipid and without a trace of romance.

If only she could have gone home and lain in her quiet, dark room with her eyes closed, completely alone, completely alone! She was very tired; she saw everything around her as if through a gauze veil.

The cotillion followed the supper. The bald assessor came up to Agathe and asked her with friendly condescension whether she already had a partner or whether he might have the pleasure.

Now that this man had gotten the notion, she was supposed to let him twirl her around, the man who had insulted her so deeply?

"Thank you, but I don't dance the cotillion," she said abruptly, and he left her with his nonchalant smile, remained standing not far from her and with a jaded look watched the ballroom through his gold pince-nez. Shortly thereafter a lieutenant came up and invited her to dance; Agathe followed him in pleased triumph.

During one of the intervals in the highly elaborate dance Mama suddenly waved her over.

"What, Agathe? You turned down Assessor Raikendorf and now you're dancing with another?" the privy councillor's wife whispered agitatedly. "That won't do! You must never do that again. Or did he behave improperly toward you?"

"No," Agathe stuttered, her cheeks flaming, "no, only — I don't like him!"

"Well, dear child, if you mean to be so choosy with your dance partners, then you can't go to balls. It was a great show of friendship on Herr Raikendorf's part to ask such a young girl to dance. Otherwise he only dances with married women. You should have acknowledged that with gratitude."

Agathe threw back her head defiantly with a disdainful jerk. She didn't understand what she should be grateful for if Assessor Raikendorf had bad taste. She found all married women monstrously old and no longer at all fit to be her rivals.

* * *

She slept fitfully the night after her first ball. Her head was dull and benumbed; she resolved not to go to another one. But when over the course of the following day she got together with her girl-friends and talked about the party, she was ashamed to own up to her opinion and protested — like all the other girls, including Lisbeth Wendhagen with her tight shoes — that she had had a heavenly time.

VII.

A great struggle had ended in victory and prosperity; a German emperor had been crowned in glory; the dream of a nation had been realized. Thousands of vigorous men lay shot to pieces and moldering beneath soil enriched with blood.

From the shell splinters that missed their mark they made inkwells and cunning little flower bowls, and young ladies decorated their boudoirs with them. Honoring the military was the right and the duty of the German girl.

Eugenie Wutrow always had a sure instinct for what was necessary, for the object of public approbation in her little circle. She wore a paletot that was practically a uniform coat. Her room resembled a wing of the armory, ceremoniously decorated for a bellicose celebration with flowers and pictures of the high-ranking generals.

Patriotism suited her like each new fashion and each ideal duty with which she adorned her charming person. She had a special touch that shaped everything to her purposes as well as a fine sense for blending colors.

How zealous she became, how sharp and animated, whenever she opposed Martin Greffinger's horrid principles! How boldly she ventured in conversation with him into areas that other girls feared! Greffinger was no longer in the good graces of the fathers and the mothers since Privy Councillor Heidling's wife had complained to her friends that her nephew was causing them considerable grief because he leaned toward those new social democratic views.[44] At their parents' command most of the young girls timidly avoided associating with the student. That was not difficult for them since he, for his part, behaved rather rudely toward them.

Despite his dislike for bourgeois society, Martin often came over to M. for a few hours, even for entire days. In the beginning he accepted the Heidlings' guest room and hospitality without much thought simply as a matter of course, given the family ties. Then the tension heightened between him and his uncle, the privy councillor. The atmosphere there became too oppressive for him, and he seldom showed his face at the home of his relatives. He went to the Wutrows' every time, however, although the views of the tobacco factory owner were surely not more democratic than those of the privy councillor.

One day in conversation with Agathe Eugenie tossed out the observation that her cousin was walking down dangerous paths, but that he was a brilliant person. Another time Agathe found on her girlfriend's table a book with a red inscription on a black cover. Eugenie tore it hastily from her hands.

"Banned!" she whispered laughing and shoved it under the lace and ribbons in a carved chest.

Then again Martin could be high-spirited to the point of madness, and when he came, he simply teased and joked with the two girls. For weeks he wore a little fur cap that he had stolen from Eugenie, and on her blonde head one could admire Martin Greffinger's knockabout hat. If he met the officers of the garrison at the Wutrows', he would sit in a corner, morose and sullen. Eugenie's most adroit attempts couldn't move him to take part in an argument about his horrid views. Usually he would leave immediately.

Agathe was convinced that Eugenie loved him.

She herself constantly felt compelled to deliberate over the question as to how she would feel if Junior Barrister Sonnenstrahl or Lieutenant Bieberitz or young Dürnheim were to ask for her hand in marriage. And what she would feel if after the wedding she were alone in the evening with one of these gentlemen and were standing at the window, her head resting on his shoulder, and looking out into a dark park. This was her involuntary mental image of the commencement of marriage. Behind them a hanging lamp would burn, and dark red curtains would flow down the windows. She would remove the bridal wreath and the veil, and he would loosen his white tie — and then he would look funny! She couldn't get past that, and the feeling of a great happiness refused to materialize.

Perhaps she was not meant to marry at all, but instead reserved for an unusual, romantic, and dreadful fate.

If only she weren't so fond of little children.

As a broadly educated man, Privy Councillor Heidling was interested in art, and along with several other educated friends he was active in establishing a permanent exhibition of old and new paintings in M. After this institution of pure and elevating delight was opened to the public, he saw to it that his daughter visited it regularly. He liked going with her himself on Sunday mornings for an hour or so and he used whatever they saw as the occasion for many an educational observation on the various schools of painting and sculpture. Agathe's taste often diverged quite radically from her father's, but of course hers was simply unpolished and childish and could be expected to become more refined. It became a sport for the young girls to gather round the privy councilor on Sundays between twelve and one and to accompany him from painting to painting, laughing, gabbing, whispering their heretical observations in one another's ears and at the same time listening attentively. The serious man's gaze rested amicably upon all these creatures clad in close-fitting little fur jackets and fluffy hats, upon the fresh, animated faces glowing with the joys of youth and the pleasures of winter.

"*Lord Byron at Newstead Abbey*," the privy councillor read from the catalogue. "Born when? What principal works? *Cain* — *Childe Harold* — good! What have you read by him? The *Prisoner of Chillon*? You can take your time getting to the other things! . . . See how excellently our painter has captured the poet's wild and mournful expression . . . . His nervous hands — very fine! Also the gothic colonnade . . . . His penchant for romanticism is indicated by the fading sunset. Leaning there in the corner, the flag with the Greek colors . . . symbol of a fate to come. Agathe, how did Byron die? Missolonghi. Right . . . . Here we have now . . . . Let's see what the catalogue says: *Grazing Cows* . . . . The work of a master of the French school from the forties . . . . "[45]

Agathe had stayed behind. With melancholy, astonished eyes she was dreaming of the English lord. She had of course seen pictures of him before . . . . What was it then that had suddenly gotten into her?

The next morning she returned to the exhibit. Only for him.

She stared at the painting so long, so fixedly and intently that before her closed eyes she saw the handsome male head clearly as if in a miniature. During the week the exhibition was usually empty, and nobody could observe Agathe. The painting became strangely animated for her. The artist had succeeded in capturing in this painted visage something of the power that in his time the poet had exercised over women. The girl stole up to it as if to a forbidden pleasure. She became intoxicated with the longing that had now found an object with which it could in fact always remain longing.

At home she read Byron's works — all of them — from the beginning to the end. Her joy in them was really an excruciating passion. She learned much here, but then again the natural relations of the sexes to one another appeared in a wild, stormy atmosphere in which everything left her, after all, with the impression of a fanciful fairy tale.

She wept with jealousy when she read in Byron's biography of his relationship with Countess Guiccioli.[46] But none of the women on whom he had wasted his ardent heart had satisfied him. None of them . . . that was a comfort!

Happiness, the unruffled serenity of the gods — the genius would have needed that, so the critics said, to become a classical author. Agathe Heidling could have given him that! The reason for the melancholy that so often mysteriously cast a pall over her became clear to her then.

Born half a century too late . . . . The romantic quality of this fate sufficed for her in the end, providing her some degree of comfort. Beneath the surface of her existence a peculiar dream life commenced. She set up housekeeping in her new fanciful homeland and from then on she transferred her deepest joys, her weird sufferings to this place — perhaps the way children create an alternative world to which they give some bizarre name and whose elaboration constantly occupies their thoughts. And parents or educators are surprised then that they muster only a weak interest in schoolwork and chores at home.

While Fräulein Heidling attended balls and coffees, went on picnics in the country and visited holiday resorts; while she went ice skating, distributed cotillion favors, selected charming spring hats, got her iron by drinking from chalybeate springs[47] and did embroidery, she was simultaneously carried off across Scotland's desolate heaths upon the dead poet-lord's breast on a wildly rearing race horse. Then she lay in oriental masked costumes upon sofas in dilapidated halls, and spirit voices sang of dark guilt and wild suffering to the wailing tones of a harp. Through renunciation without precedent she absolved her beloved. And he wept at her feet and his eyes were like burning flames . . . .

* * *

The following year Walter was transferred to M. with the rank of lieutenant. His comrades and Agathe's girlfriends spent a lot of time at the Heidlings'; there was always a merry hustle and bustle there.

But there were unpleasant scenes sometimes when the privy councillor suddenly reproached his wife and daughter severely for their wastefulness in the running of the household and declared that he had no money for such lavish socializing. But then immediately afterwards he would insist that Agathe have new boots or he would prepare a bowl of punch if six to eight young people turned up in the evening only wanting to eat potatoes and herring.

In the beginning the privy councillor found it difficult to depart from the traditions of his family and not to have his son study law. In his eyes a specious and superficial aura clung to the officer's estate. Walter had exploited the enthusiasm of 1870, which resonated for years, to get his father to assent to his wish. The privy councillor now realized that his son also had to work hard if he wished to get ahead. There was a zealous striving among young people. Each one sought to carve out a good place for himself in the new empire.

Walter and his friends laughed a great deal about Martin Greffinger's angry criticism of the newly achieved glory.

Walter had hardly been in M. three months when he became engaged to Eugenie Wutrow. That surprised even his family. Agathe had assumed that Eugenie was secretly promised to Martin. A few days earlier during a walk they had all taken together and that had ended with coffee in a public garden, she thought she had seen Martin reach for Eugenie's hand underneath the table and the girl had let him take it. Meanwhile, her head propped on her right hand, Eugenie had exchanged teasing remarks with Walter across the table.

As soon as Agathe was alone with the affianced girl she couldn't refrain from tossing out the remark "I thought it was Martin you liked!"

"A social democrat student?" asked Eugenie full of reproach. "But Agathe — ! One certainly doesn't marry such a man! And besides, he really does hate the institution of marriage, you know," she added with her frivolous little laugh.

A feeling of dislike, of contempt toward her future sister-in-law tormented Agathe even as all her acquaintances congratulated her because her brother had chosen her dearest friend to be his wife. She thought it her duty to have another serious talk with Eugenie to see whether she really did love Walter. But after her first unsuccessful attempt she didn't have the courage. What else could have moved Eugenie to become engaged to Walter? She was a rich girl and had already turned down various proposals.

The two friends faithfully reported every bagatelle of their daily lives to one another. They would have taken it amiss if one of them had purchased a bow without asking the other for advice and without engaging in protracted discussions about it. But what was going on inside her future sister-in-law remained for Agathe as alien a world as her fanciful dream life would have been for Eugenie. Each of them anxiously guarded her own secrets.

VIII.

When the children were still little, their paternal grandmother died, and Frau Heidling inherited her cook. Even back then she was called Old Dottie. Having over the years become withered and hard like a weathered old fence post and possessing a bilious temperament, she worked for the family more out of stubborn tenacity than out of gentle loyalty. They had lost track of the number of times she had quit and then despite everything stayed on. Whenever one overheard her grumbling and scolding to herself in the kitchen, one had to come to the conclusion that her employers really belonged in the lunatic asylum. Dottie displayed equal contempt toward the young chambermaids who had been hired to help her out, and all of them were afraid of her, for Old Dottie worked tirelessly and demanded the same of these young things. All the councillors' wives envied Frau Heidling the treasure she had found in Old Kitchen Dottie.

An ambition had taken shape in the old cook's desiccated heart. She wanted to receive the reward for twenty-five years of service in one and the same family. The queen presented a silver cross and a Bible in such rare cases.[48]

And because Privy Councillor Heidling's wife shared Dottie's hopes, indeed, because this public acknowledgment really brought the mistress just as much honor as it did the servant, she patiently retained her in her household even though Dottie was thoroughly disinclined to offer Agathe insight into her art.

If Agathe was unable to learn anything from Dottie, she all the more eagerly took on the education of the little housemaid who had been confirmed with her. Pastor Kandler had warmly urged upon her the responsibility for the unspoiled country girl. Thus on Sunday afternoons she gave Wiesing Groterjahn little stories by Frommel and Marie Nathusius to read[49] and subjected her to little homilies on the perniciousness and the dangers of the dance halls. While the privy councillor's wife found it appropriate to call the girl Luisa even though in the beginning tears sprang into the homesick child's eyes each time, Agathe continued to use the familiar nickname "Wiesing." If they took up a piece of work together, she conversed with Wiesing in a friendly manner and tried to make her understand how good it was for her to serve in a house where none of the care and misery that awaited working women in factories could get to her. It troubled Agathe now and again that despite her loving efforts Wiesing appeared unable to muster any real trust in her.

"The girls see all of you as their natural enemies, and at bottom they're right about that," Martin had said one day. Agathe really couldn't understand that.

Meanwhile she was more and more interested in her imaginary lover than in educating the heart and mind of the housemaid, and she concerned herself with Wiesing only when she needed something from her.

"Fräulein," said Wiesing one morning as she brought warm water into Agathe's bedroom. She stood with her eyes lowered. "There's no bolt on my door. Couldn't one be put on it?"

"Yes, don't you have a key?"

"The young master took it away," Wiesing stammered.

"The young master? What kind of nonsense is that! You've surely lost it!"

"Uh-uh, Frölen!"[50]

"Don't lie, Wiesing. As if you'd ever say anything if you broke or lost something."

"Uh-uh, Frölen. O dear God! I simply don't know what to do!" she cried, lapsing into Low German.

"I don't understand you at all. What do you want then? You've got to speak High German," said Agathe impatiently and poured the warm water into her wash basin.

"The young master — Please don't say anything to Frau Privy Councillor," she continued in Low German, "I haven't said anything either, an' Dottie, she says I'm just imaginin' things!"

The girl's round, childish face vanished into her white apron. She sobbed pitifully.

Agathe looked at her in amazement. Suddenly she flushed deep red.

"Walter probably just wanted to scare you," she said softly. "I'll tell him you don't like jokes like that!"

Wiesing raised her tearstained face and looked at Agathe helplessly with her troubled blue eyes. "Fräulein, that really wasn't a joke!"

"Oh, what else could it have been, you silly thing. Do you really think — My brother is engaged, you know!"

"I said that to the young master too. I said he should be ashamed of the sin of it, I said. He simply wouldn't listen . . . . Frölen, if he comes back — I simply don't know what to do!"

"Comes back?" asked Agathe, paralyzed as if in a frightening dream. "Where did he say that to you?"

"In my little room."

"Luisa, you're lying," shouted Agathe angrily.

The girl only sobbed more violently.

Agathe walked away from her to the other end of the room.

"My God, my God!" she stammered after a while and wrung her hands.

"Wiesing, we're not going to say anything to Mama," she whispered, tears streaming down her face. "Mama couldn't bear it; she's already so sickly . . . and she's so fond of Walter!"

"Yes, Frölen!"

"You've got to get out of the house, Wiesing."

"Yes, Frölen!"

"But how do we go about it?"

Wiesing didn't answer.

"I've got to speak with Walter. My God, I just can't; I just can't . . . . What on earth has come over him!"

"Such a fine young gentleman," said Wiesing pensively and dried her eyes.

"Damn it! Where on earth are my boots! Luisa!" Walter shouted from the hallway.

The two girls started and looked at one another in terror.

"But he's got his manservant to tend to him," murmured Agathe.

"Luisa!" The lieutenant's rumbling voice resounded anew across the hallway. Accustomed to obeying, the little housemaid ran out.

Feeling as if all of her limbs had withered and died, Agathe attended to what passed between the two of them out in the hall.

Walter, however, merely said abruptly and sharply, "Luisa, get me my manservant." Wiesing answered in her belabored High German, "Yes, Herr Lieutenant." Suddenly it seemed to Agathe that she had only dreamed what she had just heard.

But it was not so easy to disregard it.

Now she had to deliberate — without the support of advice, entirely alone, based on her judgment, on her own responsibility. She had to speak with Walter; there was no other way. If she told her father there would be a terrible scene. Papa would never ever forgive his son for something so dishonorable.

First she went to a locksmith and bought a bolt with large staples. She could barely say what it was she wanted, for she thought the people in the shop could tell by looking at her why she needed the bolt. Then with Wiesing's help she hammered it onto the chamber door, shivering in fear that Mama would happen upon her while she was doing it and ask what it was all about.

Wiesing hadn't opened the window in the cramped room since the morning. The air in it was disgustingly close. Dirty water stood in the bowl; hair that had come out in her comb and all kinds of pitiful junk lay strewn about the floor. And Walter — her scrupulously neat and elegant brother — had been here in his shiny uniform . . . how ever was it possible?

She shuddered with dread, with revulsion.

How should she approach Walter? He seemed to her a depraved person; she could no longer bridge the gap between his feelings and hers. And whenever she looked at Wiesing, she felt a violent dislike for the girl who had caused her to lose her brother.

She read her New Testament and prayed for strength. She recalled that Pastor Kandler had once told her that the seeds of every sin lie hidden in every person. She wanted to try to make a loving plea to her brother. She felt as if she were groping in pitch dark and touching something disgusting.

She tortured herself the entire day in this manner and wished that Walter would have to spend so much time at his post that a conversation with him would be impossible. Oh, she *was* cowardly!

In the afternoon Eugenie came over for a quarter of an hour. While Agathe was still sitting there and Eugenie vainly searched for something to talk about with her, Walter came in. He had been out riding. His curly hair clung damply to his forehead. He looked a little out-of-sorts. Nevertheless, he kissed Eugenie. She smoothed his hair with her pretty, nimble fingers, looked into his eyes with her cool, mocking smile and said, "Did something annoying happen?" And then she passed her hand lightly over his uniform just as her hand had once glided soothingly over Agathe's temples when Agathe had had toothache at boarding school.

This recollection turned Agathe's thoughts to the clerk who had been Eugenie's first love and to the room with the cigar samples.

Oh, if only she could have run away, far, far away from everyone.

Eugenie took her leave. Walter escorted her to the door. Father was taking his daily walk. Mama had accompanied him today because she wanted to combine it with paying a call. Walter came back

61

into the room. So Agathe was alone with him, and now she had to speak. No one was there to help her.

"What kind of expression have you got on your face today? Eugenie also wanted to know what's gotten into you?" Thus Walter unexpectedly initiated the conversation. She summoned all her might — by the way, upon hearing her first softly stammered words, he knew immediately what she was getting at.

But things went quite differently from what she had expected! He showed no trace of shame or remorse, became angry, paced back and forth in the room, his spurs jangling; and hoarse with anger, he cried softly, "Don't concern yourself with things you don't understand! Do you hear? You don't understand a single thing about this. Not a thing! And that's why you have no right to pass judgment either."

"I understand that you're engaged. I find it dishonorable . . . . "

"Don't you dare!" Agathe looked at the fist her brother raised menacingly before her eyes.

"Go ahead and hit me!" she cried. "I don't care what you do; your behavior is still dishonorable. Oh, shame on you, I'm ashamed you're my brother!"

She burst into passionate sobs. His hand sank slowly, but he was quite livid now and was gnashing his teeth.

"I forbid you to interfere in my affairs! Do you hear? You're not behaving like a lady, but like a hysterical woman. It's improper of you to speak of such things! Do you understand me?" With that he tore open the door and slammed it shut with a bang.

For a long time Agathe sat in a chair without stirring, numb with grief.

Later in the evening she asked Wiesing whether she couldn't return to her parents, whether she didn't want to say that her mother was sick and needed her. But the little housemaid shook her head and answered with inconceivable resignation, "Oh, well, Frölen, my mother would get good an' mad if I went home. An' Dottie says anyhow it's the same with all the masters. An' anyhow the young master's gonna get married soon an' then he'll be outa the house."

What more could Agathe do? She hoped that her brother would fear a scandal. But she had lost all sense of proportion for calculating the possibilities.

She couldn't make up her mind to ask Wiesing about this matter ever again; indeed, from then on she called her Luisa as her mother did. It seemed to her that an air of vulgarity clung to the girl.

IX.

Agathe was already twenty years old.

The privy councillor's wife was quite happy when in February a distant, much younger relative, with whom she exchanged short letters now and again, asked her to send her daughter to visit her for a few weeks. Agathe's picture had awakened in her the desire to get to know her.

The cousin, who had been educated as a painter, had married a Polish artist, Kasimir von Woszenski.[51] The Heidlings considered Frau von Woszenski an exciting intellectual, indeed a genius. At the same time the family situation of the married couple was so solidly established that even the privy councillor couldn't have serious objections to his daughter visiting her. But he didn't like letting her leave his side. He was accustomed to her chatter and laughter, to the comings and goings of all the young girls around him. He didn't want to do without this light and pleasant amusement in his dry and laborious life as a bureaucrat, not even for four weeks. He didn't see why he had a daughter if she were going to go on trips.

The privy councillor's wife remarked tentatively, "But Agathe might perhaps meet someone . . . someone wealthy."

The privy councillor became quite angry. He didn't need to have his daughter sold off. He could take care of his daughter himself, and she didn't need to marry at all.

His wife hadn't meant it that way. She wanted to hint at something she dared not say because it seemed to her indelicate. She was worried about Agathe's manner, which was becoming stiffer and stiffer and more and more reserved toward the young men of her set. Agathe had already hurt and rebuffed various gentlemen with her haughty disregard, gentlemen who had noticeably tried to approach her. Frau Heidling knew nothing about the run-in with Walter, which weighed on Agathe like an injustice in which she, through her silence, had made herself complicitous. Nor did she know anything about Lord Byron's relations with her daughter.

A condition of weariness made it impossible for Frau Heidling to attain an overview of the cause and effect of any circumstances, impossible to pursue a thought clearly and sharply to its logical conclusion. It had long ago taken hold in her brain, a brain tortured with worrying about a lavishly and meticulously run household, by the memories of her dead children, and by her neuralgia. But the weaker her intellect became — initially it hadn't been that weak — the more acute the intuition of her heart. With infinitely delicate feelers it sought out and suffered the most hidden moods of those she loved. She sighed the moment the conversation turned to Walter and Eugenie's wedding, and yet all the friends of the family considered the upcoming event one that brought a mother's heart nothing but joy. And now, too, Frau Heidling simply sensed that a change of scenery would do Agathe good. Her sending the painter couple the latest pretty photograph of the girl hadn't been without an ulterior motive. Since she couldn't come up with convincing reasons, she sought to reach her goal with quiet obstinacy.

Her face crestfallen, Frau Heidling revealed to her daughter that Father had decided that if she wanted to take a trip she could pay her expenses with her own pocket money.

"Papa doesn't have any idea that you've saved up something," she added in roguish triumph. "I'll give you twenty marks from the household funds. I can get along fine without it! He's got to allow you to go then! Aren't you looking forward to the trip?"

Agathe looked at her mother, troubled and frightened.

Yes, she had saved up a little treasure . . . .

For a long time now she had no longer worn kid gloves to social gatherings, but instead silk mixed with cotton, and on walks, even cotton ones. If the young ladies made a detour to the confectioner's, she always found some pretext for absenting herself. And her birthday gifts were downright shabby. There was already open talk about the alteration in her once lightheartedly generous character and about her striking neglect of her appearance, considering how well-groomed she had once been.

Since the young ladies' vocabulary was not terribly rich, two proclamations were delivered up repeatedly as the latest observation — one day by Lisbeth Wendhagen, the next by Fräulein von Henning, then once again by Kläre Dürnheim or by Eugenie.

"Girls, what *do* you think about Agathe?"

"I find it really . . . . "

The degree of disapproval, of indignation seemed to be so great that it could only be expressed properly by an uncanny pause after the word "really."

Agathe was saving for a trip to England. She wanted to visit the grave of her dead darling, to walk the places where he had breathed and sung, where he had suffered and relished delight.

Oh, and how long it took for the nickel and silver coins from her pocket money to amount to even one gold piece. At the bottom of the little box where Agathe kept her treasure lay a slip of paper with a saying in gothic letters: "Reason, patience and time make the impossible possible." Whenever Agathe read it, she felt as if she were taking a drink of cinchona wine.[52]

With nervous delight she felt the money between her fingers, the money that would finally enable her to experience something — the pivotal experience that her entire being anticipated. Perhaps her parents wouldn't allow her to take the trip, perhaps she would have to leave in secret and then would never be allowed to return . . . . She considered whether anything in her current circle of friends could exercise a pull strong enough to hold her back.

No, there was nothing there. Everything seemed to her insipid and petty. Filled with distrust or with indifference and annoyance, she turned her back on all of it.

Now she was suddenly forced to make a difficult choice.

Of course making it to England without her parents' consent was highly unlikely. The plan now seemed to her a completely crazy idea.

Frau von Woszenski wrote charming letters — just too funny . . . . And her husband was a real Pole; great artists came to his house . . . .

Agathe answered that she wanted to go; of course she wanted to!

. . . O God! Now she had to stick the gold pieces in her purse. How she thereby profaned her love.

She was a coward. She was not a great person who remained true to herself and her resolve.

But what good did it do? Now she, too, wanted to be heartily amused for once.

Frau von Woszenski was waiting for Agathe at the train station and immediately brought her over to her husband in his studio. A strong scent of turpentine and Egyptian cigarettes met them. The Polish painter pushed his glasses down on his slender aquiline nose and looked at Agathe with his sad, observant blue eyes while his long, skinny hand shook hers cordially. He had been sitting in a carved easy chair, his head resting on an old leather cushion, examining the work he had begun. On an easel before him was a large canvas.

Frau von Woszenski, who had been born in Leipzig and spoke a lively Saxon dialect, positioned herself next to her husband, put her hands on his shoulders, looked at the painting with sharp attention and then cried joyfully, "It's comin' along, Kas! Believe me, darlin'. It's comin' along."

Herr von Woszenski turned politely to Agathe and said, "I thought I'd call it the *Ecstasy of the Novice*."[53]

Agathe tried to find her way into the unfinished painting.

Before an altar, resplendent with fanciful gilding, on which candles flicker in a fog of incense and from which blood-red velvet flowed over white marble steps, a young nun has sunk to her knees . . . her dark veil, the heavy clothes flapping in the ghostly gale that is breaking through the high church window with a radiant beam . . . numerous little winged heads, angel-figures like amoretti are whirling down from heaven. And the young nun has received the Christ child in her uplifted arms.

Her figure, the blissful ardor of her gestures were sketched only in charcoal, her face an empty gray spot. But Agathe sighed deeply in pious admiration when she understood the intention.

Frau von Woszenski took her away with her as she called to her husband, "Hey, listen, today we're only havin' pancakes and a piece of ham. I need the cook."

He smiled his assent.

Frau von Woszenski had set up her studio in their apartment in order to be able to manage the household alongside her art. She was painting merry schoolgirls and blonde children who were teaching tricks to a black poodle. With this work she earned their daily bread and the leisure her husband needed for his great, unmarketable works.

The strapping maid carried Agathe's suitcase upstairs, shoveled more coal into the stove, and then removed her dress, peeling off the soot-covered cotton to reveal a splendid pair of shoulders and arms. She seated herself on a raised platform. Frau von Woszenski sketched earnestly and zealously. Agathe embroidered a tablecloth for Mama and wondered at the situation in general and in particular at the strange grimaces that Frau von Woszenski unconsciously seemed to require while she worked.

Frau von Woszenski immediately called Agathe by her first name and used the intimate form of address with her. By doing so she immediately made her feel as if she had come home.

The Woszenskis' little son Michel came home from school. He looked pale and tired. Frau von Woszenski reviled the crazy arrangements at school. She rolled the double "r" so impressively that the sound was transformed, as it were, into a lofty intimation of anger and passion.

The cook had already hidden her divine shoulders in blue gingham as before and brought the little boy his soup. Sitting in his chair, his soup bowl before him, Michel stretched his thin limbs and dropped the corners of his pinched little mouth. He had no appetite.

"The child's not eatin' again . . . . Sendin' one's child home in such a state!" muttered Frau von Woszenski. As a reward she promised Michel "the sad goat face" or "the merry African face." She explained that she could only do the "orangutan face" whenever Kas wouldn't see it; it would be too unaesthetic for him.

"Mother, now I've got a silly story," said Michel. "Do you know what our teacher does when he fishes flies out of the inkwells?"

Michel took a little piece of bread, fetched little morsels of rice from his bouillon, flung them away and muttered angrily, "What a filthy mess! Tsk, tsk, what a filthy mess!" He was able to affect the zeal and loathing of a secondary teacher's dried-up face with astounding accuracy.

His mother and Agathe burst into loud laughter. Frau von Woszenski shook with pleasure, the wild satisfaction of revenge sparkling in her eyes.

"Capital, Michel! Do it again! I've got to learn how to do it too!"

Michel's slack little features blushed as he and his mother tried out the new face. "You can do it, you can do it!" he cried enthusiastically. "And I'll eat my soup!"

Relishing stupidity, triviality, ugliness as though they were a rare delight — that was how these three refined people defended themselves against these forces, how they preserved their freedom and their witty cheerfulness.

Whenever Woszenski called his wife by her first name, he found it delightful that this unusual person, whose movements recalled those of a Japanese idol, whose short curly hair stuck out every which way like a Negro's and whose eyes glared hectically, was named of all things Marietta. The contrast of her shrill voice and her Leipzig dialect with his cultivated German and its slight touch of a foreign accent had, as a subtle and foolish allurement, perhaps influenced his decision to marry her. He had found the social and artistic conditions of the present so odious that he, hurt and weary, had turned his back on everything and had boarded with a hermit on Capri, with the only person his nerves could tolerate — until Marietta came along and with her triumphant humor brought him back into the world.

From the ceiling of the Woszenskis' living room hung a bronze lamp from a synagogue. Life-size colorfully painted saints leaned against the walls; across their folded hands they held scraps of Japanese silk. That evening as the couple sat in the living room with their young guest, Herr von Woszenski began to talk about those old times on Capri. He was wrapped in an old fur coat on whose shoulders his long, already graying hair had left traces. His expressive artist's hand caressed his tangled beard, and he smoked countless cigarettes as he spoke in a soft, husky voice.

Near Pagano a young painter had died. Woszenski and a few others had rowed his corpse over to the mainland . . . . "The sea shone quietly in the early morning light like a precious bowl lined with mother-of-pearl, and on this gray meadow a large bouquet of pink roses drifted by us; we watched it bob up and down again and again with the movement of the waves. And the black coffin in the boat was completely covered with roses . . . . "

* * *

Agathe lay awake for a long time in the unfamiliar bed in the room that was still alien to her.

She heard the murmuring of the waves between Capri and Naples; she saw the roses on the silver tide . . . . Blood-red velvet streamed over the high altar, angels' heads fluttered around her . . . . And a strong gale from heaven shuddered through her soul.

* * *

"The child ought to visit old Frau Gärtner, the captain's wife. Her mother knows her from earlier times. I'll go over with her at noon. You could drop by Lutz's, Kas. And then we'll meet." Thus Frau von Woszenski determined the agenda for the day.

Agathe felt like dressing up. She took her new Rembrandt hat out of her suitcase. It looked charming on her. Papa had found it too conspicuous, but Mama thought that for the city of artists something like that would be just the thing.[54] But Frau von Woszenski dressed very simply; she looked almost dowdy in her black knit blouse.

No, Agathe was embarrassed . . . . Frau von Woszenski would think she was a superficial, vain flibbertigibbet. And one certainly didn't just put on one's best things impromptu just because one happened to be happy, but rather when the occasion demanded it. This view had simply become second nature to Agathe. Besides a thaw had set in, and water pattered in large drops from the snow-covered roofs. The Rembrandt hat made its way back into her suitcase and she donned her fur cap. She really looked quite nice like that; since she couldn't be witty and significant, it was good that at least she had a pretty little face. At breakfast Frau von Woszenski exchanged appreciative remarks about her with her husband, a little as if she were a picture, not a living person who could become vain.

The air was oddly mild. Agathe's winter jacket became too warm for her. She unbuttoned it. She was enjoying the fact that here in this quiet little old town and at the Woszenskis' she could do more as she pleased than at home where she constantly had to be thinking of Papa's position.

69

During the visit, after answering a few questions, she sat quietly and listened to Frau von Woszenski's conversation with the old lady. To Agathe everything that Frau von Woszenski said was exciting and remarkable, even if, as now, she spoke only of servants.

" . . . Yes, I wanted to get a reliable one for once. 'A reliable one!' I say to Kas. So we take one who's got a goiter . . . . "

She rolled the "r" vehemently. "And a hump! A real hump! Like this. On the first Sunday the wench comes to me: she's been invited to the masons' ball. 'Don't you want to eat first?' I ask. So she plants herself squarely in front of me and says loftily, loftily, from above her goiter, 'No thank you. The gentlemen are treatin'!' But now I've got a pretty one. I can use *this* one as a model!" She pounded on the table loudly and triumphantly.

Frau Captain Gärtner made a face as though someone were hurting her. She remarked with a weak smile that she really wouldn't call the Woszenskis' present cook a beauty, but artists were so eccentric in everything.

Frau von Woszenski grinned with her merry African's face in Agathe's direction. She politely took her leave and said she was certain that her husband was waiting for her downstairs.

He came from the upper story and met them on the stairway.

"So I wasn't lyin' then!" the woman painter cried.

"Come on up for a moment. Lutz would like to show you his painting. Fräulein Agathe will also find the studio interesting," said Woszenski.

"She won't fall in love, will she?" whispered Frau von Woszenski and looked serious. "Child, it would be better to let that be; the man up there is not for you."

Agathe smiled, thinking of Lord Byron.

A young man held back the curtain through which they were to enter and removed his hat. He was dressed to go out and was wearing galoshes that seemed much too large and clumsy for his slender, meager body. The movement with which he greeted them and let the old tapestry drop behind his three guests exhibited a singularly delicate and charming grace.

X.

When Agathe returned to her little guest room at the Woszenskis' she hastily closed the door behind her.

She stopped for a moment, looked around her, astonished and confused. Suddenly she fell to her knees before the bed, pressed her head in her arms and remained that way for a long time, not stirring, her face hidden in the white coverlets. She was not crying. A violent, protracted shudder ran through her body. Then she felt as if she couldn't breathe. She threw back her head and looked up with parted, trembling lips.

"O God! O God! O dear God!"

She pulled off her gloves impatiently, jumped up, flung her cap, her jacket from her and ran around aimlessly in the tiny room, her eyes filled with tears.

She stopped . . . .

. . . She saw the profile, the contours of his head in the air before her like an apparition.

Gradually from out of the tortured look on her face bloomed a smile, an intoxicated shining of the eyes. Her breath fought its way out of her breast with a sigh. Tears welled up and streamed brightly down her flaming cheeks. The girl folded her hands and said softly and solemnly:

"I love him."

Exhausted, she sat on the edge of her bed, pressed her folded hands against her breast and repeated enraptured: "I love him! I love him . . . . "

So she was swallowed up in dreams. What really had happened? She couldn't recall what he had talked about with her . . . . How he had removed the little black hat from his fair hair and turned his gaze toward her — she could remember that. Yes — light and delicate — with his slender build, a little pale and tired around the eyes. Thus his apparition appeared before her imagination as if behind a light fog that slightly obscured everything.

They had exchanged few words. He spoke with Frau von Woszenski about the work he had begun. They used expressions that were alien to Agathe, that even her father never used when he spoke about art. And they waved their hands and fingers in the air, pointing out, sketching and erasing. Frau von Woszenski touched colorful lengths of cloth that lay on a little white lacquered table and excused herself earnestly as if she had been terribly inconsiderate. He smiled and said it was of no consequence. He raised one of the lengths of cloth into the air and caressed it, as it were, with his restless hands — a soft white Turkish silk, shot with cool blue green stripes. It was replicated in the painting; a bronze cupid sprang out of its folds.

Agathe ventured that she couldn't stand still lifes but that this conceit was amusing . . . . He looked at her again then — a quick, cursory glance. "Really? Do you think so? I do too."

She heard him call Herr von Woszenski "my friend Hamlet" and advise him to move to Munich. He wouldn't find a model for his nun here. "Here what is naive is always also crude!"

Agathe had looked shyly around the studio. A little chaise longue covered with blue silk plush. Pillows of faded damask, woven with a floral pattern, on gracefully curved chairs. Everything else seemed to her a confusion of soft, ingratiating colors, forms, materials, obscurities that were brought to luminous elegance with old etchings and bronzes. The decor differed starkly from the austere artist's taste that prevailed at the Woszenskis'.

Never had Agathe seen such a thing. But inside her a memory surfaced as if she had dreamed of it, as if she had sought all this unconsciously.

* * *

She raised her hand, which the painter had pressed fleetingly as they took their leave. A sweet, agreeable feeling lingered in its nerve endings. Trembling, she brought it to her lips — It was not a kiss, only a light, careful resting of the mouth on the spot that he had touched.

Her astonishment at being touched, seized, enveloped and caught by this long-anticipated, feared, and hoped-for power increasingly gave way to a roguish curiosity about everything that had to ensue now.

And her imagination with its deceptive mirages left her in the lurch.

There were for Agathe only two people left in the world. They had to be united, and the secret of union had to be revealed to her. Curiosity also receded from her. It was sacrilege.

The girl stood within the Holy of Holies of emotion; she was ready — as Juliette was ready for her beloved.

* * *

During the noon meal Frau von Woszenski's attentive gaze passed over her guest now and again. Agathe hardly ate anything. Not in the evening either. She was quite taciturn. Yet an exalted feeling of well-being vibrated within her. Her blood beat with a strong pulse in her veins, gleaming healthier and rosier through the delicate skin of her cheek. Her gait was free and easy, she carried her head more proudly, and her brown curls fluttered pertly around her temples, around her hot little ears. Whenever she was to offer some kind of indifferent answer, the girl smiled with a beautiful, happy expression at the person asking the question. Youth and life spoke animatedly from her sparkling, liquid eyes.

* * *

. . . No, of course that wasn't possible . . . . Herr von Lutz couldn't descend to her in the dark of night from heavenly heights as did Cupid when he found his way to the trembling Psyche . . . .[55] On the steps that led to the Woszenskis' apartment Agathe came to the deeply exhilarating realization that Lutz would have to ascend these same steps if he wanted to see her again. And at that moment the first apprehension as to whether that would ever happen crept over her.

* * *

Her memory of this period in her life was later almost completely blotted out. She no longer remembered when the intoxicating happiness had turned into admiration, when the admiration had turned into fear and the fear into dull, tormenting grief.

Nothing turned out as she had expected it to. He didn't come. But they just had to find one another again. Probably he was waiting for a meeting that would occur by chance.

Agathe was not beset with doubts about her impression.

She loved him.

Gradually she began to suspect that for certain kinds of people love is not happiness but rather suffering, and if it does not lead to a healthy flowering, it becomes a sickness of which youth wilts and dies.

* * *

At a concert Agathe unexpectedly saw him sitting right in front of her. She hadn't even recognized him immediately, and that gave her quite a start.

He held his head tilted slightly. Occasionally he turned it with the grace that distinguished precisely this movement of his and spoke softly to the lady at his side.

Agathe waited in suffocating tension to see whether he would turn around in his seat and catch sight of her. He didn't. He seemed very absorbed in the quiet but lively conversation that he was having with the lady at his side during the intermissions.

She was an uncommonly delicate little creature and wore a black dress embroidered with tiny beads that sparkled a bit when she moved. With it a little brown hat with white crepe. There was a certain similarity in the shape of her head to that of the painter, and also in the coloring of her skin which had nothing of the rosy tinge of a blonde's complexion, but instead recalled the matte tone of ivory. But Lutz had the profile of a real Prince Charming, and at the end of the concert she, in contrast, revealed to Agathe a funny little nose and a wide mouth.

Now Agathe recognized her. It was the actress she had admired a few days ago in the role of a boy. Her affected charm was that of a Rococo figure on a fan whose colors have already faded a little.

Frau von Woszenski hadn't gotten a seat next to Agathe and sat several rows further toward the front. Later, as they were leaving and were separated from one another by only a few people, Agathe saw Lutz walk up to her to say hello. His finely chiseled, nervous face took on a charming expression of kindness, indeed of reverence. As he followed the actress, he noticed Agathe as well and slightly tipped his hat once again. He smiled. His eyes were dreamy with the lingering memory of the music.

"Is Fräulein Daniel related to Herr von Lutz?" Agathe asked Frau von Woszenski.

"No, not that I'm aware of? Not at all, I think . . . . Why?"

"Because they look alike."

"Yes, you're right! That's really peculiar! She's his lady friend. A clever female!"

* * *

Woszenski sketched Agathe several times as a study for his novice. Lutz had given him the idea, he said. Her eyes were so pious . . . .

He heaved copious sighs as he worked, ran his fingers through his hair and his disheveled beard, stared into space over and out from under his glasses.

"Such a soft little head. There's nothing in it yet. That's fine, but difficult, difficult."

He didn't think her bright rosy coloring fit the palate of the painting.

Then he suddenly dropped it entirely with no explanation. If the ladies fetched him from his studio, they found him sitting before his work, lost in deep brooding. Marietta made a serious, worried face.

In the evenings he would tell them of the wildest plans for new works. Or he would confer with his wife about what he would paint if he actually had a talent for making money.

"Moors sell; they always sell . . . . People always like to buy hunters with dogs . . . . "

Frau von Woszenski got one of her paintings back from the Munich exhibition. "Of course no one wants to hang this stuff in his apartment. Well, it was just an idea I had," she said philosophically as she unpacked it. A window in a tower that aroused in the viewer the impression of dizzying heights, of distance from earth, and the sky close by. In the background the outlines of the large church bell. And in the arch of the window a child, his head on his round fat little arm, looks down calmly into the depths. Above him hangs a dead goose on a rough hook; the last rays of the sun shine on its downy plumage which has been treated with the greatest artistic delicacy.

"Aunt Marietta," asked Agathe, "did you mean to say perfect peace can only be represented by a goose and a child?"

Frau von Woszenski laughed. "You need to leave such clever observations to the ugly girls; you're far too pretty for that," she responded delightedly.

It became much easier for Agathe to express her ideas with the Woszenskis than with her parents. In the insecure, groping tentativeness of her sensibilities even the suspicion of contradiction disconcerted her. At home she was still enveloped by instruction. But if Frau Woszenski had a divergent view, she presented it as one human perception vis-à-vis another one. And Kas was even more tactful than his wife. Whenever Frau Woszenski discerned narrow-mindedness and lack of imagination, her entire face would immediately become cruel scorn even if she didn't utter a word.

And then a strange thing happened: Agathe found something within herself beneath the taste she had been taught, something that had nothing to do with this taste and that had led an independent, albeit modest and anxious, existence inside her, an existence of which she herself had been only half aware. She noted with happy surprise that the Woszenskis fully shared her aversion to the boredom, monotony, and narrowness of the social mores of her set, indeed, to the principles of her own parents.

Many things that her father condemned as absurd and mannered were held in high esteem here.

Agathe had discovered, for example, quite on her own that there was a great artist named Böcklin[56] whose paintings always aroused longing and happiness in her. She had listened to Walter and Eugenie's jokes about him in uncomfortable silence as if she were denying a holy thing. Tears sprang to her eyes when she heard Woszenski mention his name for the first time and when he praised with clever appreciation something she had only dimly felt. Her inner being stretched, as it were, and grew and expanded during these weeks.

But she really learned the most from Lutz. She craftily and assiduously sought to find out what he was like and what he loved and what moved him. It seemed to her that she got closer to him in a mysterious fashion by learning to understand him.

Agathe owed her first love the intoxicating experience of nature that transported her into mystical ecstasies at every sunset, her understanding for the large contours of things, and her rapturous enthusiasm for a freedom that dwelled far, far away from all earthly pain. *Don Juan*, which hurt her with its irony and which she couldn't stand except for a few parts, had nevertheless sharpened her eye for the ridiculousness of convention.

From her second love, then, she learned by eavesdropping about the refined enjoyment of the melodies of colors, of their most nuanced shading, and of the effect of light and shadow, of the strange relationships between color and mood.

Adrian Lutz was for her a narrow white band of light in a vast darkness filled with the frightening contours of huge, indistinct figures; a delicately shining pale green wild orchid.

From three etchings and a couple of landscape studies of Lutz's that the Woszenskis owned and regarded very highly, Agathe constructed for herself a taste for a certain kind of art: the most modern French school with a somewhat edgy romanticism that the artist had added from his own temperament.

That added a spicy and alien seasoning to her previous diet. Would Privy Councillor Heidling have chosen precisely these two men to educate his child?

Careful parents tend to construct a plan for the education of their daughters. But the secret influences that have the strongest effect on a young woman's intellect — they can't calculate those.

* * *

Agathe saw Lutz once more during her stay with the Woszenskis, from far away on a deserted street. She had walked up and down the street awaiting that hoped-for moment when she might run into him. It was the first time she had ever done anything like that, and she couldn't do it ever again. It was just too devastating for her.

He came out of his studio, a cigarette between his lips, ran into the mailman and got a letter from him. He tore open the envelope with those hasty movements of his, and as he read it, he came toward her. Agathe walked slowly past him without his noticing her. He looked up to the sky, his animated face beaming with joy over the news he had just received. At that moment she became profoundly aware that he stood in the midst of a rich life filled with manifold experience. And she had no part in it; it was completely alien to her.

When five weeks had passed she returned home.

77

XI.

"You know, Agathe, if these Woszenskis are so much more interesting to you than your own parents, then we might as well give you up to them. You certainly left your heart with them."

"Oh, Papa, you know I don't mean it like that . . . . "

"But, Ernst dear," the privy councillor's wife said apologetically, "it's really so nice that our child is telling us about her trip . . . . "

"As a matter of fact I insist on it," said Heidling crossly. "In the meantime I'm not going to let her leave again; otherwise she'll find us philistine and boring afterwards."

"Just believe me, my child," the privy councillor continued, "what blinded you there is a lifestyle that you with your steady temperament don't fit into at all; you would have realized that soon enough. So, now give your old papa a kiss. Even if he's not an artist, he has your interests at heart more than your Woszenskis or whatever their names are."

One evening Frau Heidling came into her daughter's bedroom. She sat down and watched as Agathe combed her long brown hair.

"Mama, would it look better if I stopped putting my braids over my part and wore them like this at the back of my neck instead? Eugenie says this is a lot more fashionable."

Mother and daughter tried out the new hairdo. As they were doing it, the privy councillor's wife looked into the girl's eyes as she used to do when she wanted to find out whether Agathe or Walter had been snacking and asked in a casual, teasing manner: "Come on, tell me, was Herr von Woszenski really so very interesting?"

Agathe laughed.

"Very, Mama — really — very — oh, he's charming. I just like him so much!"

"But, child, but he's a married man . . . . "

Dear Mama sighed and looked very worried. "You are so changed since you've returned . . . . "

"Oh, Mama, no!"

Agathe laughed even more high-spiritedly. "You think I've fallen in love with Herr von Woszenski?"

"A little, naturally only a little!"

Frau Heidling put her arms around her daughter and pulled her to her to make it easier for her to confess.

78

"Tell me, my child!"

Laughing, Agathe wriggled free.

"Really, Mama, not the slightest bit! Really certainly not! I'm just mad about both of them, you know. They're such dear, dear people!"

"If you say so, I'll believe you of course — and — and — did he never take liberties?"

"Never, Mama," cried Agathe incensed. "You've got entirely the wrong idea about him. He's really so delicate. No, no."

And after a pause, she added very softly, kissing her mother: "It was another man, Mama. I can't . . . please don't ask me to speak of it."

Mama stroked her hair silently and left with the lamp.

* * *

After Agathe wrote to Frau von Woszenski, she waited every day with bated breath for an answer. Perhaps she would write something about Lutz. Or even if not — Agathe so longed to hear something from her, to see the postmark of the dear, remarkable city where a new life had begun for her.

Finally she received a letter from Frau von Woszenski, a very friendly one, but much too short to suit her.

And later Frau von Woszenski wrote only once more: she had too much to do; after painting her eyes suffered too much to write a letter; Agathe surely knew that despite this she wouldn't forget her and that she must come again soon.

Yes, yes, yes — Agathe tried to comfort herself with the hope of a reunion.

God in heaven! Why did she always get so emotionally involved? People didn't like that at all, you know! If only she had more pride!

* * *

Early in the morning of the fifth of September Agathe read a notice in the newspaper: Fräulein Daniel had been engaged as the ingenue for the theater in M.

She saved the page and hid it in her desk with her relics: a sweetshrub blossom from Bornau which still gave off a faint perfume, the doily that had encircled the bouquet she had received for her con-firmation, Lord Byron's picture, and a review of the Berlin exhibi-tion in which Lutz was mentioned. She had already kissed the printed name a thousand times.

Had Lutz perhaps gotten his lady friend to go to M. so he could visit her there and see Agathe again?

Agathe had brooded a great deal over their relationship. It was highly unlikely that two people who loved one another wouldn't get married as quickly as possibly. So at any rate, Lutz didn't love Frä-ulein Daniel. There must be something special behind it — a mys-tery. Couldn't they be brother and sister? They really looked a lot alike. How lovely, how noble of Lutz to surround her with such se-cret, tender solicitude, a sister he couldn't publicly acknowledge out of respect for his father's honor or his mother's, how noble of him to watch over her so chivalrously in her perilous career! Yes, he would come, for sure, for sure!

The dull, dreary time was at an end! He would come!

* * *

She first heard people talking of him at the Wutrows'.

"Today I met the painter who followed la Daniel here," said Eugenie while Agathe helped her tie up her bridal linen with blue ribbons. The wedding was to take place soon. "Hertha Henning pointed him out to me. She intends to take lessons from him. Her mother is glad she doesn't have to send her to Berlin now; if they starve together, it does cost less. I find it rather inappropriate. He's still quite young — at most twenty-eight — well, and he's already got a bit of a past."

"What do you mean?" asked Agathe, her heart in her throat.

"You can just see it. But what's wrong with you? Girl, you're quite pale! Do you know Herr von Lutz?"

"I was in his studio with the Woszenskis," Agathe burst out in her confusion.

"Well, why didn't you tell me anything about it? But come on and sit down. You really *are* going to faint! Tsk, tsk — this girl! He's very good looking; he's got that debonair chic that the men of our town can only imitate. Come on, drink a glass of wine!"

So Hertha Henning was taking lessons with him .... No, Agathe couldn't be jealous of Hertha. Her nose was too long and pointy for that.

She tried to draw a chair, a flower. She botched it completely. She had no talent whatsoever, not a glimmer. Wasn't that lamentable? She had no talent for anything. She couldn't manage to produce even the tiniest verse. At bottom she was really quite an ordinary creature.

And Lutz didn't recognize her either .... When he happened upon her in the theater lobby, he looked at her fleetingly and didn't say hello.

XII.

Eugenie and Walter's wedding was a gala celebration with skits and poems and songs at the *Polterabend* and with all the ingenious fuss that Germans like to create on such occasions.[57] They reveled in the feeling of family — the most distant uncles, the most aged aunts were invited, were quite moved during the ceremony and afterwards, in various corners of the house, reheated old family feuds with their acerbic remarks.

Beneath her pink silk dress Agathe had to hide all the mute and hopeless torment that had tortured her heart for months. How easy it would have been for Eugenie to make the acquaintance of Herr von Lutz and to procure for him an invitation for the *Polterabend*. Then it would have become a festive occasion for her .... It was so unfair of Eugenie — of course — she only ever thought of herself.

She was constantly choking back her tears, but at a wedding that didn't really attract attention. Martin Greffinger was the usher paired with her. He had changed a great deal since she had seen him last. After he had given up the study of law, he had been in England for six months. No one knew what he had done there. He certainly hadn't made the journey there on account of Lord Byron. The sarcastic lines around his mouth had deepened. If his hostile gaze wandered over the wedding party, he reined it in again immediately to a spot right down in front of him, to a world that he and he alone appeared to see.

Despite Agathe's request he told nothing of his journey. What he had done and experienced over there really wouldn't interest her at all, he said. He also didn't attempt any of the teasing with which he once had habitually and cruelly tormented her; he even made an effort to be nice to her. But his efforts always lapsed into the great indifference that ruled his posture, every one of his movements, and above all his voice. And so throughout the long dinner the conversation dragged, dreary and forced, interrupted by interludes of complete silence. How alien they had become to one another, the two who had once been so fond!

During the entire day of festivities everything went smoothly, like clockwork. Only once did the dinner guests hear Frau Wutrow out in the kitchen scolding the hired help on account of the large wine consumption. When she returned, her angry face was almost the color of her red and blue watered silk dress. But with the exception of this little incident — as mentioned above — it was an ideal wedding.

The green crown of myrtle sat perfectly on Eugenie's blonde head. The bridal veil cascaded a good two and a half meters over the queenly train. During the ceremony it had also hidden her face — they found that so poetic!

She was more lively than her guests; Walter on the other hand seemed moved and quiet.

After the dinner Eugenie removed her bridal wreath from her head and put it on Uncle Gustav's head. Most people found this joke quite offensive. One doesn't trifle with a myrtle wreath.[58] Fat, pink Uncle Gustav looked extraordinarily funny in his unexpected finery. It was the only time that Greffinger burst into loud laughter. Eugenie looked over at him from out of the folds of her veil as if from out of an airy cloud. Her milk-white train rustled as she went round the table, champagne glass in hand, and touched his glass with hers. Her eyelids lowered, her golden eyelashes trembled slightly like those of a child who would ask for forgiveness. She raised her eyes hesitatingly; in them lay a gentle plea. Agathe heard her say softly to him, "To good friendship!" He made her a deep, stiff bow.

Agathe went out with her to help her change. She was more agitated than the impassive bride who circumspectly went about making the final arrangements for their journey.

After the young couple had departed, Agathe withdrew to Eugenie's bedroom and remained alone there with the bridal apparel that had served its time and that was now scattered over the chairs. She sobbed from the very bottom of her heart. Finally she dried her eyes, washed her face and returned to the lower floor.

The party had dispersed; the more distant relatives had vanished. Agathe found her parents and old Wutrow sitting in the parlor among a large circle of relatives, tired and monosyllabic. Frau Wutrow was distributing cake to the help and was beginning to lock up the silver. In the alcove of the dining room Cousin Mimi von Bär, her brother, the third bridesmaid Lisbeth Wendhagen, Uncle Gustav, and the head clerk from the business had clustered around what was left of the punch. Eugenie's boudoir lay on the other side of the long corridor facing the garden. As she had gotten into the carriage, she had asked Agathe to lock up her desk and to guard the key. "Otherwise Mama will rummage around in all my drawers. You're discreet; I know that."

Wearily and quietly, Agathe went off to keep her promise. She lifted the curtain. His back to the entrance, Greffinger stood next to the little sofa where he had often sat with the two girls, talking pleasant nonsense. He had buried his head in the woolen window draperies. His broad shoulders twitched. Agathe heard his deep, violent sobs. Full of dismay, she confronted this pain. For the first time she saw the passion that was quietly and relentlessly destroying her own health erupting in a powerful man. She made a move toward him. She would have liked to take him in her arms and weep with him, caress him and comfort him. In her weakness she now felt stronger than he. Such misery suited her better than it did rough Greffinger.

But she didn't dare give in to her desire and cautiously withdrew. He hadn't noticed her.

* * *

After the honeymoon the two young Heidlings moved into the upper story of the Wutrow house which had been redecorated for them with fashionable wallpaper, old German stoves, and parquet flooring.

Eugenie played the charming little matron now. Walter's comrades celebrated her as the model German officer's wife. The young gentlemen invented a sport: picking up Heidling for duty early in the morning so they could see Eugenie beside the coffeemaker in her new dressing gowns and her coquettish little lace caps and then gulp down a cup of mocha standing up, a cup prepared quickly by her capable hands.

In the evening one could regularly encounter one to two lieutenants at the Heidlings' and probably an unmarried captain as well.

After Walter's wedding the jolly comings and goings of the younger generation naturally moved over to the young couple's house. One got just as good a supper there and could behave in a much less constrained manner than under the watchful eye of the privy councillor.

To be sure Agathe had a standing invitation from Eugenie, but she didn't like to leave her parents alone too much. Papa liked her to read aloud. Sometimes, however, he was too tired to listen and sat in the corner sofa with his cigar, silent and out of sorts. Sometimes he still had work to do and then loved looking up from his files through the open door at her curly brown hair under the lamplight as she helped her mother do the mending. These were monotonous evenings. Agathe now had difficulty tolerating the solitude in which she had once immersed herself in endless happy dreams.

Her parents had purchased a theater subscription together with the Wutrows and the young couple. Although Agathe rarely got the ticket, each time it was an exciting experience. Previously she had displayed a mind and enthusiasm only for tragedies. That had changed. The big dramas seldom had roles for the ingenue. And only when Fräulein Daniel appeared was Agathe sure of finding Lutz at the theater.

Eugenie was of course fully aware of this, but she and her husband also preferred comedies and farces, and Agathe couldn't ask for a ticket — no. It was horrible how ashamed and frightened she was on account of this unhappy love.

Lutz usually stood in the back of the box closest to the stage. Agathe could see his head only when he leaned forward. She waited for these fleeting seconds, trembling and tense.

She couldn't imagine where Fräulein Daniel, considering her questionable upbringing, could have acquired this light and graceful superiority of manner. Beside her the other ladies of the theater appeared coarse and unrefined. One could even forgive her a certain affectation; it suited her well. If her little nose and her expressive mouth were witty mischievousness incarnate, her eyes always remained serious; their gaze could brim with emotion and sadness. Agathe didn't understand why Lutz often would come only for one scene and then disappear again. No, he didn't love la Daniel. Whenever he applauded in his careless, discreet manner, his slim and restless white hands surfaced, as it were, disembodied from out of the darkness of the theater box.

Then Agathe would hear comments from those in neighboring seats about his relations with Fräulein Daniel.

" . . . They say he has courted her for years but she has single-mindedly rejected him."

"Well, well, I've heard other things. She was noticeably absent from the stage for a while. That was by the way a long time ago."

"Yes, something was wrong with her throat back then."

"Oh, the throat problems of actresses . . . . "

"Moreover, last summer he courted Professor Wallis's wife like crazy."

"Dear God, that doesn't mean a thing!"

Such talk caused Agathe unbearable anguish. How could people speak of him as if they were talking about just any young man?

* * *

In the meantime the meeting with him for which the girl had feverishly wished at every hour of the day was vouchsafed to Eugenie. She told her sister-in-law about it; a scornful smile flitted over her mouth.

"Today I spoke to your Lutz."

"You? Where?" asked Agathe breathlessly.

"It was highly amusing. I'm picking up new music at Schmidt's music store . . . . Besides that I've got two packages, my muff, my umbrella. On top of that I have to pick up my skirt. I try to hang onto all of that with the only two hands I've got! Who comes along as I'm going down the steps? Lutz! He notices my efforts, smiles. By the way, he's got a charming smile. And just think — silly goose that I am! My sheet music slides out from under my arm and falls right at his feet, fluttering every which way. Naturally he stoops down, and we pick them up out of the snow nice and tidy. I thank him for his trouble and he answers, 'Oh, you're welcome!' If he had said this 'you're welcome' to you, wouldn't that have been something, Agathe?"

Agathe burst into tears.

"My God, does it affect you that deeply?" cried Eugenie in alarm.

"I looked him over rather carefully on your account," she ventured prudently. "He's one of the dangerous ones; there's no question about it. But, child, do you really think that you've got one single thought in common with that man?"

"I love him," Agathe murmured softly.

Eugenie sighed. She delicately pinched a little bread crumb from her new table cloth, and her movement indicated that she didn't put as much stock in the feeling that moved Agathe as in this paltry vestige of a meal that had been enjoyed and cleared from the table.

XIII.

Toward the end of winter the society people of M., mainly at Frau Eugenie's urging, put on a fabulous costume ball. They wanted to be philanthropic at the same time; the income from a roulette wheel was to be for the benefit of the poor who were suffering so from the bitter cold.

Relying on Fräulein von Henning as intermediary, Lutz supplied them with sketches and etchings and gave good advice from a distance. Shuddering, he turned down a request that he become a member of the committee.

By charging a stiff admission they saw to it that the public nature of the festivity was not abused and that undesirable elements would not be there.

A crush of people filled the largest ballroom in the city. They found the decorations, which had been patterned after the costume balls held in artists' towns,[59] hugely original.

Agathe danced with Assessor Raikendorf. They soon sought refuge from the pushing and shoving crowd and found it preferable to chat, standing side by side near the entrance. Agathe had finally mastered the techniques of her profession as young society lady, even if she had had a harder time of it than her girlfriends.

To be sure she still hit a false note now and then: manifestly disdainful, she was not forthcoming enough with her dance partner, only tossed him paltry crumbs, as it were; or in an animated, inspired mood revealed things that were much too personal, thereby acutely embarrassing the junior barristers and lieutenants who were prepared only for conventional answers. She just was not one of those simple girls whose inner self exactly fits the stereotypical mold of the sprightly dance partner and who can show themselves unabashedly as they really are without arousing astonishment or disapproval.

That shrewd connoisseur of women, Assessor Raikendorf, had discovered this by chance. Now he found it alluring. It was already known that he liked conversing with Fräulein Heidling. This secret, passionate opposition to her entire environment, of whose depth, extent, and danger the girl herself was not even aware — this was very entertaining.

Agathe had retained a substantial portion of the dislike she had summoned for him at her first ball. This furious hate made her quick and sharp.

Because her parents were always complaining that she spent too much on her clothes, she had borrowed from an old relative a Florentine costume that had been brought to Germany from Italy back in the thirties. Its colors faded, it was nevertheless perfectly tidy and intact: the dark wool felt skirt, the red jacket, the curved metal corset covered with yellowed silk, the full lace fichu around the neck and shoulders, the long silver hairpin and the characteristic headdress that framed the girl's visage with delicate white veils — she had no idea how splendidly the outfit suited her, how with her beautiful features and her deep brown eyes she reproduced the northern Italian model of a past school of art that now belonged to history.

Alien and elegant, she stood among the loud, colorful masks that were overloaded with gold and silver.

A while ago she had noticed Lutz and Fräulein Daniel in the anteroom as they took leave of a few actors. Fräulein Daniel, in a simple party dress, had evidently come for a quick turn. Lutz was already wearing his winter overcoat and a little black hat on his blonde head; he probably intended to accompany la Daniel home. Agathe thought he had left.

Suddenly, while she was chatting with the assessor, she felt something that resembled a light touch, but that was nevertheless endlessly more delicate and fleeting.

She turned her head.

Lutz was still standing at the door — by himself. He was watching her.

After a quick, shy glance she continued to speak. How good this brief notice made her feel inside! What an experience of joy it was, compared to which everything else became null and void, disappeared!

Fräulein Daniel came back to him, wrapped in a fur and a lace shawl, and addressed him softly. He made an impatient gesture; finally he followed her out.

And immediately he was standing once more on the same spot, his hat still on his head.

Agathe suddenly felt as if she had drunk vast quantities of champagne. She laughed at everything Raikendorf said and looked at him with sparkling, high-spirited glances. When they in the meantime danced round the floor, she pertly asked to be taken back to her former spot. Lutz had waited there for her, and their eyes greeted one another past the faces of strangers.

Someone asked the painter whether he intended to leave on his overcoat for the entire ball.

"Yes, well! I've been meaning to go for a while now; I've got to go," he answered.

. . . His voice — to hear his soft, precipitous, singular voice again . . . .

Now he would be roused, now he would go . . . .

No, he allowed a young man to remove his coat and to take his hat from him as well. Laughing, he indicated that he was not wearing evening dress. A couple of gentlemen from the committee applauded and pulled him deeper into the room.

Agathe was engaged by other dancers; she strolled round the rooms with girlfriends, ate a serving of ice cream and a little piece of cake under the protection of Eugenie who, as a married woman, had acquired the right of playing her mother. Everywhere she went she found Lutz nearby.

Wasn't she deceiving herself? This happy turn of events seemed so improbable.

"Sleepwalker," Eugenie hailed her. "Should we send you home in our carriage? We want to drink one more glass of beer in the restaurant. Or would you like to stay longer too?"

"Stay, stay!"

Walter laughed. Agathe's request sounded ardent as if her fate depended on it. "What will the old folks say if you behave so frivolously when you're in our care?"

"Leave the little creature alone," Eugenie said decisively. "Don't you see that she's immediately become more animated without Mother?"

* * *

Lutz had spoken to Agathe — in the tobacco smoke of the restaurant, between two and three in the morning — and asked her whether she had had any news of the Woszenskis recently. And then he asked her to introduce him to her sister-in-law.

So he did remember her after all.

The next morning Agathe had to submit to a severe lecture. It was not appropriate for a young girl to sit with men in a tavern after a ball. If Walter permitted his wife to do so, it was his affair. In future she was not to go out again with Walter and Eugenie.

The committee had arranged a kind of post-ball celebration. Lutz intended to come too.

Would Papa prevent her — ? Well, if he did, then she would go in secret. But she begged and begged Mama as she had never begged before — she found this tormenting and begging that the other young girls were always carrying on with their parents beneath her. And her good, sweet, dearest mama finally brought Papa around to saying a peevish yes.

They remained in the small ballroom only — not many people at all.

It was downright noticeable the way Lutz paid court to her. To be sure he didn't dance with her — he didn't dance at all — but leaning on the door to the smoking room, he watched her, a serene and satisfied smile on his face. He became so absorbed in this occupation that he gave all the gentlemen who greeted him distracted and short answers. Then he withdrew to have a cigarette.

"Agathe, are you coming along? I'm looking for Walter," said Eugenie when this moment had arrived. Then she took her sister-in-law by the arm and pulled her into the smoking room.

"Don't show too plainly that you like him," she whispered in her ear, and after a few seconds she left her in a long conversation with the painter. Lutz spoke a lot and animatedly; Agathe could only respond in soft, childish tones, like a fearful little girl. He surely thought her dumb and silly . . . this lovely one and only opportunity to please him passed by — unused.

Eugenie had selected a guileless ensign as her victim for the evening. It amused her enormously to annoy her husband like this, as well as the bald captain who looked in on them four times a week. She asked the apple-cheeked boy in uniform about all his passions, had him tell her about his mother and his favorite dishes. And he got very hot. His stiff red wool felt collar nearly suffocated him. Deep chivalrous admiration for this adorable woman burned a hole in his breast.

* * *

How peculiar! Agathe found herself nearly at the end of her strength now that her true life was about to begin. She was often terribly tired: on longish walks in the city she suddenly no longer knew where she was and could recollect only with the greatest effort. Moreover, the noisy streets to which she had been accustomed since childhood seemed to her uncannily alien, the buildings and the signs on the shops, as if she had never seen them before; and the people whirred and glided past her, soulless and lifeless, like machines, not propelled by their own will but directed from some secret center.

* * *

In this period Agathe learned that a young man from her set loved her. He was only waiting for a position as a judge and would then ask for her hand, her friends told her. And they had heard it from his mother. His feelings for her were discreet and modest. Agathe had known him for years, had always addressed him in a friendly manner and had never suspected that in her proximity there dwelled a serious, enduring desire to possess her.

She found the idea unbearable. It enraged her. Not a single spark of pity kindled inside her. From that moment on she treated the young man with icy arrogance. Her behavior bewildered him; she appeared to take pleasure in her cruelty. But she didn't care; he offended her. He shouldn't presume to love her; he shouldn't venture with his dreams into the magic circle that had been drawn around her and the one and only man to whom her heart belonged.

* * *

"Yesterday I ran into la Daniel in the park," said Junior Barrister Dürnheim. "Has she ever lost weight! She was coming up the stairs by the little Chinese temple. She was hanging onto the railing and barely managing to drag herself forward. What's with her anyway?"

"Nothing, or rather, no one's with her," he received as an answer. "They say it's over between Lutz and her."

"Ah, I see, well, because of him . . . . "

"He's talking of marriage now, you know."

Loud laughter ensued.

"He'll certainly make a suitable husband."

"That old Schweidnitz woman — That high-strung creature is running after him like a crazy person."

"It really was marvelous when he described the villa he intended to build with her money if he could make up his mind . . . . You should have been there. A splendid fellow . . . . "

Someone nudged the speaker. Agathe Heidling was nearby. It was not appropriate to strike such a tone in the presence of young ladies.

She had caught their meaning. These disgusting men!

No, Fräulein Daniel was probably not Lutz's sister after all. But an actress couldn't possibly presume to become his wife . . . one who herself had told how she had gone round to villages with an itinerant troupe and had played the part of old Count von Moor[60] at thirteen, who wore makeup and who every evening was embraced and kissed by who knows how many men in front of an audience . . . . She could hardly be regarded as a real human being, not as a girl like Agathe herself.

There came a Sunday when on Breitenstrasse Eugenie invited Herr von Lutz to come to her house for coffee. In this case, between noon and one o'clock on Breitenstrasse, the painter, who otherwise regarded the nature and conventions of provincial bourgeois elegance with smiling disdain, was accommodating enough to grant her his presence! If this was not a significant sign, then Agathe did not know what indications she could still be waiting for. Eugenie said she was right.

How often, since Ada wreathed herself with green leaves for Cain,[61] have girls stood beside clear streams and before metal sheets, before Venetian glass and broken shards . . . . How often have they adorned themselves for their beloved, blissful and doubting, filled with trembling insecurity or smiling self-assurance . . . . And how often have they made the wrong choice in the trepidation of their heart, selected the jewelry that appealed the least to the unknown taste of the expected lord and master! What a difficult choice between the fanciest outfit and the most becoming one, between love of finery and vanity. And he is not supposed to suspect what you have done for him; the most festive arrangements ought to appear to be quotidian habit. But your hand trembles, and sparks dance before your eyes. Why does the little curl at the ear insist on falling so willfully today — only today? Why are you unable to tie a proper bow only on this day of all days?

The little mocha cups already stood empty on Eugenie's sparkling silver coffee table. The captain and the ensign were smoking, Walter was smoking, Eugenie was holding a cigarette between her fingers, and Agathe was sitting quietly and stiffly, her hands folded in her lap. The captain proposed they take a walk together. Lutz had still not appeared. The gentlemen took their leave.

Agathe stayed with her brother and sister-in-law for the evening. After midnight she really did have to go at last.

It was probably over now.

* * *

He had planned to send his painting to Paris; the cabinetmaker left him in the lurch; it was the final deadline for the jury to accept it; he had had to pack it up himself and to take it out to the train station on Sunday afternoon.

Herr von Lutz told this to Agathe when he met her eight days later in the art club. Everything was quiet and mute inside her. Yes, that may well have been what happened. In her heart a feeling of indifference . . . . She was herself surprised at her great calm.

92

Lutz asked whether her sister-in-law received guests every Sunday. Might he come today? He would see her there too, wouldn't he?

"I'm usually there," she answered joylessly.

She didn't make any special preparations; she changed nothing in her outfit. She would have most preferred simply to stay home, so greatly did she fear that she would be forced to suffer again something like what had happened on the previous Sunday.

And today of all days her parents wanted to come along.

While she was sitting between them in the horsecar,[62] she recited in convulsive prayer verses from the old hymnal.

> One thing needful! This one treasure
> Teach me, Savior, to esteem;
> Other things may promise pleasure,
> But they are never what they seem;
> They prove to be burdens that vex us and chafe us,
> And true lasting happiness never vouchsafe us;
> This one precious treasure, that all else exceeds,
> Gives joy above measure and fills all my needs.
>
> Seekest though the one thing needful,
> Leave all cares that hindering prove;
> Be of earthly joys unheedful,
> Fix thy heart on things above;
> For where God and man both in one are united,
> With God's perfect fullness the heart is delighted;
> There, there is the worthiest lot and the best,
> My one and my all, and my joy, and my rest.[63]

If she could manage to get herself to the point of expecting nothing more, nothing whatsoever, then perhaps, then perhaps God would have mercy on her.

In the vestibule at Walter's, Lutz's familiar paletot was hanging on a hook, and beneath it stood his large, foolish galoshes.

Fearfully Agathe attended to his conversation with Mama. The two of them really had nothing in common. Why had her parents insisted on accompanying her today? How had that happened? It was completely impossible to imagine that Lutz could ever make friends with her parents, despite the fact that he really was refined and tractable. O my goodness, now Papa was even starting to talk with him about art — quite condescendingly. How pedantic it all sounded, and Lutz was only listening to him distractedly until he suddenly became animated and passionately enthusiastic about a Frenchman whom her father characterized as high-flown. In his presence Walter's intellectual insignificance was embarrassingly obvious, and Eugenie's manner seemed obtrusive, forced. If Agathe had been able to take charge of the conversation, had been able to say charming, surprising things, to captivate him, to amaze him . . . . But she knew from the start; it was all in vain. What could charm him? Him? She had also lost her voice again.

If only a few friends had been there to divert his attention. Eugenie watched her. Mama also had a presentiment. Why had her parents come along if someone hadn't revealed to them that there was something afoot?

And yet, and yet . . . having him next to her, quite close to her, having the privilege of contemplating him in peace — that was a deep joy. And she tried to feast on it, to become satiated and peaceful in this joy.

He was a stranger to her — like this, by the light of day and in the intimate, domestic sphere. He and the phantom she loved so feverishly were not quite one and the same. Under her tender care the fantasy had taken on traits that didn't correspond to life. But the living one nevertheless possessed the greater power.

He didn't look so white and delicate as in the dark theater box. Instead his coloring was sallow, his eyes slightly red-rimmed. The way in which his fingers mistreated his soft little mustache could make one nervous. It revealed a certain restlessness as did the constant fluctuation of expression on his animated face. But his Prince Charming's profile . . . .

The painter and the Heidlings were asked to stay the evening. At supper the conversation suddenly turned to marriage.

Walter said that before marriage you had no idea what love was.

Agathe looked over at her brother in astonishment. His eyes rested with fervent pride upon Eugenie.

"The marriage certificate from the justice of the peace must give you great security," Lutz chuckled. Privy Councillor Heidling furrowed his brow in disapproval.

"As it happens," Lutz remarked casually, "you see a girl a certain way so often and haven't really noticed her. Then from a distance

94

you hear a word she speaks to someone else. It hits home — somehow, somewhere. Actually you see her in this moment for the first time."

Agathe sat next to him, covered with confusion and smiling in trepidation. How strange! Surely he couldn't mean her? In everything he said she discovered a hidden meaning, one meant for her alone.

Yes, most certainly. He turned to her most often. Eugenie, who otherwise attracted men so powerfully, appeared not to interest him.

* * *

One evening Frau Heidling spoke to her daughter in a gentle tone intended to spare her feelings: "Dear child, you're a sensible girl. Papa told me yesterday: Herr von Lutz doesn't have a good reputation, and Papa doesn't want him in our house."

Uncle Gustav, however, visited Lutz in his studio and described to Agathe in detail the silvery blue chaise longue, the Louis XV chairs, and the entire interior, that — oh, for how long — had been the refuge and the home of her passionate dreams.

Agathe wondered defiantly why Adrian Lutz was supposed to be worse than her brother Walter. If her parents only knew . . . then they would surely not condemn Adrian so unfairly. They didn't care for him; at bottom that's what it was about.

Vague memories of old folk tales that were the little girl's first intellectual nourishment trickled out of the deep, hidden springs of her imagination and comforted her with tests of loyalty, perseverance, to which the king subjects his beloved; she has to walk through burning fire and pricking thorns and through deep, dark night; she has to forsake everything that was once dear to her. He approaches her at the side of the other woman, the perfidious one. And at the end the wedding bells do ring and he elevates her to his rank, elevates the woman who didn't doubt him.

> Let your love like an eagle fly
> Up to the brink of impossibility.
> If your friend's deeds comprehending defy,
> There begins friendship's credulity.

Agathe whispered these verses to herself with the penchant of the young and sentimental person for pathos, for lofty, ringing words and lofty, ecstatic feelings.

She loved Lutz — and she believed in his purity as in his beauty as in her love, believed blindly, fanatically, like the martyr who sings songs of jubilation to his God while the wild animals tear him limb from limb and he has the privilege of sacrificing his heart's blood to the glory of the Lord.

XIV.

For a long time the Heidlings heard nothing from Martin Greffinger.

After the privy councillor had attempted by means of violent scenes and sharp remonstrating letters to prevent him from carrying out his foolish and confused plans and he had only countered these paternal warnings with a stubborn resistance, his uncle banished him from his house. They let him go his way, and his relatives didn't concern themselves with him further. For he was orphaned, of age, after all, and possessed a small fortune on which he could live in a pinch. Of course given his unfortunate principles and his ridicule of any kind of authority they could only suppose that he would spend his money on the People in some nonsensical way and in the end, full of remorse, return to the family with hat in hand. Walter and the privy councillor often spoke about this prospect — angrily but nevertheless secretly desiring to experience this triumph in the not too distant future.

Martin hadn't even managed to get his Ph.D. Now he was editing a newspaper. Agathe knew nothing about it except that none of her acquaintances read it, and each time someone mentioned its name, everybody burst into disdainful laughter. So presumably it was worthless.

Once she happened to get hold of an issue; they had wrapped something in it in a shop. It was poor quality paper, miserable printing, and at the same time the rag bore the ridiculously ostentatious name *The Torch*. Agathe read some things in it. She found its tone coarse.

What a shame that Martin had fallen so low. She felt a great deal of pity for him.

He must be very embittered and unhappy. She would have liked to exercise some kind of influence over him, but how should she manage that? Although he now lived in M., after Eugenie's wedding he had sunk, as it were, into another, subterranean world to which Agathe wouldn't even have found the entrance. He was the only person besides Herr von Lutz who occupied her thoughts from time to time. She couldn't condemn him. Whatever he was doing, she could sympathize with the feelings that led him down the path to where it was dark and terrible.

When she ran into him one day on the street and he was on the point of hurrying past her with a hasty greeting, she stopped, gave him her hand and asked shyly how he was doing.

A friendly glow came into his gloomy, hardened face. He shook her hand very cordially and turned around once more to look at her. Something of her old childhood feelings of friendship for him suddenly awakened in her. She guarded the fleeting encounter as her secret.

Papa and Mama were out of town. They wanted to spend Easter in Bornau. Agathe was supposed to take care of the wash and then follow them. It had rained so much that their things hadn't dried on time, and Papa didn't want to let a few additional days be stolen from his vacation time. The doctor had urgently prescribed rest and relaxation for him.

Why did he have to be so exhausted precisely at this moment? Leave M. at this of all times . . . it was very difficult for Agathe. Now and then she told herself that the trip could also become a test for Lutz. If his feelings for her wouldn't survive a short separation then they were, God knows, worth little enough.

But you couldn't know . . . .

There was nothing left of pride and gladness in her love; anxious trepidation had consumed the last vestiges.

She had worked quite hard the entire day, had forced herself to muster a frenzied zeal for activity. Now she was sending the two hired girls off to the mangle[64] with the basket full of the dampened and folded wash.

It was a dreary evening. A fine rain was falling. Dusk arrived unusually early. Agathe lay down on the chaise longue. How little she could accomplish these days — lamentable.

A ringing startled her out of semiconsciousness. Her knees shaking, she went to the door. Her first insane thought was always the same: if only it were Lutz!

She opened the door to the vestibule a little.

"It's me, Martin Greffinger," said a familiar voice. "Please let me in for a minute, Agathe."

He pushed the door open and entered while she was still considering whether she should ignore her father's ban. And then he himself locked the door and put up the security chain. That struck her as peculiar.

"I won't disturb you for long," he said somewhat breathlessly. "Your parents are out of town. They'll never know I was here . . . . I knew the maids had left earlier. I don't want to cause you any trouble."

"Won't you come in?" asked Agathe disconcertedly.

He followed her into the living room, but when she tried to offer him a chair, he said hastily, "No, don't. I have one foot out the door . . . . I only wanted to say goodbye to you."

"Are you planning to leave town?" Agathe asked politely.

"I've been banished. Yes. By the police."[65]

"Martin, for heaven's sake!"

He guffawed. "They're after us like bloodhounds, you know. The cowardly lot!"

He clenched his fist.

"If I show my face again here after twelve o'clock, I'll be transported across the border by gendarmes. Now don't be afraid. I'm taking the next express train to Switzerland. Then all of you will be rid of me!"

He laughed again, and Agathe looked at him, confused, frightened, and helpless.

He looked at her silently for a moment.

"Listen, I want to ask you for a favor. Keep this package for me. They'll certainly search me at the border. You don't need to get upset," he added with a facetious expression. "It's only writings. But if I burn them, I'll feel their loss nonetheless. So I thought you could perhaps send them to me later. And incidentally, if you'd like to read them first, there's nothing to stop you."

Agathe shuddered as though confronted with something unclean.

"I don't want to, Martin. Won't you consider . . . . "

"It's really not dangerous! They won't make out a search warrant for Privy Councillor Heidling's daughter. You can depend on that . . . . Surely your parents don't chaperone your correspondence?"

"No, but . . . . "

"The other day it seemed to me you had some courage . . . . Yes, I really respected you for giving me your hand out there on the street . . . . Well, aren't you interested in knowing why it is I've detached myself from all of you?"

"Yes I am. Only I find it all so strange, so frightening."

"As you wish. I felt the need to show myself grateful in some way. Do you understand? I thought, 'She's surely worth a try.' Do you see? There are stories in there that will shake you up. I know it. They'll grip you differently from that idiotic stuff you normally read."

"I don't want . . . . "

"I see. You really *are* a coward!"

"No, but I think it's not right to rebel against the lawful order," Agathe answered coldly. She had it in her head that she had to do her duty by pronouncing this judgment upon her cousin's political leanings.

Martin looked at her in the gray twilight of the dreary spring evening. His face was tired and overworked. Lines stretched across his brow. There was a deeply sorrowful expression in his eyes, but this sorrow lay like a mere dusting of ash upon quietly burning embers.

He tightened his arm, pressing the package of writings closer to him.

"Agathe, it doesn't matter whether I'm in Switzerland or here. But there are poor people who let themselves be driven from their work and their families into bitter misery on account of their convictions. Yes, just go ahead and shrug your shoulders! In the service to our cause I've gotten to know women who risk their freedom and their livelihood every single day in order to help their sisters out of misery and shame. Those are women who have their heart in the right place! Whom I respect! But you don't even want to know they exist . . . . You cold-blooded, pitiful bourgeois worms. I don't think you could make a sacrifice even if the person you love most asked it of you!"

"Martin . . . . "

"Thank you for showing me what I can expect from people like you. I'll let that be a lesson to me. Farewell."

Agathe was breathing rapidly. Her face burned.

Greffinger was already at the door when she stretched out her hand and cried softly, "Leave the books here."

"You will? You really will?"

"I'll send them to you later. But that's all."

"Agathe, that's lovely! Don't forget . . . I'm your friend . . . . And you surely *will* read them. Stick them in the fire then!"

He shook her hand so hard it hurt. The door clicked into the latch, and outside the sound of the powerful footsteps that took Martin Greffinger into exile died away.

Agathe held the bundle of forbidden books in her hands and looked down at them uneasily.

Documents of a world from which great, mysterious voices rang out to her, speaking of fates that surpassed quotidian reality; from a world in which you left behind Fatherland, friends, and your soft, comfortable routine; a world in which you took scorn and danger upon yourself with such proud and happy laughter . . . . From a world in which women had to earn their daily bread, had to expose themselves at every hour to hunger or prison in order to serve their comrades and the holy cause.

Where did things like that happen in her society, in polite society? Who among all of them — among all of her acquaintances — was capable of that?

How did the fire come upon these people? In what way were they moved? How must it be to stand there so ready for action and eager for sacrifice and to surrender oneself in shuddering delight, to throw oneself into a monstrous, terrible struggle whose raging she suddenly sensed all around her.

She had to find out about it, to know, to feel . . . everything she could grasp, what was within reach of her own two hands . . . open the package, look, see . . . . Beneath the brown paper glowed revelation.

Martin — he was strong and joyous; he was saved! Was there redemption here from the power that secretly fed and fed on her vital forces so that her blood became anemic and sick, and her sinews slack, and her nerves vibrated in a painful twitching so that inside her all clear thinking turned into a dull, feverish, tormented dreaming?

Desire overwhelmed her to the point of breathlessness, desire like that which had driven her secretly in the night to the corpse of her schoolmate back when she was a child.

If only no one would disturb her now — wasn't someone ringing the doorbell outside again? . . . Eugenie? No. Whatever it was passed on by.

Thank God!

How nonsensical to thank God for something that was really wrong . . . . But she hasn't been this happy for a long time as now when the notebooks and the loose sheets of paper lie before her in the light of the lamp she has quickly lighted: black books with red writing. Red ones, adorned with black letters and strange allegories: a hand that waves a torch, a woman with a freedom cap and a naked sword, at her feet shattered crowns, crosses that have been knocked over, a throne through whose gaping joints snakes and worms crawl.

She read standing up.

Poetry . . . . My God! They had poets like this?

Yes, yes, a thousand times yes! That was beautiful. Wild, glorious!

* * *

And what if tomorrow, instead of going to Bornau, she followed Martin to Switzerland? Her father would receive a letter: his daughter had made up her mind to become a Social Democrat and to devote her services to "the cause." Martin would joyfully welcome her as his comrade. That was certain. No love between them. Two unhappy people who devoted their broken hearts to the people. Misery with misery. They belonged together! Lutz would know then what he had lost, search for her and never find her . . . . Perhaps in the penitentiary . . . perhaps on the gallows. It would come to that. Walter was always saying so. Her brother ordered to come to her execution. She — calm, smiling, without tears. God! My God!

But she couldn't continue to read standing like that. Her back was hurting her. Her arms were practically paralyzed from handling the heavy pieces of wash. There had been twelve table clothes alone.

The maids wouldn't come back for a good long while. They had taken three basketfuls and, furthermore, at the mangle they always found girlfriends to chat with endlessly. Let them have that little bit of fun. Dottie and Luisa appeared to her suddenly as if wreathed in an aura of sacred dignity. They were suffering proletarian women.

Agathe lay down comfortably on the chaise longue and pulled the lamp closer. The rest of the wine she had poured herself earlier stood there, and little cakes lay upon a small plate. She had a burning thirst and ate and drank while she read and read — of the misery and the hunger and the need of the people and their hate and their struggle for liberation. The passion that flashed from the pages went to her head and pumped her sluggish blood through her veins.

Once she started violently; she thought someone was intruding upon her unawares.

The maids returned panting. They were dripping wet, for it was raining hard. Kitchen Dottie went grumbling into her chamber. But Wiesing slipped back out into the darkness where a man was waiting for her near the door to the house and where violent kisses warmed the drenched girl. Agathe picked up the notebooks and took the lamp to go hide in her room the treasure that had been entrusted to her. She went past the large standing mirror. How she looked . . . . She stopped and lifted the lamp. She had tousled her hair; it hung in a loose thick curly mane around her face. Her cheeks looked as though they had been made red-hot by the sun, and her eyes shone with enthusiasm. She surprised herself in this luminous, alien beauty.

If only Lutz were to see her like this! Why didn't he come in this moment? Oh . . . why was that impossible!

Why couldn't she go to Martin?

A short sob. The girl threw herself down full length upon the little sofa, her arms spread wide in helpless desire for something that she could embrace, in the desire to be impregnated with strength, to receive the fructifying breath of spirit and intellect that streams over the earth in a spring storm.

All around her stood her dainty, pale furniture, silently and orderly in its place. The glow of the little light shone through a pink paper shade upon the glass and ivory trinkets, photographs, and mementos of cotillions. And amazed, she surveyed this coy little world — her world. Her outspread arms sank downwards. A wild, despairing weeping finally soothed the convulsion that shook her.

XV.

Agathe went to Bornau the week before Easter.

As she bought her ticket, a small woman in a discreet black dress stood next to her and waited for the ticket window to get free. A gray gauze veil hid her face. Nevertheless Agathe recognized Fräulein Daniel.

Where might she be going? What if the two of them landed in the same compartment? Was Lutz nearby?

He hadn't accompanied her!

A violent feeling of triumph surged through Agathe.

La Daniel was much more elegantly dressed than she herself. And Lutz placed so much importance in these external things!

The conductor pushed Agathe into a ladies' compartment that was nearly full. She was unable to observe now where Fräulein Daniel got on the train. She was disappointed when the sensational experience of travelling together with the actress eluded her. Her thoughts were occupied with painting a scene that could have ensued between them if, alone with her in the coach, la Daniel had reproached her for stealing Adrian's heart.

It was already late afternoon. Before they reached the station where Agathe had to change trains, the locomotive stopped in an open field. The conductors stood in the rain, waiting and whispering to one another.

And that's spring, thought Agathe, contemplating the landscape that stretched out flat and brown, threaded with pale green furrows and damp with fog. They say that's spring.

She was not especially interested in the cause of their unexpected stop. Somehow things would get fixed, and they would get to their destination.

A whistling and a slow starting up again. After a short time the train stopped once more. The doors were thrown open.

"Get off the train!"

Railroad officials, a couple of policemen showed them the way and answered questions.

The tracks were not free. Freight cars had crashed into one another. Passengers hadn't been killed; only a stoker had died. There to the right lay the site of the unfortunate accident. The demolished cars, like monsters up on their hind legs engaged in a fight to the death, stretching up into the gray sky, tall and black. People shouting and running. The rain beat down harder. The crowd pressed toward the station house. Between two officials, a woman came reeling, her face pressed into a blue apron, her hair dripping wet. She staggered from side to side, beside herself with weeping. The wife of the stoker who had been killed. Their gaze followed her in timid sympathy.

When they had reached the high, glass-domed hall, part of the crowd separated off toward the exit. Those who remained — among them Agathe — streamed down a wide stairway to go through a tunnel to get to the train platform at the other side of the station and if possible to reach the express train.

Young men with coquettish travelling caps and flapping havelocks rushed nimbly out ahead to secure the best seats for themselves. Shouting and scolding, porters made way for their burdens. The yellow luggage carts rattled. Mothers and fathers grabbed their children by the hand and ruthlessly yanked them onward. Old ladies with boxes and umbrellas toddled forward, panting. They needed to hurry; they were already very late.

Close by her Agathe noticed a little boy in a pretty little coat who for several seconds now had been shoved forward by the stream of people. He looked fearfully all around him. And now he stopped: for those who were pressing forward merely a tiny obstacle shoved roughly out of the way. He began to cry. Agathe turned back to him.

"Little one, I take it you're lost?"

He sobbed and nodded his head.

What to do? One really couldn't abandon the little child here.

"Whom did you come here with? With your mama?"

He shook his head.

"What's your name?"

"Didi."

Agathe led the child into the restaurant and through the large window watched her train departing outside. She turned to the woman at the buffet to ask what one could do. Clearly the child had come over from the other platform in the confusion. A carter was to make the find known to the railroad porters and to the people in the various waiting rooms of the huge central train station. In the

104

meantime Agathe took the little boy under her wing. The next train she could take didn't leave for another hour.

Over here one felt none of the effects of the accident that was throwing everything into disorder at the other end of the tunnel. Here everything went along at its normal restless pace.

New trains thundered into the mighty hall — bells ringing — whistling. New streams of people pushed down the stairs and into the waiting rooms.

Agathe withdrew with her charge to the ladies' lounge. She removed his wet little coat and wrapped him in her lap robe. She sat down on the sofa next to the child and fed him a cup of hot chocolate. It was quite still and cozy here. The waiter had turned on a gas flame and closed the door.

A child like this one. To return from a trip . . . . To be picked up by Lutz in a closed carriage, the rain beating against the window-panes. To press oneself into his arms with the sleepy little child on one's lap . . . . How did people bear such bliss? Surely it was granted to some people. But could one actually feel more than one felt imagining how it could be — surely this wasn't possible.

Agathe pulled the little boy to her — tightly, tightly — and kissed him on the forehead, kissed his fine blonde hair, his eyebrows.

Startled she let go of him as if she had done something wrong; someone had torn open the door. Two women rushed in. Agathe saw a discreet black dress, a gray gauze veil pushed back from a pale, painted little face. Didi leaped up from the sofa and out of the lap robe and ran toward them filled with rejoicing.

"Mama! My mama!"

"There he is, the silly boy! Truly!" cried Fräulein Daniel. "My precious! O you little darling, you! We've looked all over the place for you!"

She lifted him up and held him close to her — tightly, tightly. Kissed him on the forehead, kissed his fine blonde hair, his eyebrows.

The woman who had accompanied her begged Agathe's pardon. She had left the child alone only for a moment, right under the big clock where they were to wait for his mama because she wanted to see the accident. And the horror when the child had vanished!

Agathe heard nothing.

La Daniel — her — she was a mother!

And Adrian Lutz?

All of a sudden everything was crystal clear to her. Inside she was icy cold. She saw everything that had happened. She knew everything.

The actress turned with outstretched hands to Agathe to thank her. "I'm very grateful to you — "

She groped for words in the face of the injurious arrogance in Agathe's bearing.

"You were kind to my child," she stammered, unsure of herself and agitated. "It's just . . . . I'm always so worried about the child because I can't be with him . . . . If I have no news of him even for a day, I act like a crazy person."

She was devastated, worn out from crying. She was past even noticing Agathe's silent, rigid rebuff. She put the little coat on the child, put his round cap on him. The woman, in whose care the child had been placed, tried to help her, but she wouldn't allow it.

Agathe followed the motherly doings of the little soubrette with the same look with which she had often observed her on stage. No differently. All feeling seemed suddenly extinguished within her.

The little boy was ready to go.

"Come, Adrian, kiss the lady's hand and say goodbye!"

Agathe recoiled. But of course it didn't matter; nothing mattered. And she bent down and touched the child's cheek with her cold, frozen lips. She gave Fräulein Daniel her hand — quite mechanically.

An expression of alarm crossed the agitated little face of the actress. She stood irresolutely before Agathe.

"I think — Don't we come from the same city?"

"We have probably run into one another frequently," Agathe answered.

Fräulein Daniel suddenly turned very red. Her mouth began to tremble.

Agathe blushed as well and averted her eyes. Suddenly it came — the pain.

"Fräulein, I beg you. Please don't reveal my pitiful secret!"

The two girls looked into one another's eyes and suddenly their eyes flooded with tears, were suffused with an infinite sadness. They understood one another in something mysterious, in a suffering for which there was no sound, for which there was no name, a suffering that extended far beyond their own fates.

"You are good," Fräulein Daniel whispered. "It's not for my sake. Only he — it's so embarrassing for him!"

Laying her hand on the child's head, she said bitterly and hastily, "One simply can't understand why a father would deny such a boy. One learns to forgive everything in the end, if one is always afraid of losing everything."

Agathe could hardly hold herself up any longer. Shivering, she detected a vestige of theatrics in the manner in which Fräulein Daniel accented her words.

Just don't betray yourself, not to this woman! She struggled with all her might against the desire to expose her feelings, a desire that flooded over her like a dizzy spell, the desire to throw herself in pitiful lamentation upon the breast of the woman who loved him too, to scream, to despair.

But stay calm, be a lady. Agathe had practiced this her whole life long. She managed at least to do that.

She answered the actress with a grave, maidenly dignity, "I couldn't forgive someone I must despise."

"Despise? Of course you don't understand. Oh, he — He doesn't love me anymore! But he doesn't love the others either — no one . . . no one. He just tires of all of them so quickly. And when I die and they open my heart, I think they'll find his name emblazoned on it in flaming letters."

"Dear lady, don't get so upset. The child is starting to cry too," admonished the woman who had taken Didi by the hand.

Fräulein Daniel sobbed loudly one last time, dried her face and pulled down the gray veil.

"Why talk about it anyway? It really serves no purpose. Forgive me for burdening you with my troubles. Yes? I have your promise?"

Agathe nodded. The women left the waiting room with the child. After a few minutes other people entered. A bell rang. They were calling people to board.

XVI.

Frau Heidling met her daughter at the train station. As the two of them rolled down the rain-soaked country highway in Uncle Bär's

107

dark, roomy carriage, Frau Heidling seized the opportunity to ask Agathe about the wash and other domestic matters. She had been uneasy the entire time about having left everything for Agathe to do by herself. Agathe *was* of course a grown-up girl, and the privy councillor was right to be annoyed because his wife regarded travelling with him as a sacrifice and right to say that Agathe really had to learn to manage something independently. The privy councillor's wife just had the nagging feeling that upon her return she would find things different both from what she was accustomed to and from what she thought was proper. And Agathe was so indifferent, so uninterested; she answered her questions in a tired, disagreeable tone of voice. Had none of the damask napkins been missing and had the maids gotten sausage instead of roast for dinner?

Agathe had no intention of telling her mother of her meeting with Fräulein Daniel. Mama would get upset, and Agathe had forever been accustomed to sparing her mother. She was of course also afraid that Mama might voice some kind of moral objection, say something censorious about Lutz and the actress, or pity her daughter for having heard such an ugly story. And besides, that wasn't at all what was causing her such tremendous anguish. Not abhorrence. Not righteous indignation. Just envy, envy, envy!

* * *

At dinner Agathe was privy to a protracted discussion: Cousin Mimi wanted to join a Protestant nursing order, but her parents wanted her to think over the matter for one more year. The privy councillor called her plan the folly of a high-strung girl and spoke of the obligations a daughter had first and foremost to her family. It seemed to Agathe that she was separated from people, from their doings and talking and intentions, by a wide space filled with fog.

Mimi accompanied her to her room, the one Agathe had occupied during that joyous summer visit when she was still at boarding school. Not the slightest thing had changed here: the same old-fashioned white and green striped wallpaper, the same straight, high-backed chairs, covered with that same crackling, stiff, hard, shiny cotton upholstery which is to be found nowhere in the world but in the guest rooms of traditionalist landed gentry. The cool air, redolent with lavender and the smell of the stable, accosted Agathe with a thousand sudden memories of her earliest youth, of happiness and laughter.

"Do you remember?" asked Mimi and held up her candle to illuminate a strange old copper engraving. In a worm-eaten mahogany frame Sappho, in flapping robes and fleet of foot, threw herself with a splendid vault from the Leukadian cliffs into the sea.[66]

One day they had brought the boys in and oh, how they had laughed and giggled with Martin and the cadets about this theatrical agony, how they had ridiculed it.

Mimi lighted the lamp for her cousin and left her alone.

Agathe had to be quiet; her parents were sleeping in the adjoining room near the door.

Ahead of her lay the long, long lonely night.

* * *

It was so awful imagining him with another woman even as she herself belonged to him with every pulsation of her blood, with the entire rapturous feeling of her heart and all the dreams of her brain.

. . . And no thought came flying to her from him . . . . She thought she felt his spiritual proximity and his head rested contentedly on a soft, breathing bosom; in quiet darkness his ear had once listened to the joyous, wild beating of that woman's heart. Her parted lips had felt the touch of his kiss and his mouth had drunk joy from the visage of the other woman . . . .

Ugh! That was so vulgar, and moreover, so disgracefully ridiculous . . . . How her love, as it struggled in the throes of death, was desecrated by the recognition of the truth, of loathsome, miserable reality.

* * *

"Do you have a headache?" asked Mama as their relatives gathered round the breakfast table.

"I don't know — no."

The walls, the table, the chair on which she sat down — everything seemed to sway. Odd . . . .

"You're not going to get sick on me?" the privy councillor asked with a worried look.

Seeing Agathe this morning among the plump, healthy country folk whose clothes brought to the breakfast table a breath of outdoors, of grass and flowers and fresh, damp earth, he noted with dissatisfaction and wounded paternal pride how scrawny and puny Agathe sat before him in the cheery spring sunshine that beamed through the high windows of the room overlooking the garden. Indeed, his daughter was ugly . . . a gray, strained face with sharp, pointy features and dark rings around her eyes.

Mimi put ham and honey and cake on Agathe's plate.

"Dear Agathe," her nasal voice admonished sagely, "our venerable old doctor always says the first meal is the most nourishing one. Tomorrow you'll come with me to the barn and drink milk."

The privy councillor teased her. "Are your patients going to get honey and ham one day too?"

Agathe tried to eat. It had to be possible if she forced herself. There was a hard knot in her throat. She began coughing after the first few bites.

"It's nothing," she stammered with a smile, coughing and coughing harder and harder. Her face turned ashen; drops of sweat ran down her forehead and tears down her cheeks. She instinctively placed her hand on the right side of her breast where she felt a twinge. They jumped up from their chairs with concerned expressions. With great effort Agathe got up to save herself from all these sympathetic glances. She had an alien, uncanny taste on her tongue. There. That was a relief . . . .

She held her handkerchief to her mouth. It turned dark red.

Blood . . . .

Horrified, she looked at her mother for help. Frau Heidling gave her her arm and led her away. With a calm, comforting voice she said, "You lie down quietly now. It'll get better then. That does happen sometimes."

She put her daughter to bed, held her in her arms when a new attack came and had a smile on her face as she stroked her cheek and said, "Poor child, were you frightened? That always looks so terrible, doesn't it? But it happens quite often, you know."

Agathe smiled too. Yes, yes, she knew. It happened a lot.

Everything was fine this way, altogether peaceful and fine.

Only the prospect of having to bear what she had experienced in secret for years and years had worried and upset her so.

There — she felt with her hand — below the right side of her collar bone. When she breathed, she perceived a slight rattling in that spot. Hardly any pain.

Dying was indeed not difficult at all; it was a weary resignation, an indifferent turning away from everything . . . .

After the old doctor, who had been fetched from the city by carriage, had left her, she lay with her eyes closed, slightly feverish.

Not talking, not having to explain anything — oh, that was good.

Someone slipped into her room on tiptoe. She recognized her father's step, but she didn't open her eyes. He kissed her on the forehead — carefully. She felt warm drops running down her temples. Then tears welled up in her own eyes. He wiped them away and murmured, "My good child, my good little girl!"

Mama, who sat before her bed in a big white apron, gestured to him silently. Both went out again quietly and stood whispering before the door.

"The doctor says that if you're nice and careful you'll be back on your feet in two weeks," Mama told her in a cheerful voice that deviated oddly from her normal worried and weary tones and that she only assumed when a great danger threatened but could perhaps be warded off through self-control and good sense. Agathe remembered her mother's special gentle and serene manner of speaking from the sickbeds and deathbeds of her little brothers and sisters.

* * *

It did her so much good to rest, caressed by the gentle spring air that wafted in the windows, sometimes bearing the strong smell of the farm, sometimes the delicate scent of the new foliage on the tall linden tree. No pain, only a slightly feverish confusion of thought that drifted into semi-consciousness. And all that she had experienced so far away, drifting in faded colors from an earlier existence into her consciousness.

Flowers — lilacs and camellias — stood on the little table next to her. Cousin Mimi brought them from the greenhouse every day. The precious flowers that were sacrificed only for the rarest occasions. They lent an air of solemnity like a final gesture of kindness.

They hadn't abandoned her after all; they wanted to keep her with them. And she had a need for tenderness . . . .

Mimi had also hung up a picture of Our Savior by her bed. She wanted to join a Protestant nursing order, and her entire being was filled with a serene and determined faith.

Agathe liked looking at the noble bowed head beneath the crown of thorns. She prayed a great deal — silent and with folded hands. When she faced the Son of God, she felt as if she faced a lofty, wonderful someone of whom one has heard a great deal, but whom one surely never expected to come to know personally. And then He suddenly makes known His imminent arrival. Not until then does one sense what that means.

* * *

Eugenie wrote a long sympathetic letter. She told of a country outing that had taken place on Easter Monday.[67]

> It was really too bad you weren't there. Herr von Lutz asked after you and wished you a speedy recovery. He was quite crazy and courted that dumb Wehrenpfennig girl, but as all of us could tell, only for the fun of it. By the way, la Daniel has an engagement somewhere else at the end of the season and is leaving town . . . .

Mama read the letter aloud to Agathe and looked at her lovingly. A weak smile lingered on the sick girl's pinched, sharp, thin features.

Now she had withstood this trial too . . . . She felt strong in all her weakness. She had heard his name, and after the initial moment when it seemed to her as if she were sinking with her bed into cold, dark water, she had remained calm.

Thank heavens! There was no more hate and envy of Fräulein Daniel in her — and also no more hope and no desire.

How good that felt!

At bottom even happiness had been suffering.

Would she suffer a great deal more? Dying surely couldn't be that easy? She was often compelled to think about that now, especially at night when she couldn't sleep for hours. There would surely be more struggles. She wanted to be brave.

After the violent attacks that had prostrated her, her cough had nearly vanished. But one night when Mama gave her something to drink because her mouth was very dry, she had another coughing fit.

She sat up straight. Oh, it was horrible. Gasping, she struggled with the enemy that shook her and painfully lacerated her breast. Her breath whistled through her throat; her arms beat the air as she suffocated; her mother held her upright, and sighing deeply, wiped the brow that was bathed in a cold sweat.

Throwing on some clothes, the privy councillor ran in from the adjacent room.

"My child, my child, what ever has happened?"

"Let me die," Agathe gasped. "Please let me die. It'll be over soon anyway. O God! O my God!"

Now it was her father who held her. Her mother sank to her knees before the bed, took her hands and kissed them with loud, passionate sobbing.

"No, no," she moaned at the same time, "you can't, you can't die. You surely won't do that to us. Our dear Lord surely can't let that happen . . . . "

And as though it were possible for her to defy death if only she would, her father pleaded with her now — fear had robbed him of all reason — to stay with them.

" . . . We love you so very much. You have no idea. Everything, we'll do everything for your sake . . . . Please just get better again, my sweet child, how will we live? . . . You know we can't do without you . . . . "

No, she hadn't known that, hadn't anticipated this wild anguish, their stormy tenderness. That was a struggle, a terrible one that lacerated her soul as her lungs struggled for air.

She thought a stream of blood would flow again and end her suffering. But only some viscous mucus came up, and then the attack abated.

She was moved to the depths of her soul and soaked with the sweat of weakness. Her eyes streaming tears, she begged Papa and Mama not to make parting so difficult for her. She wanted so much to die and it would be so good. And they still had Walter and Eugenie, and Eugenie would also be a good daughter to them.

Finally she fell asleep sitting up, her arms flung around her father's neck, her head resting on his shoulder in exhaustion. And he held her like that, probably for an hour.

When she awoke from confused dreams, she saw by the lamplight that their two faces were still trained on her, fearful and suffused with desperate love.

Smiling sadly, she lay back on the pillows and let them settle her down and tuck her in.

No, she mustn't die; surely she must want to live.

Secretly she thought: even if she were to try, God would understand her sacrifice and would be reasonable.

But the following morning the old family doctor seemed not to be especially disturbed by their description of the nocturnal terror. He said she was healing nicely and that this was probably the last attack.

After two weeks Agathe was allowed to get up again, was supposed to eat good beefsteak and black bread and drink milk and beer, take walks or rather sit or lie outside in the fresh air.

There were daily consultations between the relatives and her parents about where they could go with her in the summer and whether for the following winter a sojourn in the South was advisable. All around her Agathe heard the familiar names — Görbersdorf, Davos, Merano.[68] They suggested nature-healers and doctors of hydropathy and a very famous man who prescribed the most successful cures by studying a piece of metal that the sick person carried on his person for a while.[69] In every letter Mama got from her friends a new remedy was touted and immediately sent along. Today Agathe was supposed to eat a jelly of snails, tomorrow rub herself with the fat of a hare, and the day after tomorrow drink donkey's milk.

In the end the privy councillor did write to a well-known luminary in the field of lung and chest diseases. When the professor answered that it came at an opportune moment inasmuch as he had to visit a female patient in the area and could combine it with a side trip to Bornau, her parents experienced a great feeling of release.

Agathe herself anticipated the examination with fluctuating moods. She no longer wanted to live and no longer rejoiced at the thought of dying. A long period of suffering interspersed with periods of ostensible well-being, Papa and Mama's misery endlessly protracted — this was terrible in a way completely different from going to sleep gently and peacefully. She no longer saw the disease that menaced her in a romantic light, but rather in a dreary, lamentable one. She suddenly saw all its repulsiveness, its unaesthetic qualities, its pain. Since she had been feeling better, she was no longer at all in that gentle, transfigured emotional state, but rather impatient, easily enraged, easily brought to tears.

She tried to calm herself by reading psalms and praying. Giving over her soul to the will of the Lord — oh, it was the only thing that could help her. But as soon as she thought herself at peace at last, her inability to get down a single bite of solid food and the unpleasant dampness that covered her hands made clear to her how vain her efforts were.

The old doctor arrived in his own carriage ahead of the professor. Finally the anticipated famous and feared guest arrived.

Agathe was with her parents in the large living room. Aunt Malvina was there too, and Cousin Mimi because the proceedings were really very interesting to her on account of her future profession. Uncle August greeted the professor down below on the stairs, led him upstairs and turned him over to the privy councillor. Everything was indescribably solemn — as in a court session.

The professor seemed somewhat astonished by the many family members.

"Oh — which one is the patient?" he asked as he greeted them all around and shook his colleague's hand.

Agathe rose trembling.

He looked at her sharply, a pale little dwarf of a man. Leaning back comfortably in an easy chair, his hands folded, he had them tell him how the attack had occurred, how old Agathe was, what diseases she had had. He also checked the age of her parents and their state of health and he especially asked whether there had already been cases of tuberculosis in the family. No, that was not at all the case. Frau Heidling answered everything with the serene voice reserved for times laden with anxiety.

Finally the privy councillor left the room.

"You are very impressionable," said the professor, putting his ear to Agathe's chest, "very unusually impressionable." Lifting his head right in front of her face and inspecting her scrawny neck in which the last weeks had dug furrows, he asked, "Did you get violently agitated before this attack?"

"Yes," breathed Agathe, and a dark red rush of blood stained her face and chest.

115

"The day before." She trembled more violently. Her heart pounded furiously to the point of agony.

"Child, you didn't tell me a thing about that," her mother began full of reproach.

The professor darted a glance at the privy councillor's wife, warning her to be careful.

"I thought so," he observed calmly. "That explains the matter. So. Now we'll tap you on the other side . . . . By the way, the wound has healed very nicely."

The old doctor received a nod of the head.

Agathe put her dress back on, and the doctors withdrew to confer.

The privy councillor and Uncle Bär looked in at the door.

"What did he say?"

They shrugged their shoulders and pointed to the door behind which the doctors had vanished.

"She got violently agitated," Aunt Malvina reported in an undertone, walking up to her husband cautiously and on tiptoe.

"Violent agitation . . . . " Uncle Bär and the privy councillor whispered.

"Agathe got very upset. I didn't know anything about it," repeated Frau Heidling to the privy councillor. Everyone looked at Agathe sympathetically and inquisitively. Only Cousin Mimi looked a little severe. How could a person get so upset she got sick?

Agathe was ashamed. She felt as if she were being tortured. Now they'd all talk about it and not rest until they'd found out what she'd gotten upset about.

Then she was seized by a wild terror. She must be very sick after all if they conferred in there about her for such an interminably long time.

It really was becoming intolerable!

To have to die, to cease to be . . . . No, no, anything but that! Just live! O God, dear, merciful God. Just live a little longer.

Suddenly they all heard the deep, agreeable laugh of the old doctor.

How that surprised them! How it broke the mute spell of anticipation!

The privy councillor opened the door. The professor's entire face was suffused with laughter.

116

"Yes, one has these experiences, my dear colleague," they heard him saying jovially.

When he saw the pale girlish face in the open door, her suffering eyes tensely fixed upon him, his pleasure in the good story vanished behind his kindly serious professional face.

He turned to Frau Heidling.

"So, I can give you good news," he said in a friendly manner. "I find no indications of tuberculosis. Your daughter is very sensitive. A blood vessel burst under the influence of violent psychological excitement. Her constitution needs to be strengthened, or else her condition really could take a bad turn. Your health, dear young lady, is in your own hands. Turn your thoughts to happy things. Enjoy your youth."

Then he gave them some simple prescriptions that in the main coincided with those of the old family doctor. Nevertheless they listened to him more attentively, and every word that came from his mouth seemed to possess a greater value.

Agathe would have liked to kiss his hand in passionate gratitude.

When the professor had left, Papa and Mama embraced their daughter. Their happiness seemed to Agathe so invaluable, so precious, and so deeply satisfying that a joyous, indeed a truly pugnacious courage to undertake every kind of renunciation came over her.

She wanted to be healthy, she wanted to live — for no one and for nothing else in the whole wide world but for her parents.

PART II

I.

Eugenie had become even prettier after the birth of her first child. She simply radiated good health and good humor. Whenever the sturdy little fellow accompanied her on an outing in the arms of his nursemaid, mother and child wore the same plate-like hat of white wool on their rosy, blonde heads. It was quite darling. Eugenie was always dreaming up something special in her dress that either made people mad or delighted them. Opinion was always divided about it.

"One of my wife's new ideas," Lieutenant Heidling would say then, and in the tone in which he would add, "yes, this little woman," one could hear an almost boyish infatuation.

If their acquaintances compared Walter with his charming wife, they were struck by his troubled and often depressed manner. He was moody. His brow, his simple youthful features could for no apparent reason suddenly darken with displeasure. At parties where Eugenie amused herself, laughed, danced and let his comrades pay court to her, he stood around silently and watched her. From time to time he cast a pleading look at her. Usually he wanted to leave early, but he always let himself be directed by her. He couldn't assert his will against hers, and then he became annoyed. He hated social gatherings. He would have been happiest spending all his time alone with his wife. But if he had revealed that to her, she would have laughed at him. And her laughter hurt him; he didn't like to provoke it. Well — and after all it was her money she made a home with, bought her clothes with, etc. Would she throw that up to him one day? He couldn't let it come to that. The fear of the words that Eugenie could speak heightened the insecurity into which his great love plunged him. He was extremely vain about his wife, her triumphs, even her coquetry. He spoke of all other women with disdain and pity. But, but . . . he had once imagined their relationship quite differently: a marriage of convenience — and she'd have to be

118

content if he didn't lose her fortune gambling. Yes, oh yes, yes, marriage sometimes brings strange surprises.

Before the baptism of the child, Agathe had witnessed a violent argument between Walter and Eugenie. Walter's captain, Herr von Strehlen, the gracious lady's most loyal admirer, was to serve as godfather alongside old Wutrow and the privy councillor. Eugenie had promised the captain months ago — in Walter's presence; didn't he remember? — her first child, if he was a boy, was to be named "Wolf" after the captain. The boy had come into the world, and Walter was quite satisfied with that fact too. Now not keeping an old promise because it suddenly didn't suit him anymore, that wouldn't do; he had to see that. An elderly bachelor placed a lot of importance on things like that. My goodness, why not make him happy? Strehlen was Walter's boss and that was that. They mustn't make him mad. Otherwise Walter's career would suffer.

She spoke very reasonably, and although Walter certainly had been angry at first, he gave in to her sound reasoning in the end.

The boy was named Wolf. Herr von Strehlen came over almost every day to inquire after his godchild. Even when he was not present, his name echoed throughout the apartment in a thousand endearments. Conscientious mother that she was, Eugenie bathed and dressed her little son herself, and as she played with him on her lap, kissing and teasing him, you could hear her saying, "My little Wolfy-mouse! My dear, old sweetie-Wolf! My little grouchy Wolf! My sweet, little lovey Wolf!"

And the young woman's piercing gray eyes would look over at Walter from beneath half-closed lids with an expression of crafty roguishness and would see that he was suffering, suffering on and on, that he reproached himself for being tormented so senselessly, would see that he called upon his honor and his trust in her and his reason, which couldn't reproach her for anything, and his delicacy of feeling, which was ashamed to express even with a single word his dissatisfaction about something that was so completely a matter of course — her playing with the little fellow — and she would see that still he suffered.

She laughed about it in secret.

Dear God — that boring captain . . . . As if he were worth her trouble . . . .

But the merciless thoughts behind the cool, gray eyes, beneath the soft mane of hair, they knew, whenever Walter took this blonde abundance in his trembling hands and kissed it with anguished joy, that passion grows out of suffering. And the consuming fire that flamed at Eugenie's side, the anxious worship that trembled at the thought of losing her, warmed her very pleasantly. It was her secret, her fountain of youth, from which she arose like the phoenix from its nest of flames with ever-renewed strength.

Perhaps there was only one person who contemplated with silent disdain the charming gaiety of the young Frau Heidling who enchanted the entire world. And that one person was her sister-in-law.

Since Agathe had given herself over completely to piety, self-sacrifice, and renunciation, she had become severe in her judgment of others who failed to adhere to the same ideal of austere performance of duty.

"You can't do anything with Agathe anymore," Eugenie declared. "She reads the Bible all day long if she's not at Sunday school or visiting her poor people. It's really too bad about the girl!"

"Last Wednesday she even went to the prayer meeting with the Brothers of Jesus," said Lisbeth Wendhagen, "out there behind the sheds where Master Butcher Unverzagt preaches! But just think — "

"If Papa knew that, he'd take care of it!" said Eugenie laughing. "My goodness! Fat Amandus Unverzagt as father confessor to the crushed souls of girls! No, Walter, we really mustn't tolerate Agathe's letting her exaggerated piety make her a laughing-stock."

On account of this sisterly consideration Eugenie began teasing Agathe with her Brothers of Jesus whenever she ran into her. When the girl went over to see the young Heidlings and wanted to pick up little Wolf from his baby carriage, Eugenie snatched him from her, wrinkled her nose and said, "I don't like you carrying him. Who knows what kind of diseases you're bringing into the house from the lice-infested children of your poor people."

She pressed the boy to her breast with a mother's proud gesture, and dandled him in her arms, far from Agathe, as if she had victoriously wrested him from a great danger.

Tears sprang into Agathe's eyes. Nevertheless she humbled herself so low as to plead with Eugenie at least not to make such remarks in Papa's presence.

Every evening Agathe knelt in her room for half an hour at a time and prayed with sobbing and weeping for the Lord to strengthen her so she could patiently bear the little martyrdom that Eugenie was inflicting upon her, just like so many other things she undertook for His sake — including visiting the poor — including going in secret to the Brothers of Jesus.

With fear and despair she felt her dull, vague dislike of Eugenie turning to hate, to a hate so deep, so poisonous, and so bitter as only those hate who are old friends and close relatives, who know one another intimately and are forced to spend a lot of time together.

How could that have happened? What evil, horrible instincts were making themselves known there? Her heart and soul should really be filled with love of the Savior and her neighbor . . . . And she didn't even have reasonable grounds for hating Eugenie. Eugenie was really the only one who had been kind enough to try — back then — to bring her close to Lutz . . . . Yes, in order to have the pleasure — such a cold, cruel pleasure — of watching her mute torment . . . said a sharp scornful voice inside her immediately. To lure Lutz into her own home . . . and at his mere wish . . . . Eugenie had probably not scattered her sheet music at his feet out of the overflowing kindness of her heart toward Agathe.

Why? Why ever had Agathe confided in her? She was ashamed even to think of it. Of course she couldn't be held responsible for her actions back then; she'd been as if under a spell.

But the spell under which she had suffered was broken now. She was liberated. The child of God, the handmaiden of the Lord. O sweet, bright Bliss . . . to sink into His wounds . . . to let herself be washed over with His blood . . . to forget . . . everything . . . everything . . . just to see His Redeemer-eyes . . . solitary above the chaos of misery . . . disappointment and misery . . . . Enveloped in His love . . . safe in His flaming heart of love . . . surrendered . . . dissolved . . . to feel oneself perishing beneath the thrill of His grace . . . .

* * *

Every other week Agathe went with Papa and Mama to the cathedral. One didn't need to hurry to get there on time; even if countless people were standing in the aisles, their pew remained empty until Agathe opened the little door with a key that she drew out of the pocket of her dress.

Eugenie also possessed a key and sat there in her most dignified beaded mantle which she only wore to go to church. All around in the reserved seats there was a glittering and sparkling in the muted, colored light that fell through the stained glass of the arched gothic windows, a sparkling of helmets and epaulets and silver tassels on swords. The heavy fur-lined winter coats made swishing noises, and the trim and beads on the women's apparel rustled. They greeted one another discreetly; they sang sotto voce along with the choir to the booming tones of the organ; they stood in solemn posture during the prayer, the gentlemen with their helmets or their black silk hats on their arms, the women with fingers lightly laced and with lowered eyes — just as is proper.

During the sermon many of the older women shed tears; a few also snoozed. And after the close of the worship service they greeted one another before the church doors, yawned a little, stood together in small groups with their acquaintances and were pleased whenever the pastor had spoken quite movingly. Agathe noticed that most of the older ladies and gentlemen really hadn't retained more than isolated phrases from the sermon. The young girls and women immediately began chatting about ice skating and parties and balls. The junior barristers and lieutenants took advantage of the opportunity to secure the most popular dance partners for the first waltzes. They only went to church regularly if they had a sweetheart whom they could conveniently meet there.

It was for this reason that Agathe had gone to the Brothers of Jesus. She hoped to find a more profound, more austere devotion there than among the majestically soaring columns, than beneath the graceful stone cupola of the cathedral where the preacher in the gold and velvet pulpit admonished high society in studied, fulsome language to take up the cross and to renounce the world and its delights.

Agathe certainly found things modest enough among the Brothers of Jesus. To get to their prayer room from the street one had to traverse a long, damp, dark corridor between storerooms and sheds. It really quite resembled the narrow portals that led to the Kingdom of Heaven. Then one came to a dirty courtyard. Wobbly stones

122

marked the slippery way through deep puddles of evil-smelling fluid that emanated from large piles of manure. Cackling chickens sought their feed here. Wretched rags hung out of the windows of the tall back houses to dry. The gathering place of the Brothers of Jesus was above a stable, reached by a perilous staircase. A low whitewashed room; on its bare walls horrid oleographs of scenes from the Holy Gospel; and as an altar, a table covered with a black cloth.[70]

Agathe usually found a little old spinster beside her who inspired a great deal of mirth at the Heidlings' because she came asking for alms — shyly and fleetingly, but as regularly as the swallows in springtime. The alms were for wonderful needy people, plagued by misfortune, who later just as regularly proved to be incorrigible drunkards or thieving women. Despite constant disappointment the wretched, tiny old spinster was blissful in her dispatch and activity, in the deprivation and hunger she suffered for those dubious fellow creatures. In her flat little bosom beneath the net mantelet she surely carried a secret treasure with which she satisfied her hunger and nourished the radiant beaming of her eyes in the tiny withered and bewhiskered face. She had told Agathe about the Brothers of Jesus.

The lowliness, wretchedness, and obscurity of the surroundings and the darkness, which was hardly relieved by the two tallow candles on the altar, recalled the gatherings of the first Christians in remote, hidden corners. Like the stumps of candles that were lit here and there to illuminate the verses in the hymnal, all this cast a flickering glow of romance over the scene. Artisans entered quietly. They emerged and disappeared in the darkness along with the muffled, consumptive figures of lightly coughing seamstresses and of shivering old ladies groping their way. Here no one could tell whether the hot drops that flowed in prayer were of despair or of love. Yes, it was as if the soul could soar more unshackled, more ardently upward to the Lord when the body, cast down and kneeling, humbled itself.

And thank God, Pastor Zacharias didn't lapse into the sentimental lamentations of the old spinster at Agathe's side.

A stout, awkward peasant figure with a ponderous head the size of Martin Luther's, the itinerant preacher stood before his disciples and interpreted God's word for them with angry urgency. The man still believed in the Devil. No euphemisms were used here, no allowances made. All or nothing, was the word here . . . . If you are half-

123

hearted, then I will spit you from my mouth — thus spake the Lord, your God, and the Lord does not suffer to be scorned.

Agathe shuddered in fear and terror. But she felt good, so good under this severity. That was something! She lacked conviction. Oh, she was a swaying reed, a smoldering candle wick, but now the Holy Spirit fanned His flames in her and warmed her cold, desolate heart.

If only they had let her simply come and go in the obscurity that she found so pleasant! But in a moment of deep emotion she had given her gold bracelet to a collection for another poor community of Brothers of Jesus. She hadn't given her name, but they had inquired after her. The pious artisans hurried to put down a straw mat on the kneeler, to bring a candle and hymnal to the privy councillor's daughter whom the Lord had brought to them. After the worship service they came up to her to shake her hand and to welcome her as a member of their little community.

Of course it was downright horrible. Whenever Master Butcher Unverzagt conducted the Bible lesson, Agathe saw the puffed up arrogance in his face and in vain sought the exaltation that initially had moved her.

Not here either? Not here either?

Was it simply her lack of strength? Why was she so frightfully sensitive to every imperfection?

The visits to the poor and sick frightened her. How could she bring comfort and help? She considered the difficulties with which these people struggled enormous and her capacity to mitigate their misery so tiny, so pitifully small. Of course all of it was nothing but an illusion. How she envied the ladies who in naive certainty preached morality, religion, and cleanliness to the poor.

Why shouldn't they steal if they were hungry? Why believe in God who didn't tend to them? How could they be clean if they had no money to buy soap? Agathe was ashamed to come to them, well shod and in her warm winter jacket. She was ashamed to give something that, as she well knew, couldn't alter the misery, something with which she wished only to purchase for herself ever more perfect faith.

Despite her ardent efforts she didn't become a brave, happy disciple of the Lord with the courage of her convictions like her cousin Mimi Bär.

. . . To shoulder the ridiculousness and vanity that clung to all of her activities like a cross from the Lord and to bear it patiently — perhaps it worked like that.

Her struggle for faith, for peace did nevertheless fill her days, did give her waking up in the morning a purpose and a goal. What else in the world did she have to live for otherwise?

Taking care of her parents . . . . Actually Papa and Mama could take care of themselves quite well. Caring for them didn't fill the immeasurable empty places in her heart. She hadn't imagined it like this when she was so full of gratitude to them for their love and their despair beside her sickbed.

Even her yearning had withered and died. She no longer knew what she should dream of. She didn't even grieve for Lutz. It had all been a dreadful delusion. She could have safely seen him again. But he was extinguished from her life like a candle. He had left M. in that summer while she slowly recovered in Bornau. She didn't know where he was living now, and she couldn't imagine that he still existed somewhere in the world.

Fräulein Daniel had married an actor. She — the woman Lutz had loved, the mother of his child . . . . Agathe understood the inner possibilities of such lives as little as she could imagine the daily existence of the inhabitants of Mars.[71]

She had forwarded Martin's social writings to him without an accompanying letter. They were sinful poison. The intoxication that had come upon her when she had read them had been a temptation to do evil.

* * *

Little by little Agathe achieved small and quiet victories. At supper at a large ball she calmly bowed her head and said grace with softly moving lips. When she took up the custom at home, her father looked at her several times full of amazement but he let her be. After the dance at the home of the supreme magistrate he reprimanded her severely for behaving conspicuously in society.

Agathe answered with a request to be permitted not to go to any more balls.

"How do you get such notions?" the privy councillor asked angrily. He put aside the paper he was reading. He had let his first admonition flow over the top of the newspaper into the conversation between mother and daughter about the previous evening.

Now it became serious.

"Papa," Agathe began with composure, "dancing's not a pleasure for me anymore."

"What nonsense! You're a young girl. Enjoy your life. I don't want to have a silly, sentimental person for a daughter."

"Yes, Papa. But . . . . "

"What do you mean — but?"

"Going to balls isn't consonant with true Christianity. Please, please, do just let me . . . . You know, it's only . . . . Then you won't have to buy me any more ballgowns."

Instinctively Agathe grasped at the reasons with which she hoped most easily to persuade her father.

The balls and the parties were torture for her. She nowhere felt herself so excluded from all pleasure in life than in the brightly lighted rooms where by this time a younger generation had come to the fore and the gentlemen crowded around the young married women who in more glittering outfits and with more uninhibited gaiety collected great circles of admirers around them.

Agathe really didn't want to play any kind of a role here anymore. If now and then a gentleman turned up who liked her, she re- proached herself for giving in to vanity. If she remained unnoticed, then she fretted about her own unworthy anger. She was never at peace as long as she served two masters, God and the world.

Mimi Bär had it a lot easier. She went her way without looking to the left or to the right. She had completed her trial year with the nursing order in Berlin, had recently been transferred to the hospital in M. and was wearing her white nurse's cap with calm pride. She had clear instructions as to what she was or was not supposed to do. Like the officer in uniform with his order of the day and his firmly ingrained sense of his estate, she lived an active and satisfied life within a clearly circumscribed space.

And Agathe was not even able to combine her filial duty and her Christianity. To be sure . . . . Mimi hadn't combined these two things either. She had simply placed her inner calling above her filial duty, joyfully leaving her elderly parents to the protection and care of God.

The privy councillor condemned her actions most sharply. He feared the influence that Mimi might exercise over his daughter and vigorously seized the opportunity to express his opposition. Agathe's reference to what could be saved by not buying ball apparel made no impression this time, although Papa otherwise readily berated the women for their spending.

"Dear child," he said getting to his feet, resting his hand on the table and directing a serious look at his daughter through his pince-nez, "you have obligations not only to yourself but also to society, above all to your father's position. To extricate yourself from them would be unconscionable. As a representative of the government I have to show myself in public and among my superiors. What would people think if I left my daughter at home? We men of the state have to look up and down, to the right and to the left in order to keep from giving offense. We are not free people who can follow their whims. I've frequently heard lately that you're creating a sensation with this oddly strict religious turn you've taken. My dear child, that will not do at all. The supreme magistrate made some intimations to me that were quite embarrassing . . . . I hear you're attending the gatherings of a sect called the Brothers of Jesus?"

"Papa, I was there only a couple of times," stammered Agathe. Her father's voice had taken on the severe tones of his office that she and her mother feared so very much.

"A certain Zacharias preaches there, a pastor who left the established church?"

"Yes, Papa! But he only comes every four weeks. He's a wonderful speaker!"

"An obstinate fellow! He's gotten into an unpleasant conflict with the consistory on account of the May Laws.[72] I remember the case. The supreme magistrate told me candidly that they frown upon the daughter of a high government official attending the gatherings of such a man."

"But Papa, they have nothing to reproach him for. He was only following his convictions. It certainly cannot have been easy for him to give up that good position, what with his five children. They often eat only potatoes and lard for dinner. Yes, indeed; it's true."

"It serves him completely right," said the privy councillor pacing the room. "You do hear what an unpleasant encounter I've had on your account. It's inconceivable to me how your mother can allow

127

you to go to these sectarians! I hereby expressly forbid you to do so. Do you hear me? You have the worship service in the cathedral. You can get yourself enough piety there. Extremes of any kind are bad."

Covered with confusion, Frau Heidling excused herself for not having kept a better eye on Agathe, and the privy councillor left for his office in a bad mood.

When he returned home for dinner the two women tried in every way possible to raise his spirits. The meal was prepared with special care. Agathe herself had to go back to the butcher to get a little piece of tenderloin. And they were lucky. Father liked it. After dinner he patted Agathe on the cheek and said in a friendly manner, "What notions a little thing like you comes up with! Oh, yes, we have to take good care of you girls!"

II.

Agathe's circle of friends had thinned during the past year. As the Fairy of Youth Agathe had handed the myrtle wreath to the little brunette who had so liked to be kissed by uncles and boy cousins. At Lotte Wimpffen's *Polterabend*, she had played the role of Family Concord, and she had hailed Kläre Dürnheim in the role of the Spirit of Happiness as the latter bid her girlhood adieu. And she had always had a heavenly time at these parties; it was a point of honor among the young ladies — especially at a *Polterabend* .... Otherwise of course people could have thought .... No. It would have been downright cowardly not to have a heavenly time at the prenuptial festivities of one's girlfriends.

Afterwards Agathe was no longer that eager to spend time with her married friends. With them she very nearly relived those times with her more experienced schoolmates at boarding school. Hardly were a couple of the young women together, when they put their heads together, whispered feverishly, laughed and shared an infinite number of secrets that Agathe was not allowed to learn for all the world. For she was a "young girl."

Lisbeth Wendhagen of course — *she* persisted and said "Ugh — you're disgusting!" over and over until she knew everything she was eager to know. With her freckled, sharp little old maid's face and her prudish little squeals she played the confidante in most of the young households. The gentlemen had great fun teasing and making a fool

128

of her. They willfully let themselves go in her presence, made risqué jokes and indulged in high spirited displays of affection. Lisbeth's delighted outrage was simply too funny.

But Agathe filled the couples with a discomfiting awe. Her mouth could twitch so harshly and disdainfully. Her eyes were so sad. And she was so pious!

Then they said, "You should be ashamed in front of Agathe!" Then the young husband went into the adjoining room and called from there, "Sweetie, come here quick!"

Sweetie rushed off.

Agathe sat alone, thumbed through an album and heard muffled giggling and the sound of countless kisses.

It was really better to spend time with older girls with high aspirations.

She was invited to take an Italian course and did in fact study the language quite assiduously for a while, although given her parents' increasing ill health she had little prospect of ever going to Italy.

She was also constantly taking music lessons. But it was even less clear to her why she was doing that. Given her nervous inhibition she would never manage a performance. And she couldn't sing at all anymore. Since her illness her voice sounded pitifully thin and tremulous. If she tried it anyway, she was overcome each time by a sadness that was now impossible to combat. She positively dreaded the dear old melodies in which she heard the ghostly voices of so many dead and buried hopes.

Now and again Agathe's teacher arranged musical soirees. She thereby combined the double purpose of examining her pupils and of taking care of her social obligations.

A whole week ahead of time Fräulein Kriebler earnestly begged Agathe, too, to do her the honor.

It was a hot summer evening, shortly before the beginning of the long summer vacation.

The piano teacher had a furnished room with a tiny sleeping closet in the apartment of a court clerk in a back house; all three of her windows were wide open. Nevertheless when Agathe emerged from the kitchen of the court clerk's wife and entered the room that was filled with ladies, she was accosted by the smell of roast, cheese, and herring salad. None of them allowed herself to be troubled by the heat. Voices buzzed in happy confusion.

129

Little adolescent girls in pale dresses who were to sing later were for the time being crammed into Fräulein Kriebler's tiny sleeping closet, sitting on the bed that was covered with a travelling-shawl. Among themselves they commented with irreverent, youthful wit on the buffet that was laid out on the wash stand.

Fräulein Kriebler's colleagues and her well-wishers occupied the living room. Besides Agathe there was one additional older pupil who had been educating herself for ten years, at first for the stage, then as a concert singer. There was even a rumor that she had once appeared somewhere in public.

For Fräulein Kriebler the musicales were an event, a very exciting affair. She had had to rearrange her little rooms completely for the occasion. The embroidered cloths with which she had covered the tables and chairs, the colorful paper flowers with which she had adorned the walls wherever there was room among the photographs, book shelves, little baskets that held things for dusting, and painted proverbs — all of this met with undivided admiration.

With two hot, red spots on the sharp cheek bones of a sickly face consumed with restless passion, she ran continuously back and forth from the piano to the tiny bedroom, whispered admonitions in the children's ears, arranged her music, asked whether her guests were ready for some tea now. She thought it would be better if they had it later, but if they wanted, she had her two oil burners set to go . . . .

A fat, hunchbacked lady schoolteacher with short hair had already asked several times why Fräulein Kriebler made such a fuss. She advised her simply to get the concert started now that they were all together.

Fräulein Kriebler cast one more helpless glance at a lady in silk who sat ramrod straight on the sofa and whose codfish-eyes followed the bashful, sighing blonde and brown-haired children who were being herded to the piano. This lady had most of the young girls in her motherly charge and was therefore an awe-inspiring and influential person in this circle.

The teacher's trembling fingers, which were clammy with excitement, struck a chord on the piano. Nervous before this circle of tough critics, thin, charming little voices began singing without expression of love and springtime and the blessed power of secret passions . . . .

130

Hardly had it ended when the pale little dresses rustled and fluttered hurriedly, hurriedly into the tiny sleeping closet. And just as there had previously been sighs and giggles of fear, so now there were sighs and giggles of relief. Oh, how good it was that it was over! And Erna snitched an open-faced ham sandwich from the buffet. Really now, how could a person be so impudent!

Linchen vanished behind the clothes closet curtain, which as a result bulged shapelessly. From time to time her bare arms emerged from behind it until she reappeared in a Zerlina costume which she had gotten on crooked.[73]

She was to sing the duet from the *Marriage of Figaro* with the lady who was being trained for the stage.

Yes, Fräulein Kriebler knew how to surprise her guests. She had actually tried to teach the frivolous countess as well as the even more frivolous pretty young chambermaid something like coquetry. Naturally everybody applauded as loudly as possible.

After a few more piano pieces the buffet was opened. The tea water bubbled on both of the petroleum burners. Fräulein Kriebler poured tea constantly. She shouted her orders at the company of adolescent girls who were helping her serve. A boisterous gaiety filled the room. They hardly had heard anything from the little ladies in the sleeping closet since the latter had begun eating little ham sandwiches and blancmange. Now the teachers began enjoying themselves. They hadn't gotten dressed up in their best clothes and white lace for nothing; they wanted to have some amusements too! The harsh, deep voices and the sharp, powerful ones of the energetic spinsters resounded in a lively confusion of conversations. Fräulein Kriebler ran around among her guests, urged them to help themselves, shrieked in her high, impassioned voice, "I hope you don't mind — it's only a gypsy tea! You've got to help yourselves. My lackeys are on vacation! We're missing a spoon? But there were enough spoons there! Rinse one off, Linchen — a young girl must be quick to help. No, do excuse me, Fräulein Heidling — a gypsy tea."

The hunchbacked teacher with the short, curly hair was telling the most droll stories and wheezing with asthma. A very nearsighted girl laughed so hard she dropped her pince-nez into the mayonnaise. Finally a pale person with a colossal nose and humble eyes that seemed to ask every one to pardon the adjacent nose commanded everyone's attention. She had a plan to found in their city a home for single girls who were no longer able to work. With their combined resources. What did the ladies think about that? [74]

Animated, vociferous applause ensued. As if she had suggested a new and glorious amusement, they hurried to make and disseminate proclamations, to organize lotteries, to approach rich merchants for contributions, to approach the magistrate about having a lot ceded to them; all this would only place new burdens on these single women who lived by the work of their hands and brains. But their days already consisted of such incessant pursuit of a livelihood that it hardly mattered if they took on additional running and rushing and worrying. It was a matter of their common interest, to the advantage of each them.

"Why ever are they all so jolly?" thought Agathe. "They really have no reason at all to be."

To pay for the roast and the sweets before them Fräulein Kriebler had had to trot through the entire town many times with her characteristic nervous haste and give at least fifteen lessons. They all knew that. But they also knew that it was a matter of pride for Fräulein Kriebler, a not insubstantial part of her human dignity, to entertain her colleagues a few times a year in her home. Each of them thought highly of this custom. And they enjoyed their food in a relaxed and comfortable fashion as they talked of the home for single girls that opened up the prospect of a secure future for them. The future that, in the best case, they could create for themselves with all their energetic work by day and through half the night, with all their anxious worrying and saving: a room with a stove in a public institution where they could gather their few mementos around them and could count on a stranger bringing them soup if they took sick. That was of course what the room was for: so they could spend their last days all alone without bothering anyone and then die.

Their cheerfulness was a little loud and forcible. All the ladies spoke with a certain importunity of their inner satisfaction, of their rewarding professional duties, of the difficulties of marriage, and the beauty of their free lives as single girls.

Beauty — O dear, good God! Where could you find the tiniest spark of beauty there? Like a secret guilt that other generations had burdened them with, the poor creatures had to drag along with them their physical infirmities, the graceless female body.

132

Agathe tried in vain to force herself to feel compassion. Her deepest instincts rebelled. Her delicate, pampered soul writhed with terror at the thought of being counted among this lot. And it had just about come to that point . . . . For surely she didn't want to join the half-grown children in the sleeping closet?

Interest and enthusiasm for the home for women? She shuddered at the thought as if confronted with the onset of decay.

. . . Prizes for the lottery? Yes, she promised to supply some, and she would be happy to buy some tickets.

She rose; she couldn't take it any longer. She felt as if the contagion of ugliness and age were stealing over her amidst this hard, barren cheerfulness.

Fräulein Kriebler was clearly hurt by her early departure.

"But we're having such a cozy time together! Of course I can't offer a lot. A gypsy tea!"

* * *

Agathe had counted on leaving with the misshapen teacher who lived near her. She felt a twinge of fear because she normally would not have been out on the street alone of an evening. But it was still almost light, and whole crowds of people streamed over the pavement. Artisans, shop girls, workers, families of townspeople with children were returning home from the beer gardens where in the heat and cigar smoke they had enjoyed the summer to the accompaniment of military music.

Summer . . . .

Was it possible that somewhere in the world, not so far away, broad fields of pale golden grain were ripening toward harvest while the fragrant evening breeze brushed long heavy waves in them, that summer was at this very hour drawing the pure spicy odor of resin out of dark fir trees in forests, where no birds twittered, that it was striding through the tall grass of the orchards, making the fruit plump and juicy?

Dust lay on the benches of the horsecar as well as on the women's skirts and the men's boots. It covered their pitiful finery, their hair whose shine it had dulled. It drew gray shadowy stripes across the faces of the children — sleepy, inundated with reprimands, pulled forward by their parents' hands toward the humid night in the disgusting air of their unhealthy homes.

Summer . . . .

Why did it dip all of nature in gold and green and ripening abundance, but make people tired, whiny, and cranky?

Was it because people alone could call themselves God's children and had to be tried, tormented, purified?

Her eyes dull with sadness, Agathe looked into the throng of people who clumsily pushed past her, steaming sweat. She was thirsty; her lips were dry and cracked. She dreamed of water that bubbled up under ferns and brightly over smooth pebbles.

But all the many people prevented her from getting to it. She was one of them, only one member of this multitude. The dust of the evening lay upon her too. Sweat steamed out of her pores too.

And she was very tired . . . . The little adolescent girls had giggled. The capable teachers had been merry. Laughing loudly, the impudent, painted girls claimed the sidewalk with their bright dresses . . . .

Why was she the only person who couldn't be happy? Never again? Why did she see more than others, who were, after all, cleverer and keener and knew the world better, people who accomplished something? Why did she see it everywhere — the frightening wretchedness and loathsomeness of every part of this social life? Why did she carry this secret knowledge like a stone upon her breast? Why did she continue to hearken to the melodious delight and ringing happiness that reached her ears from far, far away?

But that was sick too. And she didn't want to be sick. She wanted to be healthy. She wanted to be healthy with a vengeance! Whatever it cost. Just once to sit at the table of life and joyfully relish whatever she could snatch up for herself . . . . Was she really no longer capable of doing so?

In front of Agathe two women were walking down the street. One of them wore a gray dress and a little travelling hat and carried a purse. Agathe saw a knot of reddish brown hair beneath the hat. The other slouched and walked with a careless, shuffling step.

"No, no," the dainty little traveller said, "every woman can make a man fall in love with her so long as he doesn't happen to be madly in love with someone else."

"I really find that hard to believe . . . . You're saying then that every girl could get married?"

"Well, all of them *can*. If they concentrate their entire will on that one goal. Of course they mustn't . . . . "

The two women turned the corner and Agathe lost sight of them.

She had to pay attention now to the arrival of the horsecar she was to catch to complete her journey home. When she had gotten on, a gentleman made room for her next to him. She realized it was Raikendorf.

"My dear lady, so completely alone at this late hour?"

Raikendorf greeted her with a delicately hesitating press of her hand. Since Agathe had been familiar with his manner of shaking hands with ladies for well-nigh seven years, it naturally no longer made the least impression on her.

She hadn't seen Raikendorf for a long time. He was a district magistrate in a small neighboring town. But she was always glad to run into him even if at bottom she despised him. He knew how to get her to talk back. She always became animated and her cheeks flushed when she was with him.

"Oh," she said confidingly to him, "I'm in a very bad mood, completely melancholy! I was at a tea party with old maids."

"Terrible!" he cried with a shudder. "How did that happen? You don't belong with them!"

"They were all very superior girls," sighed Agathe. "No, it's awful of me to speak of them like that."

"Oh, don't be too scrupulous."

Both spoke in low voices so as to make it impossible for those around them to listen to their conversation.

"No, really. I really should be interested in their attempts to improve the lot of our sex. It's superficial and selfish of me, but — I can't explain what it is that repels me so. You see, for example, if one makes a harmless remark — I like violets — then they'll be sure to say, 'Yes if women would mobilize their intelligence, then they could establish nurseries for cultivating violets. These would make a good profit' . . . . If you make the observation 'The picture on the wall is crooked,' then you'll be sure to hear them say, 'That's what comes of having no system in women's education. When we have high schools, no picture anywhere in the world will be crooked . . . . '"

Raikendorf laughed.

"Oh, my dear lady, it's not much different with us men. Everyone simply has a hobby horse. And finally, happy is the man who has one. But seriously. Don't go there again! In the end one is seen as belonging to the social groups one frequents."

"But I do belong to them!"

"Nonsense! Pardon me . . . . Look at me. Well, for the time being, I don't see any little lines yet. Not one!"

". . . What wonderful roses you have there!"

"Aren't they? Frau von Thielen picked them for me. I was out on the river island in her garden this afternoon. Let's find one for you! One that looks like you? Shall we?"

Although his greenish eyes were merely little and not especially handsome, they could take on a friendly expression. And there was something so simple and natural about his manner of speaking.

He selected a beautiful, delicate tea rose, gave it to her silently, and she took the chosen flower with a hasty, "Oh, thank you so much."

Her cheeks flushed slightly with pleasure.

"You'll permit me of course to accompany you home?"

"Yes, I'd like that! I'm afraid at night alone on the street."

"It *is* unpleasant for a lady."

"We shouldn't be raised to be so dependent."

"Aha — the high schools? . . . You do see that you've found a protector just in time, don't you?"

"Yes, but it was only by chance."

"All good things in the world happen by chance."

"You mustn't talk like that."

"What do you want — I really would like to believe in Providence . . . but I, too, seldom see it at work. You are pious . . . . I think that's very nice! I really couldn't imagine you otherwise, with your gentle little face! We need to get off here. So — give me your hand. Careful!"

They had been the only remaining passengers for a while and had been able to chat undisturbed.

"Won't you take my arm?" asked the district magistrate. Agathe hesitated a second. Actually it was not customary . . . . She so wanted to . . . .

136

"It's easier to walk when you're in step," he said persuasively and she complied. He pressed her arm lightly to him. She felt his warm, powerful body as she walked comfortably at his side. She felt good, peaceful, and quiet.

"Are you returning to Evershagen tonight?" she asked.

"No, I'm staying in Meng's Hotel. I have a pied-à-terre there. It's how one makes bucolic isolation bearable."

"I can't imagine you at all in the country."

"Oh, now in the summertime it's pretty out there. Lots of going back and forth to the farms. And woods close by. I've acquired a pony cart. You really should visit me sometime. Then we'll have the ponies take us into the woods. How about it? Would you?"

"Oh, yes — only I don't know whether Papa . . . . "

"If I thought that you'd like to, I'd write to your parents and request the pleasure . . . . Perhaps your siblings could come too?"

"Eugenie wants to go to the shore and is in the middle of a lot of dressmaking," said Agathe. The determination to keep Eugenie away from the outing rose in her.

. . . Every woman can make a man fall in love with her as long as he isn't madly in love with someone else . . . .

And Raikendorf? Was he madly in love with someone else?

"So, when do we want to have you come visit?" he asked.

"Soon." Agathe answered quickly. "Otherwise it will certainly never happen."

Beneath the glow of the gaslight she raised her head and looked into Raikendorf's eyes. She had never before looked at a man this way. Not even Lutz.

She became completely dizzy with shame.

"Now we'll have to ask the heavens for sunshine. You're on a better footing with them. You do it for me," said Raikendorf after he had, as it were, transfixed her gaze with his eyes.

"Goodbye!" He pressed her hand. And she did not receive this slight indication of a fleeting affection with indifference as she had on countless other occasions.

When Raikendorf said "Goodbye," she was alarmed as if at an evil omen — they were the same words she had last heard from Lutz.

Was the Lord, her Savior, trying to warn her?

III.

The sunshine glanced merrily off the district magistrate's bald head when he raised his hat to greet the train that was puffing into the station with his guests. The restaurant proprietor, the two porters, and the station master of Evershagen watched, curious to see whom he would meet. He looked so pleased. A pretty picture the way he helped the dignified elderly couple out of the coach and the way the young girl lightly hopped out behind them. In her light summer dress Agathe was, despite all the sickness and hurt in her and the terrifying thoughts of becoming an old maid, still a vision that had to delight every unbiased eye. Blooming and healthy, her intelligent face rejoiced beneath the round straw hat with its large bow of blonde lace. Not a trace of fatigue after the journey. On the way she had bantered the whole time with young Dürnheim whom her parents had invited to join the outing.

She had left her puritanical side and her stern censorious expression at home. And instead this capacity to be happy, this ability to be charmed by the air and the green foliage and the sunshine. High-spirited movements, spunky little answers. All this suited her! Indeed, why didn't she display this rich and vivacious exuberance more often? It was a pretty substitute for the delicate poetry of the first bloom of youth.

A delicate, barely perceptible stamp of past suffering lay upon everything — the district magistrate with the bald head found that alluring.

How much or how little might such a girl actually know of life? How would her veiled, painfully shining eyes look if . . . .

The liaisons with the wives of his friends — they were nice of course. Certainly. Charming . . . but . . . it was all too familiar. Each of them only said the same thing the previous one in a similar situation had already said as well.

Besides, the Heidling girl was in any case a good housewife. After all, the privy councillor was particular about his food, particular about everything.

Dürnheim also fell in love with her on this day . . . . Well, well — she was exploiting the liberties and confidences of an old childhood friendship to attract him. Raikendorf noted it with pleasure. For him it increased the tension in which he had felt himself suspended in relationship to the girl since that recent evening.

If he intended to marry someday, it was high time. He calculated how old he had become in the meantime. In truth — so close to forty!

So . . . that was it . . . . Agathe simply was one of those girls who shouldn't be seen in the ballroom. The palette of her nature was much too fine for that. So naturally she had more or less the effect of an intimate water color in a vast annual exhibition. It was crazy of their dear parents to drag the poor things to places where their presence was out of place.

In an intimate circle . . . outdoors . . . at a nice coffee table like the one he had set up on the lawn behind his official residence . . . there she was charming and womanly in her pretty little light blue dress. The deuce . . . after all, you saw your wife more often at the coffee table than in the ballroom.

That painter had liked her too. She'd never be an embarrassment to his taste. That was very important.

Perhaps it wouldn't be at all stupid of him . . . . District Magistrate Raikendorf showed the ladies the beautiful old carved cupboards that belonged to the furnishings of the house, the numerous empty rooms — their ceilings were a little low but they looked fit for a lord. The house stood near the gate of the little town and had a view of a green meadow where Sedan Day was celebrated in the fall.[75]

"You really can make a charming home for yourself here," observed Frau Heidling.

"Yes, gracious lady, an old bachelor like me. Who would still take pity on me?"

"Believe me, one sometimes really yearns for a little understanding . . . . " This was said a little later to Agathe. "Tell me the future. Can you imagine that a young, pretty, clever girl would take such an old bald fellow . . . huh? Not much prospect?"

"Don't act so modest. At bottom you're really terribly conceited, you know."

"Agathe, child, come here."

"Mama, what do you want?"

"Put your shawl around your shoulders. It seemed to me just now that it was getting cool."

139

Mama Heidling was not one of those mothers who know how to get their daughters married. Of course she wanted it so badly, but the excitement made her clumsy.

The district magistrate thought it wise to reconsider the matter.

As they parted, he kissed Agathe's hand. After she had sat down in the train coach, he jumped onto the running board to clasp her thin, soft little fingers one more time.

"A lovely day," her parents said contentedly, favoring Agathe with their tenderness.

In the summer sunshine. Victory over a cool and jaded male heart. Yes — victory . . . .

And untrue to everything that seemed to her holy, right, and good . . . . The clear, pure ideal denied! Her flaws and good points consciously scrutinized to determine what could be ventured with them? Fitting together a model from experience and observation and conforming to it . . . playing out her role!

She had done what in her eyes was the lowest thing a girl could make herself culpable of — yes — she, herself.

She wanted to marry him — a man she didn't love. And it had to be precisely that man who had humiliated her at her first ball so she could never forget it, that man who had given her a foretaste of the bitter drink of her youth.

So that was how men were won over?

It was that simple? Just an arithmetic problem? And she had had to reach the age of twenty-four to find that out?

Don't keep on like that. No, don't repeat it . . . . Burning disdain, sore and bleeding hate, resigned joy . . . . And cowering in the deepest, darkest night of the emotions, the tremulous, rapacious desire to become intoxicated with what had been won.

Yes. A lovely day.

IV.

If Agathe had once pictured marriage in terms of a young couple, shoulder to shoulder, enveloped in the lily-white cloud of the bridal veil, looking out onto a dark park, now, whenever she contemplated the possibility of marrying Raikendorf, the first thing she saw before her was the coffee table in the sunny garden of the residence of the district magistrate. The carved cupboards also filled her imagination.

140

She opened them with their large ornate keys, placed piles of linens into them and little bags and tins with coffee and sugar. The many empty rooms in the beautiful old house had to be furnished. The drawing-room with the dark wood paneling; wine-colored wool felt curtains over the doors would make a grand impression; in the deep window niche, an armchair with griffin heads and soft brown leather cushions like the one in Woszenski's studio.

Did she have to tell Raikendorf about Lutz?

If she compared the two of them, she felt very apprehensive. When she was in love with Lutz, she had never thought of decorating and hiring a cook. After she had seen Raikendorf twice more and recognized that he was seriously courting her, she ceased making comparisons.

Her overstrung suffering subsided. How good it did her to feel so at peace and full of confidence. Perhaps the fact that there was a touch of resignation in it appeased the envy of the gods. And besides she really didn't believe in gods, but in a dear Father in Heaven. In the end God would grant her the happiness of good sense rather than the excessive, wild, senseless bliss she had once demanded of Him.

The district magistrate's bald head, his jaded and colorless eyes, his gold pince-nez and the incipient little paunch, the value he placed on food — Agathe accustomed herself to all this with a gentle joy. Every imperfection appeared to her almost a guarantee of her future.

Girls have to take what they can get.

Her lot will be not unlike her mother's, her friends'. She will remain in her circle. The wife of a bureaucrat — she knows very well what it's like. She knows a lot of bureaucrats' wives and all of them think and do and say and experience more or less the same thing. Whatever seeds of precious rare blossom she bore in her soul would remain hidden. But who will tell her then that the noble powers, the striving for free greatness wasn't an audacious and foolish self-deception?

Had she remained true to her first unhappy love? No.

Had she become the loyal handmaiden of her Savior? No.

In the end she was really no better than all the other girls.

Just to cease standing excluded on the fringe of the deep, holy, maturing experiences of life.

* * *

They planned to meet at the outdoor concert in the Wilhelms-garten. The district magistrate had promised to come in from Evers-hagen.

Mama had an attack of her migraine. And because Papa preferred staying home in the summer heat, Frau Heidling sent a message to Eugenie. But Eugenie peevishly refused the request to accompany Agathe.

Why hadn't they invited her to go on the outing to Evershagen? As if she had to stick with her seamstress the entire day! It seemed Agathe had set her sights on the district magistrate. Mama Heidling was making such an oddly muddled apology for that Evershagen business. She hoped Agathe wasn't getting stupid ideas into her head again! People like District Magistrate Raikendorf who are try-ing to build a successful career take a seventeen-year-old, if possible from the aristocracy, with money, or a young widow. Dear God, poor Agathe was in fact really past the marriageable age. When the opportunity presented itself, she must sound him out to prevent the dear child from making a fool of herself. Perhaps they could suggest that he come to Heringsdorf too. Actually that would be rather amusing . . . . But today? Don't think for a minute that the district magistrate will come in this heat! Give up the idea!

Agathe didn't give up the idea. She rejoiced from the bottom of her heart that Eugenie would not accompany her. She bravely sought her salvation with the Wendhagens; they were ready for fun at any temperature. With Lisbeth she felt much more secure and cheerful than under Eugenie's sharp, observant eyes. And to have escaped the loving solicitude of her mother for once — yes — terri-ble! But each time was a little holiday for her.

Raikendorf would take her home since the Wendhagens lived on the outskirts of town. From there they still had a long way alone to-gether. Would he offer her his arm again?

He did, and without asking he took hers with a cheerful, pro-prietary air.

She knew that he would speak now. She really did like him very, very much.

It happened quite naturally and was not as exciting as she had imagined. He simply told her that he wanted her for his little wife.

He used no romantic phrases whatsoever. They spoke of it like two old friends.

The door to the house was already locked. He assisted her as she opened it, and as she was about to slip away from him, he held her tightly in the shadow of the doorway and pulled her to him.

"Agathe . . . . " he implored softly.

A kiss — the first kiss on her lips . . . . A tremulous joy coursed through her senses . . . . But a light suddenly illuminated the vestibule; from the apartment on the ground floor voices and footsteps came out to meet them. Agathe pulled back. Raikendorf let go of her and shrugged his shoulders impatiently. He squeezed her hand.

"Till tomorrow, Agathe!"

"Till tomorrow! Good night!"

Agathe ran up the stairs. How fond she was of the man now! Tomorrow —

Tomorrow he will take her into his arms again so gently and firmly, and she will close her eyes . . . .

"Mama, dear, dear Mama! He's coming tomorrow morning . . . to see Papa . . . . Oh, mother of my heart . . . . I'm so very happy, you know! So happy! I really didn't think at all . . . . Oh, are you happy too? He's dear, isn't he? You know, he . . . . I can't tell you . . . what he's like to me. So kind!"

"Mama, he spoke of his income, whether it's sufficient for the two of us. I told him you had money . . . . That was all right, wasn't it? You're going to give me some of it, aren't you?"

"Sweetheart, what's mine is certainly yours too!"

"Of course I'll be so thrifty too! Really so thrifty! Oh, Mama, do you think . . . . "

"What, my child?"

Agathe laughed quietly.

"Nothing! I just thought . . . . No, I don't want to think that far ahead; otherwise I'll go crazy with joy. Tell Papa. He won't have anything against it? No — right?"

"Why should he? Papa esteems Raikendorf. He's supposed to be well regarded in high places. Go now, sleep, my dear, so that tomorrow you look nice and refreshed! Oh, my child, to think I've got to let you go!"

Gratitude, deep gratitude that bubbled up in her heart again and again, this gratitude flowed over the entire world of the girl's sensibilities like a quiet wide stream sparkling with sunshine. Gratitude was now her love; in her secret heart she called the man her savior, her redeemer.

Not a jubilant throwing of herself into all-consuming flames, no flaring up to the highest sublime beauty in intoxicated passion . . . .

No. Humble receiving, modest and busy cherishing and guarding the gift of happiness — this alone was what she desired now.

Never . . . she intended never to forget that on this evening Raikendorf had filled her . . . with pleasant hope. For that she would devote her entire existence to serving. She could never do too much to exalt him as her lord and to debase herself. Was it possible that there had been moments in which she had despised him, had scoffed at him? Him? Him whose feet she would have kissed today, bathed with her tears and dried with her fragrant hair? [76]

When she entered the living room early the next day she suddenly remembered the evening when Martin Greffinger had given her the socialist writings in order to help her.

O dear God!

She really had to laugh about that. What possible relevance could the common people have for her! They were a matter of complete indifference to her! She was as little concerned about them as she would have been if all the princes on earth had suddenly had their heads lopped off.

What she desired, what she needed, the only thing in the world that meant anything to her — she was to have the privilege of holding that creature on her lap in its helpless, soft, charming tininess: a child, a child!

My God, if, while she was preoccupied with this hope, someone had told her that she would have to endure blows, abuse from Raikendorf, she would have smiled and answered distractedly, "Yes, gladly!"

Her father sat behind his newspaper. His face, as he lifted it fleetingly in response to her morning greeting, was serious and careworn. He didn't answer her.

Agathe pursued her mother.

"What's wrong with Papa? Isn't he pleased?"

Her mother had been crying.

"Dear child, you can't ask him to relinquish you gladly. You're our sunshine. He is . . . I thought . . . he always had so many favor-

144

able things to say about Herr Raikendorf. Now suddenly . . . but it will work out! You know, Agathe, he finds it very unpleasant that you said something about my money."

"Yes, but . . . I really had to . . . . "

"I've never concerned myself with managing it. Papa knows much more about that. But Papa says we've suffered a lot of losses. Well, never mind! We'll adjust. We'll take a smaller apartment, and when you're gone, we'll also need only one maid. I've already calculated it for Papa. Your happiness is truly the most important thing for us."

The talk between the privy councillor and Raikendorf lasted a very long time. Agathe could detect irritation in her father's voice. She couldn't understand any of their words. Once again her fate was being negotiated behind closed doors — like back then when the doctors deliberated whether she would ultimately perish of a protracted illness or whether she would recover. And they didn't allow her to have a say, to ask, to hear the pros and cons. She had to sit patiently, her hands in her lap, and wait to hear what had been decided about her.

My God, my God, do have mercy!

She didn't turn to the Savior. She feared Him. He demanded renunciation and bearing the cross. Instinctively she felt herself pushed toward God, the Father, the Creator and Preserver of all life.

She kept thinking that now, as in that other terrible hour, she would have to hear that liberating laughter . . . .

A door opened. Papa and Raikendorf were speaking with one another quietly, circumspectly — so gloomily as if someone had died. Was he leaving . . . without coming to her?

She held onto the window bar and stared out onto the street. Raikendorf emerged from the door and without looking up he slowly departed.

"Mama!" shrieked Agathe hoarsely, "Do something; look what's happening!"

Her father came in to her. When he looked at Agathe and saw her little face contorted with fear, he signaled to his wife. He couldn't tell her. Her mother would probably find better words. After all, she had had to deliver the first blow once before.

" . . . You're a sensible girl . . . . Up to now Papa has kept it from us . . . he thought we wouldn't be discreet — on account of

Eugenie. Walter had debts . . . gambling . . . before he got engaged. Papa had to pay them, otherwise . . . on account of his position . . . . And he has such a strong sense of honor. We've spent a lot; there's nothing left of my money. He wanted to spare me the worry. My good, sensible girl . . . . "

Frau Heidling held Agathe's hand and caressed it incessantly as if she could thereby stroke her twitching heart into a magnetic slumber.

She feared for Agathe's health . . . . And in an almost cowardly fashion, insidiously absolving her husband of blame, she began, "If Raikendorf had really loved you . . . . "

"Mama!" screamed Agathe angrily. "He simply can't! He's got debts too! He was honest with me!"

She tore her hand from her mother's and went to her room.

* * *

That evening Walter and Eugenie ate with their parents. They were planning to go to Heringsdorf in a few days. It would be the family's last time together for a while. The privy councillor didn't want his wife to cancel.

"Doing that would only give rise to talk. It won't hurt the girl to pull herself together."

* * *

"Listen, Agathe, what's eating you?" asked Walter at supper. "You've really got such a sentimental look of misery on your face! Did your district magistrate make you mad!"

"Leave your sister alone. She has a headache," his father commanded irritably.

Agathe was overcome with trembling; her entire face contorted into a frightening grimace. She rose and hurried out. If she had remained, she would have thrown herself upon her brother. She suddenly felt something like an inner wild and terrible power that wrested itself from its shackles and that could no longer be held in check.

"That's really the limit!" cried Walter. "You can't even make a harmless joke with her any more! What a foolish, touchy female!"

146

"You're awfully hard on her," his mother said anxiously. "Agathe has her troubles too."

"But Mama, she's really unbearably touchy," said Eugenie.

"What kind of troubles does *she* have?" interrupted Walter. "She should thank God she has it so good. What then? I've got problems with my job, trouble with recruits, and ill-treatment from my superiors. Such a young girl in contrast . . . . Nothing in the whole wide world to do but fix herself up and look happy . . . . I say it's the crochets of an old maid."

"But when we pass on, there will be no one there to take care of her," Frau Heidling lamented in a sorry, wretched tone.

Her husband cast a stern look at her. It injured his pride to speak of this matter with Walter and his rich wife.

"First of all dying is still a long way off," the young officer began, "and then she has us of course."

"Yes, right, Walter; you promise me you'll never abandon your sister!"

"But of course, Mama!" This unnecessary solemnity now suddenly between salad and scrambled eggs. How hard women took everything! Well, Eugenie, thank God, had no nerves at all. "Naturally Agathe will move in with us. Right, little wife?"

"Well, she can take the children on walks if she wants to make herself useful. We could save ourselves the cost of a governess," Eugenie said carelessly.

"You see, Mama," said Walter bringing the conversation to a close with a satisfied air. "She'll find work to do at our house all right. Some day when we've got a little girl to match the boy . . . . Well, give me another slice of roast."

V.

It did appear as if with time Agathe had become more sensible. She didn't suffer a violent hemorrhage. She didn't even think that every hope for her future was at an end; rather she gritted her teeth and thought, "All right, then Dürnheim!"

More than ever before she devoted her time and energy to taking care of her body and attending to her clothes.

How had Uncle Gustav's ex-wife gotten the Majoratsherr to marry her? [77] She had no longer been young, certainly older than

147

Agathe, and on top of that she'd had a bad reputation. The daughter of a man who ran a domestics service — what attracted men to her? Indeed not adventurers but good, respectable men like Uncle Gustav and aristocratic traditionalists like her second husband, the Majoratsherr? Agathe was discovering that in these matters forces were at play that had nothing to do with what her teachers had taught her. She would have liked to get a clear picture of them so she could decide whether or not she would and could employ them.

She had always been proud to be what she appeared to be: an innocent, naive young girl. During the last few years Christianity had surrounded her with a wall even more solid and stern than that encircling her girlfriends. She hadn't wanted to hear anything about the things of this world, but rather to win a place in heaven, to force her way through the thorn-braced portals to the ineffable peace of the children of God.

Since Raikendorf had almost kissed her, she dreamed only of this kiss — no longer of him, of him as an individual, but only of the kiss that she had thought she felt before it vanished into thin air. It was her last thought before falling asleep and her first upon awakening.

Meanwhile her belief in God had almost completely melted away. The Savior whom she had striven to love so ardently had become alien and a matter of indifference to her. She didn't suffer doubt; it was just that religious feelings and ideas increasingly lost the power to influence her. She turned her back on them with quiet aversion.

A thirst for understanding what was happening around her replaced them.

Agathe assumed an increasingly animated presence. She talked and laughed as never before. Her eyes lost that look of deep spiritual rapture and focused squarely on things and people. She began reading novels — eagerly and with pleasure — the kind of novels that young girls were not permitted to read and that she hid whenever anyone approached. To her astonishment she noticed that her mother liked reading them too, even though she inveighed against them and said she didn't understand how people could come up with such nonsense.

If people were talking about one of these books at a social gathering and Agathe was asked whether she had read it, she would answer without blushing, "No, I think one simply can't."

The gentlemen of her acquaintance would explain to her then that you couldn't deny some of these works a certain value. But if they were to imagine that they had to associate with a young lady who had read that sort of thing — no, that would have been extraordinarily embarrassing for them.

Sometimes Agathe thought that if she were still to marry, it could never become an ideal marriage for her. She could never confess to any man so much of what had already gone through her head. And a true marriage was not possible without complete mutual trust. So any effort she continued to make was hardly on account of this objective, but only because an inner restlessness spurred her on to a constant search for love and admiration. To be kissed just once became an obsession.

Did it have to be a proper engagement? Other kinds of kisses *were* conceivable? Yes, certainly conceivable . . . conceivable! But the habit of a lifetime covered Agathe with a stout shield. She dreamed the most passionate adventures . . . but outwardly remained the refined, reticent girl. Not out of hypocrisy. She couldn't do otherwise, even if she wanted to. She toyed with the danger she longed for until she instinctively recoiled at a man's slightest physical advance.

Not in chaste innocence, for she was no longer a child. She was awakened, a mature, ardent woman. Her fantasy life and her feelings were no longer innocent. It was only an enduring battle between her individual nature and the creature into which she had molded herself according to a venerable ideal that was thousands of years old. And there was a wild, skittish arrogance in her: her self — this well-guarded treasure, could she give it to a man who demanded only imitation gold and who might then his whole life long consider her, Agathe Heidling, to be imitation gold?

Her parents were pleased that she seemed not to have taken her disappointment to heart. During the following winter she danced as much as she could, attracted a number of young people who came to call on the Heidlings. They flattered her, said how well-preserved she was; in the evening you might well take her for a very young girl. Only she was more charming than before.

For two whole winters Dürnheim considered whether he shouldn't court her — his cousin Raikendorf had warned him to be sure — but in the end he married the little Romme girl after all. Uncle Gustav reported that she brought thirty thousand thalers cash into the marriage.

For two winters Agathe had fought with flagging energy, not exactly for Dürnheim alone — for every new man, for a glance, for a smile. And the secret defeats that she alone knew! The regret, the shame, the boredom, finally more and more a feeling that she had lost her self, that she was tottering through the flight of appearances, a withering form without content and without spirit.

VI.

The Heidlings were celebrating a lovely occasion. Old Kitchen Dottie was getting the prize for twenty-five years of loyal service to one master and for spotless moral conduct.

All of the members of the family had gathered to honor the loyal maid. They formed a circle around Dottie as the privy councillor, on behalf of Her Imperial Majesty, presented her with the Bible and the iron cross that the empress had sponsored for this purpose. He read the accompanying official document in a loud, solemn voice.

Frau Heidling and Agathe dried their eyes. Nowadays one could say of few employers that a servant had stuck it out with them so long.

The other maids in the household who had crowded into the doorway, modest and curious, were to follow the good example of the woman celebrating her jubilee.

The privy councillor seized the opportunity to weave into the celebration a few warm words about the blessings that crowned the performance of one's duty and that granted an inner satisfaction deeper than the pleasure-seeking that nowadays was gaining the upper hand.

The maids were moved to tears: their master, the privy councillor, did speak so beautifully!

Then Dottie was led to the table with her presents. Her mole's eyes, nearly hidden by her countless wrinkles, squinted from the sparkling of the twenty-five candles encircling a splendid torte that occupied the center of the table.

With an unintelligible grumbling that was supposed to express her satisfaction, Dottie fingered the cashmere dress presented her by the privy councillor's wife, a purse filled with gold pieces — one hundred marks! — and the gifts that Fräulein Agathe, the young Heidlings, and Uncle Gustav had contributed.

Little Wolf, a sturdy little fellow, held in his fat little paws a box with a white silk shawl. He was to present it to the honoree, but because he liked the colorful picture on the lid, he would not give it up, ran away with it and bawled terribly when his mother caught him and took it from him. Thus the festive atmosphere was disturbed. Still it was the only moment when a smile, like a pale winter sunbeam through dry gray tree branches, strenuously worked its way through the wrinkles on Dottie's peevish old face.

"Hey, hey! Little Wolfy!" she said full of pious admiration, crumbling off a piece of the festive torte she had baked herself and pushing it into the little mouth which was open wide with screaming. Consoled, it closed over the sweet.

"Dottie, you really mustn't . . . . " Frau Eugenie admonished.

"Today Dottie is permitted to do what she wants, even upset our boy's stomach!" cried Lieutenant Heidling in good spirits, and the housemaids giggled.

They had to examine the presents too — Lina from the wholesale merchants' family and Rika from the professor's family above them and the lieutenant's Sophie. Perhaps it would in fact have a good influence on the frivolous, transient, lazy crew, the privy councillor's wife mused.

The Pomeranian village child Wiesing had not been with the Heidlings for some time. In the middle of the quarter they had had to send her packing and make do with a thieving charwoman. And the girl had made such a nice impression at first.

Dottie ate her midday meal at the table of her masters. The thin gray braid of her hair wound into a tiny little knot, a modest snood over the thin partings of hair, wearing her black church dress, on her breast the silver cross of honor — thus she sat quietly and stiffly upon her garlanded chair, an alien figure in the circle of the elegant middle-class family that she had served for a quarter of a century, preparing their food, in the cold of winter and the heat of summer, cooking while they were still asleep and clattering dishes after they had gone to bed — one day like all the others — for twenty-five years.

Did she feel it was a high honor once and only once to have the privilege of sitting at the table to which she had attended for so long?

Who of the family, who had lived a quarter of a century with her in the same house, slept under the same roof, had a clear and definite idea of the thoughts and feelings that dwelled behind these dull little red-rimmed eyes? They patted her on the shoulder. They squeezed her hand, which was crippled into knots with gout. They said kind words of acknowledgment to her. Old Kitchen Dottie nevertheless was and remained a stranger to them. And the conversation stagnated because they were embarrassed by her unaccustomed presence at table.

When they clinked their wine classes to her health and she had gotten a piece of torte on her plate, she stood up and made her way back to the kitchen despite everyone's protest.

Later Agathe found her there with the official writ spread out in front of her, her glasses on her nose, laboriously deciphering the convoluted officialese word for word.

So she had lived for this.

The church dress had already been taken off, the cross deposited in the chest with the hymnal, and Dottie pushed up her sleeves from her bony brown arms and poured boiling water into the bowls to wash up.

"But, Dottie, do leave that to the housemaid today!"

"She's fixin' to go," the old woman snarled. "Runnin' to the door every other minute to see if her feller ain't there. Go on back in now, Fräulein."

Agathe would have liked to say something to her that expressed respect or admiration. But it stuck in her throat. She had the vague sense of their having in some fashion used the official document, the Bible, and the cross of honor to cheat this shriveled old creature out of the best part of this existence. And it kept her from speaking as she would have wished.

* * *

From Agathe's diary:

Just once to look into oneself. . . . There the waters of the misery that lick at the weak spots of my heart plunge and churn over all

152

the embankments thrown up by good sense. Helpless struggle —
the fear of a drowning person. And all the while crocheting edgings
for curtains and embroidering doilies. How many doilies have I actually embroidered in my life?

No great suffering that elevates and purifies . . . . I know, I
know — carnal. Torturous, torturous, but common, low.

The slow starvation of a queen who has not learned to beg!

Yes, that sounds lovely . . . .

But —

Why don't you steal if you're starving, poor rabble? They laud
the victors, not the vanquished! . . . They laud Messalina . . . .[78]

* * *

A dark blue lake . . . high, high up in the Alps. Completely isolated. Barren, gray boulders — and snowcaps. And it would have to
be evening — roses strewn upon the deep blue — roses of the setting sun.

Softly, slowly, gradually . . . . How the water, warmed by the
beaming light of the day, swells upward along the limbs to the heart,
and the eyes close . . . The bottom dissolves . . . .

When the fish brush their fins lightly and silently over my forehead . . . . When long slimy water plants grow out of my eye sock-
ets . . . when the dampness down there deep in the darkness seeps
through my flesh and destroys it . . . . Will I still feel pain then?

VII.

An old woman had come up the back stairs and asked to speak with
the gracious Fräulein Heidling in person. When Agathe entered the
kitchen she gave her a stained piece of paper that had been hastily
folded.

A begging letter.

Large, clumsy letters of an unpracticed childish hand, scribbled in
pencil — Agathe could make it out only with difficulty.

The Write Honerable Frölen Heidling!

Scuse me for applyin to you with my kreat need, most honerable
Frölen my little one died on me an they wanna take it to the medical
school for the students an Ive took sick who will pay for the Coffin?

153

most honorable Frölen if youd have the kreat goodness an a pittance for that, its too hard that my little one shant lie in the graveyard most honorable Frölen Im ernestly beggin your pardon livin at Widow Krämerns.

Your servant
Luisa Groterjahn

"Luisa Groterjahn . . . . " Agathe repeated. The amiable figure of the little, round, flaxen-haired housemaid passed before her mind's eye.

"Luisa was in service in this house, ya know, an' she said she took Holy Communion together with the gracious Fräulein," the old woman explained with a ready tongue, and she looked Agathe up and down with leering cross-eyed glances. "So I says to her, Luisa, I says, turn to the gracious Fräulein. She owes two month's rent too, ya know, but I'm a good Christian an' I ain't gonna throw nobody out on the street, right Freilein,[79] may God preserve me from that, an' a course you're glad to deliver a message an' run around for such a poor gal an' at first I couldn't find the address . . . . "

"What did the child die of?" asked Agathe impatiently.

With a woebegone look the old woman raised her eyes to heaven. "Such a little angel," she lamented, affecting a distasteful sentimentality. "I always said so, Luisa, I says to her, the little kid's gonna starve on ya. Freilein — a person like me — God knows, we got our own troubles. She's been layin' there for four months now coughin' up blood. Not earnin' nothin', nothin' t'all — a little one like that packs it in soon enough. Tsk, tsk, God Almighty, that I should live to see somethin' like that happen in my house."

"I want to come," Agathe murmured. "Today. What needs to be done so that the child won't . . . . My God, I had no idea something like this could happen!"

"Oh, Freilein," Dottie said fiercely. "Poor people — no one asks whether they cry themselves to bits."

The old woman offered to speak with the gravedigger and to tend to everything that needed to be done. The expression on her face oscillated between servile humility and low cunning. She didn't inspire confidence, but one probably did have to rely on her help.

"Dottie," Agathe said in a downcast voice, "we won't tell Mama anything about these things. I'll find out first how things stand."

The old cook grumbled unintelligibly.

Four years lay between today and the evening when Wiesing departed sobbing with her box and her service book,[80] a quarter year's wages, and the colorful little pictures from her chamber.

Of course not all employers judged their maids' love affairs so harshly. The privy councillor's wife couldn't understand this. The Wutrows had twice rehired a cook. Having such a female in one's proximity — a horrible thought! To be sure she *was* an excellent cook.

Well. Frau Wutrow . . . . They were related through the children and got along politely and amicably with one another, but approve of everything Frau Wutrow did on this account? No one could demand that. Frau Wutrow often closed one eye when material advantage was at stake.

Agathe hadn't spoken a single word on Wiesing's behalf. The girl made her uncomfortable as a result of the experience she associated with her person.

Agathe went slowly down the monotonous street that was occupied by tall, dirty buildings. It led to the city limits where the barracks of the infantry lay. Here the display windows were no longer elegant and shining, but stuffed with tasteless junk. Restaurants abutted taverns and taverns abutted sausage stands and wretched fruit hucksters' shops where the sons of Mars picked up their breakfast. The children on the sidewalks played soldier. Military troops marched in and out.

After some searching Agathe found the house where the Krämern woman was supposed to live. On the threshold squatted a pale child with an infant in her arms. She eyed Agathe with curiosity.

In the entrance hall, which was like a dark, evil-smelling abyss, a glass door on the right led up a few steps to a grogshop. Agathe groped her way to the steep staircase and began climbing it. In the scant light she had a hard time reading the nameplates on the doors. The staircase became steeper and more dangerous and slippery with the damp dirt. Lost in sad thoughts, Agathe hadn't paid attention to how high she had climbed and didn't know at which of the many doors she should knock or ring; up here there were no longer any nameplates. Then she noticed that the child from the threshold had followed her. She limped and nevertheless was carrying the heavy infant.

"Can you tell me whether Frau Krämern lives here?"

She didn't respond.

In the end Agathe just picked a door and knocked. A man in a woolen shirt opened the door.

"Frau Krämern?" Agathe asked shyly. "Or Luisa Groterjahn?"

"Her, ya wanna see her?"

His tone of voice expressed scornful disdain. "Over there."

He stared after her until she vanished behind the door he had indicated. The limping child pushed through the door along with Agathe.

"Krämern ain't there," the child said then.

"But I'd like to speak with Luisa Groterjahn."

Silently the little girl indicated an interior door.

Agathe entered an attic room with a slanting ceiling. It held nothing but a bed and a wooden footstool. Light entered from a hatch in the ceiling and fell directly upon the sick woman on her straw mattress. She lay motionless. Agathe thought she was sleeping because she didn't turn her head when she entered. But her eyes were open and were gazing at the gray wall at the foot of her bed, if one could call this indifferent staring a gaze.

Not until Agathe stood right next to the bed and placed her hand quietly and gently upon that of the sick girl and said a heartfelt "Wiesing, poor Wiesing," did the dull eyes turn toward her.

Agathe had imagined that Wiesing would be happy to see her. But the sick girl didn't smile. She didn't cry either. Her features remained completely impassive.

Agathe thought of the round face of the child who had peered into the world, healthy and happy . . . . Health had hastened from it; it bore a cadaverous hue with greenish yellow shadows around the mouth and the eyes, and it was very emaciated. But that wasn't what shocked Agathe so deeply; it was the expression of immeasurable, dull indifference upon it.

She was surprised that this creature had still cried out for help.

Pain sent tears spilling out of Agathe's eyes. She bent over and kissed the girl on the forehead. Then she sat on the edge of the bed, took her hand and caressed it softly.

Wiesing silently let her do what she wanted with her.

"Thanks a lot for comin'," she murmured after a long while.

"Wiesing, why didn't you send a message sooner?"

"The Frau Privy Councillor was so angry."

"Oh, that was a long time ago; it's long forgotten." Agathe knew she was lying. Her mother was still angry.

"Wiesing, why didn't you go into service again?"

"I was always a little weak. The birth of the little one was so hard. An' then he was always sick — We intended to get married too. If he could get out after two years."[81]

Wiesing was silent and stared at the gray, scratched-up wall that was smeared with names and disgusting graffiti.

"Didn't he get out?"

A slight shake of the head.

Agathe tried once again to fathom the story of this life. Then she ceased trying. It was useless cruelty.

The sick girl's pale lips, which were covered with a dry crust, remained firmly closed as if over a dark secret.

"Is this Krämern woman good to you?"

Wiesing withdrew her hand from Agathe's and turned her face to the wall.

Both girls were silent.

Outside there was a shuffling. The door was unlatched. Frau Krämern barged in hastily and with her the limping child with the dirty infant.

"Well I'll be, the gracious lambkin took the trouble to come here! Well I'll be, Luisa, what an honor! I've taken care of everything — a coffin for the child, an' the reverend pastor'll say a prayer; the little angel's already in the mortuary. Here, everything's written down. Not a penny too many. Tomorrow your little one'll be put in the ground. Oh, such misery. Well, I tell ya."

She blew her nose into her blue apron.

A soft whimpering emerged from the straw mattress.

"Shall I bring you a lovely wreath for your little one?" whispered Agathe, bending over the sick girl.

Wiesing opened her closed eyelids. "Oh, Frölen!"

"Yes, I'll bring it tomorrow. You can count on it."

She gave the old woman money for soup and wine.

On the way home she got flowers. She wove the wreath in secret in her room. Her conscience was severely tortured.

In the afternoon of the following day just as she was leaving someone paid a call. She was held up until five o'clock and had to search for a lot of excuses simply to get away.

157

She strode hurriedly through streets swept with a harsh, sharp easterly wind. It was already getting dark so early.

As she was about to pass by the grogshop on the ground floor of the building, a couple of male heads appeared in the doorway. "Fräulein, come in!" they called to her.

Breathless, she ran up the stairs. Up there she took the wreath out of her bag and laid it on the bed before Wiesing. The sick girl didn't say anything; she softly fingered the bright flowers. A moist gleam gathered in the staring pale eyes. Two teardrops trickled down the gray cheeks.

Frau Krämern came as soon as she heard Agathe. And immediately thereafter the limping child entered noisily. With a knowing, spiteful laugh she stationed herself in front of Agathe and said, "Greetin's from the gentlemen downstairs, an' the Freilein should come on down an' eat roast goose."

At first Agathe didn't understand the girl. The Krämern woman had to explain the offer. "Well, Freilein, don't I always say it! Every good deed does immediately bring its reward! For visitin' Luisa the good Lord immediately gives ya the roast goose!"

Agathe froze in the face of this naive vulgarity. Wiesing had lived here . . . throughout these four years.

How should she get past that ghastly door downstairs? Her father was right to forbid her visits to the poor on her own. Fear and hopelessness descended like a fog over her thoughts.

"Shouldn't I write your mother to fetch you home?" she said irresolutely.

Wiesing shook her head very slightly. She began to cough, tried in vain to sit up and catch her breath. Agathe took hold of her and held her. Her throat had once rattled like that; she herself had once struggled like that . . . . Think what all had been done for her!

"Wiesing, I want to send a doctor to you . . . . "

Oh! The terrible smell in the chamber. And the icy cold . . . . How dirty the bed was.

"No doctor!" the sick girl stammered, and her hands waved through the air with a febrile restlessness.

But Agathe wanted to ask their family doctor to look in on the girl.

The Krämern woman, eager to serve, tried to accompany her downstairs, but Agathe put her off stiffly and haughtily.

On the stairs the man with the roast goose came to mind again.

He stood waiting at the glass door and laughed loudly when he saw her. Agathe became dizzy with fright.

"Not so fast!" he roared and reached for her arm. She tore herself loose and plunged out onto the street. Booming laughter sounded after her. She ran more than she walked — just get away, away from this part of town.

She arrived home with a stupefying headache.

For several days she couldn't make up her mind to visit Wiesing again. She was sick and miserable. She couldn't really help her either. With frightening clarity the roast goose affair suddenly showed her pictures from life in the filthy abyss into which the unfortunate girl had plunged.

She no longer dared to communicate with the family doctor, as if she alone had been informed of the horrible world there and must not speak of it to anyone — no one.

But it gave her no peace. She had to get the girl out of this environment. She had at least to see to it that she got something to eat. If she went early in the morning, probably there wouldn't be any men sitting in the tavern who would bother her.

This time a woman emerged from the door opposite Frau Krämern's apartment and came toward her. She looked clean like a decent working man's wife. So Agathe stopped politely when she spoke to her.

"Fräulein, are ya fixin' to visit that there gal again?" she asked.

"Yes. Do you know Luisa? She seems very sick to me."

"They took her away yesterday."

"Away? Where to?" asked Agathe.

"Well, to the mortuary."

Agathe was aghast and said nothing.

"My husband says the Fräulein certainly don't know what kind of person that one was."

Agathe sighed.

"Oh, dear lady, she did have so many troubles."

"I certainly ain't denyin' that — Well! When Krämern gets her hands on a gal like that . . . . "

"You mean she wasn't kind to her?"

"Her? That old beast? Fräulein . . . she slurped down your soup out here, well, an' she drank the wine right away down there in the grogshop. Well, the gal didn't swallow a drop of it. Yeah, if the rich people knew who they was givin' their money to. My husband an' I don't ask nobody for alms; we tough it out, we work, yeah, but that rabble, they have their ways of gettin' by!"

"Oh, but she's dead now," Agathe said sadly.

"Well, I won't say nothin' against the gal. That's how it goes. That Krämern really exploited her. What was she s'posed to do? Her little kid hadta eat. No, my husband says we're leavin' too. The police is always comin' here. What a mess!"

Agathe turned around and went back down the stairs. Perhaps envy drove the woman to speak like that. But who could ever learn the truth of the matter!

VIII.

If Mama hadn't been so outraged back then, if she hadn't so mercilessly sent Wiesing packing — of course Agathe herself had also turned her back on her in disgust — if they had tended to her in her hour of need and seen to it that the child was placed with decent people and if perhaps they had raised the girl's wages so that she could pay the child's board, would she have fallen then into the hands of this Krämern woman, would her young life have ended with that dull gazing at that dirty, gray, scratched-up wall with the hundred names and the revolting pictures?

But that would have been immoral and so it simply couldn't have been permitted.

Indeed a girl had to be terribly frivolous to forget herself to such a degree.

And if Lutz had wanted to . . . .

O my God! Why was that wrong, and then suddenly after the pastor speaks a few words, the terrible infamy became a well-earned right? It was a ghastly secret.

Agathe had seen the misery now, the lethal misery. And the police had been involved too? Who could know what disgusting things remained hidden there?

And this little girl, who on the same day together with her had happily embarked on life's journey, had seen, experienced and suffered all this in the few years since she had lost sight of her.

And she and her mother were guilty. Yes, yes, yes. They were guilty.

But Mama would never understand that. Agathe went to her and told her about Luisa's death and of the torment that she herself suffered on her account — and Mama remained calm and cool. "Yes, those females! They're all good-for-nothings; they're created to torment us," was her response.

How could it be? Her mother was otherwise such a good-natured woman. Why was she so completely blind in this one respect?

She recalled the severe judgment that Martin Greffinger had once pronounced upon the women of the bourgeoisie, upon their ossified narrow-mindedness. But *he* was a Social Democrat or some such thing. He couldn't be right! He couldn't be!

Agathe truly had no cause to be constantly so out of sorts or to lament her lot. That is, as of yet her ill humor was not visibly noticeable; thank God, she still had this degree of self-control. Of course she had it so good in comparison with that poor creature. And now she saw where it led when you indulged those thoughts of love and didn't keep up your guard against them. Naturally no man would dare tempt *her*, Agathe Heidling, the daughter of Privy Councillor Heidling. O dear God! Of course the gentlemen all treated her with the most refined respect. It verged on boring.

Yes — but — wasn't it an indication of appalling moral depravity, the fact that she in truth was on the verge of wishing . . . . Had she sunk so low? Who knows how quickly she will sink lower, lower . . . with nothing to stop her, with no return!

No fallen woman can ever reinstate herself, Papa once said, and as he said it, he was the picture of relentlessness like the angel with the fiery sword at the gate of paradise.

Probably nothing they could have done for the little housemaid would have helped — So just disappear, and quickly, into the mire.

And Eugenie? And the clerk in the room with the cigar samples? It was horrible that Agathe was still compelled to think of it.

All her dreams and fantasies were defiled with the poison of sin. How awful she was, how rotten through and through!

High time to put it behind her! All her praying and wailing to the Lord God for help had been fruitless. Who could know whether there was a God? In any case He had not revealed Himself to Agathe, had left her in the lurch.

She only had to get it through her head that her youth was over and that it was simply disgraceful to give herself over — in her more mature years — to such stupid ideas. Just give up hope, once and for all! She was already losing some of her hair. And when she laughed she no longer had a cute little dimple, but a genuine wrinkle.

So many girls never marry. Life did after all offer so many other beautiful things! And she had plenty of responsibilities; she really didn't need to seek any outside the home. Had she completely forgotten her vow to live only for her parents? She needed to be much more amiable and cheerful.

* * *

If Papa were to be transferred to Berlin . . . . That really would be another new beginning! She just didn't want to feel too happy about it; otherwise it would not come to pass.

And it didn't come to pass. Some minister of state had differences with another minister of state, or he supported a law that was not passed in the Reichstag — In short, he had to resign his post, and Papa didn't become superior counsellor in Berlin but was dismissed instead.[82] Naturally Agathe didn't learn how all that fit together. She wouldn't have understood it anyway, and it never would have occurred to the privy councillor to initiate a young girl into professional matters.

They had to make do with his pension. And besides that Papa had to pay a lot for life insurance. They let go of the second maid and took a smaller apartment where they rented a room to Uncle Gustav.

Uncle Gustav hadn't had much luck with *Fountain of Youth*. Besides Agathe's girlfriends to whom he gave it away, no one had inquired about the beauty wash. And so humanity hadn't become more beautiful nor Uncle Gustav richer. He still did think a lot about marrying some charming young heiress in order to promote his invention with her fortune. But in the meantime he boarded with his sister-in-law, for his stomach could no longer tolerate hotel food. Agathe calculated that the modest allowance her dear old uncle paid for board didn't begin to cover his needs. But every time he delivered up two gold pieces on the first of the month, Mama always thought she had put her hands on an inexhaustible treasure.

162

As a result of the alterations that were necessary on account of Papa's dismissal poor Mama had lost any semblance of composure. She burst into tears at the slightest provocation and was tortured by the fear that in the end they would all starve to death. If, however, a lace maker came by she couldn't resist buying tatted inserts for pillows for Agathe's hope chest. One had to deny oneself the smallest pleasures — and yet, always, the peculiar idea of putting things by for the hope chest.

Agathe had to work hard to keep the house clean and to keep the household running smoothly. One couldn't really rely on Dottie anymore either. Agathe was unaccustomed to real work and suffered a lot of sick spells that she concealed even from her mother, for Papa might hear about them, and that would have been horribly embarrassing for Agathe. Also he always became terribly irritated when something was wrong with either of them. It was important not to darken his mood still further; he was irritable enough already. No wonder! He had worn himself out working, sitting over his files late into the night in order to serve the state. Now the state suddenly tossed him overboard like a burdensome, superfluous piece of furniture — this vigorous man who didn't know what to do with his time now except pace all the rooms, looking for something to find fault with. What good had it done Papa, this incessant fear of giving offense, either upward or downward, either to the right or to the left? But heavens! If Agathe had ever held that up to Papa . . . . The face she would have seen!

The entire world was chock full of sanctities one was not permitted to touch as in her childhood when she had reverently contemplated the contents of Grandmama's trinket cabinet through the glass panes. She was tortured by nothing but thoughts for which she had to reproach herself. Within her boiled a continuous rebellion against every word her parents spoke. As long as she waited and kept on waiting, as long as tomorrow a new life might dawn for her — it had been easy to be patient for that long. But now that she saw this new life would never come, now that she had to adjust to things as they were as best she could — now she could scarcely bear it any longer — still being treated like a dear, stupid child whose opinions were laughable, the object of their jokes, or a child to be lectured and guided.

She had to muster a great deal of finesse to keep Mama from noticing that she was actually running the household. She had to consult with her continuously and at length about the simplest things because only then was Mama convinced that she herself was in charge and that she was guiding Agathe. The wishes, needs, and whims of three old people — actually it was four, for Dottie, too, was old and moody — needed to be catered to. Whenever they directly contradicted one another, one had to appear to do the bidding of each of them or to try to placate them in a tactful and kind manner.

Papa became angry at the slightest imposition on his comfort and the slightest marring of the elegant veneer of the household. Uncle Gustav had all kinds of habits from eating in restaurants, and it was hard to convince him that these cost them dearly given their limited budget. And Mama's scrimping verged on pathology. If she spent time with Frau Wutrow, she would get new recipes for saving money from her. At the Wutrows' they always mixed mashed potatoes with the butter for the seamstresses. The privy councillor's wife planned to put that into practice too. Agathe had quite a row with her because she felt ashamed in the presence of the maids. Recently Mama had demanded that the living room rug be swept with a light brush and rolled up every evening so that it would retain its color longer. Frau Heidling intended to do it herself in order to set her daughter a good example of humility. Agathe couldn't stand by and watch her do it. Unfortunately, just as she was sliding around on the floor on her hands and knees, Eugenie came upon the scene and made mocking remarks.

Of course she didn't have to do any such thing. If Mother Heidling felt such hankerings, then that was her own private pleasure and didn't much concern Eugenie. The young Heidlings had a manservant, the cook, the housemaid, and a nursemaid for little Wolf. Old Wutrow had to pay.

"You know, as an officer's wife, I . . . , " Eugenie said and in this fashion got whatever she wanted.

Every evening Agathe wept a few secret tears onto the rug; she found it so shabby and completely unnecessary and impractical to keep on rolling it up and rolling it out again.

Oh, life was so boring, boring, boring in this abundance of pointless work!

At least they spared her the balls now. She simply was no longer invited. But the two or three dinners to which she continued to be invited weren't exactly a heady pleasure either.

And the socializing with her girlfriends, with those who like her had remained unmarried? In the very moment she intended to visit this or that acquaintance she was often seized with such an aversion that she couldn't make up her mind to go.

She really couldn't speak a word of what she thought. She constantly had a guilty conscience. If anyone had suspected the terrible hours the elegant, serious, steady Fräulein Heidling suffered through! Just once to say everything you felt — that had to be a relief. To hear what things were like for others, how they managed to get by, whether they were resigned or sad, whether they bore their lot bravely or whether they lost heart . . . .

Strange. As little schoolgirls the friends had whispered in one another's ears whatever they could ferret out about the secrets of life that people hid from them. As pert adolescents they had conversed audaciously and happily about everything imaginable, and each of them had contributed something from the reservoir of her knowledge. Now that they had wandered this earth for twenty-eight to thirty years and none of them had had the misfortune to be born blind or dumb, they had forgotten all their experiences. They knew nothing; they hadn't a clue about anything — even when they were alone together.

Sometimes they even complained that they were still so ignorant.

". . . Just imagine. Recently I embarrassed myself terribly," said Lisbeth Wendhagen. "I asked about the affair with the Russian woman everyone's been talking about so much lately.[83] Do you think there's anything wrong with that?"

Naturally Agathe didn't think there was anything wrong with it.

"Eugenie said afterwards that as a young girl I wasn't allowed to ask about it in the presence of gentlemen. I don't have a clue what she meant."

"Oh, well, young married women, naturally they're *au fait.*"

Agathe was often downright disgusted by her friends. But one really did have to be very careful oneself.

IX.

Recently she had discovered a wonderful book in Papa's library. She had come across it during the big fall housecleaning. After she had read a chapter kneeling before the bookcase in the dust and draft, she couldn't put it down, took it with her to her bedroom and read it every evening in bed — they didn't turn on the heat in her room — and also after the midday meal when Mama was sleeping.

She had thought it would simply be incomprehensible to women. To her great astonishment she could follow the author quite well. She needed only to pay attention to what she was reading and then mull it over in her head during the day while she went about her various activities.

How it shook her out of her intellectual torpor, out of discontented semiconsciousness, so that she rubbed her eyes, planted her feet firmly on the ground and looked around her inquisitively.

In its effect it was comparable to a trip around the world, one with sublime backward glances into frightening past times and with telescopic views into a future filled with powers of development, oblivion of the self, and astonishing knowledge of one's own becoming as the result of countless series of ancestors, a trip with the discovery of new affinities . . . with thunderstorms and breaking masts, with the loss of luggage and the gaining of unsuspected riches.

To think that such a book existed and she hadn't known it! It stood ignored in the glass cupboard; she had seen its title while dusting who knows how often:

Haeckel's Natural History of Creation.[84]

And her father hadn't whooped for joy when he read it? How strange!

For a time one was always hearing those jokes about our descent from the apes that were all the rage until people had a surfeit of them and one no longer talked about it in polite society. Agathe also recalled having heard from the minister who preached in the cathedral that scholars had long since disregarded Darwin and Haeckel's viewpoint.

How could that be? Agathe couldn't believe it. One doesn't simply turn from such a fabulous new world view back to the same old boring agenda.

Oh, men who immersed themselves in the subject, men who had the opportunity to continue researching and brooding over it — how lucky they were! How lucky! Of course for them stupid love need only be a matter of little consequence! In the end she, too, found peace in these new ideas. She did see now that it had to be this way, that Nature was shockingly cruel, that millions of sprouts continuously perished so that the others had room to grow. So she was just another of the weak, useless sprouts — so what? She had, to be sure, already known that such waste existed. But she had never related it to herself; she had always sought a place for herself outside of Nature and had wrangled with a God who could work miracles and just didn't want to work one for her sake!

To sink into this manifold, immeasurably rich universe! To be completely at rest, completely at rest. And yet somehow alive! How interesting Nature had become to her. How wonderfully one could recover from disagreeable people among the beetles and flowers and marvelous rotifers.[85] And then again their incredible connections to human beings. She had to learn much, much more about all this.

When Christmas arrived she was finally looking forward to the new year again.

On the last page of the *Natural History of Creation* Agathe found a list of recommended books in case one wished to educate oneself further in the area of natural science. Recommended by Haeckel himself, by this splendid man!

She wrote down a lot of the names.

If only she had had an allowance as she used to! It had been a silly, good-natured gesture to forgo it in the first fright over the necessary restrictions her parents had to impose upon themselves. Now she asked for money only when a purchase was absolutely necessary.

She therefore deliberated for a long time before writing down two or three of the books on her Christmas list. Which were likely to be the most interesting? Which ones the most necessary? Actually it was like playing the lottery. Well, in any case she would ask for books again for her birthday and so on. She was already so old; in truth she needed to hurry in order to acquire even a part of this vast storehouse of knowledge.

She couldn't have had that; she wouldn't have found the time if she had been married. At last it seemed to her good for something that she had become an old maid!

Would Papa perhaps give her all three books? Or only two? He had been astounded when she had handed him her Christmas list.

"You've set your sights enormously high," he had said with a smile. "What kind of incomprehensible stuff do you want to cram into your little head?"

"Oh, Papa, I've got to educate myself a little!"

"Well, yes, I've nothing whatsoever against it."

"I understood the *Natural History of Creation* quite well."

"Hm. So you read that? That was quite unnecessary. Next time you'll ask me before you fetch something from my bookcase. Do you understand? Young girls often misinterpret works like that."

"The book with the terrible illustrations?" asked Frau Heidling. "But Agathe, I really wouldn't want to read anything like that."

"Mama, it's really very interesting. And if, if one doesn't get married, one has to have something one enjoys doing."

Agathe was ashamed of the childish manner in which she spoke about an issue that was truly difficult and more than serious. But there was no avoiding it; she felt it would seem affected to speak as she really felt.

"Well, we'll see," said the privy councillor.

She threw her arms around her father and kissed him stormily.

"You little whirlwind," he observed tenderly, patting her cheek. "And they call that an old maid!"

Agathe had the loveliest expectations. No. Her parents couldn't be so cruel, so cruel . . . they would surely fulfill her wish.

On her Christmas table she found a charming jabot of pink crepe — she had once admired it in a shop window — and a deluxe volume with colorful pictures: *The Flora of Central Germany, for the Use of our Daughters*; beside it, a carved flower press.

"You see, dear child," her father said amicably, "I've found a very pretty book here that suits you better than the books you wrote down there. I flipped through them. They didn't strike me at all as something for my little girl. You'll find instructions here about drying flowers. You girls are making the most charming lamp shades out of them these days! You'll enjoy that."

Agathe stared silently at the ground before her. She was compelled to think of the Herwegh they had exchanged for "Pious Pearl" back then . . . . Did everything always repeat itself in her life? And would it repeat itself in the same manner again in ten years?

168

Did everything in this world evolve into higher forms of existence and only she and her kind remained excluded from it? She was "the young girl" and had to remain so until they laid her in her coffin, withered and desiccated, with gray hair and a shrunken brain?

Didn't anyone know that it was cruel to tie a silk ribbon around a burgeoning flower in order to keep it a bud? Didn't anyone know that in the interior of the calyx it rotted and moldered?

Hot anger toward her father boiled up in Agathe every time she went through his study and her glance brushed past the bookcase that was now locked.

Of course he doesn't know what he's doing, she thought, defending him against herself.

Each day he took her in his arms and kissed her, in the morning and at night, but of what she had felt and struggled through her whole life long, of that he had no clue. How delicate and practiced the hand would have had to be, how kind and adroit the hand that could have coaxed out the dark instincts, the seething powers that in a silent battle were churning her soul to pieces, could have coaxed them out into the form of words.

X.

Uncle Gustav had died. Mama had found him dead in his bed this morning, almost in the same position in which she had tucked him in the night before. He had been poorly recently, but the doctor always assured them that with good care he could live months, even years longer. Mama and Agathe sat together in silence and wove a garland. Frau Heidling handed her daughter little bunches of greenery and flowers, but she often made mistakes. Both of them looked tired and wasted; Mama especially could hardly hold herself upright. Her energy had been consumed down to her last reserve by the demands of the sick man.

No matter what she and Agathe had come up with in the way of fortifying bites to eat, nothing tasted good to him. He pushed the plate away peevishly and told of this or that hotel cook who knew how to prepare the dish in question amazingly well. He constantly demanded to be entertained but usually interrupted his niece's efforts with the gloomy observation, "Oh, child, that doesn't interest me at all!" He took an interest in nothing in this world. It could almost be called a piece of luck that grooming himself filled many hours of the day. The "cherry blossom," as Agathe's girlfriends had called Uncle Gustav, remained clean and well-groomed till the end. Of course afterwards poor Mama, the only person allowed to aid the weak old gentleman with his toilette, always sank down on the sofa fainting with exhaustion.

Now the large easy chair in which Uncle Gustav had sat for six months, dressed in a long, gray dressing gown, was empty. On the table lay his pretty blonde wig. He had never let his niece see him without it.

His next of kin spoke sadly of this life which had melted away so silently. Frau Heidling told of the shining bloom of her brother-in-law's youth. At the time they had thought he couldn't fail to succeed. Everyone had prophesied that he would marry well.

The privy councillor paced the room gravely.

"That was his misfortune," he observed coming to a halt. "Gustav set his hopes and his plans on women instead of on himself. Naturally only a failed, foolish life could come of that. One should not speak ill of the dead, but what did human society, the state, what did he himself get out of his existence? No duties, no profession, no seeking his own perfection . . . . It was always the women, only the women! In the end women only made a fool of him!"

The privy councillor was silent. It was not a good idea to pursue his thoughts out loud in Agathe's presence.

Agathe picked up her garland and carried it into the room where her good Uncle Gustav had died and where he lay in his coffin. With gentle, careful movements she wrapped the greenery around his white pillow. How his face had collapsed now that they had removed his false teeth! A very old man — and yet he was not yet sixty.

No one grieved over his death — in the whole wide world, no one. Women had only made a fool of him.

Who will one day grieve for her? No one — in the whole wide world, no one. Love had only made a fool of her too.

* * *

Mama caught a cold at Uncle Gustav's burial and then completely collapsed.

This required a different kind of care from Uncle Gustav's. Waking nights, weeks of lethal agitation, a trembling fearing and waiting . . . . O God! O my God! Did she have to depart this earth?

Agathe nearly despaired at the idea.

No, then life would no longer be bearable. She, too, would end it then! Yes, for sure! Papa could move in with Eugenie and Walter.

"O Lord God, O merciful Savior, do not punish me for my faithlessness! Spare me my dear little mother! You know she's all I've got, all I've got!"

She didn't even ask for understanding, no spiritual community, just that she not lose this little bit of love and tenderness.

The same struggle, day and night . . . . It often seemed to Agathe that she wrestled, body against body, with death, seemed as if she would certainly win if she harnessed all of her forces to the extreme, didn't let up for a second, remained constantly vigilant . . . .

"I don't understand how Agathe bears it all," said Eugenie. "I wouldn't have thought the girl had so much strength."

"You don't discover what a person is capable of until you're in need," Walter remarked respectfully.

She ought to enlist the aid of a protestant nurse.

Well, then, all right! But what did the nurse know of this secret struggle? Would she, in the throes of mortal terror, rack her brains for the ruses that must be employed to drive away the terrible thing that stood invisible and waiting in the room right next to Agathe? Agathe felt it. She smelled it. She felt its presence, intangible and close by her and shuddered with chills of terror that penetrated the very marrow of her bones . . . . And yet she always found kind and comforting words for the sick woman.

No, the hired nurse wouldn't do that. She simply couldn't. She really couldn't know how vital it was that the tired and sad old woman not die! And thus her presence didn't help Agathe either. Agathe had to see it through alone.

Recently Agathe had stopped praying. Her heart had become numb as in all of the crises of her life. She didn't believe either that she would see her mother again. She couldn't imagine this patient visage, this tortured body transfigured, not the body she cared for with a thousand tendernesses. It would really no longer be her mother.

The sick woman often spoke of heaven and of her dead little children who awaited her there. Her eyes then took on such an expression of yearning that one could surmise how much of her emotional life the woman had laid in the grave with them. She hadn't grown with the living son and daughter. She had remained the mother of the little children. In lucid moments when she was free of pain she told Agathe little stories from her babyhood and whispered the terms of endearment with which she had once dandled the oblivious, wriggling little creature on her lap.

Agathe had to promise her innumerable times to take care of Papa, to make certain that he got everything just as he was accustomed, to stay with him always, to tend to him and to love him. And Agathe promised everything. How could she not? She was now united with her father in shared sorrow.

When Mama died, they clung to one another and wept together — at least in the first hours after her death. Later Papa recovered his peaceful, dignified composure, and Agathe hid her tears to keep from distressing him still more.

The memory of the dead woman now cast a shadow, as it were, over her entire daily existence, her slightest actions. Invisible ghostly hands ruled in the house and managed things as always according to the will and the idiosyncrasies of the dear departed woman.

As during her lifetime Agathe swept the rug in the living room every evening and then rolled it up. And now tears of longing for the past fell upon it.

She could have managed the household now as she wished. But this thought no longer gave her any pleasure. And she was not managing it for herself, but rather regarded it as the dead woman's venerable legacy. The responsibility she had assumed tormented her, and she wore herself out in feverish activity so that no one could reproach her with not being up to her holy task.

XI.

Agathe climbed the stairs to the attic. She had begun inventorying the old things that had been placed in her care. The boxes and crates up there were to be examined for this purpose as well. Eugenie took advantage of the opportunity to ask her to give her some of the little children's things that Mama had continued to hang on to — in the winter she had at last given birth to the little daughter Walter had so wished for in addition to the two boys. Mama had been so stubborn in that regard. She would not give up the least little thing. And of course these things were no longer of any use to Agathe.

As Agathe ascended the last steep flight of stairs, she suddenly felt the same affliction that had plagued her mother for many long years: on her body, spots the size of a thaler, spots raging with pain as if a mad animal had clamped its teeth into them.

Her mother had known why she suffered these torments. She, this delicate woman, had given birth to six children and had to watch four of them die. It was understandable then that her energies were exhausted and that abused Nature took revenge. In a certain respect Mama had always been proud of her suffering. She bore it as a part of her life, as woman's crown of thorns, destined for her for all eternity.

But why Agathe, a young girl who had been coddled and protected and had never done even the slightest thing for the human race, why should she attain to this terrible inheritance? It was of course downright unnatural. It was as if fate were maliciously mocking her! Was it the grief over her mother?

Wasn't it also unnatural that the death of a tired old woman who had fulfilled her destiny plunged her into such bottomless despair, unnatural that she wept whenever she was alone and couldn't pull herself together?

It couldn't go on like this! Indeed she was destroying herself.

She knew it. She felt it!

And suddenly she resolved to vanquish all her corporeal and spiritual suffering with the strength of her will. She mustered all her energy and spurred it into battle, directed it toward a goal.

She began to smile and to convince herself that nothing hurt her. She picked herself up and went about her work with a light, elastic tread, like a happy person suffused with desire for activity.

Warm, musty air filled the attic. Agathe pushed open a hatch. A beam of sunlight shot inside and spread out over the maze of rafters, among all the dusty objects that had wandered up here over the course of the years. She looked out the little window. The shingled roofs of the city were surrounded by a light, bluish-golden vapor. From afar the green plain of the open countryside with its yellow fields of rape plant and the flowering trees along the roads beamed amicably at her.

Agathe began humming to herself:

> The farthest, deepest dale's in bloom
> Now, poor heart, forget your pain
> Now must it all, all of it must change . . . .[86]

As she hummed she pulled out a box, opened it and knelt down before it. On top lay her dolls. When she saw the faded, tousled little wax heads again, she was transported back with powerful clarity to the day when she had packed them up.

Although it was a different attic, the sunbeam danced just as merrily among the gray dust balls, and the box had not been opened since. Beneath the pink blanket she found the delicate little lace-trimmed shirt, wrinkled and crushed, as she had stuffed it in there in the blissful excitement of her seventeen years.

She wanted to be brave. She didn't want to weep any tears . . . . Blanching in the effort it cost her, she hastily packed all the pretty little things in her apron to take them to Eugenie. And all the while she hummed to herself quite pointlessly:

> The farthest, deepest dale's in bloom
> Now, poor heart, forget your pain
> Now must it all, all of it must change . . . .

When she righted herself, she bumped into another little box. There was a tinkling in it like shards of glass. It was filled with empty little bottles, all of the same size. Among them lay bundles of dusty labels. Agathe pulled out a handful. All of them bore the same inscription:

Heidling's Fountain of Youth

This was all of Uncle Gustav that was left on earth.

Agathe bit her lip. Just don't leave the empty shells of dashed hopes behind you like that.

Just be brave and wind it up at the right time!

Eugenie was waiting for her in the dining room. When she began holding the dear little things against the light, examining frayed spots with her fingernail, and when many of them didn't meet her standards, when she said disparagingly, "Children don't wear caps nowadays; you can embalm them with piety," Agathe felt like slap-

174

ping her face. But this dull anger was foolish. It, too, had to be vanquished.

Agathe kindly put aside for her the things she had chosen. The sisters-in-law kissed one another and Frau Heidling junior departed in her elegant mourning clothes with the crepe veil that billowed, long and solemn, down her slender, supple back. She would send over the manservant to fetch the basket.

Now the toys. Cousin Mimi Bär was the head nurse of the children's ward at the hospital. She could always use things like that. Mimi was pleased when Agathe arrived and asked her to distribute the things among the little ones herself. This way some children — even if they couldn't be one's own — would certainly derive benefit from them. In the large, whitewashed room they sat or lay in rows in their iron cots, wretched creatures, some with gauze bandages around their little heads, disfigured with scrofula and rashes, or consumed with fever, prematurely old, with suffering expressions on their pale little faces. But everything here was bright and clean; the little beds, snowy white. It did make a cozy impression. When Sister Mimi entered, all the little heads turned toward her. Impatient little voices called her name. She went from row to row with an agreeable cheerfulness on her large features beneath the stiffly starched cap. She bantered here; she scolded merrily there — Agathe envied her as the peace-loving ruler here in this kingdom of sickness and death.

To conquer oneself, to be happy with others — to the point of self-oblivion, to the point of self-destruction — that is the only thing, the true thing!

And she distributed all her beloved mementos among the poor afflicted children of the common people. She joked and played with them. There was a little girl, ugly as a little brown ape, but as lively as could be. Look how she had poor faded Princess Holdewina turn somersaults in her little bed. Really, it was just too funny! Agathe burst into loud laughter. She laughed and laughed . . . .

"But, Agathe, don't get my children upset," admonished Mimi in her placid manner. Agathe tried to pull herself together. Tears spilled out of her eyes. The laughter hurt her; it shook her like a convulsion. The little ones looked at her fearfully. The sounds she emitted didn't much resemble gladness.

Mimi took her by the arm and practically carried her out. She opened a window and tended to Agathe carefully and considerately until the latter finally calmed down and rested upon Mimi's bed, exhausted to death.

"Poor child," said Mimi with her superior goodness, "you've got to do something for yourself. You're quite overwrought."

XII.

Privy Councillor Heidling heard from all sides that his daughter needed some rest and relaxation. He himself had noticed nothing of the sort; she certainly wasn't sick and she did her duty. But of course since the family doctor thought so too, something had to be done. A little distraction would do him good too. He missed his poor wife more with each passing day. Agathe did try hard of course, but a young girl like her couldn't really replace his wife. His routine had been hopelessly upset.

So he traveled to Switzerland with Agathe.

On the way they visited the Woszenskis for a few hours. The Woszenskis were still engaged in a harsh struggle with the malice, nastiness, and stupidity of their surroundings, living and dead. Malicious cooks afflicted with strange infirmities of body and spirit were still preventing Frau von Woszenski from working. On the art market laughing Africans and hunters in full regalia were still more in demand than naked anchorites and ecstatic nuns. It was still a torment that Michel didn't want to eat anything. The idiocy of his earlier schoolteachers had, however, been surpassed by the obtuseness of the professors at the academy where he was studying now. Herr von Woszenski still had the most baroque of plans and notions, and still he lacked the disposition to realize them.

His long beard and his disheveled hair had turned gray; his aquiline nose protruded even more sharply; his blue eyes peered, full of melancholy, out of deep hollows into the foolish world. More than ever he resembled his anchorites plagued with strange visions.

While Agathe sat on the divan, which was covered with a faded Persian rug, her gaze glided over the rigid, colorfully painted saints; the dark etchings on the walls; and the yellow bindings of French novels upon the carved chairs. When she smelled the sharp scent of turpentine and Egyptian cigars in the apartment, she felt as if she had returned home after a very long, bleak and meaningless period of banishment.

176

But it was folly to surrender herself to that. She would have to depart that very evening. And now she could hardly even bear the memory of such deep feelings as she had once experienced in this house.

She learned that Adrian Lutz had married her old boarding schoolmate Klotilde, the daughter of the Berlin writer. The marriage was not happy; people were already talking divorce. In Agathe there was a stirring of the disdain and aversion of the well-brought-up middle-class daughter toward the insecure, roving quality of such an artist's life. A divorced woman. Would it have ended like that if she had become his?

As a painter Lutz had failed by far to realize the potential he had once demonstrated. His pupil, Fräulein von Henning, had effectively surpassed him, they said. "That is, the woman hasn't got a glimmer of wit and grace," said Frau von Woszenski. "But what energy! She accomplishes more with that than if she had talent! She's exhibitin' her work in Paris . . . ."

"Well, she does have talent too," said Woszenski kindly.

"Oh, my husband's not so exactin' with the ladies," cried Marietta and laughed sharply and loudly.

Agathe saw perfectly well that her father was not in sympathy with the Woszenskis' manner. How *could* he be?

She asked what had become of the painting that Herr von Woszenski had been working on back then — *The Ecstasy of the Novice* — whether he had sold it.

"Oh, sold it! I'm still working on it."

He peered pensively over his glasses at Agathe.

"Why ever didn't I use you as a model back then?"

He brought out a color sketch of the new project. Over the course of time it had become a completely different picture.

Instead of the heavenly radiant gale that rippled the rich red and gold splendor of the high altar and in which thousands of angels' heads fluttered in blissful riot around the bride of Christ who had sunk to the ground, a cadaverous blue moonlight now glided through the colonnade of a convent. In the quiet, ghostly light a pale child with a crown of thorns floated down to her. The nun was no longer the rosy creature who had received the tiny redeemer into her arms and pressed him to her heart with an innocent, beaming smile. She lay on the ground with lockjaw, her arms stretched out stiffly as if she were nailed to the cross, the red stigmata on her pale forehead and her waxen hands.

"One just tries to express what one thinks in various ways," Woszenski said softly. "Over the years one's ideas change in the process."

He sighed deeply and put aside the canvas that Agathe had contemplated silently and at length.

Lutz had once called the brooding painter "my friend Hamlet." And the day on which she had seen Lutz for the first time appeared once again before her. Between then and now lay her life. And now nothing more? Slowly growing numb in coldness and renunciation?

She glanced down at her waxen hands and she almost thought the bloody stigma had to become visible there . . . .

What strange, foolish thoughts sometimes came to her . . . .

* * *

A week later Agathe sat on the veranda of a Swiss pension and looked out over pots of geraniums and carnations at the high mountains. They were dipped in brownish violet tints by the vanishing evening light, their powerful silhouettes etched against the warm blue southern sky.

God, how beautiful! Great Nature had a calming, uplifting and healing effect on all serious and profound people. So Agathe would have to be calmed, uplifted, healed. It was the last resort. It had to help!

If it was in vain . . . then . . . well, what then?

She didn't want to think about it, about the terrible fear that always lurked nearby, ready to pounce on her . . . .

Only the nights . . . .

As a result of the long period of waking beside her mother's sickbed she had lost the ability to sleep peacefully. To be sure, after the long walks with Father she sank into her bed, exhausted, intoxicated by the mountain air, and immediately lost consciousness. But after a short time she sat bolt upright in sudden terror; it was as if she had received a blow. Something terrible had happened . . . . She couldn't recollect what it was . . . . She was dripping with sweat; her heart pounded . . . . O God! Whatever could it be?

Someone was in her room, right close by her! Something evil was going to happen to her. She felt it clearly.

Her eyes wide open, she stared into the darkness.

She had to pull herself together violently to keep from screaming out in fear and horror.

Then she talked herself into being reasonable. After all, her father was right next door. She listened. No sound reached her. Papa was sleeping quite peacefully.

Thieves? . . . In the strange hotel. It could be . . . . It was even likely.

She strained her ears again.

But she had gone through the same thing the night before and also the night before that. Imagination. Everything was only her imagination.

Hardly had she lain back down on her bed when it was there again . . . . That alien thing, that ghostly, incomprehensible some-thing . . . . What ever could it be?

"O God, dear, dear, God, please help me," she prayed shudder-ing and put her head under the covers. "O God, dear God, do let me go back to sleep at last!"

But no thought of sleep. And she lay and listened to the hard splashing of the fountain before her window.

It spoke a language, but she didn't understand it. It had a rhythm; surely she would be able to identify it in the end . . . . In vain. Always the same hard splashing. If only it would stop just once, just for a second . . . . She felt as if she lay there in the fountain and the water splashed down upon her forehead, ceaselessly — How it hurt her.

At noon today . . . the gentleman across from her at the table d'hôte . . . . He had looked at her oddly . . . . What if he ran into her on a deserted path?

And the ferryman who had ferried her over had also followed her with his gaze. Actually he was a handsome fellow . . . .

My God, my God! What had gotten into her?

Had she fallen so low that she was thinking about a deck hand?

Was God punishing her for loss of faith by turning her over to the power of the Devil? What if there *were* a hell? Eternal damnation, eternal . . . . Eternal consciousness of one's torment . . . . She had a presentiment of her terror in this abandonment, this self-loathing.

Adrian . . . . Adrian Lutz . . . . Yes, she had loved only him. O you one and only handsome, sweet man . . . .

No, it wasn't Adrian at all she was thinking of; it was Raikendorf. And not Raikendorf either . . . . Martin, Martin Greffinger! Back then in Bornau he had really loved her! If she had given him the kiss he asked her for . . . had then become engaged to him! So many girls become engaged to schoolboys . . . . Martin would have taken her with him into his alien, adventuresome life . . . . They would have fought for a great cause, and they themselves would have become great and free and strong in the process. Oh, yes. She would have made quite a good socialist!

How could she have remained so unmoved by his warm, beautiful young love back then?

What if Adrian had seduced her — like Fräulein Daniel?

O my God!

She sat up and turned the light on. The endless night was unbearable! She ran to the window in her bare feet, leaned out it and breathed the fresh mountain air that was redolent with perfume.

How tired, how tired . . . .

In the light of the dawn she sometimes was able to fall asleep again.

Unfortunately Papa had a passion for undertaking early-morning excursions. Thus she was often awakened a half hour later. And she didn't dare tell him that she slept badly. It would have ruined his summer holiday.

The beginning of the day was indeed precious. But at ten o'clock the girl was already in a state of exhaustion and nervous agitation that could be concealed only by a desperate exertion of all her powers of self-control.

The air was so oppressive too. In the morning the sun burned and beat down on the wide, exposed valley that was enclosed by the high craggy mountains. In the evening heavy thunderstorms exploded. They barely cooled the air. Only a damp steam rose from the alpine meadows and from the orchards and floated over the wild, rushing mountain stream that flowed through the town, and the warm haze sank down again exhaustingly upon the people who were thirsting for refreshment.

At that the privy councillor lost the inclination to undertake further excursions. They sat on the veranda or beneath a sweet chestnut tree in the little hotel garden, Agathe with her needlework, Papa with a cigar and the newspaper — more or less as they had also sat at home in the garden of the Harmony Club.

If the thunderstorm had already occurred around midday, then one would stroll out to the lake around sunset.

They had found the family of a justice with an oldish daughter for companionship; thus one remained neatly in the rut of customary activity.

Agathe wondered sometimes why they had bothered to travel to Switzerland.

She looked at the craggy mountains in their mute and powerful greatness; she stared into the rapid, roaring waters; she contemplated the chestnut and walnut trees, the ferns sparkling with dew, the pomegranates in the gardens, all the vegetation that suggested southern climates to her. And she asked the same question of all of them. The cliffs remained silent in stony calm, the water roared down into the lake, the pomegranates bloomed, and the trees ripened their fruit. They gave Agathe no answer. And the obtrusive beauty, the rich splendor of this Nature exhausted, offended, enraged her.

XIII.

Papa was playing dominoes with a gentleman who had spoken to him recently, an all-around educated man, a professor from Zurich. Today a few of his pupils who were passing through had looked him up. The young men were also drinking their wine and eating their cheese on the veranda.

The doors to the dining room were open.

Suddenly one of the students hastily put his pince-nez on his nose and leaned forward. Inside a man in a gray suit with a straw hat was passing by.

"Professor," the student cried eagerly, "there he is. I *was* right! Wait. He'll come out the door down below any minute."

The Zurich professor knocked over his dominoes in the haste with which he jumped up and leaned out over the iron railing. The young men looked out over it too. Then the professor turned back around and sat down.

"Well, well, so that was Greffinger . . . . Seeing him really was interesting!"

"What was that name you mentioned?" asked the privy councillor.

"Greffinger!" said the professor as if that sufficed and it was unnecessary to add further explanation.

"Papa!" cried Agathe with the sudden liveliness that sometimes seized her, "could it possibly be Martin?"

"I have a nephew by that name," explained Privy Councillor Heidling perfunctorily.

The Swiss students observed the old gentleman and the lady with interest. It seemed they truly were relatives of Martin Greffinger . . . and yet they themselves weren't sure of it!

Heidling's hand toyed with his soft gray beard.

"I haven't heard anything from the young man for a long time," he said, deliberating how much he should communicate to these strangers about his relations with Martin. "It pleases me, however, to see that you speak of him with respect. If we do in fact mean the same person . . . . "

"Haven't you read Martin Greffinger's latest book?"

"Do you think it's any good?" inquired the privy councillor.

"Without a doubt! I don't agree with everything. But it's a sound and significant book. It will make its mark. In twenty years people will talk about it more than they do now. This Greffinger is a complete and solid personality. I wish we had more like him."

"Well, I'm glad to hear it. I'm glad to hear it." The privy councillor resolved to take a look at the work sometime. He thought it better to leave open the question of whether or not he was familiar with it.

"I imagine Greffinger will drop by again this evening," said the student who had called attention to him as he passed by.

"Let's ask our landlady whether he's taken lodgings for the night," the professor cried animatedly. "I really would be delighted if you were to afford me the opportunity of meeting the man in person!"

"We're rather out of touch," the privy councilor remarked evasively.

Agathe was secretly amused. Her father had become significant to these people because he was Martin's relative! They were requesting of him the pleasure of making Martin's acquaintance! Who would ever have thought it . . . . Her warm feelings for the friend of her youth reawakened. If only he would come!

Her silent waiting made the afternoon seem long. She grabbed her hat to take a little stroll through the village.

Now the students were standing together in front of the hotel, talking and laughing.

"A pompous old duffer," Agathe heard the oldest one say as she went by.

She knew that he meant her father, her father who, despite everything he had done to grieve her, seemed a man whom no disapproving judgment would even dare to approach.

The student had called him a pompous old duffer . . . . His words cut Agathe to the quick; she found them coarse. But this young man didn't impress her as coarse. On the contrary. He looked intelligent and inspired.

Filled with sadness, she walked along high stone walls. They enclosed the gardens of the wealthy Swiss citizens who had villas here, locking them up against all things foreign. Thick old ivy hung down from them. Thus the town consisted of a vast labyrinth of narrow corridors. Agathe could never find her way and seldom knew in what part of it she would emerge.

At the end of the damp, gray street the lake glistened bluish.

Agathe walked faster and faster toward this distant blue light as if she were fleeing something that lay behind her. Of course it would be too late to reach it today, but she wanted at least to get an unimpeded view. And she could no longer be sad. When she got home, she would find Martin! She was completely certain that she would see him! Suddenly she dropped the thought of the lake, turned around and hurried back toward home. But now she had taken a wrong turn and it took her a rather long time to reach the hotel.

When she got back, she saw a gentleman standing next to the waitress against the railing of the veranda and looking down at her over the red carnations. She recognized Martin immediately although he had put on weight and had gotten older. He came toward her with outstretched arms.

"Agathe! I'm so happy to see you here!"

Laughing, moved, and flushed with excitement, they stood beaming at one another. It was as if the years had been obliterated and they were once again the inspired schoolboy and the lively young girl who had lain in the tall grass and dreamed of freedom and human happiness.

Martin didn't let go of Agathe's hands.

"You haven't changed at all," he asserted boldly.

"Has it really been that long since we saw one another last? Unbelievable!"

They could no longer figure out how long it had in fact been.

"Since I brought you the banned books? Oh, what nonsense that was! You were too firmly tethered. Tell me. Are you here by yourself now?"

"No, with my father of course," answered Agathe in astonishment.

"Oh, yes, naturally! I forgot. Young ladies certainly don't travel by themselves."

He cast her a mischievous sidelong glance. A grinning irony, which Agathe liked quite a lot, had replaced his previous acidity.

"Well — so just imagine. I return from my walk and the waitress says to me that a party is waiting for me and a young lady went out to meet me!"

"But — nothing of the sort . . . . I didn't go out to meet you," cried Agathe.

"What? Nothing of the sort . . . . And I'm standing here and dying of curiosity as to who the beautiful young lady who's looking for me can be! Perhaps you don't want to have anything to do with me?"

"Oh, yes we do. A little while ago a few gentlemen told us you had written such a significant book."

Martin Greffinger burst into loud laughter.

"And the two of you thought I was sitting in prison somewhere? That's rich! Who were the gentlemen?"

"Professor Bürkner from Zurich."

"Well, yes! He reviewed my *Book of Freedom*.[87] Is he still here?"

"Yes, he's made friends with Papa. Tell me, Martin, are you staying this evening?"

"This evening?" cried Greffinger cheerfully. "I just booked a week's room and board."

"Oh, how nice!"

"You're staying here too?"

"Yes."

A shadow passed over Greffinger's firm and steadfast face. His eyes gazed thoughtfully at the ground. And when they rested once again upon his cousin, the joy and brightness had vanished from them.

* * *

The Swiss professor's judgment of Greffinger did not remain without influence on the tone with which Privy Councillor Heidling greeted his nephew. Martin really seemed to have worked his way out of his former bewilderment! Besides they were abroad and there was no career left to be damaged. The privy councillor undertook to make the gentlemen acquainted with Greffinger.

They had a jolly evening beneath the sweet chestnut of the hotel garden by the flickering light of storm lanterns.

With golden Asti in his glass Greffinger clinked glasses with Agathe and drank to their reunion in free Switzerland. An abundance of childhood memories came over the man without a country, a remembrance of the first oppressive sweet feelings, of the first intoxication of the senses that the girl next to him had awakened . . . . What had he felt when they declaimed Herwegh in the park in Bornau that was hot with summer! His interest in all the people of whom he hadn't thought for years was suddenly rekindled.

"How's Eugenie doing?"

"Three children — and Walter will become a captain soon."

"Mimi? A nurse? If it makes her happy. Tastes vary!"

"And you, Agathe, how are you getting on?"

"The way one does . . . . Uncle Gustav was sick for half a year, then Mama for three months."

"You've had a hard time."

No glance answered him. She lowered her eyes, and her faded features became still more meager and sharp.

"Agathe, shall I take you rowing on the lake tomorrow?"

"Oh, Martin, do you really want to?"

* * *

They rowed on the lake or they sat on the veranda of the little restaurant down by the lake and talked about various things. Agathe was eternally grateful to Professor Bürkner for persuading her father to undertake long excursions in which ladies couldn't take part. Martin also held back. He had to work. Then he would come by later and pick up Agathe. The oldish daughter of the justice's wife watched their departure with envy.

Greffinger treated Agathe like an old friend whom one could trust.

And she wasn't in love with him — thank God!

But what he told her of his life and of his striving and thinking was of burning interest to her, and she became nearly as excited as she would have if he were courting her. Everything was so new, so surprising to her, so completely different from what she had imagined.

He had long since burst the party bonds of social democracy.

"That, too, is a delusion and a form of tyranny that impoverished humanity must savor fully to the last drop and then overcome . . . . "

Why did he allow Agathe to see so deeply into his singular brooding? She asked herself that in amazement. She could seldom respond to him; she didn't speak his language. She often didn't even understand his expressions and imagined his words to mean something different from what he meant.

And yet his friendship filled her with deep, fervid satisfaction.

. . . No, she didn't love Martin — thank God.

That's why she could tell him a lot about the things that weighed on her. Not everything. But she did talk about her relationship with her father, and he heard the pent-up anger resonating in her voice.

"That old man will always prevent you from doing everything you mean to do to help yourself. If he locks up his bookcase and if he bars you from life . . . . You have to free yourself from him! Leave him and look for work and joy that satisfies you."

"Oh, Martin! That's quite impossible."

"Yes, but you're unhappy with him. One can tell by looking at you. Your existence is unbearable. Good. Then change it."

"But, dear Martin, do be reasonable. How am I supposed to leave my father all of sudden and go out into the wide world with no

186

money, knowing nothing? He needs me. Who would cheer him up and take care of him? Out there away from home no one needs me."

"No!" said Martin very seriously. "No one needs you there, and you'll finally have the time to think of yourself for once, to find yourself again — you who have completely lost yourself!"

"That would be quite a find, wouldn't it!" Agathe lamented meekly.

"It's really impossible for you to tell now! Believe me, it's very surprising getting to know oneself."

She did want to show him that she was worthy of his caring about her well-being. If he walked beside her in silence, tired and worn out from work, she began making chitchat. She employed all the little arts she used to entertain her father; she was practiced in this. With harmlessly droll remarks, she could often make Martin laugh too and shoo away his bleak moods.

The privy councillor was not unhappy about his daughter's association with Martin. He had found it deeply offensive that the son of his only sister had so completely removed himself from his influence. Perhaps he could be won back by means of his daughter.

"In the end, spending time again in the company of refined women no doubt does benefit these extravagant young men who try to take life by storm," he explained to Agathe. "You have a lovely task to fulfill there, my child. I'd be pleased if you were able to draw Martin back more into our circle."

Thus in the quiet mountain retreat two worlds strove to save one another.

Sometimes it seemed to Agathe that Martin was pursuing a secret plan. In conversation he often sank into thought or cast long, searching glances at her.

Many a girl would have presumed a lot from his friendship. Didn't he go through the garden, climb over the fence and come up into the forest where she sat and read while the professor from Zurich was waiting to converse with him out in front on the veranda?

No, thank God — she was not in love with him. She liked looking at his hands when he accompanied his words with expressive gestures. She was glad that he had well-manicured white hands that were at once powerful and manly. But one couldn't call that being in love.

She examined herself honestly. Completely certainly not? Under no circumstances? She still had some resistance! Fortunately. Now it was a matter of something quite different from love.

* * *

Her relations with Martin ran through her entire life! Her first childish liking and yearning — they had been for Martin even if she hadn't admitted it to herself back then. The first test of her demure young virtue — by him. The grand passion had torn them apart; they had experienced the same agony at the same time. And then the lonely struggle to keep up one's courage: he out there in the wild, blustering thunder and lightning, his soul expanded and free; she at home in the narrow space, her soul battered and crushed.

Oh, it was something far loftier than love that brought them together now.

Nothing of what she had feared and expected of Martin had become of him. Not a demagogue who roused the rabble to wild deeds, not a conspirator and thrower of bombs — and not a politic and cowardly backslider either, no weary renouncer. He had simply become a free person. Nothing more.

And what was that supposed to mean? A free person? What a gap there was between the circles of her society and a personality that relied solely upon itself, that led its own life according to its own law and own choice! Measured by such a standard, did any of the deeds, any of the thoughts of her life still have any value at all? Not until now did she have an inkling of this. She was filled with awe as her soul awakened with impatient beats of the wing.

Whenever Agathe observed Martin associating with her father, she was particularly struck by how mature and solid and calm he had become. Nothing more of his angry bravado. To be sure Martin did not seek to spend long hours with his uncle. And the gaiety, the youthfulness of his nature only emerged when he hiked alone with Agathe into the mountains. But he knew how to come up with topics of conversation that posed no danger. He also knew how to hold his tongue at the privy councillor's sententious invectives against the immorality and lack of idealism of the new generation.

"You have to give me a lot of credit for staying here," he said one day to Agathe. "But I still have a lot to do to get all the maggots out of this stupid little girl's head. Me, the maggot killer! If only you were serious about it!"

"I *am* serious, Martin."

"Are you really? Oh — I'm wasting my time with you. In the end you're just like all the rest."

"If you think that, why do you bother?"

"Yes, that's what I ask myself! One morning I really will take off."

* * *

Finally he suggested to her that she let her father return home alone and herself stay in Switzerland — with him in Zurich. She should get a room there. He had work she could help him with. That is, if it suited her; in case she wanted to try her strength alone, she was of course free to do so. Just no pressure, no deference to one another's feelings.

Agathe sat opposite him, disconcerted, her eyes lowered, her needlework resting in her lap, her fingers pressed against one another, shuddering inwardly. What was he proposing? What did his offer mean?

He proposed it in such a calm tone of voice.

Didn't he know that he was demanding something monstrous of her?

He had reflected on it. That became apparent in the self-possession with which he began to speak of the practical side.

He knew a restaurant with good plain fare. A lot of female students frequented it, capable girls who took life seriously, one or the other of whom would appeal to her.

Her father would surely not deny her what it cost to support her at home?

"Oh, Martin, he would most certainly do that. He would be beside himself!"

"Yes, a step like this isn't taken without battles. When he sees that your resolve is unshakable, he'll surely relent. For the moment speak only of a year, for all I care, only of a winter!"

Agathe was silent.

. . . In the end her father would not leave her without means of support. He deferred too much to the opinion of others and was accustomed to glossing over hard facts.

But didn't Martin sense that he himself, his presence in Zurich, would give the greatest offense? He didn't sense it. How strange . . . . She really couldn't possibly point it out to him. This step was a break with everything that had gone before it. Once it was taken, there was no turning back — at least no turning back inwardly. Did she even want to turn back? Certainly not.

"Your father's not sick, you know. If you were to marry, he'd have to fend for himself then too!"

"You're right about that!"

"You don't have to decide right now. But do it soon. And then act quickly! Just don't let yourself return to your old situation."

He really was greatly agitated. She saw it when he stood up from the bench, where he had been sitting across from her at the long plank table, and called the hostess to pay for the wine and bread.

Silently they returned home, a long way over pale green, fragrant alpine meadows that sparkled with sunlight. Martin's eyes were deeply serious, his glance turned inward, his countenance void of amiability. Occasionally Agathe raised her head and silently questioned his profile. But he strode on silently. He had spoken. She had to choose.

Just one more encouraging, persuasive glance!

She was afraid of him. The obdurateness, the domineering aspect of his nature had often repelled her. Now she felt it again.

For his sake . . . .

No, not for his sake; she must do whatever happened for herself. Couldn't she absorb this, let her thinking and feeling be permeated with it? She kept forgetting. And the habit of her previous way of seeing things prevailed. Anything one did that wasn't for the sake of another was reprehensible.

For her own sake . . . .

How did he imagine their working together? Didn't he know what everyone would take her for?

It was probably a matter of indifference to him; he had never placed much stock in the opinion of others. In Zurich social intercourse between young men and single girls was perhaps freer than at home. And of course she was no longer young. Did he think she was so completely harmless? But what would people say about her back home?

She had always believed that the great human being who was capable of making heroic decisions was merely sleeping inside her. Now Martin called upon that person in a powerful voice. Now it had to come out whether that person was still there at all and not long since shrunken and desiccated.

It was frighteningly exciting and appealing to imagine — the entire world thought her a fallen woman; only she herself carried the awareness of her cool purity within her. And Martin — naturally he had boundless respect for the quiet strength with which she continued down her chosen path despite all the false accusations. He had really never ever encountered such a woman.

He begged her for love, entreated her again and again, pled, became impassioned . . . . She saw him before her as after Eugenie's wedding, his head pressed into the curtains, sobbing, thoroughly agitated with wild desire . . . .

But he would probably never consent to a civil ceremony and certainly not to a church wedding.

Thank God — she didn't love him . . . .

Only somehow the wish came over her to lean her cheek against his hand, to let herself be stroked over her forehead and eyebrows by this strong white hand.

She must not dream of such feminine weaknesses if she wanted to venture to carry out her plan.

All possibility of sleep that night was completely at an end now.

XIV.

"Girls with talent are enviable," Agathe lamented to her cousin. "Everyone finds it understandable that they cultivate it. Even poor old straight-laced Frau von Henning sent her daughter to Paris. If my father asks me what in the world I want to do in Zurich, I haven't actually got an answer. And who knows whether I won't feel more superfluous there than at home. To be sure — it *is* wonderful to stand on one's own two feet for once!"

"I should think so," cried Greffinger and laughed heartily.

Agathe was more or less in the same mood in which, as a child, she had sat on the chains on Kasernenplatz and dangled her legs — a little fearful, a little oppressed, but really so secretly impudent and happy.

She sat next to Martin on the deck of the steamer as it rushed through the blue foaming waters toward the opposite shore of the lake.

Agathe intended to climb the Hörnli with her cousin.[88] They said you got a gorgeous panoramic view even at the moderate height of the plateau at the top of the cliff. The outing had been planned for a while. But with Papa and Martin and the justice's family — no, Agathe didn't expect it to be very pleasant given the composition of the party. Now Papa had undertaken a two-day excursion with the professor and a few other gentlemen. Martin had enticed Agathe on their morning walk further and further toward the shore. There the steamer lay ready. And Agathe herself suggested that he cross over with her.

"You're already starting to emancipate yourself," he cried happily.

Agathe regretted that the steamer was not departing immediately for Zurich. Today it would have been easy for her to bid farewell to her entire past, father and friends — and her respectable reputation.

They were both very cheerful and amused themselves with silly prattling. Martin posed the insidious question as to why Agathe hadn't married. She must certainly have turned down a lot of men. Agathe shook her head.

She must have always been too reserved toward men? He told her of a schoolboy who had tattooed the initials A. H. on his breast with a pin and blue ink. Agathe plagued him for the name. He didn't reveal it, only added, "But it wasn't me."

Nevertheless Agathe thought he was the one.

Martin promised her that when they were on the Hörnli she would get Asti to drink. Today he was behaving completely like a young man whose head is full of crazy ideas. Up on the Hörnli he wrote in the visitors' register of the inn: "Mark Anthony Grausinger, Underwear Manufacturer and Spouse." Agathe burst into giggles like a schoolgirl.

Before them the chain of the snowcapped mountains, the enormous craggy masses whose colors dissolved in the brightness, lay in deathly silence in the atmosphere of noon day. Deep in the valley dark forests stretched down to the water and the smooth lake slumbered pale blue. Walnut trees shaded their heads and clematis climbed up the trunks sending forth its delicate clinging tendrils with the white blossoms, creeping from branch to branch. Now and then from out of the dark thicket of larch and pine, through which the path wended its way upward, a breeze wafted over them like a cool fragrant drawing of breath. Cyclamen were blooming amid the lichen there.

It was hot, and as they rested and looked they became tired and taciturn. Martin had removed his hat, his face was flushed, and he mopped his forehead with his handkerchief.

A little waitress brought them their food and tended to their needs. The lively thing, round, white and red like a little Borsdorf apple, was an appetizing sight in her black velvet bodice and her bright apron. Agathe and Martin watched as a bulky, greasy man with a large signet ring on his index finger who had already finished his meal beckoned the cute little woman to him, pulled up a chair and pushily urged her to sit with him and drink a glass of wine.

She answered impatiently; one could tell that it was not the first time she had had to defend herself against him. He tried to hold on to her by her skirt. She freed herself brusquely, gave him a coarse scolding and ran off.

Agathe turned her head away. Nature and her own happy mood had been desecrated.

"I'd like to give that fellow a piece of my mind," Martin fumed. "What a poor girl like that has to put up with!"

The fat old vulgarian departed, snorting peevishly after his attempt to kick over the traces had failed.

How lovely! Now they were alone and could chat unconstrained.

Agathe liked to hear Martin get worked up and explain to her that above all she had to get to know Life as it really was, not as well-bred daughters of privy councillors were told it was. Then interest in that manifold, dreadfully powerful and glorious monster would grow so strong within her that she would learn to love it again, in its precipices and depths and rugged, terrible heights, and she would become healthy and happy in the air of knowledge.

"Haven't you made progress during these two weeks?" he asked. "Haven't we spent lovely hours together? Wasn't that better than your parties and your junior barristers and lieutenants?"

Agathe affirmed it with a deep shining glance of her brown eyes.

193

How splendidly he spoke! What luck to have found him again! She had been practically at her wit's end — this miserable existence of the last few years frayed into nothing but minute suffering and minute worries and unnecessary labor.

She told him about it. Never would she have believed she could speak so frankly and on top of that with a man — a young man. But it was no longer a man and girl here; it was two good comrades who would help one another in loyalty and sincere conviction.

"What you're telling me is very interesting, Agathe," cried Martin. "Write it down — in the very same words you've just used."

"Oh, Martin, you know I'm no writer."

"I don't mean you'll create a work of art. That's a matter for a chosen few."

He continued speaking slowly. "I don't know at all whether it's important to create works of art nowadays . . . . All of us are struggling so hard! Don't worry about the form! Just tell your dear sisters honestly and clearly what their lives are truly like. Perhaps they'll have the courage then to take their lives into their own hands instead of letting their parents and society dictate to them how to live, instead of becoming sick, sad, hysterical females whom, when they are thirty, one would just as soon strike dead — every last one of them! Well, doesn't that tempt you? Working with others for the right of the self? Come, let's drink to it. Long live freedom!"

He said it in a powerful voice. His sunburned face beamed in joyful emotion. Agathe lifted her glass to him. A fine, shrill sound resonated through the stillness of midday. It seemed to the girl that in the reverberations she heard her own heart and nerves ringing, so poised was everything in her to devote herself enthusiastically to the work that he showed her.

Greffinger slowly sipped the shining wine. Agathe noted half unconsciously that his gaze flowed over his glass toward the little waitress who, not far from them, was occupied with her crocheting. She perceived it even as her thoughts were completely filled with a new something that was beginning to take effect within her. She propped her head on her hand and looked at the great depth that stretched down to the lake. Silently she submerged herself in this new thing that promised her future something that was coming to be.

Something that was coming to be! Therein lay emancipation . . . . This was why living with her parents had made her so unhappy despite all her love and faithfulness to duty: it was without hope. She saw nothing but withering all around her. She, with her lively energies and young blood, had been fettered to existences that had already blossomed and born fruit and that lived only with the memories of the time when they were at the height of their powers, with memories that really didn't concern her. She had had to content herself with the achievements of the previous generation.

Something that was coming to be . . . a child — or a project — for all I care a delusion; in any case something that raises expectations and promises joy, something that one can hope to give the future. It's what human beings need, and for that reason women need it too!

Agathe was very proud and happy when she finally disentangled this core from dark feelings. She had to tell Martin about it. She turned back to him.

He didn't notice . . . .

What had happened?

He was still looking at the waitress. Were those his eyes, the ones into which she had just been gazing as if into two lucid stars that proclaimed a proud and lofty message?

Had she gone crazy if she suddenly perceived Martin as transformed? The loathsome fellow whose disappearance had so relieved her — he looked like him . . . . The half closed, squinting eyelids, out from under which a greenish light flickered toward the girl over there . . . the smile hovering upon his lips — his lips spoke not a single word; nevertheless they enticed and entreated . . . .

And — he had better luck than the old fellow. Without a sound a connection had been established between him and the young thing while Agathe had brooded with her back turned. She disturbed the whirring back and forth of their wooing.

Martin poured himself some wine and raised his glass with a flourish of candid homage in the direction of the little woman. "Fräulein!" he cried and drank it down to the last drop. Then he leaned over to Agathe and whispered confidingly, "Charming gal, don't you think?"

Her mouth twisted oddly.

He paid no attention to it but rather began to converse with the little Swiss girl. Cheerful, dumb, harmless stuff, but there was an undercurrent in his voice that Agathe knew — from a time long since vanished.

When she stood up to leave she was surprised that the sun was still shining.

* * *

Was Martin only trying to test her? Conquer herself, not let him feel her huge disappointment and outrage! But suddenly all her self-control had vanished. He had become repugnant to her, but she was still more repugnant to herself. What could she have seen in such a man? How had she been so deluded as to think him great and important? And why did such a cruel pain tear at her heart? She tormented herself and him with an obscure coldness.

In the evening after supper Martin invited her to take a little walk with him. "We can't say a single thing to one another here," he added with a glance at the justice's wife and daughter.

Agathe understood that he wanted to have it out with her. And she also felt clearly that it would be more advisable for her to avoid him today. But despite this she stood up and took her shawl from the hook on the wall.

"Where are you going, Fräulein Agathe?" asked the justice's wife.

"I'm going to take a little walk with my cousin."

"Now?" the justice's wife asked in astonishment. "But you were already on the Hörnli today! And it's almost dark!"

"What does that hurt?"

"It's already past nine!"

"I'll bring my cousin back in one piece in half an hour," Martin said in an indifferent and scornful tone of voice.

He led the way, leaving it to Agathe to follow him. He knew of course that she would follow him. She did it although it seemed to her that she was acting like a woman who was no longer in possession of her senses. She knew full well of course what the justice's wife and daughter and the landlady and the waiters must think of her when she went out into the night with a young man. It really was quite odd that the justice's wife said nothing further. Probably she was simply too stunned by the young girl's scandalous intention.

Why ever did she go, and with her head bowed and an unbearable shaking of the knees, trot along behind Martin who didn't turn around even once to look at her? In any case he didn't care whether she hurt herself on the stony path.

Alongside them the mountain stream roared in a deep bed, swollen with the downpour of the thunderstorms of the past few weeks, dragging along in its raging whirlpools large branches and bushes that had been ripped out of the earth. Masses of clouds once again covered the sky. It was so dark under the trees whose branches arched over the path that one couldn't see one step in front of one-self.

Benumbed by the wild raging of the water that sent up cold va-pors from out of the obscurity into the sultry night, with a pounding ache in her head and above her eyes, with uproar and misery in her breast, she continued on her way.

Why had she followed him? Why, oh, why?

She felt like throwing herself upon him from behind, throwing herself upon the dark silhouette of his body, seizing him and drag-ging him into the wild water — a few days ago he had remarked, "I wouldn't be able to get anyone out again who jumped in there!"

And she smiled with cruel delight at the thought of him stretch-ing out his arms just as the dead branches stretched out of the whirl-pools . . . . At the same time she felt that it was no longer a smile but rather a grimace that twisted her features. How horrified he would be if he turned around now and the lightning showed him her face . . . .

But he didn't turn around.

Once he said, "Keep to the right; otherwise you'll fall in the stream."

Ugh! How heartless, how cruel he was. How she despised him!

They didn't have a very long way to go before they came to a bridge without a railing that went over the stream. Martin walked across it and went into the courtyard of a country inn that was fre-quented only by people from the area and for which he alone had a partiality. A stable lantern hung on a large tree. It cast a meager cir-cle of light upon the table and the two benches. Above it the leaves shone a hard, metallic green. Darkness was all around it. The din of the water separated the spot from the rest of the world and created the impression that one was alone on an island in the midst of a wild, roaring deluge.

"No one will bother us here," Martin said.

The innkeeper appeared in his slippers and sleepily set down two glasses of beer in front of them.

"Just run along. We'll call if we need anything."

Agathe had sat down. She propped her head on her hand and stared at the gray wood of the table before her. Silently she suffered Martin's reproaches.

He hadn't thought her so petty and sentimental and such a vain female as she had shown herself to be today. He wanted to win her for freedom. But he would not bend to the tyranny of a prudish and foolish female.

What did his liking for the pretty, vivacious Swiss girl have to do with their friendship? If she imagined that in future he would forgo associating with pretty young girls, then she had fundamentally misunderstood the feeling that had drawn him to her; they would have to come to an understanding about this.

Finally he was interrupted by Agathe's sobbing.

"Stop crying. You're acting like a child," he said in a hard voice.

It could hardly be called crying anymore. Long, rattling screams from deep down burst from her breast and were lost in the roaring of the water.

She jumped up, threw back her head and wrung her hands wildly as if in danger of suffocating and struggling for her life.

She was starting to worry him.

"So let's go home! Perhaps one can have a sensible conversation with you tomorrow. Why in the world are you so upset?"

"Because I love you!" she screamed at him shrilly. In that moment she knew of no greater insult to hurl at him. And she was gone — like a bolt of lightning shot out into the night and the darkness. She raced over the bridge, following the course of the stream —

"To the lake, to the lake . . . . " It was the only thought that raged within her, that hammered in her pulses, that panted in her breath.

"I want to be free! Free from him, free from him — "

A loud peal of laughter . . . .

Trembling, she stopped and listened . . . . Was it her?

She dared not take one step further in the terrible, lonely darkness. Was someone behind her? Her teeth chattered in terror.

She had forgotten that she wanted to reach the lake.

Close beside her was the raging water; the banks plunged down so deep, so deep . . . .

The panting and laboring in her breast, the rushing and ringing in her head let up. She was dead tired. Her eyes closed. She almost lost consciousness.

Only a movement . . . .

"Mama . . . my dear Mama . . . ," she stammered, stretched out her arms and leaned far over.

A bolt of lightning struck blindingly. She opened her eyes wide, saw the whirlpools raging in confusion below her, illuminated by the pale light. She reared back. Shaken through and through with fright, she stood breathless, stared into the night and heard the crashing of the thunder.

She really mustn't, she really mustn't . . . care for Papa, she had promised . . . . She mustn't run away. Mama had called her . . . .

Her knees shook. She felt she was going to keel over and simply let herself sink to the ground. She lay there, cowering and letting the roar of the water stupefy her. All kinds of senseless stuff went through her head. She didn't know for how long.

Finally she rose and crept back through the night. Now she was afraid she would get lost and strained to recall the direction she had to take. And then she ran as fast as she could.

Shuddering with inner chill, her face covered with sweat and tears, she stopped before the door to the hotel. She opened it softly and flew through the vestibule up the stairs. There on the first landing she met Martin.

"Agathe, how could you!" he called out to her. "I've been running around in the dark for an hour looking for you! You gave me quite a nice little scare!"

She dragged herself on by, her back to him, and bolted herself in her room.

And that's how Agathe's jaunt into freedom came to an end.

XV.

Frau Lieutenant Heidling was summoned to Switzerland by a telegram from her father-in-law. The privy councillor met her down by the lake at the steamboat landing.

"My God, Papa, what happened?"

"Yes, poor Agathe. . . . " The old gentleman looked at his daughter-in-law, troubled and distressed. "Can you imagine? She sits all day long and cries. All day long! And if you try to calm her, she has a fit. I didn't think she could get so angry. I have no idea how to handle the girl any more. I'm at my wit's end . . . . She's also had a falling out with Martin, and she really had been showing a distinct partiality for him . . . in any case . . . he departed suddenly."

The privy councillor seized Eugenie's hands. Tears flowed into his beard.

"Don't be cross with me . . . the long journey . . . . I thought if you — You really were always such good friends. If you could speak with her! Something has to — You really have no idea how the poor child looks."

"Well, Papa dear, we'll certainly do something. One is happy to make sacrifices for one's family. Just leave everything to me. I'm sure I'll bring Agathe back to reason."

When Agathe spied her sister-in-law, she had a crying fit.

The privy councillor ran for the doctor. And the doctor explained: The patient was very nervous and very anemic. Anemia came from overstimulation of the nerves and the overstimulation of the nerves was founded in anemia. Something needed to be done for her nerves and something for the anemia — moreover, a little iron would certainly put everything in order.

"You know, Papa," said Eugenie, "I ought to drink a little iron too. So I'll take Agathe along to Röhren; everyone's singing its praises nowadays. Lisbeth Wendhagen is there too. It's supposed to be run by an excellent doctor. Then I'll have Wolfy join me. The boy still looks so wretched after his scarlet fever. And we'll have a heavenly time together! Heavens, everybody has times now and then when nothing suits them, and Agathe really has taxed her energies. Leave her to me and don't worry a bit."

The privy councillor kissed Eugenie's hand in warm gratitude. How clever and practical she was. He was already no longer so pessimistic . . . everything would of course be all right again!

"I don't want to go with Eugenie! I don't want to! Leave me here by myself, Papa, all by myself," Agathe begged her father. "You'll see. Then I'll come round! I just have such a longing to be completely alone for once, not to have to speak at all, not to hear any voices at all. I can no longer bear your voices. That's the whole story. I don't want to go to a doctor."

Eugenie and Papa exchanged meaningful glances. The privy councillor sighed deeply.

"Sick people aren't up to making decisions," Eugenie said energetically and packed the suitcases.

Agathe watched the young woman rummaging through her things, opening her boxes, thumbing through her letter case as if she were a dead person of whom one no longer need be considerate.

And then again the constant chatter to cheer her up, to distract her. Or Eugenie posed adroit questions to find out whether something had happened between Martin and her.

. . . Perhaps she had already written to Martin behind Agathe's back, and he would reveal everything . . . . And Eugenie would hear about her humiliation, the secret misery that was destroying her.

She did want to live; she did want to do her duty, but they didn't have to torment her so terribly. Even when she was healthy, she had found Eugenie's light, sure, complacent manner boundlessly irritating. And now, dead tired and worn out as she was, she was supposed to be in her company day and night for weeks at a time? Submit to her surveillance and prying? It was inconceivable.

And Papa would not be reasonable.

She really couldn't say to him that she loathed Eugenie, could she? If he were to ask why? She knew of no reason why.

But she herself was guilty; she alone. She wanted to bear everything as a punishment from God for her insane desire for happiness. How He must delight in martyring her like this . . . .

Respectable girls never have any blasphemous thoughts . . . . At thirty respectable girls are no longer jealous of waitresses . . . . Respectable girls — do they behave as she had behaved? What ever possessed her?

She is not at all a respectable girl. She has played the hypocrite her whole life long. Played the hypocrite out of cowardice. And if in the end it's revealed after all . . . . Oh, poor Papa — such an irreproachable man of honor . . . if it comes out what kind of creature his daughter is . . . .

Just endure everything patiently . . . . Pull oneself together with all one's might, be calm, not make any more scenes! Then the doctor would have to declare her fit. Everything depends on it now.

201

Agathe's terrified soul clung in genuine desperation to the consultation with the physician at the spa in Röhren. He had to send her home — he had to. But when they arrived, he immediately prescribed a six-week course of treatment for her.

Might she be permitted to stay here alone?

No, she was too weak for that; her sister-in-law would have to care for her and divert her. How fortunate that she had such a cheerful, amiable sister-in-law with her.

* * *

The women's spa lay on a green, treeless plateau. The spa hotel and the living quarters of the doctor constituted the center. A single long street, lined with guest cottages covered with grape vines, extended from here out into the meadows. At its end crowded the dilapidated huts of the native population. There haggard women and coughing girls sat day and night bent over their lace-makers' pads and with feverish haste threaded the little wooden bobbins through the delicate and precious mesh of lace that came into being beneath their fingers.[89] Little of the sharp, pure air penetrated the holes that served as windows and were sealed with paper. The natives did see that you could drink something besides coffee made of chicory, that you could bathe, but they observed this like alien, incomprehensible customs. The goats' milk belonged to the foreign guests; the iron springs, the spruce needle baths, and the mud baths were for the foreign guests. One saw little of the natives; one saw only the foreign female guests. They sat together under the arbors of the wretched gardens where a few heads of cabbage and a row of straw flowers grew.[90] They stood in groups on the village street and complained to one another of their sufferings. One could follow their figures across the wide expanses of the meadows, could see how they walked, alone or in pairs, along the banks between the fields, collecting little bouquets of grasses and pale scabiosa for a thoughtful gift for their friends or for the doctor.

Women, women, nothing but women. They streamed by the hundreds from all parts of the Fatherland to gather at this iron spring as if the abundance of blood and iron with which the German Empire had been forged to a great power had been leeched from the

202

veins and bones of its daughters, as if they could not recover from the loss.

Nearly all of them were young, in the summer of their lives. And they were divided into approximately two equal parts: the wives who were exhausted from the demands of their spouse, from their social obligations, and from the birth of their children, and the pallid spinsters who had been consumed by doing nothing, by yearning and disappointment.

Men rarely visited the spot. An hysterical artist was in residence now, a retired colonel who never allowed his wife to travel alone, and the doctor.

They didn't concern themselves very much with the first two. But the doctor! What Dr. Ellrich had said, the mood he was in, the nature of his character — that constituted the stuff of conversation in the morning at the mineral spring, at the noon meal, and at the social events in the evenings. Some thought him a demon; others thought him an angel. Twenty ladies found scandalous the lack of restraint that twenty others displayed in his company, and a dozen others declared the censors themselves insidiously coquettish and opportunistic vis-à-vis the doctor. The young wife of a banker wanted to get a divorce on his account, but it was of course simply inconceivable that he would marry her; indeed, he knew better than anyone how sick she was.

A highly charged moment ensued every evening as soon as he entered the salon and they didn't know which group he would join. It was perhaps foolish, laughable, but it remained a point of honor to have the doctor at one's table. There were so few points of interest in this narrow community; under the influence of the stimulating baths and the sharp air of the high altitude, these morbidly unbalanced souls attached an unnaturally heightened significance to every mood, every feeling, and every notion, and it had a dangerously contagious effect on all of them. They all expected so much from this doctor: he was supposed to restore health, good spirits, courage and hope, and trust in life to each and every one of them. So one really had to court him a little.

"I find this doctor offensive," Agathe announced right after her first appointment. Under his sharp eye she shuddered like a mimosa.[91]

Eugenie thought him amusing. "A little ruthless and impudent, but well, otherwise he probably couldn't manage here."

How everyone watched them when he joined them that evening! Lisbeth Wendhagen immediately came running up from the other end of the salon. Naturally Eugenie flirted with him; it was of course the fashion here, and she was always ready to take up a new fashion. Ugh, ugh, disgusting.

This Dr. Ellrich had such a trace of cynicism at the corner of his mouth. He saw through the women utterly; he despised them . . . . The frivolous jokes and intimations about the other patients that he exchanged with Eugenie! Probably, about her too, behind her back. You needed to be on your guard against him; he didn't have good intentions — Just get away, get away from here . . . . A place, a dark, quiet corner where the voices wouldn't pursue her, where no color, no light, and no sound could penetrate. Hide yourself there and sleep, sleep, sleep without dreaming . . . .

* * *

Since Eugenie had been watching over her, Agathe could no longer sit cowering on a chair at night, staring into the darkness. Nevertheless she didn't sleep. She had to keep on brooding about how she could get away from Eugenie and the doctor and all the many women who observed her with curiosity.

At the same time this ringing and resounding, as if a large church bell were continuously being rung in her head. That disturbed her thinking; she simply couldn't get a grip on things. And yet something had to happen, very quickly . . . .

Before Martin departed, he had said to her, should she still wish to remain in Switzerland, what had happened would not change in the least his readiness to help her. His bearing had been forced and his tone of voice cool. She had given him no answer.

She became boiling hot inside when she thought about it. But never, never to see him again . . . .

What if she did go to him after all? Secretly, completely in secret?

She had to prove to him that she was not as pitiful as he thought.

Justify herself . . . . That was no longer possible now.

Help him by doing quiet, hard work . . . . Yes indeed! He would only think her forward.

204

And with this mad loathing, disgust, and hate . . . . It could come over her again as on that evening . . . . She — she — and still want something? Something that required self-confidence and strength . . . . Sneak off, hide where no human being saw her or heard her, where she felt no one close by her —

* * *

No, the only thing she wanted was to stay quietly with Papa. She certainly didn't want to jostle the old accustomed yoke again.

She had seen now that she couldn't breathe in the pure air of the heights. She was not made for the mountain peaks; she simply suffocated there.

Men of course . . . they brought along what they wanted up to the heights, what seemed pleasant to them; she alone — she was to grow numb in ice and snow. At bottom it didn't matter whether she sat down below or tried to climb the rocky slopes of truth and freedom in peril of her life; for girls it was more or less the same thing — renunciation at every turn. There — there — she encountered it there again, the great betrayal that everyone had committed against her — Papa and Mama and her relatives and girlfriends and her teachers and pastors . . . . Love, love, love was supposed to be her entire life, nothing but love, the purpose and goal of her life . . . .

. . . Woman, the mother of future generations . . . . The root that bears the tree of humanity . . . .

Yes, but if a girl only raises her hand, if she wishes merely to drink just once from the cup continuously and seductively held to her lips since childhood, if she even merely shows that she is thirsty . . . . Humiliation and shame! Sin — shameless sin — wretched weakness — hysterical madness! they scream at her — the severe ones as well as the gentle ones, the old ones and the young ones, the pious ones and the free ones.

* * *

She had shown that she was thirsty and thereby robbed herself of the only person who could have saved her.

205

And she longed for him so terribly. She wanted to run to him. She would become strong and healthy with him . . . . She knew where Eugenie kept the travel money . . . . Papa didn't even trust her with that anymore . . . .

She began crying again.

By all means let him despise her . . . . She will ask him quite humbly: dear, dear Mani, let me stay with you, just protect me — from the others . . . . Especially from Eugenie! How she hated her — the woman who drew everything to her with her icy power . . . . She ruled over the entire world!

The doctor had also fallen in love with her. Naturally they were conspiring against her — and they would reveal everything to Papa, everything — these bad people . . . .

Oh, the fear, the fear!

Agathe runs around her room — back and forth, back and forth again and again. She is alone.

Eugenie has left her for an hour. She is supposed to lie down on her bed and rest in the meantime. Eugenie is going for a ride with the doctor in his open carriage that he drives himself. How she reigns supreme there — that mischievous line that lurks around her mouth, the little black hat upon her blonde hair. They watch her from all the windows. Riding with him was the highest honor the doctor could bestow. Out on the street the ladies come running and make envious, sarcastic comments. But Frau Eugenie does nothing to damage her reputation. Between her and the doctor sits Wolfy, bolt upright in his military pose, wearing his little soldier's cap.

And she had triumphantly nodded a greeting all around and waved as the doctor slapped the reins and had the horses merrily lengthen their stride.

The hypocrite . . . the hypocrite . . . . Agathe laughed in her loneliness, clenched her fists and shook them menacingly.

They didn't take me along. They're probably afraid of me — But the little boy, what do they care about *him*?

When they're out there where no one can see them, then they'll kiss — the doctor and Eugenie — ha ha ha — and she kisses Walter and Wolfy too — all of them kiss. Martin and the waitress and the clerk — all of them, all of them . . . ugh! Why are they coming into her room. It's so wicked.

206

She keeps her eyes closed. She mustn't see that. She's a respectable girl, after all.

No, no! Don't point your fingers at me! Do have mercy. At least spare my dear papa . . . .

When Eugenie returned, she saw that the blinds of her sister-in-law's room were still closed. Cheerful and refreshed, she stepped out of the cool, bright autumn air into the half-darkened room.

"Girl, what's wrong with you?"

In the corner between the wall and the stove stood a needle-pointed easy chair. Agathe was cowering here, her knees drawn up, her bony shoulders hunched forward, her elbows pressed against her, her yellow, hollow-eyed face staring, with an inconceivable expression of horror, straight ahead into space.

"My God! Is something wrong with you?"

Eugenie grabbed her arm and shook her.

"You have such a look, you know. One could really be frightened."

Agathe stared into her eyes, silent and menacing.

"Listen, hey," cried young Frau Heidling. "I'm sending for the doctor . . . . "

A piercing scream. A wild sound and the cry "Help, help!"

The women in the neighboring room, waiters, and the landlady rushed to the scene in wild confusion.

Agathe had thrown her sister-in-law to the floor. She was kneeling upon her and trying to strangle her. She laughed. She screamed and raved.

The raging woman had to be subdued with brutal force; her tender maidenly body, restrained and fettered.

* * *

The ladies sat together and stood together in front of the spa hotel late into the night, discussing what had happened.

A young girl had lost her reason. It was not anything that unusual at the spa. They counted the cases of the last few years. And they whispered shuddering, pointing out this one and that one who probably were not far from it either.

They crowded around Eugenie in sympathy. She wore a scarf of tulle over a red abrasion on her neck and supplied information in a low voice mixed with sympathy and gravity.

Two aides guarded the sick woman. No one could go to her. In the morning she was to be taken away.

No, they knew of no reason, absolutely none!

An unhappy love affair? God forbid — in her younger years — but Agathe had always been a sensible girl . . . . God — you could rather call her prudish, reticent. Right, Lisbeth? And the two of them had always gotten on so well together. They had been friends since childhood . . . .

Too frightening, too horrible . . . she whispered to Lisbeth Wendhagen. Poor Agathe was accusing herself of having done things — in front of the doctor and the nursing aides — it was really completely insane, not a word of it true! She hadn't had even the tiniest adolescent crush . . . . And she called herself names, used expressions as if an evil spirit were speaking out of her. Eugenie didn't understand where she could have ever heard these loathsome words . . . .

That spring evening under the old yew tree where she had whispered dirty secrets in her little playmate's ear, secrets she had overheard from the cigar workers and the servants — Frau Lieutenant Heidling had forgotten that long ago.

* * *

Over the course of two years, with baths and soporifics, with shock treatments and massage, hypnosis and suggestion, they brought Agathe to a state in which she could return to human society from the remoteness of numerous sanatoriums without creating a disagreeable sensation.

She lives with her father, and what with faithfully following the directions the doctors have given her, has so much to do that her days and her thoughts are more or less filled. You see her taking a walk with her father every day at three o'clock; she is dressed simply and elegantly. From far away you can still even take her for a young girl. Because the doctors have told the privy councillor that his daughter needs a little intellectual stimulation, he tells her what he read in the paper that morning. After coffee Papa goes to the reading room at the club. In the evening he plays whist with a few old gentlemen, and Agathe plays solitaire.

In this manner they live on quietly side by side, full of consideration and inwardly alien to one another.

Agathe's memory has suffered. There are segments of her past she can no longer recollect. It is not possible for her to follow a lengthy discussion. She has acquired a collection of crochet patterns and is pleased when she can add a new one. The future no longer worries her nor does she understand why so many things once were able to upset her. Now everything that doesn't concern her health leaves her completely cold. She often sighs and is sad, especially when the sun shines brightly and flowers bloom, when she hears music or sees children playing. But she would hardly know how to say why . . . .

Walter and Eugenie are trying to get her a place in the newly founded home for women; if Papa should be taken one day . . . they can't really take her into their home where she'd be around the children — not a girl who was in a clinic for nervous diseases . . . .

And Agathe has perhaps a long life ahead of her. She isn't forty yet.

Notes

[1] Low German belongs to the West Germanic language group. In the Middle Ages it was the language of the powerful Hanseatic League of Northern Europe. By the nineteenth century, however, it had become a regional language, spoken in the Northern German territories around the North Sea and the Baltic, in such provinces as Pomerania where this scene takes place. With the standardization of education and consequently the teaching of only High German in school, Low German came to be associated with less educated groups, with peasants and workers, though in point of fact the social range of daily usage of the language varied from location to location. In chapter 8 we encounter Wiesing speaking Low German once again. Here the text again marks the class issues surrounding the usage of Low German in the Second Empire. The peasant girl Wiesing has been imported, as it were, westward from the countryside of Pomerania to the industrial city of Magdeburg in the heart of the new empire.

[2] Reuter quotes three of the seven verses of "Schmücke Dich" by Johann Cruger (1598–1662). The English translation takes some liberties with the original German hymn and is based on a translation by Catherine Winkworth (1858; Rev. 1863). Hymn 224. *Lutheran Book of Worship* (Philadelphia: Augsburg Fortress Publishing, 1978).

[3] 1 Cor. 11:27–29. "Whoever, therefore, eats the bread or drinks the cup of the Lord in an unworthy manner will be guilty of profaning the body and blood of the Lord. Let a man examine himself and so eat of the bread and drink of the cup. For anyone who eats and drinks without discerning the body eats and drinks judgment upon himself."

[4] The title *Rat* (Councillor) was used both as a designation for high-ranking officials in various contexts and as an honorific, as in the title given to industrialists, *Kommerzienrat* (literally: Commercial Councillor), or that given to doctors, *Medizinalrat* (literally: Medical Councillor). *Regierungsrat* (Privy Councillor) identifies Agathe's father as a very high-ranking official in the bureaucracy of the provincial government. We never learn, however, exactly what it is he does, except that he serves the state and the emperor. More important for understanding the mentality of the age is, however, recognizing the general significance lent to titles in the Second German Empire. The wives of government bureaucrats were addressed by their husband's titles, usually in the feminine form (*Rätin*), e.g., in the case of Agathe's mother, *Frau Regierungsrätin* or *Frau Regierungsrat*. In essence the hierarchy of the public sphere in which the titled husbands functioned was reproduced in the social life of their wives.

[5] *Liebesfrühling* (1844): poetry collection by Friedrich Rückert (1788–1866).

[6] *Palmenblätter:* popular collection of religious poetry by Protestant theologian and poet Karl Gerok (1815–90), first published in 1857 (English translation, 1869). An expanded edition was published in 1863 and this is presumably the edition to which Reuter refers.

[7] This title could not be confirmed. Either Reuter remembered the title incorrectly or she simply invented a title to evoke a genre of instructional books for young women that was current in the nineteenth century, for example, *Das Weib als Gattin und Mutter. Seine naturgemäße Bestimmung und seine Pflichten* (Woman as Wife and Mother. Her Natural Destiny and Duties, 1899), Johann Ludwig Ewald's *Die Kunst ein gutes Mädchen, eine gute Gattin, Mutter und Hausfrau zu werden* (The Art of Becoming a Good Girl, a Good Spouse, Mother and Housewife, 1798), *Das Weib als Gattin* (Woman as Wife, 1872), and Julie Burow's *Das Glück eines Weibes* (A Woman's Happiness, 1860).

[8] Paul Thumann (1834–1908): popular German illustrator who illustrated for magazines such as the widely circulating family journal *Die Gartenlaube* (The Garden Bower) and for editions of books by well-known German writers.

[9] M.: Magdeburg

[10] Johann Heinrich Voss (1751–1826). The fragments of *Luise. Ein ländliches Gedicht in drei Idyllen* (Luise. A Bucolic Poem in Three Idylls; translated by J. Cochrane as *Louisa*, 1852) appeared between 1782–94, and subsequently in 1795 as a complete volume. The poem takes place in a vicarage and describes a girl's eighteenth birthday, courtship, and marriage.

[11] 1 Cor. 3:21–23. "For all things are yours, whether Paul or Apollos or Cephas or the world or life or death or the present or the future, all are yours; and you are Christ's; and Christ is God's." In this passage Paul talks about the division between Paul, Peter, and Apollos, and how different factions are forming according to who baptized whom. The point is that Christ provides the center, not the group or faction to which the Christian is connected.

[12] In the context of his dinnertime homily, which is based on 1 Cor. 3:21–23, the pastor means to say that one should not be envious of the lives of those who are not godly.

[13] Georg Herwegh (1817–75): poet who became one of the leaders of the Revolution of 1848. Following the failed revolution, he lived in exile in Paris and Switzerland until 1866.

[14] Robert Blum (1807–48): German political leader who was a spokesperson for the radicals at the Frankfurt parliament during the Revolution of 1848. Georges Jacques Danton (1759–94): French revolutionary who was one of the main figures in the overthrow of the French monarchy, first president of the Committee of Public Safety. Barbarossa (1122–90), Friedrich I: One of the most celebrated emperors of the German Middle Ages who was glorified by the Romantics. Rückert's poem "Barbarossa" (1814–15) helped to popularize the myth that the sleeping emperor would awaken and resume his reign when his empire needed him again. National myths, like this one, contributed to the forging of German national identity and increased German yearning for political unity. As becomes clear in chapter 7, Reuter's novel opens just before German unification in 1871. "Freedom, equality, and unity" had been the battle cry of revolutionary movements in Germany throughout the century. In the second half of the nineteenth century, however, parties advocating German unity increasingly ignored the call for social equality. A Prussian bureaucrat like Agathe's father might typically have welcomed German unity, that is, especially unity under Prussian hegemony, but have rejected left-leaning social and political movements of any kind.

[15] These are the opening verses of Georg Herwegh's poem, "Aufruf" (Appeal, 1841) from *Gedichte eines Lebendigen* (Poems of One who is Alive, 1841–44).

[16] German children receive a large paper cornucopia filled with sweets on the first day of school.

[17] In the nineteenth century girls sometimes collected and played with spools of thread or other such everyday items. In her autobiography Reuter herself mentions playing with string and patches from her grandmother's various little boxes and baskets (*Vom Kinde zum Menschen*, [Berlin: S. Fischer, 1921] 43). Presumably this is what Reuter means here when she refers to patches of silk (*Seidenflöckchen*).

[18] In 1856 William Henry Perkin discovered a method of creating chemical dyes that revolutionized the textile-dying industry. Lilac was at the forefront of the new, fashionable colors. I thank Meghan Barnes for calling my attention to this historical detail.

[19] Gottfried August Bürger (1747–94): German poet and professor. His sister-in-law, Auguste Leonhart, was the Molly of his erotic poetry.

[20] The prototype for Dr. Engelbert was Karl Breymann, the principal of Neu-Watzum, the boarding school located near Wolfenbüttel that Reuter herself had attended. In her autobiography she describes him as an idealistic liberal theologian.

[21] Protestant Union (*Protestantenverein*): organization founded in 1863 in Frankfurt am Main for the purpose of promoting the union and progress of the various established Protestant churches of the German provinces in harmony with the advance of culture and on the basis of Christianity. It met with fierce opposition from the orthodox sections of the Lutheran Church, especially in Berlin. Dr. Engelbert's membership in the society signals his liberal theology.

[22] Egmont: the eponymous hero of Johann Wolfgang Goethe's play *Egmont* (1788). Amalia: the central character's beloved in Friedrich Schiller's play *Die Räuber* (The Robbers, 1781). Thekla: the daughter of the general Wallenstein of Friedrich Schiller's dramatic trilogy, *Wallenstein, ein dramatisches Gedicht* (Wallenstein, a Dramatic Poem, 1800).

[23] Agathe seems to share here in the reflexive anti-Semitism of the Second Empire. In her autobiography Reuter presents herself as more open-minded; she fondly recalls, for example, a brief friendship with a Jewish girl in Dessau (*Vom Kinde zum Menschen*, 59). In fact Reuter's portrait of Eugenie as a young girl appears to owe something to her memories of this Jewish girl. More importantly, Reuter attempts in her autobiography a passionate defense of the Jews, over the course of which she refers scornfully to Nazi phantasies about the pure race of Aryans (*Vom Kinde zum Menschen*, 260). On the other hand, as is perhaps not surprising, she also reveals her own thinking about this minority to be influenced by cultural clichés that she does not call into question.

[24] Ottilie Wildermuth (1817–77): German author especially beloved for her children's stories such as *Bilder und Geschichten aus dem schwäbischen Leben* (Pictures and Stories from Swabian Life, 1852) and *Aus der Kinderwelt* (From the World of Children, 1853). Elise Polko (1823–99): German author whose productive career stretched from the 1850s to the 1890s. Polko wrote children's stories and works that affirmed the status quo for women. Eugène Sue (1804–57): French author known especially for his sensationalist social novel *Les mystères de Paris* (The Secrets of Paris, 1842).

[25] The prototype for Frau Engelbert was the wife of Karl Breymann, Luise Breymann, née Mirow.

[26] In the nineteenth century typhoid fever, caused among other things by drinking contaminated water, and typhus, spread by lice (though this was not known at the time), were both termed *Typhus* in German. Whereas typhus was known to be highly contagious and would have required quarantine and whereas it was thought possible to contain typhoid fever, it is probable that Reuter means typhoid fever rather than typhus here.

[27] Empire: the period of the first French empire (1804–15), which was dominated by the neoclassic style of art, architecture, and decor. Biedermeier: a style of furniture and interior decoration especially popular with the middle class during the Restoration in Germany (1815–48).

[28] Macaroni pudding: a steamed casserole.

[29] As a result of industrialization the population of Magdeburg had increased from 50,000 to 70,000 between 1840 and 1865. Around 1870 the ramparts were pushed outward, making possible the laying of new train tracks and the building of a new train station that has served the city ever since. Additionally the suburbs, Sudenburg, Buckau and Neustadt, where many of the new factories were located, were incorporated into the city between 1867 and 1887.

[30] *Fromme Minne* appears to be an invented title. It means pious love, in the sense of religious love. Minna was once a popular woman's name. The pun has been rendered by slightly altering the title of the book.

[31] Cretonne (from the French village Creton where it was first made): a heavy unglazed cotton or linen fabric, colorfully printed and used for draperies and slipcovers.

[32] Eugenie presumably alludes here to the Darwinian struggle for survival, which the girls vaguely, and in fact correctly, associate with sex.

[33] Supreme magistrate (*Oberpräsident*): the highest civil official of the province within the Prussian bureaucracy.

[34] Breitenstrasse: Reuter presumably alludes here to Magdeburg's main street, the *Breite Weg*, literally Broadway.

[35] Gymnasium: an elite secondary school (formerly for boys only).

[36] Glacis (French: "slope"): the former fortifications of Magdeburg converted into a four-kilometer-long stretch of park, known as the Glacis.

[37] Cotillion (French: *cotillon*, meaning "country woman's skirt"): an elaborate dance (a variation of the quadrille) with frequent changing of partners carried out under the leadership of one couple at formal balls. In the nineteenth century it was often the concluding dance of the evening.

[38] Painting on wood (*Holzmalerei*): a fashionable decorative art. Flowers and various designs were painted on small wooden household objects such as little boxes, plates, and picture frames, usually with water colors, and coated with shellac.

[39] Hoffmann's drops: ether spirits of wine named for the physician, Friedrich Hoffmann (1660–1742).

[40] Ruching (French: *ruche*, meaning "beehive"): a pleated or gathered strip of fabric frequently used for trimming the highly elaborated ballgowns of the period.

[41] Assessor: a man who has passed the state examination that qualifies him to assume the office of a judge or an administrator in the government, but who does not yet have a permanent position.

[42] Extra dances: dance numbers played in between the scheduled formal dances, i.e., dances that do not appear on the dance card.

[43] Benzoin: a hard fragrant yellowish balsamic resin from trees of south-eastern Asia that is used as a fixative in perfumes.

[44] The Social Democratic party, the party of the workers' movement, had its origins in Germany in the Revolution of 1848. In 1863 Ferdinand Lassalle (1825–64) founded the General German Worker's Union in Leipzig, calling for universal suffrage and supporting German unification. A few years later in 1869 Wilhelm Liebknecht (1826–1900) and August Bebel (1840–1913), followers of Karl Marx, founded the Social Democratic Workers' Party in Eisenach, the party of a workers' movement rooted in international socialism and based on the idea of class struggle. Whereas the former party welcomed German unification in 1871, the latter party opposed it. When in 1874 representatives from both parties were elected to the imperial parliament, the government began to take harsh measures against both of them. They then joined forces as the Socialist Worker's Party of Germany, a party eventually dominated by the Marxist wing. In 1878 Bismarck seized the occasion of two assassination attempts against Kaiser Wilhelm I to press the passage of the so-called Socialist Laws, laws that empowered the government to dissolve social democratic organizations, to ban social democratic agitators, to suppress social democratic publications, etc. Martin's social democratic views, obviously in line with the Marxist wing, can only make him suspect in Agathe's set, a set invested in preserving the power and privileges of the upper middle class.

[45] George Gordon, Lord Byron (1788–1824): English poet. *Lord Byron at Newstead Abbey*: Reuter appears to have invented this painting. Newstead Abbey in Nottinghamshire, England: the ancestral home of the Lords Byron since the sixteenth century. *Cain: a Mystery* (1821): verse drama by Byron, based on the biblical story of Cain, that questioned traditional religious beliefs. *Childe Harold's Pilgrimage* (Cantos 1, 2 [1812], Canto 3 [1816], Canto 4 [1818]): Romantic poem about a young man in search of adventure in foreign countries. *Prisoner of Chillon* (1816): Poem about François Bonivard, a sixteenth-century Swiss political prisoner in the Chateau de Chillon on Lake Geneva. Missolonghi, Greece: Byron died here of a fever on 19 April 1824 while seeking to assist the Greeks in their struggle for independence. *Grazing Cows* (*Kühe im Grünen*, literally, "Cows in the Green" or "Cows in a Natural Setting"): This could refer to any number of paintings from the Barbizon School, a French school of landscape painting that was active from the early 1830s to the 1870s.

[46] Countess Teresa Guiccioli: Italian Countess who met Byron when she was nineteen. She and Byron had an adulterous relationship from 1819 until he left for Greece in 1823.

[47] Chalybeate spring: a spring impregnated with salts of iron.

[48] The *Brockhaus Conversations-Lexikon* noted in 1884 that the value of servants and hired hands prompted governments, communities, and private organizations to offer prizes for special loyalty and longevity in service (*Brockhaus' Conversations-Lexikon*, 13th edition, s.v. "Gesinde").

[49] Emil Frommel (1828–96): Protestant theologian and popular writer, military pastor in the Franco-Prussian War (1870–71), pastor to the imperial court in Berlin. His publications (1865–95) include among other things fiction, essays, sermons, recollections, and musical biography. Marie Nathusius (1817–57): Reuter's cousin by marriage, writer of pious Christian stories.

[50] Frölen: Low German for Fräulein.

[51] For her portrait of this couple Reuter borrows traits both from her Uncle Behmer and his wife, Elisabeth, and their friends the von Suchodolskis, a Polish painter and his Saxon wife who was also a painter and known for her rich humor.

[52] Cinchona wine: a popular wine for the stomach made of tincture of cinchona, the source of quinine, which was used to treat malaria in the nineteenth century.

[53] Kasimir von Woszenski's artistic sensibilities recall those of the Nazarenes, a group of young German artists who in the early nineteenth century sought to imitate sixteenth-century German painting and the early works of the Italian High Renaissance (i.e., the works of Perugino, Raphael, and Michelangelo).

[54] Reuter never names this town, but the reference to it as a city of artists suggests that she does in fact have Weimar in mind. Her own personal experiences there somewhat resembled those of her protagonist.

[55] In this well-known love story from Greek mythology, Cupid, the god of love, falls in love with the mortal Psyche, whom he visits only in the darkness of night.

[56] Arnold Böcklin (1827–1901): Swiss painter whose highly idiosyncratic paintings of fanciful figures from Greek mythology created a sensation in the 1870s. Known for his expressive use of color, he also established a reputation as a landscape painter.

[57] *Polterabend*: festivities that take place the evening before a wedding and that include, for example, a banquet, skits, jokes, and dancing. The word comes from *Abend*, meaning "evening," and *poltern*, meaning "to make

noise," probably as a result of the folk custom of breaking pots to frighten away evil spirits.

[58] The myrtle wreath symbolizes the bride's virginity.

[59] "Artists' towns" probably refers here to picturesque places like Weimar that attracted artists. Reuter was at any rate familiar with costume balls from her time in Weimar.

[60] Count von Moor: the elderly father of two sons who is a principal character in Friedrich Schiller's *Die Räuber* (The Robbers).

[61] Cain's wife is not named in the biblical account. "Adah" appears in Byron's *Cain: A Mystery* as Cain's sister and wife.

[62] Horsecar: a tramcar drawn by a horse or horses, in use in Germany from 1865 to 1925.

[63] Lutheran hymn by Johann Heinrich Schröder (d. 1699), based on Luke 10:42 and 1 Cor. 1:30. Reuter supplies the first two verses of ten. As the third verse makes clear, the hymn refers to the story of Mary and Martha. Jesus says that by choosing the spiritual life Mary has chosen the better part. This translation is from Hymn No. 227, *The Lutheran Hymnary* (Minneapolis: Augsburg Publishing House, 1935).

[64] Mangle (*Rolle*): the large wooden roller of the machine used to press large items at a laundry.

[65] Reuter's time frame is somewhat vague, yet we know that Agathe is now just over twenty years old and that she experienced her first ball at about age seventeen before unification in 1871; the year must therefore be approximately 1874. Thus Greffinger's banishment coincides with the first harsh measures taken by the new imperial government against the two workers' parties (see note 44).

[66] Sappho (ca. 610-ca. 580 B.C.): Greek poet. According to legend, she cast herself into the sea as a result of her unrequited love for the much younger Phaon. The Leukadian cliffs are the marble cliffs on the southern tip of the Greek island of Levkas.

[67] Easter Monday: the Monday after Easter, still observed in Germany as a legal holiday.

[68] Görbersdorf: a spa near Breslau (Wroclaw) in what was then Lower Silesia (now Poland), famous as a place for the treatment of lung diseases. Davos: a resort-town in the mountains of the Swiss province of Graubünden, known for its sanatoriums for treating tuberculosis and other lung diseases. Merano: a town in Northern Italy (then part of the Austro-Hungarian Empire) that on account of its relatively mild winter was a popular place for the convalescence of those suffering from heart problems or nervous disorders.

[69] Hydropathy: the water cure or Kneipp cure was a holistic treatment employing a natural diet, cold water, and exercise in the fresh air according to the prescription of Sebastian Kneipp (1821–97). Piece of metal: metal had long been used in homeopathic folk medicine to diagnose illness; the sick person was to touch the metal which would then turn a certain color depending on the illness.

[70] Oleograph: a picture printed in colors from a series of lithographic stones on cloth to imitate an oil painting.

[71] Inhabitant of Mars: What may seem merely a manner of speaking here is rooted in the moment of the genesis of the novel when Mars figured in the popular press and the question of life on Mars was debated, fueled by Giovanni Virginio Schiaparelli's description of the so-called canals in 1889.

[72] May Laws: the four laws that were passed in Prussia, 11–14 May 1873, and that constituted the climax of the so-called *Kulturkampf* (Culture War, 1872–87). These laws were aimed at the Catholic Church, but also affected the Lutheran Church. They limited the power of churches to punish laymen, demanded German citizenship for clergy as well as a German high school diploma, three years at a German university, and the taking of a so-called *Kulturexamen* (cultural examination) which covered history, philosophy, and German literature. They put seminaries under state supervision and also made the appointment of clergymen subject to review by the highest state official of each province. In addition the laws regulated leaving the church and limited the ability of the church to take disciplinary action against clergymen.

[73] The peasant girl in Mozart's *Don Giovanni* (1787) is named Zerlina. Reuter means the chambermaid, Susanna, in *The Marriage of Figaro* (1786).

[74] Reuter refers to a trend of the times, namely for members of professions to found rest homes for their members, as did, for example, the *Verein christlicher Lehrerinnen* (Christian Women Teachers' Union).

[75] The Battle of Sedan (1 September 1870) was the decisive victory of the Germans over Emperor Napoleon III during the Franco-Prussian War and made possible the unification of the Second Reich under the leadership of Prussia. Sedan Day was therefore a highly patriotic, even jingoistic event.

[76] An obvious reference to the woman who washed Christ's feet with her hair (Luke 7:37–38) and who is traditionally conflated with Mary Magdalene.

[77] Majoratsherr: the aristocratic owner of an entailed estate.

[78] Valeria Messalina (d. 48 A.D.): the adulterous wife of the Roman Emperor Claudius.

[79] Freilein: dialect form of Fräulein.

[80] Service book: a book, issued by the police, containing a record of a servant's positions and including references.

[81] The father of Wiesing's child was apparently in the military and tried in some fashion to get an early discharge. In Imperial Germany every able-bodied man was expected to do military service that as of 1875 ordinarily consisted of three years' active duty, beginning at age twenty. During that time the soldier was not allowed to marry.

[82] Reichstag: German parliament consisting of 397 representatives, elected for three years by so-called universal suffrage (women did not yet have the vote) and representing the whole people. The position of superior counsellor (*vortragender Rat*) would have been a step up the bureaucratic hierarchy for Privy Councillor Heidling; as superior counsellor he would have reported directly to a minister of state.

[83] "The Russian woman" may refer to La Paiva, a denizen of the French demimonde, who left her tailor husband in Moscow to come to Paris. There she made her fortune by seducing wealthy noblemen and bilking them of their money and possessions. In France in the early 1870s she was under suspicion of being a Prussian spy. I am indebted to Meghan Barnes for tracking down this information.

[84] Ernst Haeckel (1834–1919): professor of zoology, who specialized in lower forms of aquatic life; best known as the German popularizer of Darwin. His *Natürliche Schöpfungsgeschichte* (Natural History of Creation, 1868), his most famous work, went through numerous German editions and was translated into many languages.

[85] Rotifers: minute, usually microscopic, but many-celled aquatic (chiefly freshwater) invertebrates. Haeckel researched largely primitive aquatic life and frequently used these organisms as his examples as he attempted to lay out the laws to which nature was subject, these laws being, among others, Darwin's theory of natural selection.

[86] The last three lines of Johann Ludwig Uhland's (1787–1862) "Frühlingsglaube" (Spring Faith) (*Frühlingslieder II* [Spring Songs, 1813]), set to music by Felix Mendelssohn (1809–47) (op. 9 no. 8) and Franz Schubert (1797–1828) (D. 686 b op. 20, no. 2). This translation takes some liberty with the final line in order to make it conform to the melody of the Schubert rendition. Reuter appears to have quoted from memory here, for she quotes two of the lines incorrectly. The point of the poem is that spring is fast approaching and that it will bring about a change that will comfort the tormented heart.

[87] Martin's final transformation and appearance in the novel owes much to Reuter's friendship with the writer and anarchist John Henry Mackay

(1864–1933). Reuter later claimed in her autobiography that Mackay, an ardent admirer of the anarchist and individualist Max Stirner (1806–56) and author of *Die Anarchisten* (The Anarchists, 1891), taught her the real meaning of freedom. The title of Martin's book recalls that of a book by Rudolf Steiner (1861–1925) who belonged to Reuter's Weimar circle, a circle that in the early 1890s was, like many intellectuals in Germany, avidly reading the works of Friedrich Nietzsche. Steiner's *Die Philosophie der Freiheit* (The Philosophy of Freedom) appeared in 1894, a year before *From a Good Family*. In the Germany of the 1880s at least two anarchist movements grew out of and subsequently separated themselves from the Social Democratic party, a development reflected in Martin's political history.

[88] Hörnli (Swiss: "little horn"): mountain near Rapperswil on Lake Zurich, 15–20 miles from Zurich.

[89] Reuter's description of the making of lace with a pad rather than a pillow corresponds to the type of lacemaking for which the Saxon *Erzgebirge* is noted. This mountain range runs along the border between present-day Germany and the Czech Republic.

[90] Straw flower: flower that because of its durability was placed on graves or used in funeral wreaths in the nineteenth century.

[91] The mimosa closes its leaves when touched.

Upon publication in 1895, Gabriele Reuter's *From a Good Family* (*Aus guter Familie*) became something of a cultural event, making its author one of Germany's most talked-about women of letters. Set in the first two decades of the Second German Reich, this story of a Prussian bureaucrat's daughter caught between conformity and rebellion struck at the core of the class that upheld the empire, revealing the hypocrisy and misery at the very heart of the bourgeois family. It recorded the conflicted and ultimately interminable adolescence of a middle-class girl who failed to fulfill the destiny prescribed for her by her gender and class, a young woman who, despite an incipient high-spiritedness and independence of mind, internalized the attitudes of her culture to the point of lethal self-censorship. The feminist Helene Stücker remembered Reuter's novel as a wake-up call that gave such voiceless women the voice they desperately needed.

Reuter's novel was timely in many respects. Not only was it published at the beginning of a decade of heightened productivity by forward-looking German and Austrian women fiction writers, its account of what might now be called repression appeared in the same year as Freud and Breuer's Studies in Hysteria. Reuter did not, however, see her protagonist's failed life as the mere result of individual pathology, but instead understood it as embedded in the cultural politics of Imperial Germany.

Gabriele Reuter, whom Thomas Mann would later call "the most superior woman living in Germany," was born in 1859 in Alexandria, Egypt, the daughter of an import/export merchant. After her father's death the impoverished family resettled near Magdeburg, Germany. Reuter began writing in her teens but did not experience a literary and commercial breakthrough until the publication of *From a Good Family* in 1895. This success enabled her finally to live as a freelance writer. In addition to a string of popular novels, she wrote essays and sketches for German and Austrian newspapers; in the 1920s and 1930s she regularly reviewed German books for the *New York Times*. Reuter died in Weimar in 1941.

Lynne Tatlock, Hortense and Tobias Lewin Distinguished Professor in the Humanities at Washington University in St. Louis, has published widely on German literature and culture from 1650 to the 1990s, edited an anthology of seventeenth-century German prose in translation, and translated Marie von Ebner-Eschenbach's best-known novel *Das Gemeindekind* (1887), also published by Camden House as *Their Pavel*.

CPSIA information can be obtained
at www.ICGtesting.com
Printed in the USA
LVHW101933020722
722646LV00003B/52

CPSIA information can be obtained
at www.ICGtesting.com
Printed in the USA
LVHW101933020722
722646LV00003B/52

9 781571 134066

From a Good Family

Studies in German Literature, Linguistics, and Culture

Edited by
James Hardin
(*South Carolina*)